Winnabow

For Idlewild
and Pleasant Oaks

Part 1
August 5 and 6, 2010

I

Mexico City
Southern Bahamas

The tallest building in Mexico City is on the north side of Paseo de la Reforma, eight hundred meters east of the towering palm trees that line the middle of the avenue. For generations the trees dwarfed the buildings, until a Swiss bank decided to build something big. Ten years ago, fifty floors of steel and glass, emblazoned with the bank's acronym, rose above Reforma. Floor by floor, the tower narrowed to a flat roof with satellite dishes. From the roof, a cell phone tower continued like the point of a needle another three hundred feet into the air, and it sent and received almost all of the transmissions in the city.

The building's glass reflected the sky. When the winds were strong, they swept away the haze, and the glass was blue. But mostly, it was the color of the yellow air that hovered over Reforma. An enclosed bridge fifteen floors above the pavement connected the tower to a shorter building to the north—the back office—surrounded by a chain-link fence and guarded by a military detail.

On the tower's twenty-eighth floor, the two outer walls of Leandro Dufau's office faced east and south. Below, cars swirled around the gold Angel of Liberty, Mexico's monument to independence, and pumped exhaust into the haze that floated over the capital.

The tinted glass encased Leandro in warm light. The interior walls of the office were covered with two electronic touch screen maps of the world, one for each hemisphere, and three flat-screen televisions that transmitted business reports, cable news, and US-government media releases.

On the morning of Thursday, August 5, Leandro watched two computer screens on his desk and waited for an electronic report that in a single-coded sentence would assure him that the movement of cargo had occurred as planned. In the eastern Caribbean, from Venezuela to the Grenadines, to the Dominican Republic and then to the Bahamas, the cargo moved due north from Caracas, along a familiar route of transporters, couriers, dead drops, and landings. He had developed the communications systems, created the routes, hired the transporters, and provided security. A strict hierarchy made it work. Flawless enforcement meant flawless transport into the eastern seaboard of North America.

He pulled on a cigarette. Smoke rolled from his mouth and nose as he spoke over a telephone. He had taken a cold shower, a morning ritual that kept him focused and clear; it tightened his skin and cleaned away the particulates that descended through the air during his walk in the gardens of Chapultepec. He was on a speakerphone reviewing a spreadsheet of cash payments for the prior month when an orange light at the left corner of the main monitor began to blink. It was the first signal that something was wrong.

He ended the call, rolled his chair to the screen, and tapped in a series of pass codes to an encrypted site buried in the dark web. A call from a Bahamian satellite phone waited, highlighted with an image of the caller on the upper left corner of the monitor. Arnold Glass looked out from an inset box. It was a three-second mug shot video Arnold had taken of himself on the dock of Guana Cay, a rocky island in the southern Bahamas. The video looped automatically when Arnold appeared. With blue water and sky behind him, he tilted his head back from the camera lens and smiled. His mouth showed white teeth and a few gold caps that reflected highlights from the sun. His skin was the color of a coffee bean.

Leandro opened the line with two keystrokes and said nothing. Three pings sounded and told both men that the line was clear. Arnold had reached the bank. He spoke after the last ping. "It's me," he said.

Leandro had taught employees that every call, even encrypted ones, could be sucked up into American military satellites, automatically searched for keywords, processed, and located. Patterns deemed important were routed to US Navy interdiction sections, which operated radar balloons and planes throughout the Gulf of Mexico and the Caribbean. Employees used the language of the hotel and fishing businesses, the two most common occupations throughout the islands. Nonspecific language camouflaged the conversations within millions of calls made every day by hotel managers, fishing boats, and private yachts.

Arnold kept to protocol. "I'm twenty miles out," he said, and gave no name or location. "No one's answering." His voice was large and loud; it filled Leandro's office from speakers on the desk, walls, and ceiling. Arnold stood on the upper deck of a deep-sea rig, fifty feet long, with hoists for shark cages. He traveled north at twenty-five knots on the western side of the Exuma Land and Sea Park over aquamarine water with visibility to one hundred feet. On the northern horizon, a slip of rock was the nearest island of the Exuma Cays. North and west of the Dominican Republic, they formed a three-hundred-mile arc of green scrub forest, white-sand beaches, and rocky coral: a marked path from the Turks and Caicos to Nassau.

Leandro watched the screen; it pinpointed Arnold's location as a blinking blue light twenty miles south of Guana Cay. He leaned forward and crushed the cigarette into an ashtray. On the keyboard, he tapped a code into the website, which linked him to Arnold's guidance system and scheduled route. The blue light turned into a pulsating ribbon with an arrow. It moved up the screen and plotted a path north to Guana Cay's main dock; then it turned west across the water to the uninhabited southern tip of Andros, a labyrinth of mangroves and creeks. The screen registered the longitude and latitude of Arnold's location, refreshed and updated every ten seconds as the boat moved north.

"We're evacuating for the storm," Arnold said. "I have the big boat. Everything goes out...to avoid floodwater." He stood on the upper pilot's deck in denim shorts and a blue T-shirt with a jumping marlin printed on the back. An Atlanta Braves baseball cap and black wraparound sunglasses shielded his eyes. The sun beat through holes in the canopy. The boat engine and wind roared behind his voice. "It's on the schedule, boss. Check it."

Leandro tapped on the keyboard and called up the transportation log for the eastern Caribbean. On the log for Guana Cay, he clicked twice. In bold green type, the entry from the previous day appeared with notes of each scheduled event. The manager of the Guana Cay Bone Fishing Club, Noah Rolle, had entered it onto the system at 3:58 p.m. Noah's face in a still photograph was next to the entry; within it, he smiled and stood next to his purple Cessna, a two-seater parked on the island's landing strip. Behind him, the cream-colored buildings of the Bone Fishing Club were bathed in hot sunlight and framed by coconut trees. Coral stone paths wound among lawns and led to a portico.

Noah's entry reported the material was ready. Written in less than full sentences, he acknowledged a delivery one month earlier and identified the product by weight. From a few words, Leandro knew that Noah had separated the cargo into one-kilogram plastic bags, put the bags in paper sacks, and filled each sack to the top with precise proportions of flour and vanilla. Sealed with glue and wrapped in plastic sheeting, the material was prepared for transport to the southern tip of Andros.

Leandro scrolled to Arnold's entries below Noah's. His first entry showed he had delivered the product in twenty-kilogram packages in early-morning darkness at the beginning of July. Designated by the letter "A" in Arnold's report, the product was the most pure stimulant that came through the system. In its refined form, "Amy"—the name used by distributors in the United States—entered the bloodstream on contact and had an instantaneous effect. A handful, if thrown in the air, would disperse and disappear in the wind like a $50,000 cloud of talcum powder. Mixed with pure methamphetamine, it was the accelerant to designer street drugs and sold for twice the price of any other product Leandro's clients manufactured. Amy was the most profitable retail drug in North American cities.

Noah had stored the packages underground in abandoned dry cisterns next to the landing strip and under the floor of the club's main room. Delivery and storage occurred during a scheduled two-day gap in the calendar when the Bone Fishing Club was unoccupied. The two-day window was essential to the operation and provided Noah enough time to repackage the powder for transport off-island and sale. Outside of the two-day window, the club was busy with men who flew in for fishing and gambling. During the mornings, he took them onto the shallow flats for bonefish that darted and disappeared. In the afternoons, he captained larger boats over the trench to the east for blue fin tuna that ran one thousand feet deep. In the early evenings, the private games of cards began. By invitation only, they drew the men to a round felt table in the club's main room. The games attracted hundreds of thousands of dollars and euros, lost and won by German, American, and British men who appeared during storm season when families stayed away. They spent hours around the table risking stock-trading accounts and insisting that Noah and his two employees replenish their drinks, cook them food, and contact their pilots.

Leandro clicked on Noah's more recent entries; they showed he had identified tropical storms off West Africa that moved to the northwest. He'd warned of floods on the island and tracked the storms daily. When one storm gained strength and headed over the Turks and Caicos, Guana Cay was in the projected path. Noah had contacted Arnold, who had responded and scheduled to relocate the material— twenty-five hundred pounds of Amy—in sealed containers to Andros. It was on the schedule. Noah had prepared Amy for transport and loaded her into three boxes of heavy plastic, four inches thick on each side and reinforced with steel wire. With proper gaskets, the boxes were waterproof to 150 feet. Sunk at coded locations off Andros, they were the perfect storage system. Only Leandro and Arnold knew where to find them.

Leandro rolled his chair to the other end of his desk, hit the speakerphone function, and pressed a speed dial button for Noah. The phone blinked, uplinked to the encrypted site, and dialed a satellite phone that rang three times. The encrypted site scrambled Leandro's number in Mexico City and the one in the Bahamas. If someone tracked the phone, the call would register as random ten-digit sequences with no identifiable phone or caller, buried and indecipherable within the data accumulated from the needle on the roof. The call went to voice mail; Leandro lifted the receiver and put it back down. Noah had never failed to answer an encrypted call. He was careful, a private pilot who didn't take chances. Leandro looked at Noah's photograph on the screen. He stood in front of the Cessna with the satellite phone on his belt. He was a good employee, a high school graduate with family throughout the islands. Leandro dialed Pedro Martel, Noah's assistant, and received the same result. He terminated the call and rolled his chair back to the screen where Arnold was waiting.

"Stay on course. What's the weather like?"

Arnold looked behind him. Large clouds rose in the South Atlantic, where the third storm of the season had formed a circular eye with wind speeds of 115 miles per hour. A thin black line painted the horizon.

"It's coming. I can see the edge."

Leandro flicked through the channels of a television monitor attached to an interior wall of the office. He landed on an American weather channel and turned up the volume. Hurricane Chloe was a few miles west of the Turks and Caicos and followed a projected path over the Bahamas; wind speeds were category two. The channel showed sections of the islands already underwater. Scrolling text predicted an uptick in strength to category three through the Exumas. The storm surge would be twenty-two vertical feet, enough to swamp the landing strip and buildings.

"It's about eight hours out," Leandro told Arnold. "You're in its way, so stay on schedule. I'll call Noah. Is there anything else around you? Take your time. Use the field glasses."

Arnold perched the sunglasses on the bill of his cap and held binoculars up to his eyes. He pivoted in a deliberate circle, like the second hand of clock, and searched for a coast guard ship. He'd seen the Americans before; in the distance, they were a tiny glint of light on the horizon.

He saw nothing, turned again, and raised the field glasses above the horizon line, where spotter planes flew like a speck in the distance and projected a radar beam for one hundred miles. The sky was empty. Arnold said, "No, nothing," and Leandro terminated the call.

II

US District Court
Foley Square, Manhattan

On Thursday morning, the sun rose on Foley Square in lower Manhattan. It shone on men who shot water from power hoses onto the sidewalks and sprayed away mounds of litter that had accumulated from the day before. Dressed in rubber boots to their thighs, they powered the junk onto grates along the streets and through them into sewers, where it became food for members of the vast underground population of rodents that, depending on the year and who did the counting, could outnumber the human population of the city. The light started low at the East River and then flashed up like a fluorescent lamp. It moved in an arc across the sky and pushed the temperature to ninety degrees by ten o'clock and one hundred by noon. The rodents stayed underground. The people escaped. Some drove to beaches, rented hotel rooms, and rearranged calendars to delay their return. Those who stayed fled into air conditioned buildings and hoped for rain. It was a day when the residents of Manhattan wondered why they lived there.

Most of the courts had adjourned for the first two weeks of August, but some were still in trial mode. On the sixth floor of the federal courthouse, cool air vented from registers with a constant loud hum. The ventilation system was on overdrive to keep the marble free of moisture and the jury in courtroom 6A awake. Alone at one end of the hallway, Peyton Sorel and Eric Olsen stood under a register, felt the cool air, and spoke above the whirls rushing through the ductwork. Peyton had dressed Eric in an inexpensive gray suit, white shirt, and a blue print tie she had bought in the garment district. They had agreed to tailor the suit, which hung gently on square shoulders over a tight build. It was the twentieth day of trial, and there was a ten-minute recess. She had brought him out of the courtroom to tell him he'd be the next witness. She wanted one last private look into his dark eyes to find a flicker of light and make sure he understood what he needed to do.

He'd grown tense when she told him he'd be next. His midsection flexed, ready to be struck. She'd seen it before, a subtle involuntary movement in preparation sessions. When he felt threatened, Eric tightened his muscles and tendons like the strings of an instrument. "Relax" was a useless word; she'd given up using it months earlier. Seven hours of sleep, she had told him. Every night, throughout the trial, make sure it happens—and regular exercise. No coffee; just water. She appealed to his vanity—it would make him look younger and feel better, more handsome—which he liked. She'd written the instructions on a pad for him. Like a prescription, they became part of his daily routine. He added them to the directives she'd given earlier: how he would sit, where he'd place his hands, and how he would turn to the jury and address them directly.

In the hallway, she stepped back and assessed the image. "The jacket—button the middle button only," she said. "And no tie clip." She held out her hand. Compliant, he removed the clip and dropped it into her palm. It was the right effect, unpretentious and fit. Any heavier, Peyton thought, and he would project as too well fed. Weeks earlier, he had argued with her about the suit, and she'd told him—politely, in her view—to shut up and wear it. The cheap and unassuming tie too. It had to be simple, blue print, not striped or red. She had bought it from a job lot. At first, he had insisted on something expensive, a silk tie he wore to work. She told him no; he relented. Peyton had discarded other witnesses for many reasons, but $4,000 suits and long, meandering answers were at the top of her list. Extravagantly paid executives provoked the worst instinct in jurors. Perfect clothes and thirty pounds of fat made it worse. Juries inflicted penalties that dragged corporate careers into abandoned lots, beat them unconscious, and left them for dead. Every piece of research confirmed it.

She stepped forward and adjusted the tie. "This is the first time they will hear you speak, so remember what we worked on."

Eric flexed. "Why would he call me?"

"He's gone through his entire witness list. There's no one left. He sees you every day. Trust me. I know him. You're next."

"Why now?"

"The man needs a new strategy, and he's poking around. But today, you're a delay tactic. Remember that. He doesn't want to close his case, not in the next twenty minutes. He wants the rest of the day to think things over. If he closes now, he gives us the evening to prepare." She offered a brief smile— *confidence, Eric, and stick to the script.*

Her face was twelve inches away as she straightened the tie. Peyton had shoulder-length chestnut-brown hair pulled back in a clip and wore a navy-blue suit with a skirt hemmed just above the knee. In conservative heels, she was Eric's height. Her blouse was off-white with no collar, buttoned in front, just below the nape of her neck. A uniform: simple and effective. She wore a gold wedding ring, no stones. Eric had spent months with her preparing for trial. He liked her face. It was symmetrical with broad cheekbones, and her nose had a prominent bridge. Her lips were full and bore a subtle stroke of color: deep-flesh tone in a gloss that reflected the light. Her eyes were blue.

She straightened his lapel.

"Can you close it out?" Eric asked. He referred to a dismissal, an end to the case. They had discussed it. It was the reason he'd hired her.

"He doesn't have enough evidence, and he knows it."

"Dismissal. We're talking about a dismissal and no jury, right?"

She nodded.

"So you'll make the motion?"

"Yes."

"When."

"Soon." *Relax, Eric.*

He looked at her, insistent for a complete answer.

"Tomorrow or Monday," she said. "And I'll serve it cold." She said it with a smirk.

He emitted a laugh—small, hopeful, and short. He liked the description; she made it sound like the poisonous plate from a summer menu, as if she were preparing to murder the opposing lawyer. It was why he had hired her—she thrived on the fight and lived within it. "Yes," he said, smiling, "that would be best."

Peyton nodded.

———

Eric wanted a directed verdict, when the judge took the case away from the jury, dismissed it for insufficient evidence, and didn't require the company to put on a defense. It would stop the case with no further evidence or testimony—a perfect end. Peyton had explained the term to him when he'd sought to hire her two years earlier. It had happened across a conference room table with her partners, all men, gathered around to watch and listen. He had asked her to replace the lead lawyer a year into the litigation. It caused conflict within the firm—a partner had to be replaced on a case that wasn't going well. The company wanted her, and Eric was the messenger. It had to be her. She had won other trials in front of the judge, and he respected her. He had published opinions in other cases that word for word followed the memoranda she had written.

At first, Eric had spoken with her privately, a quiet request over the telephone; he had asked her to take over the case. She wouldn't agree if one of her partners would be replaced. Then he was frank. In a conference room on the forty-fourth floor of the firm's building with five of her partners at the table, he told her she had to do it—the partner would be replaced anyway. Peyton would agree, but only if the company accepted her terms: $5 million in cash up front for her to take the case and another $10 million if she obtained a dismissal or jury verdict in the company's favor. It was a signing bonus and success fee for her alone, not her partners, on top of the hourly rates and costs charged and payable month to month.

When she made the demand, faces around the table went slack. She sat across from Eric and looked in his eyes. The revised agreement was in front of him. She had pushed it across the table, the new terms inserted in red type.

Eric choked; Peyton didn't react. Whenever a defendant asked for her skills in front of this judge, she demanded an extra $5 million dollars if she won. In this case, she'd doubled the price and added an additional $5 million cash payment up front. Eric told her he liked the existing contract. He asked her to step in, show loyalty, and follow the agreement already in place: straight hourly rates, an automatic discount of 15 percent on all invoices, payable four times a year, no performance bonus. He looked around the room at her partners, as if they had the power to persuade her. The company was a long-term client; Eric could go to other firms and seek bids. He told them he would.

Peyton refused. Her partners were silent. If the company wanted her to clean up the case and step into the trial cycle— sixteen-hour days and weekends—the new terms were required. Everyone around the table knew why. To take her away from her children for two or more years, Eric would have to pay. Those were her new market rates. He was lucky she hadn't demanded more.

"Eric," Peyton asked, "you know what the opposing lawyer is seeking, don't you?" *Of course you know.*

He stared back at her.

"It's a one billion dollar case. His fees will be about twenty-five percent of that if he wins. I'm cheap by comparison."

"I don't care about him."

"You should. He's motivated."

"We'll settle before we lose."

"You may not be able to."

"We want to win, Peyton. That's why I'm talking to you."

"If you want to win, ask yourself, what's the risk of not hiring me?"

Eric stopped talking. He thought about reaching across the table and smacking her. If she hadn't been so earnest, he'd have walked out. But he stayed, looked at her unblinking eyes, and thought of a price far above what she was asking—he would have paid that too.

"It's a fascinating question," Peyton said. "Can you calculate that?"

Eric already had. Before he could respond, Peyton stood up, shook his hand, and walked out of the conference room. One of her partners wanted to grab the back of her skirt to make her sit down, but she crossed the room too quickly. The next sound was the small click of the door latch. Eric had watched it close, blond wood varnished to dark honey with a polished-brass handle. He looked at her partners. Fifteen million dollars was a rounding error in the company's monthly cash-flow statements. He knew it; they knew it. It was a good deal—an easy deal. One of the men shrugged. Eric signed the contract.

———

On the sixth floor of the courthouse, Eric looked at Peyton and swallowed. He would have paid her far more. "And you'll make the bonus." It wasn't a question.

"Success fee," she corrected him. "It's why you hired me. I earn it; you benefit—if Stapleton dismisses the case."

"You feel good about it?"

"No guarantee." She smoothed his lapel with the back of her hand. "You'll see. With Joe, there's always something more: a different angle, a surprise witness, some new document. He knows what he's doing, so don't think it's over. And remember the work we've done. When a company has as much money as yours, jurors think you live outside the law, as if you're clever enough not to pay taxes or a mortgage like they do." She stopped speaking for a beat and watched his eyes. "I can make those twelve people trust the company. You have to show them why. What's the answer?"

For weeks, Peyton had prepared him with jury consultants and witness experts. Role-playing lawyers had cross-examined him on every fact and argument the plaintiffs could raise.

"I am," he said.

"Why?"

"Enlisted military, an officer, honorable discharge, family man, and middle class, regardless of my income."

"And?"

"I'm one of them, and I'll never forget it."

"Nice." She smiled. He had learned.

"And I've worked hard, had some luck."

"What else?"

"I'll always tell them the truth."

"Always?"

"Always."

"Do it the way we rehearsed. They'll see themselves in you. This is our first opportunity, so in the next twenty minutes, nothing comes out on the witness stand we haven't discussed. And it's always the truth. Got it?"

"Yes."

"Good." She turned him around, pointed him to the court-room door, and whispered in his ear. "You'll be fine." She had some doubt.

Eric had a strong voice and enough gray hair to convey years of experience as the chief financial officer of an international real estate company. He had sat next to Peyton throughout the trial. She had chosen him as the image of the company. If the jury decided that the company recruited and promoted people who had served their country, even better.

Peyton and Eric entered the courtroom and took their places at the defense table. She was right—the plaintiffs' lawyer called his name, and Eric rose on cue. He walked to the witness stand to the right of Alfred J. Stapleton, US District Judge for the Southern District of New York. Standing, with his right hand raised, Eric swore to tell the truth, every bit of it, in detail and with confidence. Peyton liked the look. In the gray suit, he was every woman's good husband and every child's even-handed father—still lithe and young enough for all the play a wife could want but accomplished with an authority and discipline that came through in the voice. He sat down, adjusted the height of the microphone, looked to the judge, and nodded. Then to the jury, he nodded again. His hands were scrubbed clean; his fingernails were clipped and even. He was what Peyton wanted the jury to see: confident, informed, and fair. She'd beaten it into him, like bread dough on a wooden table, until the imperfections were gone.

III

Guana Cay, Southern Bahamas

Noah Rolle lay on the Guana Cay dock, his head over the edge and black eyes open, as if he were searching the turtle grass below for something he had lost. Blue light reflected onto his face, which had turned from Sudanese black to bloodless gray. Jesse Forbes, a younger Bahamian who did contracting work on Guana Cay, lay by his side, eyes bulging toward the water. Piles of oilskin tarpaulins lay next to him.

Under a thatched palm roof at the end of the dock, Pedro Martel stood in front of a sink and washed his hands in a bucket of seawater and bleach. The August sun scorched the palm fronds; a hot breeze blew from the South Atlantic and pressed his shirt against his back. The dock pointed north to mangrove islands and rocks on the horizon. At a right angle to the main dock, a long section of boards built on steel-and-concrete pilings pointed west to the Caribbean and a dredged channel deep enough for a sixty-meter yacht. Under the roof were aluminum sinks, benches, and an outdoor bar. Next to the sink, a folding fish knife with a serrated blade stood upright, stuck into a scaling board. Martel had scrubbed the knife and soaked it in bleach. The handle was etched aluminum with paisley designs and lined top and bottom in faded brown leather for a good grip. The nine-inch blade caught a shaft of sunlight that entered a gap in the roof.

Moored to the dock was a modified open hull military boat, sixty feet in length, with no cabin. Covered with a deck at the bow and open at the stern, it was stripped of every fixture and cleat that could reflect the sun or moonlight. The hull and deck were streaked in patterns of gray, blue and green, light and dark ocean camouflage that broke up the outlines of the boat from a distance. Twin diesel engines were at the midline below deck with extra fuel tanks on either side for extended trips over the open ocean. The bow bore no registration numbers. On the side of the boat in crude graffiti paint strokes was the blue image of a beetle and the word "Scarab" underneath.

Sweat beaded up on Martel's brow as he scrubbed his arms with soap. Blood covered the front of his shirt like a red bib. It splotched his shorts from arterial spray and ran down his legs in stripes to his sneakers. Around his feet, the blood pooled up and clotted like enamel on the boards. The amount had surprised him. He had become accustomed to the leaking cold blood of large fish caught on a gaff; it mixed with seawater in the stern of the club's motorboat and was easy to clean. He had never seen the pumping blood of a major human artery. It was hot and relentless. Instinctively, he'd put his hand in the wound to stop it. It had worked, but when he'd removed the hand, the severed tube sprayed into his face and over his chest and pants. He had tasted the blood and spit it out. It had splattered his shirt, which now adhered to his body like glue.

Martel had wanted to vomit. He cleaned himself as quickly as he could. With a hose, he sprayed his chest, pants, legs, and shoes. He doused the dock under his feet with a steady stream and pushed the pink liquid and red clumps through the slats of the boards and into the seawater.

A short Guatemalan with thick arms picked up a bucket of bleach from the sink and walked it to the main part of the dock near Noah and Jesse. He had a thin mustache and wore a faded red shirt with the image of a gold scarab beetle across the chest. His shorts were ragged, and on his head he wore a black baseball cap turned backward. Dark goggles protected his eyes from the sun. He released a surge from the bucket over the red stain on the boards. It ran from Noah's body at the edge of the dock to cut-coral steps under a canopy of trees that led up to the Bone Fishing Club. The Guatemalan threw Martel the empty bucket, and Martel handed him another, brimming with seawater and half a bottle of bleach.

The work with Noah hadn't gone well. Martel had tried to convince him to come to the dock, but Noah had opened his phone and dialed Arnold. The Guatemalan chased him up the steps, tackled him at the top, and rolled him into the bushes. He continued to resist. Martel had discharged a bullet into his leg, which ripped open Noah's thigh and severed the femoral artery. Blood poured onto Martel and the top step. When they dragged him down to the dock and heaved him next to Jesse, they left a smeared red ribbon sixty feet long. Martel had used the fish knife to make things certain, over the edge of the dock, ear to ear, a long quick cut that opened Noah's neck to the seawater below. He had done the same with Jesse, but the knife had caught a bone. Martel pulled it free and heard the bone crack. Then he cut Jesse through to the ear and let him bleed out into the water.

With buckets and brushes, Martel and the Guatemalan washed and scrubbed the steps until every stone smelled of bleach. Some of the blood had run off into the soil, which they turned with shovels and hoes. On the dock, the Guatemalan scrubbed as Martel shot water from the hose onto the planks. When the dock was clean, they returned to the bodies. They dragged them onto tarps spread flat on the dock and rolled them up in long cloth tubes tied with rope and duct tape. They pulled them across the dock to the club's motorboat, a wide fiberglass model twenty-two feet long with two three-hundred-horsepower outboard motors for reef fishing on the calm western side of the Exuma Cays. Lashed to the inside of the gunwales with rope and netting, the bodies wouldn't move.

Martel had thirty more minutes to stay on schedule. He walked up the steps to the Bone Fishing Club and collected the things Noah had been carrying on the steps: an aluminum briefcase filled with cash, binders of club records, and computer hard drives, all of which he'd brought out of the club for Arnold. They were strewn among rocks at the top of the path, with Noah's satellite phone at the edge of the veranda, the back cracked open and battery in the sand. Martel brought the items into the main room of the club and dumped the records and pieces of Noah's phone into a plastic bag that lined a trashcan behind the bar. He pulled the bag out of the can and set it aside.

Light from open windows lit the room. The walls were steel-reinforced cinderblock covered in plaster and painted powder blue. There was a high ceiling with exposed beams of stained teak. A common table twenty feet long ran parallel to the bar. In the corner was a circular poker table with green felt and red leather. The floors were terra cotta tile under Persian carpets. Modern paintings purchased in Miami hung on the walls.

Martel put the aluminum briefcase on the bar and opened it. It contained $2 million wrapped in paper sheaths: one hundred stacks of crisp, newly issued twenty-, fifty-, and one-hundred-dollar bills. On top of the money was a box with a Bahamas Telecom satellite phone, a charger, and a timing device. Two Florida driver's licenses were in a zippered cloth compartment within the open lid. Martel removed the licenses and slid them into his pants pocket. He closed and locked the briefcase with a key.

He took the Bahamas Telecom receipt to the bar sink and sprinkled water on the paper. He returned to the empty trash can and pressed the receipt against the inside of the can. He had to get it right, and he did. It looked good on the upper inside edge, as if someone had thrown it in and missed the plastic bag. It would be seen as a mistake, inadvertent, there to be found by an investigator who never overlooked details. The receipt provided just enough information to find the cell phone number and track it. Martel crouched down, positioned the trashcan toward the light, and examined the paper. The blue ink was legible and hadn't run. He smiled as he read it. It was the purchase record with the serial number of the phone. It bore the name Jennifer Glass, Arnold's cousin, the sales agent at Bahamas Telecom who had sold him the phone in Georgetown, Great Exuma.

In the business office, Martel removed the guest register from a standing desk and all of the paper records from file drawers. He pitched everything into the trash bag. The hard drives of the two computers were next; they recorded transactions and charges of the club's guests. Martel punctured them repeatedly with a screwdriver and threw them into the bag. From a desk drawer, he pulled out some baggy athletic shorts and a new navy-blue tennis shirt embroidered with the club's lettering on the upper-left chest. He removed the two driver's licenses from the blood-stained shorts and took off his clothes. Naked, he rolled up the bloody clothes and threw them into the trash bag. At the bar sink, he washed his hands and face with cold water and stuck his head under the tap until every inch of his scalp was wet. He put on the new shirt and shorts. In the mirror they looked good; they would have to do for the next two days. He put the licenses in his pocket, tied the top of the trash bag in a knot, and pulled the briefcase off the bar. He left through the screen door.

When Martel returned to the dock, the Guatemalan stood at the pilot's console of the Scarab. The engines were on, and the water churned. The boat's bow now pointed away from the island, north to the mangroves, and the stern faced the dock. The Guatemalan put the Scarab in reverse and moved it into position, rattling the boards and blowing back the palm fronds on the roof. The transom, on hinges, descended and lay flat. Like a hand below the edge of the dock, it waited to receive the cargo. Along the transom and stern floor, rows of thick rubber rollers were mounted on steel brackets.

Martel walked along the dock and threw the trash bag into the club motorboat. He continued to the bar sink, where he rested the briefcase on top of the first of three translucent plastic cubes, forty-eight inches on each side and set on dollies. Each one was packed with cargo, measured, weighed, wrapped, and sealed the day before. Martel crouched down, pushed with his shoulder, and rolled the first cube across the boards to the end of the dock. When the dolly struck a raised piece of wood, the container kept moving and slid onto the rollers attached to the transom. It glided downward onto the stern floor, where the box rolled for a few more feet. The Guatemalan looped braided rope around the container and attached it to a winch near the pilot's console. He turned the handle and pulled the box over the rollers. It moved across the stern floor and into place, where he fastened it to the floor and sides with wire cables. He set the aluminum briefcase on the pilot's seat and returned to the transom for the next container.

When all three cubes were on the deck, the transom rose to its normal position, and the Guatemalan locked it in place. He returned to the console and pushed the throttle forward, which moved the boat west past mangroves into the deep channel.

From under the bar sink, Martel removed an electric drill and a box of drill bits. He pulled the fish knife out of the scaling board, folded it, and slid it into a front pocket of his shorts. In the club motorboat, he secured the drill under the passenger's chair with the trash bag, removed the ropes from the bow and stern, and turned the key. One at a time, the outboard motors came to life. He backed the boat into the channel, where he turned it west into the big boat's wake.

At full speed, the Scarab and the club motorboat moved over calm water. In minutes, they were beyond the island and into a sea that rolled with the wind. The color of the water changed from pale blue to transparent ultramarine. Eighty feet below, the reefs were black.

Two miles west, Martel pulled back the throttle, turned off the engines, and let the motorboat float over a reef. The Scarab circled. Martel stood in the middle of the boat and inserted into the drill a twenty-five-inch bit with heavy cutting teeth. He pointed it into the air and pulled the trigger; it spun in a blur. He spread his legs a few feet apart for balance, bent his knees, and lowered the drill. It cut through the floor and spit bits of white curled plastic around his feet. As the drill penetrated the hull, water leaked up, first in a trickle, then in a plume. One after another, he drilled eight times through the hull. Water pushed up through the holes in spouts that flooded the stern and rose over his shoes. He sloshed through the rising water and admired his work.

The boat listed to port and backward to the outboard engines. Martel dropped the drill and checked the bodies. He pulled at the ropes to make sure they were tight and that neither Noah nor Jesse would float away. Satisfied, he stepped onto the right gunwale and then to the Scarab, which had pulled alongside. He stood on the Scarab's bow and watched the smaller boat fill with water. Minutes later, the bow rose as if reaching for air, and the stern went down. For a few seconds, the bow bobbed above the surface, and then it rolled to the left. The last thing to go under was the rounded nose and aluminum railing. The boat floated three feet below the surface, held up by an air pocket. Martel stood on the Scarab and watched the snow white hull in blue water. When some air released, the boat descended in a slow crawl, sixty feet down, until it came to a stop above the reef, where it floated like a specimen suspended in blue liquid.

Martel instructed the Guatemalan to circle the sunken boat, which discharged traces of gasoline. The Scarab moved around the spot twice and then churned over the water to disperse the stain on the surface. Satisfied the boat wouldn't rise, Martel spun an index finger in the air. The Scarab turned west and north in a long arc with Martel balanced on the bow, looking back to the spot where the boat had descended. He stepped down and pushed the throttle forward. The boat flattened out across the water at fifty knots and pointed north to Abaco.

IV

Foley Square

Eric laid his hands flat out in front and raised his eyes to the man at the lectern. He faced Joseph K. Boyle, a bald-headed bantamweight in a perfectly creased black suit, starched white shirt, and black tie. Boyle looked like he was on the expensive side of the burial business, as if embalming fluid and mahogany caskets were part of his inventory. Light from the courtroom ceiling reflected off an unblemished bald head. He had beautiful, straight capped teeth. When he looked up from the lectern, Eric thought of the dead German art-house-movie actor, Klaus Kinski. He couldn't help it. He had told Peyton during a break in the trial. Boyle, he had said, had the same jutting jaw but softer features, good dental work, and no hair. His eyes were too close together and deep set under the brow. When he spoke, they moved in his head like blue marbles rolling on a dinner plate.

The description had made Peyton laugh during an adjournment. She couldn't stop and had turned away. Eric had watched her walk to the other end of the hallway. From behind, he could see her shake, hands over her mouth and head in the air. She couldn't stop and took minutes to refocus. It was the first time Eric had seen her laugh.

Boyle had a voice made for radio, and he used it in every trial. In a lower register, he conveyed authority and reason; in a slightly higher register, an acute sense of justice, fairness, and decency. Sometimes, he used a stage whisper that urged jurors to lean forward and listen. At other times, he swelled his voice in a slow crescendo to propel them to a conclusion. He mixed in humor and indignation and always looked in their eyes. The voice humanized him and made the graveyard apparel look like the choice of a serious man—less the uniform of one who buries the dead and more the attire of a professional who administers relentless punishment. His method was excruciating in its detail and inexorable in its movement, like an implement of torture, a slow, unstoppable wheel. Boyle at trial could stretch a defendant into an unrecognizable shape but leave him sufficiently alive to pay the verdict. The black suit was no accident.

———

Peyton had explained Boyle's method to Eric four weeks earlier, before the opening statements. It wasn't a trick. Formula was the better word for it. He combined the voice and an acute visual memory for documents and writings to create a performance without any notes. Boyle's only references were the evidence on a projection screen and the witnesses on the stand. Perfected for years, the method was difficult to resist. At the beginning of the trial, Boyle presented his opening statement without any cards or papers. During the first week of testimony, he had stood in the center of the courtroom and questioned ten witnesses about the company's financial data and forecasts. Full pages of records scrolled on a screen behind him, while Boyle referred to the details of line items from memory. He knew the figures as if they were his own social security number. He quoted text from company records but never looked at the screen or made a mistake. With a comic's timing, he posed rhetorical and indignant questions to the witnesses that made the jury laugh. The jurors leaned forward for more, eager for entertainment, for things they'd never heard before. It was a show, and he smiled for them with white teeth.

A woman with honey-colored hair and pink lipstick sat in the front row of the jury box, one knee over the other. She followed him with her eyes and took notes, a writing pad on her lap. When he paused, she wrote. Peyton had identified her for Eric as the foreperson. She filled an entire writing pad in the first week.

At a break after the first eight days of trial, Eric had asked Peyton if Boyle could obtain a verdict against the company by intellect and personality alone, without sufficient evidence.

"Yes," Peyton had told him. She'd seen him do it. "He can sell anything to anyone: juries, judges, and people on the street. It should be illegal, but it's not. And don't be fooled by the smile. It's for the courtroom only."

Peyton hated him. She described Boyle to Eric as a dangerous and brilliant sociopath who spun beautiful narratives to juries as if he were spoon-feeding medicine to children at the end of an evening. He had perfected the craft over thirty-five years. Downloaded into her brain was every Boyle story from every defense lawyer she could find who was willing to talk, usually over several drinks and always off the record. For background, she'd read seven Boyle trial transcripts. His work was always well presented, but there was a consistent dark aspect to every case.

"Stuff that makes a trial go sideways," Peyton told Eric. She reminded him in the hallway before he entered the courtroom and took the witness stand. "That's his thing. He always has something new designed to kill. No matter how courteous and pleasant he seems, it's a mask. That's not him."

What worried her most was what she couldn't see coming: the surprise witness, the newly discovered document, and the questions that seemed irrelevant at first but were almost always a prelude to something ugly.

"Forget the voice and smile," she said in the hallway. "This is a Louisiana knife fight. He invented it. It's what he does best when he's backed into a corner."

She looked down the hallway to make sure no one was looking and then swiped an index finger across her throat. "He'll go for you—and me. Don't play a game. It's what he wants. He's aching for it. We have twenty minutes left. For now, you're a delay tactic, nothing else." She shook her head. "Don't make it easy for him."

Six weeks before the trial, Peyton had described a case in New Orleans that had made Boyle's reputation. The result was the eventual disbarment of the opposing lawyer, a member of the Louisiana bar for thirty years. Peyton had read the entire trial transcript. There were two rules in a Louisiana knife fight: stealth was the method of attack, and litigation death occurred by a deep cut to the opposing lawyer's largest artery. The merits of the case mattered little.

Toward the end of the trial in New Orleans, Boyle had accused the defense lawyer of suborning perjury and manipulating expert testimony. The lawyer was as astonished as the presiding judge. He was forced to defend himself, not just his client. Two years later, the lawyer had abandoned his practice and all but disappeared.

During the trial, the lawyer had put on an expert witness, a young financial analyst from a firm in Mississippi, who provided a compelling economic-market analysis of why a company had gone bankrupt. It had damaged Boyle's case against the company's officers and directors whom Boyle had accused of destroying the value of the company. Unannounced, the financial analyst returned to the courtroom a week later and sat in the back row. He smiled to the defense lawyer for whom he had testified and claimed he was merely curious about the proceedings and outcome. At the close of the case, Boyle called the analyst to the stand as a rebuttal witness. The defense lawyer objected, but the judge allowed the testimony. The analyst testified that he had discovered material evidence as part of his investigation. He wanted to include it in his opinion, but the defense lawyer had told him to forget about it and never asked him about it on the witness stand. Boyle hadn't either. The expert was angry. He came forward to disclose the full truth, assist the jury, and achieve justice. He wanted to add the information to the trial record.

The "flipping expert," as he became known, caused chaos in the courtroom. The result was a verdict for Boyle. It didn't matter that the defense lawyer had no obligation to reveal the new information or that the flipping expert had sworn that he'd always told the truth. The new evidence made the jurors angry, and they penalized the defendants with millions in punitive damages for litigation abuse. Immediately, Boyle began disciplinary and disbarment proceedings against the defense lawyer.

Everyone involved suspected that Boyle had contacted the analyst during discovery and trial. Some thought Boyle had made a deal with the man and staged the entire scenario. The defense lawyer subpoenaed the expert's e-mails and text messages but found nothing. Investigators scoured airline and hotel records and the digital files of security cameras from hotel lobbies, businesses, and restaurants all over New Orleans seeking evidence of a meeting. They interviewed waiters, bar owners, and bellhops and showed them photographs of Boyle and the expert analyst. There was nothing. The flipping expert sat for a second deposition during the trial and denied ever speaking with Boyle, until he personally reached out to clear up the record. He was a man of truth and conscience, he told the presiding judge, implying that the defense lawyer was not.

Two years later, the analyst purchased twenty acres of waterfront property on the Gulf for $6 million and built a mansion and boathouse.

"How," Peyton asked Eric, "does a thirty-five year old analyst from a midlevel financial firm in Gulfport, Mississippi buy a property like that and build an extravagant complex on the water? No one ever got an answer."

———

Eric sat in the witness stand and looked across the courtroom. From behind the lectern, Boyle seemed smaller than he did at the start of the trial and hardly able to wield a knife. Beads of sweat accumulated across his upper lip and the top of his head, as if he'd walked through mist. The tips of his fingers had blue ink stains. According to Peyton, he had no more witnesses on his list and needed a new strategy. Overnight. His performance for the day was over, no more lines to say or marks to hit—a shiny bald head and a perfect black suit. Twenty minutes left.

Boyle looked at the courtroom clock, moved papers around the lectern, and tried to find a place to begin.

V

Guana Cay

Arnold dialed Noah's phone when he first saw the mangroves south of Guana Cay. Three rings and it kicked into voice mail. He accelerated the fishing boat to thirty knots and approached through the deep channel.

The fishing boat glided to the place where the Scarab had been moored ten minutes earlier. The dock was immaculate—a clean bone dried in the sun. Arnold tied the fishing boat to the concrete columns, stepped onto the boards, and circled the dock. At the base of the steps, he stopped at the shed and opened the doors. It was empty. Missing were eighteen wire-reinforced forty-eight-inch squares of heavy, unbreakable plastic, six for each cube. The gaskets were gone. Arnold had stored and locked them in the shed one week before. He dialed Leandro by pressing one button on his satellite phone and spoke as he walked up the steps. "It's open," Arnold said, as he arrived on the terrace, "but the club boat isn't here, and the shed's empty." From the terrace, he walked into the main room. "Bar's clean. Someone washed it. They stepped out and left."

"The floor?"

Arnold put the phone on the bar and pivoted the common table over the tiles. He pulled back a Persian carpet and knelt down. With an index finger, he traced a wet line of grout between the tiles. He stood up and walked to the bar. "It's wet," he said into his phone, code for the fact that tiles had been removed, the pit opened up, and the floor sealed with new grout in between the tiles. "Want me to check it?"

"Not yet. Are the planes there?"

Arnold walked out of the front door, through the gardens, and onto the tarmac, Two small planes were parked in the distance.

"Yes," he said. "The seaplane and the Cessna. You want me to make any more calls?"

"I want you to look in the old cistern."

Arnold walked along the edge of the tarmac toward Noah's purple Cessna and the pontoon plane. Fifty feet from the planes, he turned into a forest of coconut trees and over a carpet of rotting palm fronds. He walked through dead wood, pieces of chopped-up furniture, logs, and downed trees until he arrived at piles of loose rocks and coconuts that had cracked open and dried in the heat. A bicycle wheel Arnold had thrown among the junk was the marker. He put the phone on a rock and removed the wheel. He cleared away the trash, opened up a patch of sand and rock, and dropped to his knees. In fistfuls, he cleared away dirt and sand until he found the steel plate and pushed his fingers into gaps in cracked masonry that had crumbled around the opening. With a firm grip, he lifted the plate, stood up, and pushed it just past vertical onto a tree trunk.

He lay down, pivoted his legs, and lowered himself into the cistern. His eyes adjusted to the dark as he scanned the walls and shelves. They were empty. Eight hundred sealed plastic bags, one kilogram each, were missing. Noah had arranged the bags, packed with pure powder, on the shelves the day before. He'd run his fingertips along each one, flicking the bags as he counted into the recording device on his satellite phone. They had been in the cistern and later in his electronic logbook. Arnold had seen the photos and video, downloaded to the encrypted site operated in Mexico City. Arnold pulled himself out of the hole and picked up the phone. "It's empty."

———

Guana Cay was a "landing," as Leandro called it, one of six storage facilities along the route across the eastern Caribbean to the world's largest market. Landings one and two were in the southern Antilles, just north of the Venezuelan coast. Landing three was a series of caves at the eastern end of the Dominican Republic. Landing four was the Bone Fishing Club at Guana Cay, and landing five was a collection of shallow underwater spots along the eastern seaboard that changed constantly, depending on the date of delivery and time of year. They were known only to Leandro and the individuals designated to pick up the boxes.

The route had been closed in the 1980s and 90s, because the US Navy had tracked and stopped shipments using a radar network that blanketed the Caribbean. Leandro had reopened it ten years later with better technology and a secure group of employees he had hired and trained. Guana Cay and the caves in the Dominican Republic were the critical links, and he watched them closely. Arnold moved from landing to landing to inspect the records and make sure the flow of product was efficient and safe, usually at night, and in swift boats. Navy ships were a constant presence within two hundred miles of the North American coastline. Every transporter carried a satellite phone, kept it charged, and reported daily to the encrypted site in the dark web. If interdiction was a genuine threat, the transporters dumped the cargo at sea and sometimes scuttled their boats. If a phone went out of service, reports were not timely, or a voice didn't clear the recognition system, Leandro provided an immediate response. He pursued the missing transporter until he obtained satisfaction, the shipment, or both.

It had happened before in the Dominican Republic and more recently on an island north of Venezuela. As he listened to Arnold, Leandro brought onto his screen images of a burned house on an island south of Mustique and Canouan in the Grenadines. He had snapped the photos on an overcast day. The house was charred black, with a single wall standing. Parts of the gardens bloomed with red and blue flowers. The hills in the distance were thick and green. He flipped through images of the house and surrounding hills. A Caracas street gang had stolen a shipment as part of an inside job, arranged by a low-level employee, a boy Leandro had hired to pack boxes and prepare transport boats on the other side of the island. The robbery was born of stupidity. The boy had known that some of the product was stored at a villa on a remote side of the island. Two retired Scandinavians rented the home for four months a year, unaware of an underground concrete vault beneath the kitchen. It had been Leandro's idea. The house was rented to the unsuspecting couple and kept up by caretakers, who stored the product under the kitchen floor and moved it in a truck when the couple was away. They gave the home a tranquil, occupied feel, like any vacation property with gardens and flowers tended by local people. The retirees parked a modest car in the driveway, read books in the garden with their friends, and hung white sheets on the clothesline to dry in the wind.

As Arnold walked the Guana Cay tarmac and reported things found in the cockpits and storage compartments of the planes, Leandro clicked through pictures of faces and corpses. Some were in apartments; one, an image of the boy, was among garbage in a landfill. The young employee had told the thieves that a cache of Leandro's best product was beneath the kitchen floor and the home was unoccupied. The elderly woman had walked into her kitchen at night and came upon the bright beams of flashlights. Four Caracas gang members were prying open her floor. She received a shovel to the head. A bullet went into her chest while she lay on the floor. Her husband died in bed, beaten with the shovel. The gang members found only a small amount of product—twenty kilograms below the floor—and with rage set fire to the house. With no fire department on the island, the structure burned and smoldered for days. Leandro, posing as an insurance adjuster, investigated the destroyed home with a local constable and encouraged him to conclude that the double murder was a robbery gone bad. The home was razed to the ground. The garden grew up. In a year, the ruin was covered with weeds. An insurance claim was paid through a local Grenada bank that acted as agent for the property owner, a Swiss bank located on

Paseo de la Reforma in Mexico City. As with many properties in the Caribbean, the bank held the title by virtue of a mortgage in default.

After the theft and fire, the employee failed to report. Leandro found him two days later in an apartment block on the outskirts of Caracas, newly employed to manufacture thousands of rocks from the twenty kilograms his people had stolen. The Caracas gang was converting Amy into crack cocaine. Leandro abducted the boy on his way to a coffee shop and took him to a garbage dump on the south side of Caracas. He gave him a modest dose of sodium pentothal and scrolled through his cell phone for the names, phone numbers, and addresses of the four accomplices. Groggy, the boy told him everything. Leandro gave him enough sodium pentothal to stop his heart and buried him in the landfill. For the next twenty-four hours, Leandro traveled through Caracas, located the four men who had robbed him, and executed them.

VI

Foley Square

Boyle stood at the lectern, unprepared for the first time. Julian Smythe, the tanned lanky presence next to Boyle during the trial, had placed in front of him some notes on what to do next. Some were handwritten, others typed. They had no order and weren't for Eric Olsen, who had never been on Boyle's witness list. They were for some other witness of marginal relevance, an analyst named Mrs. Nesbit, whom Boyle had mentally dropped from the witness list six months before the trial; somehow, pages with her name were in front of him.

He looked back at Smythe, who searched the first row of benches for a box. When the younger man rose, box in hand, Boyle gave him the look he had perfected across conference room tables and offices. It was a cold blue-marble stare. He'd seen it from a big cat behind bars at a zoo. When the animal recognized a passerby as potential prey, its languid face transformed, and it locked eyes with the individual. No longer part of an indistinguishable group of moving objects, the passerby had become flesh and a bone to be chewed. Boyle liked the look. He adopted and used it on employees. It motivated them, particularly at trial, and they understood immediately what he wanted.

Smythe kept his eyes on Boyle's. He set the box on the table and opened a briefcase that held a manila folder with sheets of paper from a legal pad. He had written questions on the papers and clipped them to documents with selected words, sentences, and sometimes whole passages highlighted in yellow. Together, they were a road map, a strategy, according to Smythe, that could win the case or prevent a loss. Either way, the trial would enter a new phase. He had told Boyle about it in the courthouse hallway.

Judge Stapleton cleared his throat, took off his glasses, and asked the two men if they would move the case along in the interest of time.

Smythe walked to Boyle and handed him the manila folder. In block letters, the word IBERIA was on the front of the folder. Boyle nodded. He turned his head to the judge and politely asked for a moment to review what he held in his hands.

The judge looked at the clock at the far side of the courtroom.

————

Joe Boyle had filed the lawsuit three years earlier based on the precipitous decline of the stock price of a California real estate trust owned primarily by Eric's company, Maynard Inc. The stock price had fallen from an all-time high of sixty-five dollars per share to nearly zero and then climbed back to eighteen dollars by the time the lawyers began to pick a jury. As far as Boyle was concerned, it was a winnable garden-variety securities case with a huge potential return. He had invested $10 million of the firm's money to bring the case to trial with a team of lawyers and paralegals. In exchange, he would receive 25 percent of whatever he recovered by jury verdict or settlement. His clients had calculated the losses as slightly more than $1 billion. If he won, his attorney's fees would be $250 million, 25 times his investment. Even if he settled the case for half the alleged losses, Boyle would make a fortune.

Boyle had happily admitted to the media that his firm was a litigation hedge fund, but it enjoyed immunity from the business cycle and investment returns no financial manager ever imagined. He had chosen the cases well and built his reputation by trying to verdict hard-fought litigation against teams of defense lawyers who rarely, if ever, gave up and settled. At age sixty, Boyle selected cases based on the potential returns and jury appeal. He knew jurors couldn't understand complicated securities claims—he'd seen them struggle before—but he knew they understood arithmetic and the roller coaster ride of a stock price, particularly one that had risen to an all-time high and then fallen to nearly zero in less than two years. They knew something terrible had happened, and Boyle had the talent at trial to convince them who was to blame.

In his opening statement, Boyle had led with the decline of the stock price and the concept of deception. Maynard had cheated his clients, he said, and he had pointed at Eric. Maynard executives had lied to the North American Machinists' Pension Fund—"the Fund," as Boyle called his main client—which once owned $900 million of shares in the California Real Estate Investment Trust. CIT was a Maynard-controlled company with a stock price that had soared and then fallen like a plane from the sky.

According to Boyle, Maynard had played a game for six years with CIT. Eric had told everyone, including the Fund, that CIT was the centerpiece of Maynard's business in North America. According to Boyle, Eric had pumped up the stock price in two ways: by giving CIT loans to invest in California commercial real estate and by telling investors that CIT was Maynard's most valued asset, now and forever. The stock price kept going up, and Eric had fed the frenzy. He had predicted an endless uptrend in California real estate and urged the public and large pension funds to buy more. CIT was the investment future; that had been Eric's message in Maynard's media releases and government disclosure statements. As buy orders for CIT had flooded brokers and online investment sites, the CIT share price tripled to an all-time high of sixty-five dollars a share.

But in 2006, Eric began a slow and deliberate plan to liquidate. Early in the trial, Boyle had looked across the courtroom and told the jury that Eric had lied from the beginning. Maynard hadn't merely changed its mind and started to sell. Since 2002 Maynard had pumped up the CIT share price and then, with a clear plan, let it fall. Boyle loved homicide analogies. He had said in his opening that Eric had pushed CIT off a ledge, like an unwanted employee from the fiftieth floor of Maynard's office building in Stamford, Connecticut. The plan was premeditated: inflate the stock and then liquidate for profit.

The CIT share price had fallen gradually at first, but descended quickly in the later months of 2007. Once Maynard had liquidated half of its CIT holdings, the share price had dropped to less than forty dollars. Before the market saw the liquidation for what it was, Maynard had sold everything, and the share price was in a free-fall.

"Gone vertical" was how Boyle had described the 2008 share price. The jury had watched with wide eyes. He had the numbers to prove it. On the big screen, he had provided visual vertigo: a day-by-day 2007-2008 calendar side by side with the share price. By June of 2008, the stock traded at less than two dollars per share, and CIT had become a financial graveyard for retirement accounts and pension funds. For the Fund, the losses hovered at approximately $700 million dollars. Boyle's five other clients had suffered the balance of the losses for a sum in excess of $1 billion.

In some ways, Boyle was right. The facts he recounted were true. The high share price was based on Maynard's good work developing CIT and well-timed speculation in California real estate. After the Internet boom, people and companies had made money, and the profits had to go somewhere. The stock market had collapsed, and investors looked to California real estate. Eric had predicted the flow of capital and wanted Maynard in first. The company made a $4 billion loan to CIT in early 2002 and directed CIT to use the loan to acquire large holdings in Los Angeles, San Diego, and San Francisco. The new buildings generated colossal rents every month, which CIT used to pay Maynard a 5 percent fixed-interest rate on the loan and make a profit for itself. As more money flowed into California, the value of the new properties had gone up, but the CIT share price had risen faster. When Maynard had crowed about its long-term strategy for CIT, it had fed the speculation, and the "California bubble" was made. It was a term Peyton had in her opening statement. Too much investment money had flooded California, raising real estate prices to irrational heights. Maynard had known it would happen, but according to Peyton, so had the Fund and every investment manager in the business.

Eric had seen the bubble coming and likened the frenzy to hundreds of millions of mice moving all at once from a few old office towers that had lost their heat to the new plush building nearby—the new digs were wonderful but not big enough for all of them. Peyton had told him to keep the simile to himself—comparing investors to rodents could blow back on him—and never ever put it in an e-mail or text message. He followed her advice.

Eric began the liquidation in 2006. He had sold off the first small block of CIT stock as a test. Nothing happened. Trading volume had remained the same, and the price stayed stable. At the end of 2006 and throughout 2007, the company had phased in a series of sales every month that liquidated two-thirds of its CIT shares at the highest prices in history. At the end of 2007, the market had reacted, and the price had dropped. In one year, CIT shares had lost 50 percent of their value. Maynard had kept selling and executed the full liquidation, which had forced the share price into the vertical fall Boyle had described. By February 2008, the stock price had fallen to twenty-six dollars a share, back to its 2002 price before the bubble had expanded. By September, shareholders had panicked, and CIT shares had been worth less than two dollars.

Maynard was pleased. It had made an exponential profit from the stock sale and still collected a 5 percent fixed-interest rate on the $4 billion loan to CIT, just as the entire economy entered the worst recession since 1929 and interest rates dropped to zero.

The Fund hadn't sold fast enough and had lost $700 million. The other plaintiffs had losses, but the Fund's losses were the largest.

Boyle had compared Eric's plan to creating an aneurysm in a patient on purpose and then opening the bubble, at first with a leak and then a pop. It was Boyle's second homicide analogy and had turned Eric cold. In a whisper, he had asked Peyton whether she could object and stop him. She had shaken her head, kept her eyes on Boyle, and never changed expression. Years before, Eric had used the word "aneurysm" in a directors' meeting to describe what would happen to the CIT share price. He'd been graphic. A few directors had cringed. One had laughed. A year before the trial, Peyton had ordered him to comb through the directors' minutes and notes looking for the discussion. He couldn't find the word or any reference to the CIT share price. Either the secretary had purged the minutes or left the discussion out, as if it had never happened.

"All those men," Boyle had said in his opening statement— he wrote the names of the Maynard and CIT executives on a dry marker board in front of the jury with Eric's name at the top of the list—"every one of them approved a plan that cheated investors. When Maynard sold, it made a fortune, and the stock price plummeted. The Fund lost hundreds of millions, and so did everyone else—everyone but Maynard."

More than anything, Boyle was infuriated by Eric's buy-back plan. In January 2010, seven months before the trial, Maynard had begun buying back CIT at less than two dollars per share. By the time Boyle and Peyton had picked the jury, Maynard had reacquired control of CIT for a fraction of the profit the company had made between 2002 and 2007. Business schools loved the strategy and had asked Eric to lecture on it. Peyton had instructed him to decline the invitations. Boyle had pointed across the courtroom when he described the buy-back plan. It was, he said, the final element of the scheme against the investing public. He had used the word "fraud," and his voice had dipped into a baritone. He paused after he said it so it would float in the air. Standing in front of the jury, he had said it again in a conversational tone, as if the jurors had been in his living room. He looked at them and scanned their eyes.

Eric had felt sick.

VII

Mexico City
Guana Cay

Leandro told Arnold to walk back to the club and open up the floor in the main room. Arnold stayed on the satellite phone and walked along the tarmac. He talked about the wind in the trees and the time it would take him to lock down the club, how the planes had to be bolted to the tarmac or they'd be blown away. As he listened, Leandro pulled up pictures and files of Noah Rolle and Pedro Martel. Noah's smile beamed from the computer screen. He was a native Bahamian and a private pilot. He had a wife and children and family members throughout the central Bahamas. If he had ever had an unhealthy ambition, he'd abandoned it long ago. Leandro clicked on a video of Noah on the tarmac next to his Cessna. Long limbed, Noah spoke of the weather, laughed, and patted the purple fuselage like the flank of a horse.

Martel was younger and ran Guana Cay day to day. At twenty-seven, he had proven himself. Arnold trusted, promoted, and vouched for him. Years earlier, Martel had sat on the transom of Arnold's fishing boat, miles off the western side of Great

Exuma, and answered questions. Leandro had sat in a fishing chair attached to a thick stainless steel column at the center of the stern. He had held on his lap a file of Honduran police reports, prison documents, and photographs. On the screen in his office, Leandro scrolled through photographs and a video taken that day. In the video, Martel had hollow cheeks, floppy black hair that fell over a hazy sloe-eyed face, and ragged clothing on a thin frame. Arnold had found him on Great Exuma lying in a cultivated row of onions and digging for food. He was less than one hundred pounds, too weak to run away. He lay on his side in the small garden with an onion in his hand. Arnold had stood over him with a shovel and considered his options.

Leandro clicked on the video and watched Martel explain himself. His head was Mayan, but he was taller, more Mexican in height, with an emaciated frame, crooked teeth, and an underbite. He sat in the sun, far from land, and rocked with the boat on a windy day. With only water behind him, he brushed back his hair and said that he had been born along an unused road on a hillside at the edge of Tegucigalpa, Honduras. The road was approximately one mile long. It stopped short of its intended connection at the edge of the city. Around it were shanties made of cinderblock, wood, and corrugated fiberglass. A culvert along the road had become an open sewer, and the shanties sent waste and trash down the hillside into a ravine. It was the smell, Martel had said, as he sat on the transom, that he remembered most. Whenever he encountered rotting fish or a malfunctioning septic tank, it reminded him of the road and shanties. Every few years, the Guardia came with bulldozers and destroyed the homes in a single day. In a few months, the people returned and rebuilt.

He had attended school through the eighth grade and had done well but left home at fourteen for something different. With friends, he had squatted in an abandoned building at the edge of the city and engaged in street theft for fun and money. On the video, he described how difficult it was to break into expensive homes in Tegucigalpa, because of gates, dogs, and guards. He turned to hijacking cars, which was safer, quicker and a high-volume business. He had hijacked Toyotas and Nissans throughout the city and sold them to men who stripped them for parts. But the American Express office on Boulevard Morazan was where the real money rolled to a stop. He said it with a small smile that came and went.

Leandro rewound the video and played it back. He watched Martel say the words "real money." He stopped it, rewound it, and played it again. Martel looked away, formed the smile around his crooked teeth, and emphasized the word "real." Then his mouth relaxed. Leandro let the video play out. Martel explained that he and a friend had dressed in good clothes, brushed their hair, and brought knives tucked inside their pants. A white Mercedes Benz sedan had come to a stop at the American Express office. The boys had moved across the street, distracted the driver with a question, and pulled him out through the window.

"I cut him on both palms," said Martel. "Deep, hit the bones, so he couldn't use his cell phone. The driver held his hands, looked at the blood, and screamed. When I cut the women, they screamed the loudest. It was crazy." He said the last sentence with a smile.

One day later, Martel was in a windowless room somewhere in Tegucigalpa. The Guardia beat him and broke his legs. They put him on a prison road project, where he spent three years limping, recovering, and shoveling asphalt. He was, he had told Leandro, reformed. He had learned from his mistakes and wanted a new life, something peaceful that allowed him to eat. He had joined work crews in the Caribbean that built hotels. His last stop was Great Exuma, where he lived in a locked trailer at night and built cinderblock walls for the Four Seasons Resort, now bankrupt. He escaped the work camp and nearly starved. Arnold had spared his life. Martel was willing to do anything.

Leandro stopped the video. Seven years before, he had left the stern, entered the cabin of Arnold's fishing boat, and closed the door. He'd removed a nine-millimeter semiautomatic pistol from his waistband, handed it to Arnold, and told him to shoot Martel. "Push him overboard," he had said. Arnold had put the weapon on the pilot's chair and spoken for the boy. He could be trained, Arnold had said. Martel would be grateful, loyal, and effective. Arnold had done it before with young men in the Dominican Republic; they were like stray dogs in need of food. It would work with Martel, because he was young and alone, not a gang member, nothing like the Mexicans along the Rio Grande who cut off each other's heads and stuck them on pikes like mile markers along a road.

Leandro had looked back at Martel through the glass windows of the cabin as Arnold spoke for him. Martel never turned away. He watched and waited.

"He's yours," Leandro had told Arnold. "Anything goes wrong, you fix it."

For seven years, Landing Four had operated well; now something had gone wrong, and Leandro would fly east.

"Search the island," Leandro said to Arnold. He clicked on the video again, which brought Martel's shy smile onto the screen. "Start with the perimeter. Walk slowly along the foot-paths and the runway, then to the water. Look along the rocks and beaches. You're looking for anything—anything that might tell us something."

"What do you think happened?" Arnold asked.

The question was annoying. "Figure it out. The island is your responsibility. I'll be there in four hours. Contact me if you find anything."

He ended the call and tapped Martel's satellite phone into the keyboard. A dial tone sounded, and a recorded voice answered. He terminated the call and tapped in Noah's number. No answer.

Leandro rolled his chair to the other end of the desk and picked up his office phone. He punched in four numbers and entered a prompting system that led him to Gregorio Gonzalez, who answered the call with a perfunctory, "Sat-Com."

"Can I come in?"

"For how long?"

"Thirty minutes."

"For what?"

"I need a tracking program for the next forty-eight hours."

"Come in now but not later. Only thirty minutes. I'll register you under the bank's name."

Leandro rose from his desk and walked down the hall to an elevator that took him thirteen floors down to the sky bridge that connected the glass tower to the smaller building two hundred feet to the north. He walked across the bridge and used his cell phone to dial the same number. He arrived at a door that read "Military Security—Sat-Com." On the other side, Gregorio Gonzalez rested his full hand within a molded plastic casing formed to fit a palm, thumb, and fingers. Green lights flashed, the machine read his hand, and Gonzalez's face and name appeared on the screen. The bolt on the door opened with a metallic thump. Leandro entered and followed Gonzalez through a narrow hallway into the secure area, surrounded by light that poured in from windows on three sides. He presented a bank identification card to an official at a desk and signed a logbook. Through a maze of cubicles, Gonzalez guided Leandro to a private office with a door that opened with the swipe of a card. Inside, computer servers lined the walls in glass cases. Five oversized monitors mounted above a workstation showed satellite images from the Gulf of Mexico, the Caribbean basin, and the Pacific. Gonzalez put on a headset and sat in a rolling chair. Leandro gave him a sheet of paper with three phone numbers.

"I want a broad search," Leandro said. "Code it in as bank security. Start with the first number. Tell me who he called and who called him over the past week, day by day, hour by hour. We need a written report that has all the traffic on that number, everything for the week. After that, let's pinpoint every spot where a transmission occurred. Again, assemble detail for the week up through the present."

Gonzalez looked up at Leandro. "Who are we tracking?"

"A thief."

"What did he..."

"Don't ask."

"How do you think he's moving?"

"By boat, but it's a guess."

Gonzalez entered Martel's satellite phone number into the servers for the eastern Caribbean. Within thirty seconds, he received a full report on the phone for the last seven days. There were sixteen hits that appeared on the screen. Over Gonzalez's shoulder, Leandro recognized each one. All were calls to or from Arnold Glass. Next to each number was the time and duration. The last one, transmitted that day, was from Arnold to Martel in the morning. It lasted four minutes.

"How about the geographical work?"

Gonzalez downloaded the list of calls into another server. The list reappeared on the screen with a new set of data to the right that showed the latitude and longitude of each call. He downloaded the data into a mapping program and produced a satellite image of the central Bahamas. A blue light blinked in the Exuma Cays. Gonzalez descended and stopped at an image of Guana Cay. The two planes were parked on the tarmac. The blue light blinked at the dock.

"He made the first call at the end of the dock, seven days ago: July thirtieth at 11:02 a.m."

"Next one," said Leandro.

Gonzalez called up the locations where Martel's satellite phone made or received a call. Each location was on or near Guana Cay, except one. On August 2, Martel was in Georgetown, Great Exuma, fifty miles south, and had received a call from Arnold.

"Georgetown."

Gonzalez looked up. "Unusual?"

"Maybe. Now do a search of all satellite phone transmissions in the last two hours. Make the search within a one-hundred-mile radius of the island."

Gonzalez looked up. "All units?"

"Satellite phones only."

"Nassau is within the radius. We'll get tens of thousands of hits."

"You're looking for a moving shipment. It's a phone that turns on briefly and turns off. It moves quickly over the water and turns on again. It's tradecraft. He doesn't want to be found."

Gonzalez looked up at Leandro. "How do we know he's on the water?"

"It's how we trained him. If I'm right, the pattern should be obvious. Most people turn on a satellite phone and leave it on, particularly at sea. They think of it as a locator and a safety device. Our man is different. He wants to disappear. If he turns it on, he'll do it only because he has to. Then he'll turn it off and keep moving." Leandro put his finger near the screen that showed a satellite image of the Bahamas. He pointed just south of Nassau. "If Martel is here and heading north into the Florida Keys, he'll make a single call, turn the phone off, and then move across the water, maybe fifty or one hundred miles. Then he might use it again. That's what you are looking for."

Gonzalez gave a low whistle. "Don't be too hopeful."

Leandro sat down in a second rolling chair. "Narrow the numbers any way you can. Don't look at the units on the islands. Filter them out. That will remove everything in Nassau and Freeport. When you identify a transmission within the radius, record the number, the location, and the length of the transmission. Keep the search live and continuous; slowly expand the radius. Sort them by frequency and location. If he's got a high-speed boat in open water, it will show up. The transmissions will be many miles apart during a short time period. Contact me over the encrypted site if you find anything. I'll feed you information when I can."

The men stood up, and Gonzalez escorted Leandro back to the security desk and then out of the door to the sky bridge. Leandro reentered the glass tower. At his desk, he logged in to the encrypted site on his desktop and redialed Arnold, who answered immediately.

"Have you found anything?"

"The earth next to the steps was turned with a shovel. There's a stain on the stones. It could be something. Other than that, it's clean."

"Get the place ready for the storm. I'll be there while it's still light."

Leandro terminated the call and lit a cigarette. A plume of blue smoke curled up and around his face. He removed a soft leather briefcase from a lower drawer of his desk. From the middle pouch, he pulled a 5.7-millimeter semiautomatic pistol with a four-and-a-half-inch barrel. It was an FN MK52 manufactured by FN Herstal in Belgium, exceptionally accurate and for military use only. He looked through the barrel to be sure it was clean. He checked the hammer mechanism, squeezed the trigger, dry-fired it, cocked it again, and squeezed the trigger a second time. A slip in the briefcase held a suppressor, six inches long and nearly two inches in diameter. Leandro screwed it tightly in place over the barrel. Five magazines were in other slips. One was empty. The other four had twenty rounds each. In the desk's middle drawer, a cardboard box contained hollow-point bullets with blue polymer tips. Individually wrapped in smooth tissue paper, they would expand on impact and tumble through the target. He unwrapped the bullets and inserted twenty into the empty magazine, which he then slid into the handle of the Herstal and locked in place. Leandro flipped the switch on the side to the safe position and set the weapon within leather straps on the inside of the briefcase.

Behind the desk in a wooden cabinet was a safe bolted to the wall. Leandro swiveled on his chair, spun the combination lock, and pulled open the door. A thin stainless steel box rested on the top shelf and shone bright when he brought it into the light. Inside were items labeled in Spanish: a bottle, a scalpel, four syringes, eight needles, and numerous vials of clear liquids with bands of different colors to identify each substance. The vials had red rubber tops that a needle could penetrate to remove the liquid. One at a time, Leandro held the vials up to the window and shook them. They were full. He arranged them in the steel box, closed it, and stowed it in the briefcase.

On his computer, he returned to the encrypted website and dialed a number. A tired voice with an Irish lilt, not yet awake, provided an annoyed greeting in one word: "Yes."

"I want you at La Paz in one hour," said Leandro. "The plane will be ready. A package has gone missing, so bring someone who knows what he's doing."

Sean Fallon sat on the edge of his bed with the phone at his ear and rubbed the top of his head. The shades were drawn. Behind him in the bed slept a woman. He looked at the clock; it was mid-morning. He confirmed he would be at the plane, hung up the phone, and dialed. In an apartment in a leafy section of the city, Joseph Dominquez lay in bed, awake, staring at the ceiling when his phone rang. He answered and listened to the instructions. It would be like the Grenadines, Sean told him, three days, in and out, just like two years ago. Joseph rolled out of bed, packed a small bag, and left the apartment.

In an anteroom to the office, Leandro opened a closet that held a folding suitcase, suits, jackets, a blue blazer, some ties, and pressed pants. He packed the blazer and pants in the suitcase. He added socks and shoes from a chest of drawers. In the top drawer were two Texas driver's licenses, both with Houston addresses, and two US passports bearing Leandro's face but with different names. He slid them into compartments in the briefcase and left his office.

In an elevator from the twenty-eighth floor, Leandro descended to a garage where he had parked a Range Rover for trips to the airport. He drove out of the garage and up onto Reforma. He turned east around Chapultepec and followed the access roads to 195D, east to the private airports at the edge of Mexico City. When he was not in the hills, he drove the car at eighty miles per hour on the highway toward La Paz. In forty minutes, he walked up the steps into the fuselage of a Citation, fueled and ready to fly, at one end of a private runway. Sean and Joseph sat in leather chairs and sipped coffee. Leandro took a map from his pocket and spread it across a table in front of the two men.

VIII

Foley Square

The folder from Smythe was thick, but the word IBERIA meant nothing to Boyle. He heard of it first from Smythe two weeks into the trial and then in the courthouse hallway when they paced and decided to call Eric Olsen as a witness. It was Smythe's strategy—to delay the end of their case and "save the trial." It would open up discovery again, Smythe was certain of it.

Boyle opened the folder. The first sheet was a series of questions that related to the 2002 Maynard financial statements and compensation paid to the company leadership over the last eight years. He looked at the attached document, a real estate closing agreement. The remaining questions were standard but not related to CIT. They focused on the required disclosures under the securities laws and compensation Maynard paid to executives years ago.

Judge Stapleton removed his glasses and wiped them with a cloth. Boyle watched the judge and wondered how Smythe's questions were relevant to a drop in CIT's stock price years after the date on the documents. Nothing in front of him related to the original Complaint and his theory of civil liability. His whole case had been in his opening statement—Maynard had misled the investing public about CIT—and every wrong flowed from that. It was simple, which is what Boyle had told the jury. Stapleton would find the new approach puzzling, possibly desperate. Peyton would object; the judge would agree. Boyle would lose the jury, if he hadn't already. He looked back at Smythe, still standing at the defense table, and wiped moisture from his upper lip with a handkerchief.

Judge Stapleton interrupted his thoughts. "Mr. Boyle?"

Boyle turned back to the judge. "Yes, Your Honor?"

———

Peyton had exposed the weaknesses in Boyle's case from the beginning, and it had unraveled earlier in the day. She had scoffed at Boyle's opening. "Simple? Yes," she had said. "Lies and deceit? No." CIT was always the centerpiece of Maynard's US strategy— of course it was—but not the way the Fund expected. Maynard had planned the loan and liquidation to take advantage of what it thought would happen in the near future. Maynard recognized the California bubble, and the Fund should have too, because CIT stock was publicly traded.

Early in the trial, she had walked to the projection screen and asked Boyle to put up his own calendar of events and stock-price list from 2007 and 2008. She recited the prices day by day for November 2007. "Were these publicly known?" She had asked. "Yes, of course they were." The Fund's financial advisors knew the price of CIT stock "by the minute," she had said. "They subscribed to every investor information service on the planet and paid people to watch price monitors. They used their own judgment not to sell in a high market, and they turned out to be wrong."

"Maynard protected itself, which is what it's supposed to do," she said. "The Fund sat on its hands as the bubble deflated and the share price dropped. Now it wants a bailout." Maynard, she had said, had predicted what would happen and preserved its assets. Like many other corporations, it sold off CIT shares at their maximum value to protect its own shareholders and maintain financial stability. Many other investors had sold when Maynard did, and Peyton named them. It was a long list of pension funds, mutual funds, and wealthy individuals. Peyton inserted a thumb drive into Boyle's laptop and projected their names in blue block letters onto the screen. Next to each name were entries for the number of CIT shares owned and the dates of liquidation, all of which occurred in 2006 or early 2007.

"Did the company speculate in the California real estate market?" Peyton asked. "Yes, it did. That's not illegal. Just because Maynard succeeds out there"—she pointed to the west—"doesn't mean it has to insure the CIT stock price here"—she pointed south to Wall Street. "There is nothing in the law that requires Maynard to send up a warning flare every time it sells stock on the public markets. The Fund should have used better judgment like everyone else"—she pointed to the list on the projection screen—"and sold when Maynard did."

Peyton identified a man and woman in the first row of benches behind the counsel tables. The Fund's investment advisors had watched the markets every day but did nothing as the share price dropped. "The Fund should look to them for the lost money," she said, "not to Maynard." And in the inter-vening years, the price had gone up to eighteen dollars a share. Eric's buy-back plan had worked. "The stock is coming back," Peyton had said. "It's no different from the price of a building or a farm—it can go up, and it can go down—but Maynard doesn't insure the price, and certainly not for those who fail to act."

Peyton had torn at Boyle's case when she cross-examined his witnesses. In the first week, Boyle had done well; Peyton hadn't made progress. The second week was mixed. In the third week, she had asserted control over every witness Boyle had called. Smythe had warned him. She was executing Maynard's defense using the Fund's own people. She had them agreeing with her about what the Fund knew and when it knew it, the obligations of the Fund's financial advisors, and the other in-vestors who had sold promptly before the bubble had burst. It was the persistent problem in the Fund's narrative—the Fund paid people to watch the markets, and they knew what was happening. Peyton exposed it to the jury in her opening and with every witness Boyle called.

Smythe had talked to Boyle at the end of each trial day. He likened the cross-examination to Peyton pulling at the case's main problem like a thread in a tapestry. Boyle tried to weave and knot it; Peyton wouldn't let him. She pulled only as much as necessary with each witness, depending on what the witness knew and when. But with each one, she succeeded, and Boyle couldn't tighten the weave. The knots were loose, sometimes with threads hanging, ready to be pulled apart, and incapable of forming the image Boyle wanted.

It all unraveled on the twentieth day of trial, moments before Eric took the stand. Boyle had closed his narrative with Professor Daniel Chrepto, a financial expert from the Massachusetts Institute of Technology. The professor's testimony was positioned to bring the case together and rebut the points Peyton had scored in her cross-examination of other witnesses. Boyle expected Chrepto to be the capstone, the lid of the strongbox, slammed shut, convincing, and sound—perhaps an epiphany for some, but generally enough to make the jurors collectively nod to each other in the deliberation room and agree that Boyle's version of events was correct. In his direct testimony, Chrepto had succeeded. Like the other jurors, the woman with pink lipstick kept her eyes on him and glanced away only to write notes.

Professor Chrepto was rumored to be on a shortlist for the Nobel Prize. He specialized in economic projections and the value of marketable securities. Boyle had asked him all of Smythe's prepared questions, and the professor had responded. He offered the jury a series of equations that rebutted Peyton's common-sense approach. According to the professor, the CIT stock price would fall so rapidly the moment Maynard sold a designated percentage of the stock that no act by other stockholders could possibly have avoided massive losses. Best of all, Chrepto had relied on Maynard's internal documents that showed Maynard's plan to liquidate CIT stock as early as 2004. Maynard had known in advance exactly what the professor established in his equations: massive and unavoidable losses for investors.

Like any good teacher, Chrepto had a gift for presenting his work to those who knew nothing about it. He explained in simple terms a complicated set of circumstances and assured the jury that Boyle's case was unassailably correct: Maynard's scheme was intentional and timed so perfectly that no investor could have avoided large losses. Anyone who did was lucky, not smart.

Boyle's last question had been beautifully staged. "Professor," Boyle had asked, "what was Maynard doing when it told the public that CIT was the centerpiece of its long-term growth strategy?"

Chrepto answered on cue: "Maynard lied," he said. "All along, the company planned to liquidate. Their statements show it. Their documents prove it. But they never told the public for one reason. They wanted to keep stock and real estate prices at all-time highs as they liquidated. When Maynard sold rapidly, CIT shareholders took huge financial losses, but not Maynard. The company made a fortune at the expense of everyone else."

"Your witness, Ms. Sorel." Boyle gathered his papers, snapped a folder shut, and left the lectern.

With his thin white hair and avuncular baritone, Chrepto was someone the jury could trust. He respected and spoke to them directly. They came alive when he looked at them. No longer randomly selected members of a jury pool, they were students attending a presentation by a future Nobel laureate.

When Peyton stood up to cross-examine, Boyle rocked back in his chair, hands together, fingers at his lips. He expected her to argue with Chrepto for hours and drown in a sea of numbers. It was his ideal scenario. It didn't happen.

At first, Peyton asked general questions. She asked Chrepto about the documents and testimony he reviewed to prepare for trial. They were on a forty-seven-page list he had attached to the back of his expert report. The list included every document and piece of sworn testimony in the case. Chrepto affirmed he had read them, every sentence and word, the testimony, documents, charts and graphs. He knew them all.

"You read all fifty-five depositions?" Peyton asked.

"I did."

"Every page?"

"Every one."

"And you read your client's testimony, correct?"

"Yes."

"You relied on that testimony to form your opinion?"

"Of course."

"Then you understand this case?"

The professor had no choice. He responded with a confident yes.

"You're certain that the Fund never knew the risks of the bubble before 2007?"

Chrepto paused and provided an equivocal answer. "I believe so, yes."

Smythe folded one leg over another and adjusted his chair. He looked down and listened for the next question.

The jurors sat up. Some leaned forward. The woman in pink lipstick looked at Smythe and then at Chrepto.

It was the answer Peyton wanted. "You wrote that in your expert report."

"Did I?"

Peyton turned to the defense table. "Rachael, please put Exhibit 10 on the screen."

Peyton's associate, Rachael Hill, touched a key on a computer, and Chrepto's report appeared on the screen directly across the courtroom from the jury.

"Take us to page three, second paragraph. Highlight it, and bring it out."

Rachael enlarged the text and highlighted it in lemon yellow. Chrepto had confidently written in his report that the Fund had never known the risks of holding CIT stock beyond 2006, because Maynard had lied. Peyton read him the entry.

"Did I read that correctly?"

"Yes."

"You wrote that?"

"I did."

"That's your carefully considered opinion?"

"Yes."

"You wouldn't have written that if you didn't think it was true?"

"That's right."

A southern lilt crept into her cadence, and Peyton went for his throat. "Professor, in forming your opinion, did you consider the sworn testimony of an officer of your own client"—Peyton pointed just beyond the defense table to the first row of benches—"who testified that the Fund knew the long-term risks of the California real estate stock but elected to invest anyway?"

Chrepto froze. The jury saw it. He didn't know what she was talking about and couldn't summon anything in memory. He had chosen to stay positive, as Smythe had instructed. He leaned forward, his mouth at the microphone, and gave the wrong answer. "I know of no such testimony." His voice filled the courtroom.

Smythe locked his jaw. He had prepared Chrepto for everything but this and had hoped that Peyton would not use the troubling exchange buried deep within forty-five thousand pages of deposition testimony.

"Rachael, please call up Smith clip six." In seconds, the presentable head and shoulders of Dexter Smith, vice chair of the Fund's investment committee, appeared on the screen. At the trial, Smith sat in the first row of benches, directly behind Boyle. He wore a bowtie and khaki suit. The woman in pink lipstick looked at Smith's image on the screen, to Smith in the courtroom, and then back to the screen. Smith was one of five men who presided over the Fund's portfolio, a sum in excess of $15 billion. Within the video clip, the jurors heard Peyton's voice ask a question: "Mr. Smith, did you analyze the risks of the California real estate market?"

"I did."

"For the Fund?"

"Yes."

"In 2002?"

"Yes."

"In 2004?"

"Yes."

"And the years beyond that?"

"Yes."

"Did you analyze the risk to the CIT stock price if Maynard decided to sell?"

"I did."

"And at that time, did you know the term 'California bubble'?"

"I did."

"Did you report your findings to the Fund?"

"Yes."

"Did you inform the Fund of the risks?"

"Yes."

"The Fund decided to hold the stock?"

"Yes."

"And buy more?"

"Yes."

"The Fund knew the risks?"

"They did."

The video clip stopped, and the screen went black. In the courtroom, Peyton addressed Chrepto. "That was Dexter Smith's testimony, Professor, wasn't it?"

"It was."

"And he swore to tell the truth, correct?"

"I suppose so."

Smythe never ordered the DVDs from the court reporting service for Dexter Smith's deposition, so Peyton took a chance. "You've never seen that testimony before, have you?"

Chrepto was annoyed. "I read the depositions, Ms. Sorel, but I've never seen the video."

Peyton repeated the question. "Before today, you have never actually seen that testimony, have you?"

He had to answer her. "No, I have not."

Peyton faced Boyle and Smythe. The woman in pink lipstick turned her head and followed Peyton. Peyton turned back to Chrepto, and the woman's gaze went with her. "The lawyers for the Fund never showed you that testimony, did they? They never gave you the DVD of Dexter Smith."

"That's right," said the professor. "They never showed it to me."

Chrepto was more compliant than she expected. In defense of his own integrity, he gave up without a quarrel. For four hours, he had testified for Boyle about every issue in the trial. In ten minutes, he admitted for Peyton that Boyle and Smythe had withheld evidence and manipulated his opinion.

Smythe's face flushed. His even tan turned to hot sunburn. The rant Boyle would inflict would be punishing.

Peyton continued. "Let's go back to your report, sir."

Exhibit 10 re-appeared on the screen.

"Professor, isn't it true that you wrote in your report that the Fund would not have held onto CIT shares unless Maynard gave assurances that there would be no sell-off? You remember writing that?"

"Yes."

"'Unusual and out of the ordinary' is how you wrote it. Do you recall that phrase?"

"I think so, yes."

"Professor, it's right on the screen in front of you."

Chrepto looked at the screen. Rachael enlarged the phrase and highlighted it in yellow. Chrepto read the phrase and nodded. "So it is. Yes, I wrote that it would be unusual and out of the ordinary for the Fund to take a risk and hold the CIT stock without assurances from Maynard."

"Did you consider, Professor, testimony from the Fund that it was neither unusual nor out of the ordinary for the Fund to take an investment risk that Maynard might sell off CIT shares at their all-time high?"

Smythe felt cold.

Chrepto sat lower in the witness chair and smiled weakly. "I do not recall the testimony."

"I do. Rachael?" Peyton asked her to play a clip from the deposition testimony of Sharon Urban.

When her face appeared on the screen, Sharon Urban, who sat next to Dexter Smith in the first row of benches, stiffened. She had worked with Smith and educated the machinists on the Fund's portfolio. On the screen, her face was three feet high.

Peyton's voice came through the audio portion of the clip. "Ms. Urban, was it unusual or out of the ordinary for the machinists to take an investment risk when they knew that Maynard might sell off CIT shares at their all-time high?"

On the screen, Sharon had paused and waited. Twice, she had looked off-camera to her lawyers, then back to the papers in front of her, and up to the camera. For forty-five seconds, she was silent and waited.

Peyton had been patient. "Sharon," she had said within the film clip, "your lawyer can't answer the question for you. You have to answer it yourself."

The juror with pink lipstick wrote on her notepad.

In the courtroom, Sharon closed her eyes.

"No," she said on the screen, over the audio part of the film clip. "It was not unusual or out of the ordinary."

On the screen, Peyton drove in a nail: "Why, Sharon? Why was it neither unusual nor out of the ordinary for the Fund to take the risk?"

"Because the Fund's long-term growth strategy required some risk. We knew there could be a large sell-off as the stock price soared. The Fund would sell if, you know, if it needed to. We didn't sell. I'm not sure why."

The screen went black. Peyton looked at Professor Chrepto. She'd always liked him. Long before the trial, they had met at his deposition and spent a full day together.

"You never saw that testimony either, did you, Professor?"

"No, I did not."

Peyton looked back at Boyle and Smythe and then directly to Chrepto. "The lawyers for the Fund never showed it to you?"

"No, they did not."

She wasn't finished. "How much do you charge?" She knew his rates.

"Two thousand dollars."

Peyton feigned surprise. "Per hour?"

"Yes."

"How much did Mr. Boyle pay you for your testimony?" She knew the answer.

"More than one million."

"Your yearly salary at MIT is less than one-third of that, correct?"

"Correct."

Peyton smiled. "You bought a beach house on Cape Cod with that million, didn't you?"

Before Boyle could stand and object, Chrepto had agreed with Peyton, who gathered her papers at the lectern, looked at Judge Stapleton, and said that she had no further questions.

Smythe had worked against Peyton for two years. In ten minutes, he watched her destroy a future Nobel Prize winner. Chrepto stepped down from the witness stand, and no one asked him to stay. Smythe imagined him as the only living victim of a terrible highway accident. He choked at the possibility that the professor might turn on Boyle in the courtroom, take the stand on behalf of Maynard, and rip another hole in the Fund's case. Smythe exhaled when Chrepto continued to the back of the courtroom, gathered his belongings, and left.

Peyton returned to her chair and waited for Boyle to call another witness. Smythe watched her. Everything she did distracted him. At forty, she looked younger, as if she should not replace the lead lawyer in a massive securities case. Two years earlier, Smythe had wondered if other attorneys would appear, and they had. Each one reported to Peyton. Her face was symmetrical but set off by the aquiline nose. When he wasn't looking at her face, he followed her legs, cut and shaped for speed. He watched her walk back from the lectern as Chrepto gathered his papers, pressed them to his chest, and fled the courtroom. It was as if she'd done it all before, every step, with an easy stride.

At the defense table, Peyton whispered in Eric's ear. "If that's all he has, this could be over." Eric could smell her perfume. She was five feet, eight inches in bare feet, approximately 140 pounds with no clothes. She rocked back in her chair as Boyle stood and asked the judge for ten minutes. Eric stared at her profile and the small gold studs she wore in her earlobes. She wrote a note on a yellow pad and slid it to Eric: "Pay attention."

IX

Foley Square

When Professor Chrepto walked out of the courtroom, Boyle and Smythe had nothing left. Boyle asked for a recess and walked the long hallway on the sixth floor. Smythe had warned him throughout the trial that the witnesses hadn't done well under cross-examination. At breaks in the trial, Boyle had snapped at him and asked what he intended to do about it. In the hallway, Smythe gave him the answer.

Peyton spoke with Eric at the other end and watched Boyle and Smythe over Eric's shoulder. For five minutes, the two men spoke in animated whispers. Boyle was threatening, his index finger tracing lines in the air in front of Smythe's face. The discussion ended when Boyle walked away. Peyton watched him disappear toward an elevator and then turned her eyes back to Smythe, alone at the end of the hallway. He looked up and walked away.

In the courtroom, with Eric on the witness stand, Judge Stapleton broke Boyle's thoughts. "Counsel, shall we proceed?"

"Forgive me, Your Honor, was there a question pending?"

From his perch above the courtroom, Stapleton finished cleaning his glasses and rested them at the end of his nose. "No. You haven't asked one."

The woman with pink lipstick laughed. Other jurors smiled.

The judge pointed to the clock. "Will you finish your side of the case today?"

"Probably not, Your Honor."

Boyle looked down at the open folder and the questions Smythe had written. Behind him, he heard Smythe arrange the box on the table so the same word, written in block letters, faced the jury. Boyle looked back and saw IBERIA stenciled in black letters on the front of the box.

Boyle ignored Smythe's written questions and moved forward on his own. "In your opinion," Boyle asked Eric—Peyton rose from her chair—"were Maynard's statements to the investing public the result of intentional desire to mislead?"

"Objection, calls for an opinion," Peyton said, standing.

"Sustained," said Judge Stapleton

"In your opinion…"

Peyton: "Objection."

"Sustained."

Boyle felt an expletive move up his throat. "Your Honor," he said, "may I approach?" Judge Stapleton motioned for Boyle and Peyton to approach the bench. Boyle pleaded. "The witness is the chief financial officer of Maynard. He is fully capable of stating his opinion on Maynard's motives and misconduct."

"We object," Peyton said. "The Fund couldn't have been misled about facts it already knew. That's been established by Mr. Boyle's own witnesses, including his expert. Mr. Olsen hasn't been qualified as an expert about whether any of Maynard's statements were misleading or intentionally misleading, which we deny. Mr. Boyle should be asking questions about what Mr. Olsen knew and when he knew it. Otherwise, we'll continue to object."

The judge looked down at Boyle. "Objection sustained."

Peyton continued. "By the way, Mr. Smythe just put a box on counsel table with a word on it. It's a demonstration, inappropriate and prejudicial. We request that Mr. Smythe remove the box."

Judge Stapleton had a thin, razor-like nose and a patch of uncombed white hair. He looked at Boyle. "Remove the box."

Boyle turned to Smythe and shook his head. Smythe complied.

The judge spoke. "The objection is sustained. You have to seek facts from this witness, not opinions. Ask him what he knew and when he knew it. You already presented an expert, such as he was. How many more witnesses do you have?"

"Mr. Olsen is our last witness today."

"May I respond to that?" Peyton asked.

The judge turned to her and nodded.

"Mr. Olsen is not just their last witness today, Your Honor. Mr. Olsen is their last witness, period. They've called everyone on their list. There isn't anyone else, unless they plan to call every witness on my list."

The judge raised his hand, and Peyton stopped. "Mr. Boyle, is this the last witness in your case?"

"Technically, yes."

"Technically? It better count. I haven't seen anything that looks like fraud. Your clients were free to read the stock pages every day. The jury might not get this case."

Boyle's mouth went dry. Judge Stapleton referred to the directed verdict Peyton wanted. If the judge thought Boyle's evidence was insufficient, he could take the decision away from the jury, grant a verdict for Maynard, and send everyone home. Directed verdicts were almost unheard of, but when they happened, clients sued law firms. They could begin the irreversible decline in a firm's practice.

Judge Stapleton sent Peyton back to the defense table, and Boyle met Smythe at the lectern. Boyle received a second folder from Smythe and opened it to a few pages of questions written by hand. He read them; they were new. Smythe returned to the plaintiffs' table, sat down, and looked up at Boyle, who pursed his lips. Smythe nodded.

Eric watched from the witness stand.

Boyle cleared his throat. "You reviewed the books and records of Maynard from 2005, didn't you?"

"Yes."

"In 2005, the Maynard executive committee received approximately fifty million dollars in bonus compensation, correct?"

"Approximately."

"Twelve people on the committee, correct?"

"Yes."

"And all compensation is reported in the audited financial statements?"

"Yes."

"The reason compensation is reported in the audited financial statements is so the investing public knows what the executive committee is paid year to year, including bonuses, true?" Smythe had provided a new path, and bravado crept into Boyle's voice.

The woman in the pink lipstick sat up and leaned forward. "Of course." Eric tried to deflate the moment.

"So it would be wrong if the Maynard executive committee failed to reveal to stockholders that they had received more than fifty million in bonuses for that year, true?"

Boyle had just changed the nature of the case, but Peyton chose not to object. Eric handled it. "If executives receive a bonus, Maynard must report it in the audited financial statements. We did that. We reported compensation properly."

Boyle focused. "In 2002, did the Maynard executive committee receive compensation other than what's set forth on the audited financial statements?"

The question asked for information before the 2006 stock sell-off. Peyton objected, but Judge Stapleton overruled the objection and told Eric to answer the question.

"I began work for Maynard in October of 2002, so I'm not fully aware of everything that happened in that year." It was an incomplete answer. He had no script for 2002.

"You're the chief financial officer, correct?"

"Yes."

"Starting in 2002?"

"Yes."

"The financial historian of the company?"

"For some things—not all."

"At any time in 2002, did Maynard operate offshore companies whose assets were not reported in public filings to the Securities Exchange Commission?"

Eric hesitated and looked to the wall at the back of the courtroom. Instead of a confident no, he paused. Peyton stopped her pen in midsentence, and it bled through the writing pad. Maynard had created hundreds of subsidiaries over the years; each one had a purpose related to the finance, purchase, or sale of real estate. Eric adjusted his body in the chair, leaned forward, and spoke into the microphone.

"I don't think so, no. I can't say that there were." He was equivocal. It was exactly what she'd told him not to be, but he wasn't ready for 2002. All Peyton could do was listen and wait.

"What about Iberia Company?"

Peyton wrote the word "Iberia," underlined it, and pushed the pad to her left. Rachael shook her head.

"What about it?" asked Eric.

"Have you ever heard of it?"

"Just the name."

Boyle turned to the jury. "Do you recall what the company did?"

"No."

"Tell us. Where did Maynard get four billion dollars in 2002 to loan to CIT?"

Boyle had done it. He'd linked the case to 2002. Eric paused again. Peyton stood and objected. Judge Stapleton told Eric to answer the question.

"I don't know specifically. We're an international real estate company. We have revenue every day. Over time, it accumulates. But I wasn't with the company when that revenue came in."

Boyle smiled and nodded. "That's good," he said, "you're the chief financial officer, and you don't know where four billion dollars came from." Peyton stood to object, but Boyle withdrew his comment. He looked to Judge Stapleton: "I'd like an adjournment, Your Honor, and I'll resume with this witness tomorrow."

Peyton asked to approach the bench. Out of the jury's hearing, she directed her statements to Judge Stapleton: "Your Honor, we'd like to know the relevance of these questions and where Mr. Boyle is going with this witness."

Boyle nearly lunged at her. "I don't have to tell you anything."

The judge raised his hand and asked the lawyers to take their seats. He turned to the jury. "You are dismissed for the day. Please return to the jury room tomorrow no later than nine thirty in the morning. We appreciate your patience. As I instructed, you are not to discuss this case among yourselves or with anyone else, including your families. Have a pleasant evening."

The jury filed out, and the court clerk closed the door.

X

Foley Square

The judge motioned for Peyton and Boyle to return to the bench. He drank water from a paper cup. "Mr. Boyle, you will resume your examination tomorrow morning at ten o'clock." The court clerk tapped the instructions into a schedule.

Peyton asked to speak, and the judge nodded. "Your Honor, Maynard intends to move for a directed verdict."

"Understood, Ms. Sorel." He didn't discourage her.

Boyle interrupted. "We may be able to locate other witnesses and documents, Your Honor. We need an adjournment of one week."

"One week? What basis do you have to hold up this jury while you seek other witnesses?"

"With respect, Your Honor, former Maynard officers will establish an offshore subsidiary in Bermuda that Maynard used to funnel unreported income to the executive committee, now and in the past. We also suspect the subsidiary was the source of cash that became the CIT real estate—four billion, never reported. These are false statements to stockholders, the Securities Exchange Commission, and the Internal Revenue Service. We need more time."

The judge was curt. "This is about a stock drop between 2006 and 2009, not an offshore company in 2002. How is that relevant?"

Boyle looked back at Smythe, who nodded. "We can link it up, Your Honor. The whole scheme was ongoing."

"Who are you looking for?"

"George Harwood, Maynard's former treasurer and chief financial officer. He orchestrated an illegal compensation structure. The speculation in the California real estate market through CIT was a small part of it. We need his deposition."

Peyton was stunned. Boyle had to be making this up. She had never even heard of Iberia. "Your Honor," she said, "I've never heard of this company. None of this is in the Fund's Complaint. I can't see how this relates to the case we've been trying for the last twenty days. Mr. Boyle submitted his witness list three months ago. Mr. Harwood's name is not on it. He retired eight years ago. Now, the plaintiffs want a fishing trip in the middle of the trial." She looked at Boyle. "How would an offshore company from 2002 be relevant to the CIT stock losses four and five years later?"

———

The accusation was as personal as it was unsettling. George Harwood had hired Peyton. He was a family friend who'd grown up with Peyton's father in North Carolina. She'd encountered him at family events in the summers and known him since her childhood. He'd paid attention to her, followed her progress through college and law school, and helped her when she had arrived in New York.

George had gone to college in the Northeast and, as a young man, had helped found Maynard in the 1960s. He had built it into an international holding company with assets in Europe, South America, and every major American city. For forty years, George personified Maynard, becoming the single most powerful officer in the company. He hired and fired CEOs, chose when to issue or buy back stock, and developed the strategies for expansion on a global scale. George created Maynard subsidiaries every year for many different partnerships and joint ventures. Peyton knew the method and purpose. It was the routine way Maynard owned and developed real estate. George was shrewd, political, and often manipulative, but he was honest and way too smart to be a tax cheat.

George had chosen Peyton from among many to litigate and try cases for the company. He had recommended to her father Edmund that she interview at Stewart & Stevens, Maynard's firm of choice, while she was in law school. She met with George's primary lawyer, Arthur Konigsberg, who hired her immediately at the top salary in New York for any first year associate. She wasn't vain enough to think she deserved it, but Edmund had told her to enjoy it while it lasted; it was the only solace to offset the endless nights, early mornings, and lack of sleep.

At George's request, Arthur made certain she was on every Maynard assignment in the firm. At first, her role was to support others, but soon she had an opportunity to try a case. No one else wanted it. When other lawyers heard the case name, they excused themselves from conference rooms or walked the other way, as if to avoid infection. Everyone expected a loss. She recalled Arthur showing her a room full of evidence boxes and telling her that she wouldn't win. "Sometimes," he said, "bad cases have to be tried and lost. Think of it as training." The firm wanted to force plaintiffs to win their cases, not just litigate to jury selection and a settlement. Even if she lost but kept the damages low, Arthur had told her, she could declare victory. Arthur and George had come to the trial and sat in the last row of benches. She presented the evidence clearly and connected with the jury. Her cross-examination was unexpected. It appeared innate, fully developed with little or no experience. She won a defense verdict, and her training ended.

George started to work with her directly, and Arthur made sure she was part of the trial team on every major Maynard case. In time, Peyton became Maynard's trial lawyer of choice at Stewart & Stevens, the one person with whom George wanted to speak if litigation was a threat.

George sat with her through trials, offered suggestions, testified, and taught her the business. Earlier trials had involved real estate valuations, international acquisitions, tax disputes, and contracts. She'd won them all. He had taught her how to simplify for a jury the complex nature of financial transactions. "They're actually simple if you keep an eye on the abstract design," he had said. On a single sheet of paper, he had drawn schematics to explain how the transactions worked. "The execution is often complicated, but if you remember the original design, you won't get lost, and neither will a judge or jury."

It had taken a few years, but George had taught her what he described as "the art he practiced." In a trial on an international acquisition with which French investors were unhappy, George had sat with Peyton at the defense table and testified for Maynard. It was ten years ago, and he had been sixty-seven. He was short and thin, with close-cropped hair at the top of a high forehead. He looked great in a dark-gray suit, but he understated everything, as if he were the company's beneficent uncle, not just hers. She remembered he'd opted for a camelhair jacket with suede patches on the elbow and brown leather shoes, slightly scuffed. When he turned to the jury and spoke, he was a professor—more Chrepto than Chrepto—and explained the essential facts of the transaction so they could understand it. He'd instructed her to ask questions that allowed him to explain and repeat the essential facts three times. At the trial, she had asked him to step off the witness stand and walk to a marker board. He had stood at the board like a teacher, not an international real estate baron, and drew simple designs with colored pens. He made it easy for her. And when the jury rendered the favorable verdict, he gave her all the credit. By the time George had retired in 2002, Peyton was in a corner office at Stewart & Stevens. The money came with it.

The last time she had seen him was at her husband's funeral more than three years ago in Pennsylvania. He had flown in from the Caribbean and hadn't looked well. There was a brace on his leg, and he walked with a cane. She'd first seen him in a small stone courtyard next to the church. The ground was covered in light snow. He rose off a bench as she approached. She kissed him on the cheek, and he offered sympathy. With tears, she'd described the climbing accident that had taken Paul on Mount Hood, a fall onto an ice ledge during an early December climb up the north side along the Elliot glacier. George patiently held her hand and listened as she told him what had happened. When she described the inside of the morgue, he wiped tears from her cheeks. He listened without saying a word. When she was finished, he reminded her how lucky she was. He asked about the boys, her father, and the practice and reminded her of the security of an excellent profession, outstanding colleagues, and the money. He told her she would survive, that she had to survive, and that too many people depended on her. "Take a month," he had said. "Take two or three. Then come back, and you'll know what you need to do."

She took off two months and called him on his mobile phone; it was an international number and the only way to reach him. They spoke about what she would do, and he suggested that she contact Eric, told her that the company had a proposal regarding litigation that wasn't going well in front of Judge Stapleton. She said she wasn't certain about resuming the extended hours of trial practice and wanted to be with her two boys. He gently asked her to make the call and explained that Joe Boyle was the plaintiffs' counsel. He knew the details of the case. She could tell he'd spoken to others about it, as if he'd never left. An expression of distaste and frustration was in his voice.

"We need a win here," he had said. "Make a demand. They'll pay you whatever you want. Then you can retire. Go back to the boys; maybe move away, if that's what you want."

"It's that serious?"

"This kind of scrutiny is not what we want. Once lawyers and regulators start looking, you don't know where it will stop. I know this is a difficult time for you," he had said, "but the company needs to clean this up."

She was surprised. The damages were large, but the company could settle the case for less than half that figure. The self-insurance would cover it. "If it's that bad, why not settle it and walk away?"

"You know, that might happen," he said. "But they'll need you to do it. The other guy's not working out. Joe Boyle's too talented for him."

The conversation had become strange. He was retired for five years, but the case bothered him. She was a widow for two months, and George wanted her to call Eric to help the company. He had suggested that he'd already told Maynard to accept her demand, whatever it would be. There was authority and control in the words and tone he chose, as if he were compelling her to take the assignment. She remembered how he had looked at the church, tired, sickly, and out of place in the cold weather. He was old and delicate, his eyes ice blue against sunburned skin. The voice on the telephone was different; he had summoned it from the past when he was younger and she was his lawyer, when he could tell her what to do.

"I doubt I'll have any effect."

George was blunt. "Make your demand," he said. "They'll pay it."

———

In front of Judge Stapleton, Boyle wanted to grab Peyton's throat but stayed calm. He answered her question by summoning Smythe to the bench. "Mr. Smythe," Boyle said, "will tell Your Honor why an offshore corporation dissolved in 2002 is linked to CIT."

"This is new information," said Smythe. "It was improperly withheld. We can prove it's relevant to the claims we've already made. But we need time. The preliminary evidence shows that Maynard used untaxed illegal assets from offshore to make the CIT loan. It was part of a scheme to funnel profits to the executive committee, in the past and, we think, right now. That is relevant."

The claim was surreal, but the conversation with George had come back. Peyton remembered the tone of his voice and alarm. *Step in and stop it—this must be why.* She felt blood run up her neck and into her face. Before she could speak, Judge Stapleton gave a ruling.

"Mr. Boyle, discovery is over. If you have something compelling, put it in writing and submit it no later than nine o'clock in the morning tomorrow. We will continue this discussion at ten o'clock. Put Mr. Olsen on the stand and anyone else on the witness lists. I'll decide what's relevant and whether the case goes any further."

"Your Honor," asked Peyton, "may the defendants submit something as well?"

"If you feel it's necessary, but neither one of you should submit more than seven pages. After seven, I stop reading."

Peyton and Boyle returned to their tables. The judge departed, and the lawyers remained standing at attention. Peyton turned her head to Rachael. "Put together three good directed-verdict cases," she said in a whisper, "all published in the last eighteen months and in the Southern District of New York. Make sure they're securities cases. Look for something Stapleton wrote." Rachael scribbled the instructions. "Then give me seven pages. I'll edit it tonight. The overall theme here is that the Fund admitted they knew the risks of a stock liquidation, sat on their hands, and did nothing as Maynard executed the sell-off. They have to prove actual deception, and they can't. The Fund wasn't deceived about information it already knew."

Rachael finished writing and nodded her head. Peyton instructed two young men in suits to gather up the exhibits and place everything in boxes for the night. Eric waited for Peyton at the back of the courtroom.

"Is this a win?" he asked and smiled as she approached.

The question was smug. George had hired Eric as a successor, not a custodian. "Work with him," he had told her, "make him present as I do and avoid the projection of wealth. He's former military and has no pretense. That will help you. We can't avoid showing people the revenue numbers, but we can be modest. No jury ever punished companies for that."

She looked at Eric. In the inexpensive suit and tie, he projected the way George had wanted—the way she had wanted—but he was uninformed. He had visibly hesitated when he answered the questions about Iberia. He offered up something about not being sure, that he wasn't fully aware of what the subsidiary did, and then perhaps he didn't know anything at all. It was drivel; the correct answer was "no." But without a script, he was lost.

She smiled to put him at ease. "Joe will use what he has," she said, "so I need to know as much about Iberia as you can tell me. What did Maynard use it for? What information might Boyle have, and what does he intend to do with it?"

Dennis Upton and Morton Shaw, two of Peyton's partners, stood next to Eric. Shaw tapped on an electronic tablet. "There's never been a directed verdict against Joe Boyle, not even a dismissal," he said. "If you win, it will be the first one, which means it could be his last case." He turned to Eric. "Maynard will look bulletproof. You can't buy that. Plaintiffs won't bring cases against the company, just because they'll have to face her."

Peyton wanted to smack Shaw. He looked away.

"We'd be lucky to get it," she said. "Iberia, Eric—what is it?"

"It's what I said. I don't know. That's it. It's all I know. The money used for the CIT loans are accumulated earnings over many years. There's nothing to this."

"Did you ever discuss it with George?"

"No."

She turned to Dennis. "How about you?"

"We're reversing roles, Peyton. I mean, you're Maynard's lawyer."

He was tedious. "I do the trials; you and Mort do the transactions. Help me with this."

"I know what Eric knows."

She held up her phone. "And if I call George?"

"That's above my pay grade."

"Call him if you'd like," Mort said. "But he's old and not well. This was a risky case for Boyle from the beginning. He should never have taken it to trial. Now, he has nothing left. Dangerous and clever? Yes, he's all that. But on this one, you have him."

She remembered the conversation with George in the snow. "I hope you're right."

They walked to the elevators and descended to the entrance. On the marble steps above Foley Square, the summer heat hit them. Mort asked her to go for a drink and decompress. Peyton thanked him and declined. "I have two boys to pick up." She turned on her phone.

Peyton walked down the white steps to the line of taxicabs parked in front of the courthouse. Boyle and Smythe watched from the sidewalk. When she arrived, Boyle stuck out his hand. Peyton shook it politely, felt the sweat on his palm, and wondered where she could wipe it clean. She walked along the curb; Boyle followed.

"I want to keep this face to face, totally professional," Boyle said. "Can we talk?"

She walked to the taxi first in line. "You have my number; I'll always talk."

"You're on the wrong side. Have you ever even heard of Iberia?"

She pretended disinterest. "Not until today."

"Your guys are hiding things."

Peyton turned and held up three fingers. "You had three years of discovery; that's a long time in federal court. You deposed fifty-five witnesses. You issued sixty subpoenas, obtained millions of pages of documents, and spent a fortune. Now, on the last day of your case, you name a company my client knows nothing about and I've never heard of. The box? Big trial moment, Joe! I've seen better; you've done better. Are you going to give me those documents, or do I have to serve a trial subpoena?"

"They're your client's files."

For a moment, Peyton stopped breathing. "If you illegally obtained Maynard documents, you're in trouble."

"If you illegally withheld them, I'll take your license. Give me the rest of them, and we'll call it even."

She changed the subject. "Maynard never misled anyone. There's no fraud here. Your guys could have sold the stock as the price dropped. It's a free country."

Boyle pursed his lips in a smile. "They haven't given you everything."

"I have. I've given you everything. Everything I know about. And there is no way we will agree to a continuance."

Peyton stepped forward, and Boyle looked up at her. She had pale-blue eyes and square shoulders. If he had ever wanted to touch her, this was his chance. He pointed a finger at her chest. "This case is not what you think. There's real trouble here."

She told him to take his hand away, and he did. "We withheld nothing," she said. "You received a million e-mails. What else do you want? The stock is priced well and is coming back. It's not Enron, and it's not Madoff." She turned away, opened the door of the cab, and looked back at Boyle. "I'm a Girl Scout. You know that; Stapleton knows that."

"Maynard's no Girl Scout."

Peyton entered the cab. "Eighty-Second and Fifth Avenue, please." As the taxi moved into traffic, she dialed Rachael.

XI

Manhattan

The phone rang in Peyton's ear as the cab weaved through traffic on its way north. Rachael Hill answered with a brisk greeting.

"Iberia," Peyton said. "We need something by tonight."

Rachael's response was immediate. "I've called the office, and they're running searches now."

"Look for everything: Iberia Company, Iberia Corporation, Iberia LLC, and any variation on that name. It was Maynard's, so we probably created it. Search our archives. Get everything you can find, scan it, and e-mail it to me. I'll get it on my laptop at home. If you find anything, send an e-mail or call me right away."

"Yes, ma'am, right away."

Peyton thanked her, ended the call, and pressed the speed dial for Maria, who answered. They exchanged cheerful words about the weather. Peyton told her that she could take the rest of the day off and laughed at her response. No, she wasn't kidding—it was an early day, and the jury had gone home—but Maria would have to return tomorrow at 7:00 a.m. Peyton thanked her and turned off the phone.

At Eighty-Second Street, she stepped into the light. The wide steps of the Metropolitan Museum of Art were filled with people—some seated, some lying down, and all of them enjoying the August air. She waded through the crowd and into the main hall, where tourists moved in a throng up the central staircase. Tintoretto dominated the landing with an operatic scene of horses, chariots, clouds, and sky. She reached the top of the stairs and turned left down a hallway where beams of light illuminated nineteenth-century images of London at night, shrouded in fog. They were small paintings of buildings and horse-drawn cabs on cobblestone streets, punctuated by the glow of gas lamps. Every image was a silhouette. Peyton slowed her pace to look across the cobblestones, past black carriages, buildings, and streets. A picture pulled her east up the Thames to bridges in the middle distance and the river at the horizon. She had walked the embankment for miles and knew the bridges, docks, and tidal movements. As she came closer, she reached out to touch the image. The bridges merged with the river and disappeared. She drew her fingers back and stepped away. The bridges returned, and the river was distinct again, at the horizon, flowing to the North Sea. She stood with her hand at her chest, read James Whistler's name on the adjacent plaque, and moved on.

At the end of the exhibit, a ramp took her into open rooms lit from above. French paintings surrounded her with summer fields, ponds, flowers, and women in hoopskirts. Boys and girls with large drawing pads on their laps sat in front of paintings by Monet, Vuillard, Pissarro, and Manet. Some sat in front of Georges Seurat's preliminary study for *Sunday Afternoon on the Island of La Grande Jatte*. They marked their pads with colored pencils and listened to a man explain in a whisper how the color vibration worked, how the painter positioned one piece of paint next to another without blending them and created a simultaneous separation and cohesion. He brought his finger up to his eye, pulled down the lower lid, and explained how color and light splash across the retina.

Peyton's younger son, Frank, sat on the floor and drew a copy in crosshatched marks with colored pencil. He copied Seurat's figures, static in the sun like Egyptians on a frieze. She watched as he added colored pencil strokes of violet and blue to the large figure of a woman with a parasol escorted by a man in a top hat. It was almost finished. His gift was obvious; he had his father's talent. He'd captured the vibration of the pieces of paint laid next to each other. In blue, red, violet, and yellow cross-hatched pencil marks, Frank had realized the woman with the parasol and the faint image of the monkey, leashed and poised to jump across the lawn, where men and women lounged on the grass. Passersby in the galleries stopped and looked from the original to Frank's copy. An older woman leaned down and whispered to Frank: "Is that for sale?" Frank swiveled, looked up, and smiled; politely, he said no.

Peyton found her older son, Ben, in the distance wandering in socks and a gray baseball uniform marked with dirt and grass. In dark blue, the number 7 on his back floated through the gallery. At fifteen, he was taller than his mother and had discovered his legs. Painting to painting, he moved with a glide and stepped through circles of boys and girls without touching them. She followed him. In two years, he had changed. Now, he was a younger version of Paul, with his father's shoulders and black hair pressed against his head and matted by sweat. He was far from shaving—his cheeks still had a young red glow—but the transformation made Peyton stop and watch. She had turned a corner in the apartment earlier in the summer, found Ben standing in a room, and seen Paul, still young and alive. It had happened in June when she was preparing for the trial. She was holding some documents and had turned the corner to enter the living room. Ben had looked up, the phone at his ear, speaking to someone in a low voice. In the partial light, he was Paul, young, distracted, and laughing. Her hand had relaxed, and the documents had fallen away. She didn't hear them hit the floor, and she watched Ben's eyes as he looked at her and then bent down to pick up the documents. He handed them to her and continued to speak to the party on the other end of the line. She had thanked him and walked to her desk in the office beyond the living room. Unable to focus, she looked out over Seventy-Seventh Street, the rooftop of the Museum of Natural History, and Central Park beyond.

In the galleries, she watched Ben circle, stop at summer fields in western France, and continue. He passed Frank. His uniform was streaked with dirt from his chest to his knees. She'd seen it before, timed perfectly. He had taken advantage of a catcher too involved in the count who hadn't checked whether Ben had moved down the third baseline to the plate. When the catcher had lobbed the ball back to the pitcher, Ben sprinted in a delayed steal. He had practiced, measured, and timed it: eight long strides and a headfirst dive to the plate. Peyton had watched the ball float softly in an arc to the pitcher and heard the dugouts erupt. In the third-base bleachers, she had covered her mouth with her hands and inhaled as Ben sprinted down the line. In an instant, the ball had returned to the plate. Ben collided with the catcher headfirst. His helmet flew off his head and spun out in the dirt. The throw was late, and the ball rolled to the back of the cage. She had remembered Ben lying on his chest, slapping the plate, looking up at the umpire. Smiling, he bounced up, arms in the air, and received hands from his teammates, who had unloaded onto the field.

She followed him into the galleries of nineteenth-century academic painting, past armies on horseback and clouds that towered over fields. He stopped at a huge tableau of wild horses running through dust. They had turned sharply, as if to race out of the picture and into the gallery.

She stood behind him. "Were you safe?" she asked.

He turned around with the same small smile that barely escaped his father's mouth. He nodded and with a finger traced the streak of dirt down the center of his uniform. "Winning run." Peyton stepped forward and kissed him on the cheek.

They walked back to Frank, gathered his things, and headed to the first floor and main entrance, to Fifth Avenue, which they followed south to the Central Park Zoo. Peyton dialed her secretary and arranged tickets for the Friday flight out of LaGuardia Airport to Wilmington, North Carolina. Her return ticket was early Sunday morning to prepare for trial; the boy's tickets were open-ended. Then she dialed Rachael.

"Do you have anything on Iberia yet?" *Please tell me you do.*

There was nothing so far, but she expected all search records later in the day and promised to forward them. Peyton asked Rachael to transfer her to Dennis Upton, and she was connected in seconds.

"Peyton?" asked Dennis. He put her on the speakerphone, and his voice seemed to come from across his office. He handled

Maynard's corporate transactions and had attended every day of trial. "What's on your mind?"

"Iberia, Dennis. Tell me. What do I need to know?"

"Well, I, I'm not..." He stumbled into silence.

Peyton persisted. "Where's Boyle going with this?"

"Olsen doesn't know, and you really don't want to get into this."

"Dennis, I need to know what it is."

He was silent.

"Were you in the courtroom today?"

"You know I was."

"Then you saw what happened."

"I did."

"Boyle's case could disappear."

"It might."

"I may not have to put on a defense."

"I was there."

"There are members of the bar who would pay money to see that."

"You could sell tickets."

"So where is he going?"

"I'm not sure."

"Are you saying you know nothing about a subsidiary for one of our largest clients?"

Upton was silent.

"You're not Eric, Dennis. You've been working with these people for fifteen years."

"What are you getting at?"

"I need information, and I would expect you to have it."

"Not always. They don't tell me everything."

"And if Iberia is the knife Boyle wants to put into my chest, what then?"

Dennis knew Boyle's reputation. "Peyton, you're a little over the top here."

"I can't defend myself if I don't know what's coming."

Dennis didn't respond. The conversation had become an interrogation.

"What's wrong," she asked.

"Sorry, multitasking. What was the question?"

She issued a threat to draw him out. "Rachael Hill is doing searches, Dennis. She's running things through the computer to see if we formed Iberia or ever did any work for the company. If we did, Rachael will know."

Dennis interrupted. "You may want to leave that alone, Peyton. Whatever you do, you should have Maynard authorize it."

"Authorize what?"

"Maynard wants this buried. Don't dig up dead stuff."

"Dennis, I'm sure we created Iberia. Do we need Maynard's authorization to look at our own files?"

There was only one answer. "No."

"If it makes you feel better, tell Eric what I'm doing. You can also tell him I can't look stupid in front of Stapleton. And I better not look evasive."

"Evasive," Dennis said. "Good word. We can't be that."

"Dennis?"

"What?"

"Is there anyone else in your office?"

"What?"

"Is there anyone in your office listening to this conversation?"

In his office on the 45th floor of the firm's Park Avenue building, Dennis rocked back in his chair. He looked at Morton Shaw, who sat in a red leather armchair on the other side of the desk. Shaw shook his head and pointed to the computer screen.

"No, Peyton, it's just me. I'll do what I can, but no one is allowed to wander off, including you. You know, stay on the reservation. If Maynard wants it buried, it stays buried. Boyle's information is irrelevant, unverifiable, and too old. We want you on board. 'It's irrelevant'—say it to yourself, and chant it like a mantra. If Maynard doesn't want this, neither do you."

"Take me off the speakerphone."

Dennis picked up the receiver.

"This won't go away," she said. "Joe wants George as a witness, and he will never stop."

"We've looked at that. George is out of the country for the rest of the trial and beyond the subpoena power. Boyle can't get him."

Mort nodded.

"Have you spoken to George?" Peyton asked.

"We want you to stay to the playbook."

"How do you know George is out of the country?"

He lied. "It's a hunch."

"Whose playbook?"

"Maynard's."

"Have you spoken to him?"

"George? Personally, no."

Mort stood and pointed to the computer screen. Dennis looked to Mort and then to the computer. "I have some documents for you. They're from Bermuda. That's all I have, and you'll get them."

"By tonight?"

"Yes."

"What about Maynard? What do they have?"

"Nothing. Everything was destroyed in 2009. They operate like we do—seven-year document destruction policy."

"You're sure it's been seven years?"

"Yes."

"For every document?"

"I counted the days."

"I'm sure you did. Send me what you have. We'll speak later."

Dennis said good-bye, pushed the button, and ended the call.

"Give her the incorporation and dissolution record," said Mort. "Not one page more."

"You think she'll win, don't you?"

"She's never lost a trial. If she gets a directed verdict, she gets a ten-million-dollar premium. They've already paid her five just to take the case." Mort waved his hand in the air. "She'll never let the ten million go. She's about to make a publicly traded real estate company look bulletproof to the plaintiff's bar. Who's done that? No one. Ever. We'll pitch that to every *Fortune* 500 company. It will put us at the top of the list for every bet-the-company case out there. Think about it. She'll command a higher premium to try a case, and she knows it. Basically, she'll get any price she wants."

"You're certain she can win it?"

Mort stood up, walked to the window, and looked down at the tiny human figures racing along the Park Avenue sidewalks. "She's a flawless trial lawyer," he said. "And the world's most beautiful widow." He looked back at Dennis. "Stapleton loves her."

The boys had walked out in front of their mother. Frank jumped up on the Central Park wall and raced along the top. Ben followed and pushed him into the park. Frank rolled through grass and broke into the trees. Ben chased him through the brush, back up to the wall, and down onto the sidewalk. Frank was exhausted, with a film of dirt on his hands, knees, and shoulders. He ran to his mother, a last line of defense, who saw a missed called from Rachael and dialed her back. His grass-stained shirttail hung out over his shorts, which were wet and covered with dirt. He was breathing heavily, and drops of sweat rolled down his cheeks. He bounced on the balls of his feet and dodged his brother's attempts to reach beyond Peyton and grab him. Peyton kept walking.

"I have something in front of me," Rachael said as she answered the call.

Peyton stopped and asked her to describe the document.

Rachael looked at an image on her computer screen. "They're client intake records. One is from a card file dated 1975. Someone named Konigsberg took out a matter for an entity known only as Iberia and closed it six months later. Maynard is not listed, and there's no name listed for the client contact."

Every case and legal matter handled by Stewart & Stevens were recorded on computer records that listed the client, dates of invoices, the responsible partner, the fact of a conflict of interest, if any, and the date it was identified. The records were also required to list the parent corporation and the person to contact at the client. This one didn't list anything.

"Look on the right column," said Peyton. "Do you see a category titled 'INV'?"

"Yes."

"When were the first and last invoices sent?"

"It's blank."

"Then Arthur never billed for his time."

"Who?"

"Arthur Konigsberg, George's lawyer. He's a deceased partner."

"Is that unusual?"

"Maybe. What's the other record?"

"Same, but for 2002. Konigsberg opened a matter in January 2002 and closed it in August. No invoices."

Peyton looked up into the trees. "Rachael, I know you haven't had much sleep, but I'm going to ask you to drop what you're doing and drive to New Paltz. There's a document depository. My secretary will get you the address and number. Have her call a driver. Without traffic, it's one hour. I want you to go there and find Arthur's personal files. He died in 2002, but we should have retained them. Call the depository now. Ask them to search for his personal records, things like chronological day-to-day files his secretary kept for him. Those don't get shredded after seven years. Ask for Iberia too. The Iberia files should have been destroyed after seven years, but ask anyway."

"You want me to call you when I'm up there?"

"Yes. And if you have trouble, call me right away. Then send me everything you find. I'll be at home."

"Should I let Dennis know?"

Peyton was at Sixty-Ninth Street and began to walk. "No. Send me what you find first."

"You sure?"

"Yes."

"Okay." Rachael had a rasp in her voice.

"One more thing, I want you to look up the contact information for Ted Heilman." Rachael quickly wrote as Peyton spoke. "He's a former US Treasury and IRS agent. Anything on Iberia you send to me, copy him. But do not copy anyone else—not Dennis and not Mort. I'm going to have Ted clear his calendar for the next two days if he can. Boyle can't be making this up. Ted will help us."

"Okay. Writing it down."

Peyton could hear exhaustion in her voice. "And, Rachael, you've been terrific. Stay with me. We're real close. We just have to get to the end."

"I'm with you, Peyton; I'm grateful to be on this."

"I hope you feel that way next week." Peyton thanked her and said good-bye. She immediately dialed a number. The voice mail recording of Ted Heilman came across her phone. She left a message asking him to catch a flight to Bermuda and gave him the details about Iberia. When she looked up, the boys had not returned. She scanned the park wall and then across Fifth Avenue. She dialed Ben's cell phone, which rang in her ear. Two blocks away, he answered, walking with Frank, whose powder-blue shirt shone through the crowd at Sixty-Fifth Street. Peyton watched them disappear into the zoo.

XII

Guana Cay

The plane flew past the northern edge of Cuba and descended to three hundred feet, just above the water. It pointed to the southern Bahamas, two hundred nautical miles away, and landed on the Guana Cay tarmac in the early evening.

Leandro, Sean, and Joseph entered the Bone Fishing Club, where Arnold sat alone at the common table. The windows were closed and the hurricane shutters sealed tight. Decorative bar lights lit the room. Arnold had pushed aside the table and opened up the dry cistern, now a pit, in the center of the floor. Four large terra cotta tiles lay next to a black hole. The pit was empty and Amy was gone, two and a half thousand pounds of her. A steel safe in the pit was open and empty; it had contained the briefcase and money. Arnold rose, and Leandro told him to sit.

"Tell me what you've found."

"It's professional," Arnold said in a Bahamian cadence. "The computers were dismantled. All the hard drives and paper records are gone. I've looked at everything, all over the buildings. No bullet holes, maybe some bloodstains, but I'm not sure. Nothing's broken. Same with the dock and around the tarmac; there's nothing. Everything's gone."

"The planes?"

"They're empty, except for equipment, tow rope, and a few floats."

Leandro turned to Joseph and Sean. "Go through all the rooms in the buildings. I'll be at the dock with Arnold."

On the veranda, Leandro looked down the path. He stepped off the right side and touched a branch, cracked and hanging, barely attached to the trunk. He ran his index finger along the branch until he arrived at the base of the tree. A triangular three-inch slice penetrated the dirt, where the corner of an office binder had hit the ground during the assault on Noah. Nearby, another binder had fallen flat and left a square outline in the soil. The third binder had hit the branch and cracked it at the base.

The steps were narrow. Leandro looked to the left side. Two branches were broken where the Guatemalan had caught Noah and pushed him into the trees. They had dragged him back to the steps, where Martel had discharged the weapon into Noah's leg. Leandro crouched and looked at the first step. It had a one-inch overhang. He laid his hands flat on the step and glided them over the stone. He held up clean hands to Arnold.

"No dust. It's been washed."

He moved his fingers under the one-inch overhang. Every few inches he pulled them out. Black specks littered his fingertips. Halfway along, he touched a soft patch that felt like glue. He worked it and opened up a soft liquid center. It oozed onto his fingers as he pulled it free. The clotted lump lay in his hand, covered in a red smear.

"They did it here and cleaned it up." He stood up and pointed down the steps. "The blood must have been everywhere. There should be traces, but not in plain sight."

Leandro walked two steps down the path and turned. On his knees, he looked at the riser of the first step. Just below the overhang where he had found the blood, a circular hole broke the tan coral. It was the circumference of his index finger, which he used to penetrate the hole and feel the remnant of the bullet. He lay flat on the step, pulled out his reading glasses, and examined the hole.

"It's from today," he said. He took a folding tool from his back pocket and dug with a file. As the bullet loosened, he guided it out onto the step. Between his thumb and forefinger, he held it up to Arnold. It was large, flattened by impact, and splayed apart. "That's a forty-five caliber, hollow tip," Leandro said. "It makes a big hole in a human being."

They moved down the path from side to side. Arnold turned over loose stones near the steps, and Leandro examined each step and riser as they approached the dock. They walked out into sun, which hit the tops of their heads and baked through their hair.

Leandro turned in a full circle and then dropped to his knees. He looked between the planks for traces of dried blood. He smelled the wood. "Bleach," he said. "They used bleach and took the time to scrub the steps and the dock."

Leandro walked along the perimeter and looked into the water and turtle grass below. He lay on the planks with his head over the edge. On the posts under the dock, arterial spray had left spots of blood, now dry and black. Some had washed away, but a few remained. In the grass below, fish pecked at a pink-and-white object. Leandro rose off the dock and ran up the path two steps at a time. He returned with a flat net attached to a pole. He dipped the net into the water, and the fish scattered. He guided the net under the object in the sand, raised it up, and laid it on the dock. The bone was bright white with pink flesh attached. Leandro picked it up and held it out for Arnold. He asked if he knew what it was, and Arnold shook his head.

"It's part of a human neck bone." Leandro positioned the fragment as it would be in life, described the vertebra, and with his finger drew an outline in the air of the neck and where the cervical vertebra would fit. Part of the transverse process was still attached, and it bore a serrated cut mark where the fish knife had caught Jesse's vertebrae and sliced off a section. "You see that?" Leandro asked. He touched the serrated marks. "That's from a knife."

Leandro turned to the other side of the dock and pointed to the empty cleats. "I want the boat."

"The club boat?"

Leandro nodded. "Let's fly around."

At the Bone Fishing Club, Leandro searched the equipment closet and picked out field glasses, snorkeling equipment, and a scope for viewing underwater. He walked to the tarmac and tossed the equipment into the rear compartment of the seaplane, where there were boxes of fishing gear, coils of rope, two small anchors, two life preservers, a bottle of drinking water, and a large gaff hook with a handle for pulling big game fish into a boat. He climbed into the pilot's seat and turned the key. "Get in," he called over the noise of the propeller and motioned to Arnold, who stepped onto the pontoon and climbed into the passenger seat. "We need to see this place from above." He pushed the throttle forward and taxied down the tarmac.

"Why do you want the club boat?" asked Arnold, as loudly as he could.

"It has to be here," Leandro shouted back. "It's not big enough to go beyond the reefs; no one could use it to transport a ton of the product. Take the binoculars, and scan the sea. Look everywhere. It could be floating in a cove near a beach. They may have scuttled it."

Arnold took the binoculars. The propeller spun in a blur; the seaplane climbed off the runway and rose one thousand feet in circles over mangrove islands. From the air, Arnold scanned the sea. The plane turned north, then west and south and banked to the passenger side; it turned in an arc toward the sun over sandbars and rocky cays. Two miles west of the island, marine fuel glistened on the water. Arnold shouted over the noise and motioned to the spot. Leandro nodded and circled the plane back until he saw the streak. He flew west and then east, so the sun was behind him, and put the plane into a slow descent.

When the pontoons hit the sea, the roar of the water rose above the propeller, and white spray erupted in a double wake behind the plane.

"What are we doing?" Arnold shouted. He gripped the safety handles on the dashboard and door.

"We're landing, Arnold," Leandro said with a rascally grin. "If the boat's here, we'll bring it up." Arnold looked out of the window and grimaced. Chloe's winds had increased, and the pontoons rose and fell over larger swells. Leandro shut off the engine; the cabin was quiet. "Get onto the pontoon so we can find out what's in the water."

Leandro pulled the viewing scope from the back compartment and handed it to Arnold, who opened the door, stepped onto a pontoon, and lay down. He pushed the glass bottom of the scope into the water and lowered his face over the cone. Below, sharks swam through a coral bed sixty feet down. In the upper left of the scope, he could see the overturned hull of the boat, suspended above the reef. The sharks swam slowly beneath it and above, circling in silence.

He removed his face from the scope, rolled over on the pontoon, and looked up at the sky. Leandro had moved to the copilot's seat and was leaning out of the open door. His face, with aviator sunglasses, appeared above Arnold.

"Is the boat there?"

Arnold nodded as he sat up on the pontoon. "Yes," he said. "It's drifting over a reef. There are sharks."

Leandro stepped onto the pontoon, removed his sunglasses, and pushed the scope into the water. The momentum of the plane had moved the pontoon directly over the hull. He climbed back into the fuselage and pulled equipment from the rear compartment. Back on the pontoon, Leandro brought with him a heavy steel fishhook thirty inches long and several lengths of nylon rope. He tied the ropes together in standard square knots and fastened one end of the connected ropes onto the handle of the fishhook. Arnold stood on the pontoon and steadied himself with his hand against the fuselage of the plane. Leandro threw the hook into the water. It sank to the hull below.

He watched through the scope as the rope ran through his hand and the hook descended. Leandro tried to thread the hook into the gap between the bow and the guardrails, but the swells rocked the pontoon. The hook swung gently near the overturned bow without success, and the hull drifted away, out of reach.

Leandro stood up and handed the rope and viewing scope to Arnold. He climbed into the cockpit, picked up his satellite phone, and accessed the global positioning system, which gave him the longitude and latitude of the seaplane. He dialed Sean, who answered in one ring. "Get out here now. Bring the big boat west about two to three miles from the dock. We've found what we're looking for. I'll give you the coordinates." He read Sean the coordinates, terminated the call, and looked into the plane's rear compartment. He pulled out two life preservers and an empty plastic Clorox bottle.

Leandro stepped back onto the pontoon and faced Arnold, who held onto a wing strut and looked at his own distant image in Leandro's sunglasses. The older man's hair was cropped close to his head, and the skin on his forehead had begun to burn in the sun. His lips moved calmly. He told Arnold to descend and secure the hook to the boat below. Arnold stared at his image in the lenses. The pontoon bobbed on the swells.

"Secure the chain and hook," Leandro said. "We can't lose the boat."

Arnold smiled in disbelief. "I can't do it, boss."

Leandro threaded one end of the rope through the life preservers and tied the end of it to the bottle's handle. In the back of the seaplane, he retrieved a diving mask and a pair of large black scuba fins, which he held up to Arnold on the bobbing pontoon.

He spoke quietly. "More than one ton went missing. Martel had sixteen calls last week. All were with you. Unusual? No, except for one thing. You called him a week ago, and he was in Georgetown. What was he doing in Georgetown?" Leandro handed Arnold the mask and fins. "One hundred million dollars does not just walk away. It takes planning, secrecy, and help.

I have a discharged bullet on the steps and a human neck bone near the dock. Are you going to tell me what happened?"

Arnold stared back.

Leandro was brief. "Put on the mask and fins, and get in the water."

Arnold sat down on the pontoon. He took off his shoes and put on the fins. He felt cold in the heat.

Leandro went back into the plane and returned with a small anchor. "Take this with you; you'll move down faster. Drop it when you arrive at the hull. Wrap the hook and line around the bow. Cleat it if you can, but make sure it's secure. The sharks will circle, but they won't attack. You're not food to them, not right away."

Arnold pushed back nausea he felt in his throat. He looked to Leandro for a reprieve.

Leandro put his face near Arnold's. His voice was urgent. "They scuttled it. That makes me want it. Right now it's all we have."

Arnold removed his shirt and handed it to Leandro. He put on the diving mask and tightened it. He cradled the anchor in his left arm and lay flat on the pontoon, face first. Without a ripple, he slid into the water and downward next to the rope, pushing back and forth with the fins to speed the descent.

The hull had drifted away from the plane; it floated in blue shadows and shafts of sunlight. Sharks disappeared into the distance and reappeared instantly into the light, sometimes alone, other times in groups, moving under the hull, waiting for the cargo to release.

The anchor pulled Arnold down along the rope to the steel hook, which hung fifty feet below the surface and away from the hull. When he arrived at the hook, he dropped the anchor and kicked his fins until he reached the bow.

The sharks darted back and forth, circled Arnold, and swam near him. He was out of air and imagined the end, his own blood in a plume around him. He wrapped the line around the bow railing, secured it to a cleat, and swam under the hull, the large fishhook in his hand and still attached to the line.

Arnold rose up into the air pocket that kept the boat above the seabed. He took a huge breath. The stench of dead bodies filled the space, lit by reflected light from the sand below. The corpses were wrapped and fastened to either side of the boat with rope. Parts of the tarps had fallen away, torn by adventurous sharks that had snapped at the bodies. Noah's face looked upward into the boat. His mouth was open, as if he'd been stopped in midsentence. His throat yawned wide to the vertebrae. Jesse's face was turned away to the gunwale.

Below, the sharks moved up. Arnold pulled himself out of the water and wrapped himself around the steel column of the cockpit seat. Like a dog, a prying shark stuck its nose toward a body. Arnold tied the remaining rope around the column of the chair and put the hook over a steel bar on the pilot's console.

He ducked his head into the water to see whether the sharks had moved away from the hull. When they were at a distance, Arnold slipped into the water and under the side of the hull. He released, swept the fins back and forth, and climbed to the surface at an angle to the pontoons.

Leandro gripped Arnold's arm as he breached the surface and slid him onto the pontoon. Arnold spit over the side. "The bodies are there," he said. "It's Noah and Jesse; they're inside the boat."

Leandro held the rope, pulled it taut, and felt the hull at the other end. He dropped the life preservers and bottle into the water, where they floated as markers.

In the distance, the fishing boat approached. As it closed on the plane, Sean appeared at the transom and called to Leandro, who pointed to the markers. The boat slowed to a crawl at three knots. Leandro watched as Sean pulled the markers from the water with a gaff and tied the rope to a wire line on an electric winch for a shark cage. It turned, one revolution per second, and the club boat began to rise.

Leandro and Arnold stepped up into the cockpit of the seaplane and watched. When the motorboat's hull breached the surface, Leandro called Gonzalez in Mexico City and asked for the tracking results.

"We have some units," Gonzalez told him. "North of Guana Cay. They have turned on, then off, then on again. Some are British and German; most are U.S. and Bahamian. A few are Cuban. You'll like this: two Bahamian accounts, one right off Guana Cay, and another near Eleuthera. There's a Venezuelan unit that transmitted twice in the same area about forty and thirty minutes apart. That's faster than anything I've seen yet, about forty knots in the open ocean."

"Tell me about the Bahamian numbers."

"One of them transmitted four hours ago. It was due north of Guana Cay, less than two miles. The other is a different number. It transmitted an hour ago, less than a kilometer north of Harbour Island, right off of Eleuthera."

"And the Venezuelan unit, was it nearby?"

"Yes, same location, two minutes apart. They could have come from the same boat."

"Can you track the numbers all night?"

"Yes, but the hurricane is moving in. It affects the results. The closer the storm gets, the more limited the information."

"Focus on the Bahamian and Venezuelan numbers, but look for more. Give me regular updates. Anytime those numbers light up, I want to know."

Leandro started the engine. Arnold put on his shirt and stared through the windshield as the plane taxied, took off, and climbed. Leandro shouted over the noise, told Arnold to place the contents from the motorboat in the main room of the Bone Fishing Club and take a complete inventory. He wanted every scrap of paper from the club boat and everything in Noah's and Jesse's pockets. "Once you have a complete list," he said, "have Sean call me, but not before nine o'clock tonight. I'll be in Eleuthera."

XIII

Harbour Island, Central Bahamas

The seaplane landed in Eleuthera on an old airfield lined with weeds and rusted planes. Some had crashed; others had been abandoned and left to fall apart. Trees and bushes had grown up through the wreckage and bloomed through broken windows. At one end of the field, a plane had overshot the runway and lay at the edge of a bay. Its cockpit was above the water and its wings below. Leandro taxied to the opposite end and stopped among small planes tied to the tarmac. He glided the seaplane to a section where steel loops were embedded in the asphalt. He stepped out of the cockpit and into the wind. In the storage compartment at the nose of the plane, braided cables were coiled around a tube. Leandro removed the cables, looped them through bolts on the wings and fuselage, and locked them into hooks on the tarmac. The plane was secured for the night.

The only building was a one-room clapboard structure. Boarded up and locked, it stood at an angle to the runway, as if the wind had picked it up and turned it around. Leandro left the seaplane, walked around the edge of the building, and found the car he had ordered parked under an oversized sea grape tree. He slid into the backseat and gave the driver the destination, the Princess Hotel. The car pulled onto the road as dusk set in.

In twenty minutes, Leandro arrived at the Princess, a two-story pink-and-cream structure; it faced the bay that separated Eleuthera from Harbour Island, one mile to the east.

"I want two rooms, please," Leandro said to the concierge, who sat alone behind a desk in the lobby. There wasn't a guest in sight. "I'll pay now."

The concierge nodded and smiled—snow-white teeth against black skin. "We have rooms, sir, but the hurricane will be here later in the night. Are you sure you want to stay?"

"A suite." Leandro handed him ten one hundred dollar bills.

The concierge counted the money and stood up. "One night?"

"Depends on the storm."

"Is there anything else?"

"A boat to Harbour Island."

"Sir..." the concierge hesitated and looked into the visitor's eyes. "The Princess launch is all we have."

Leandro handed him another roll of bills. "Let's have a look."

The concierge took the money and removed a key from a desk drawer. He motioned for Leandro to follow. They walked to a patio and stepped down to a concrete bulkhead where boats were moored to iron cleats. The largest was a thirty-foot wooden rig painted powder pink and blue with an open cabin and wide stern with wooden benches.

"Do you have your own dock?" Leandro looked across the water to the lights of Harbour Island.

The concierge handed him the key. "At the Princess Beach Club." He pointed across the water. "But I have to go with you. At night, if you don't know the harbor, it's dangerous."

Leandro stepped into the launch, turned, and showed him another roll of bills; he held it between his index finger and thumb. "I know the harbor. You'll have the launch later tonight."

"How much?" he said.

"Two thousand. Where's the dock?"

"Straight across, sir, with a large gazebo and a sign." The concierge pointed again. "There's a green light at the peak of the roof. Point straight. You'll find it."

Leandro threw him the money. "You never saw me."

"I know."

Leandro turned the key on the dashboard of the launch. The engine rumbled, and the lights went on. The concierge untied the bow and stern ropes and threw them on board. With his foot, he pushed the bow away from the bulkhead. Leandro moved the boat into the harbor and crossed the water, far from the ambient light of the hotel. In a few minutes, the glow of the green light on the gazebo appeared. Within fifty feet of the dock, he turned off the engine and let the launch drift slowly into a slip next to the gazebo. He tied the bow and stern lines to cleats and climbed a ladder to an empty patio. A few yellow lights illuminated the doors and windows that were locked and boarded for the storm.

He moved across the patio to flagstone paths covered by trellises and hanging flowers that gave off familiar perfume. At the front of the beach club, he entered onto the corner of Bay and Hill Streets at the south end of Dunmore Town and turned north on Bay. For thirty minutes, he walked through the Dunmore settlement along the harbor and into the darkness of the northern end. The forest grew across the road as it narrowed and lost any trace of macadam. At the tip of the island, Leandro turned east onto two dirt tracks with a ribbon of grass in between. He followed the path and began to run when he saw the black silhouette of a steel gate and stone wall. He accelerated to a sprint and leaped onto the wall. He grasped the top, pulled up, and pivoted to the other side, where he landed on a lawn.

Beyond the gate, a peninsula stuck out like a snake into the ocean and curved north. It rose up as a rocky promontory with cliffs that faced west to a small bay. To the east, it sloped to the road and the unobstructed Atlantic. At the highest point, lights of a single house shone in the darkness. For eight hundred yards, Leandro followed a road along the curve of the peninsula. To the east, the ocean had developed a chop. Salt spray slammed against rocks and a retaining wall and spilled water into the potholes of the dirt road. At a gatehouse, the road turned north.

Leandro veered off the road to a path and moved up through the forest onto the cliffs, where he could see Eleuthera to the west. In the distance, the lights of the house lit the water below. He stayed to the path and made his way to terraced lawns lined with flowers and coconut trees. The wind blew petals off the bougainvillea and rattled sea grape trees at the edge of the cliff, where stone steps in the coral rock led to a dock and boathouse. With the light behind him, Leandro thought of the report from Gonzalez. He looked along the cliff and across the bay for a boat but found none.

He stepped up through the terraces to the house and into a brightly lit room with open glass doors on either side. Hot wind poured from the east and blew curtains up into the room like loose sails. A maid in a light-blue uniform and white apron cleared a table.

"I'm here to see the gentleman," he said.

The maid looked up and dropped a glass. Leandro opened his hands to her and bowed. "Forgive me," he said. "I thought he was alone, so I let myself in." He took a napkin from the table, knelt, put the pieces of glass in the napkin, and handed it to her.

"Please tell him that the businessman from Mexico City would like to see him. He does not expect me."

"Yes, sir." The maid looked at him, bowed her head, and put the napkin on the table. She walked through the room of flying curtains to the end of the house. In a doorway she spoke, looked back to Leandro, and waved for him to approach.

Leandro walked to the far end of the house and entered a library lined with polished wood bookcases packed with leather-bound books. Paintings hung on the walls. An elderly man with a trim white beard sat in a cane chair with a book on his lap and one leg in a steel pan filled with water. He wore a pressed pink shirt with each sleeve rolled up just below the elbow. A crystal glass, a mobile phone, and a black leather case were on the table next to him. Tracy McPhee watched Leandro enter the room, nodded to the maid, and asked her to leave.

"May I sit?" asked Leandro. He placed a cane chair in front of McPhee and sat down. Over the old man's shoulder, two paintings hung on the wall: a framed watercolor of wind blowing through coconut trees and a large oil painting of an open sailboat tossed in a storm. Leandro recognized the long spontaneous strokes of the watercolor.

"Winslow Homer?" he asked.

McPhee looked at the visitor. "Why?"

Leandro ignored him. "Eleuthera?"

"Bermuda." McPhee couldn't resist. "The original."

"Beautiful." Leandro stood and walked to the larger painting of the storm-tossed boat. He flicked a switch on the wall and stepped back. Lighted, the painting dominated the room. It had the deep, dark tones of the northern European Renaissance. A full moon lit the boat like a stage spotlight. Every figure and wave was fully described. The central figure was a man in robes to the left of the mast. Sails billowed in wind that blew left to right across a black sky. Green water churned and pushed the open rig up on a wave and put the crew in peril. One figure in the stern with a puffy face and bulb for a nose turned toward to the viewer to cry out.

The painting was familiar. He'd seen it before.

"Dutch Renaissance, right?"

McPhee sat up, closed the book, and put it on the table. "You didn't come here to discuss pictures."

"No, I did not." Leandro prodded him. "The original?"

"It's nothing."

It was perfect. The brush strokes were without a false move or overlay of paint to hide a correction. It was a masterful depiction of light and deep darkness, the roiling water, and fear. It drew him in. If the watercolor was Winslow Homer, this was more. He had seen it in a museum or auction-house brochure.

"Let's talk about why you're here," said McPhee.

Leandro returned to the chair. "Shall I call you 'McPhee,' or is there some other name you'd prefer in the tropics?" The question was obnoxious.

"Whatever you'd like."

"Then down to business; I'm tracking a shipment."

McPhee licked his lips. "You've lost something?"

"Two and half thousand pounds."

The old man was silent for a moment and stared at Leandro. "That's quite a sum of money."

Leandro nodded.

"How much?"

"One hundred million, at least."

"Ever happen before?"

"Not like this."

"One of your cowboys take it?"

"It would require more than one or two cowboys."

"Why come to me?" He motioned to his foot in the pan of water. "I can't even walk."

"Gout?"

McPhee lifted his foot. "Guinea worm." It was swollen, the size of a rugby ball. "It's as bad as it looks, but it never gets worse." He extended his hand with tweezers, grasped a small white growth just below the ankle, and pulled. A long, flexible white string stretched out of the foot into the air. McPhee returned the tweezers to his foot and pulled again. Three feet of the white string emerged and lay floating in the water.

Leandro leaned forward. "That's the worm?"

McPhee took a breath, sipped whiskey from the glass, and nodded.

"Where did you get it?"

"Safari in eastern Congo, years ago. Mountain gorillas, militias, and disease. Your kind of place."

"You drank the water?"

"There's no other way to get it." McPhee said it through clenched teeth as he leaned forward again and pulled at the worm. "Once you have them, they never go away. They lay eggs in my flesh, and gravity causes them to fall to my feet. The worms grow and break through. Then the swelling subsides."

Leandro reached across to the table and picked up a black leather box. He opened it and found a syringe, needles, and vials of phenobarbital. He read the labels on the vials.

"It's for the pain," McPhee said. "Answer my question. Why did you come here?"

Leandro put the leather box back on the table and picked up McPhee's mobile phone. He turned it off and returned it to the table. "Whoever stole the shipment knows how we work," he said. "He knows our methods, timing, locations, and finances." Leandro pulled a cigarette out of his shirt pocket and tapped it against his thigh. "We trusted him. He stole it between noon and two o'clock today. We tracked a satellite phone transmission north of Harbour Island, right off your beach. Can you tell me about it?"

McPhee took a swallow from the glass of whiskey. "How do you track phones?"

"Not for you to know."

"Can you get real-time transmissions? Record conversations?"

Leandro bluffed. "I've recorded you."

McPhee leaned back in the chair. "Then you know I've nothing to do with this. You know I can't help you."

Leandro smiled. "My people won't like it if you don't." He looked over McPhee's head to the Dutch painting. It glowed in the spotlight. The painter was Rembrandt, and the picture was unusual. It wasn't a portrait of a wealthy merchant or guild leader of Amsterdam; it was a major event from the New Testament, Christ on the Sea of Galilee before he calmed the storm. Leandro recognized it from Interpol notices on a website that reported crimes, warrants, and arrests of international interest. He monitored the reports for interdictions and Interpol tendencies. He stood up and walked to the painting. It was from the Gardner Museum in Boston, stolen years ago in the most conspicuous heist of fine art in history.

McPhee picked up the tweezers and pulled at the worm. "What could you possibly want from me?"

"The Rembrandt," said Leandro.

McPhee stopped pulling.

"What's it worth? One hundred million? More? Did you buy it from a desperate fence for six figures?" Leandro lit the cigarette and sat down.

"Why not kill me and take it?"

"I might. It's magnificent. But I need information, not a picture."

"What do you expect me to tell you?"

"Even if you weren't involved in this, you may have heard something. Did you?"

"No."

"You're clever," said Leandro. "You know how to plan well and disappear. How would you do it? Tease it out for me. My target helped run a landing for seven years. He disappeared with one hundred million dollars in cargo and took the time to clean blood off the dock and steps. Why? Where would he go?"

McPhee drained the glass into his throat. "For this assistance, you leave me in peace?"

"If it helps."

"Is he a transporter?"

"Yes."

"A delivery man?"

Leandro nodded. He watched the old man for a trace of knowledge of Martel and Guana Cay.

"Where's he from?"

"Tegucigalpa. Breaking and entering. Carjacking. Spent time in prison, then as a guest worker for hotels in the Caribbean. Last stop was Great Exuma. He disappeared from a work crew and started working for us seven years ago. Smart enough to operate one of the landings."

"Why did you hire a street criminal?"

"That's my business. I'm fixing it."

"How are transporters paid?"

"On delivery."

"You want to know where he would take it?"

"Yes."

"As far away from you as possible." McPhee laughed; Leandro didn't.

"Think of a fast boat moving north."

"Think of the accomplice," said McPhee. "Find the accomplice, and you'll find him. Even I had an accomplice."

Leandro nodded. "Now dead."

"Nice work."

"How about a thank-you?"

"It was one of your better moments."

"You're welcome."

"Your target—you think he's in a boat?"

"Yes."

"If he's moving by boat, to whom would he take it? With whom would he talk? He'd have to talk to someone. Who competes with you? Who can receive all that material, handle it, cut it, and sell it?"

Transporters in the eastern Caribbean worked for Leandro. Everyone else was out of business, buried, or frightened into different work. Since the Grenadines, things had been quiet. Losses were rare and almost always to the US Navy and Drug Enforcement Agency—a cost of doing business.

"The individual transporters out here work for us. This was well organized and quick. My target killed two employees, cleaned it up, and buried the bodies at sea. I don't see any of our transporters doing that and taking thousands of kilos over open water."

McPhee looked up at the ceiling and thought. "Then there's an organization willing to pay him on delivery. Who on the eastern seaboard has a distribution network other than your people?"

Leandro liked the way he thought. "Dominicans in New York; Mexicans in North Carolina. They buy in bulk from the people who buy from us."

"Where in North Carolina?" McPhee asked.

"Asheville."

"Would the thief go that far north?"

"He could, with a big enough boat. Some of our contractors operate north of Florida. They're local and use fishing boats to move packages offshore and up the Saint Mary's River; sometimes the Savannah River."

"Do they use Cape Fear?"

"That's north of Charleston, but they might. You know the river, don't you?"

McPhee moved in the chair. He had offered too much. "I know the region, but not the boat channels."

"You own property on the river."

McPhee shook his head, annoyed with himself. He poured more whiskey and drained it into his throat. "A private home."

"Even better. I want you to fly there."

McPhee breathed out and adjusted his body. He laughed malevolently, angry at himself.

"Put your people near the river," said Leandro. "Have them photograph every yacht and fishing boat that passes Wilmington. The boats will be coming in to avoid the hurricane. Record the numbers and names. Have them start in twelve hours."

"What if your thief chooses a different destination?"

"That's my problem. Call your people now, and make sure you're in Wilmington by tomorrow."

"What if I say no?"

"Then the Rembrandt is mine."

"You could take it anyway."

"You have my word I won't, as long as you're in Wilmington by tomorrow."

Leandro stood up and smiled at the painting; he knew a buyer to whom he could sell it. Before McPhee could speak, he had walked into the room of curtains, once flying in the wind, now stationary, as caretakers closed sliding doors and locked hurricane shutters in place with wedges and mallets. Over the terraces on the western side of the house and along the cliff, Leandro walked in the dark until he arrived at the road, which he followed to the stone wall and front gate. Before mounting the wall, he sat on the grass, turned on the satellite phone, and saw a missed call. He dialed Sean.

"What do you have?"

"Everything," Sean responded. "We pulled up the boat. There was a trash bag with the guestbook and business records for the last month. Everything's wet, but we have a list of every guest and credit card and the hard drives that contain the last month of video from the security cameras. But listen to this: Arnold found a receipt in a trashcan near the bar. It's from Bahamas Telecom, Georgetown office. His cousin Jenny works there. She sold a satellite phone to Martel last week."

"You have the number?"

"Jenny gave it to us."

"Send it to me. And make a list of people who were at the club in the last month. I want their credit card numbers, addresses, phone numbers, and the dates they were there."

Sean sat at the bar of the Bone Fishing Club. He peeled the receipt from the interior edge of the bar's trashcan, exactly where Martel had positioned it. He flattened it against the bar, took a photo, and attached it to a text message. He tapped into the message the phone number provided by Jenny Glass and sent the message to the encrypted site.

Leandro stood up and scaled the wall. On the other side, the satellite phone vibrated in his chest pocket, and he looked at it as he walked. A notice from the server said that the message was available on the encrypted site. He notified Gonzalez in Mexico City to log on and find the number. He turned off the phone and walked south along the unpaved road, half the length of Harbour Island to Bay Street, Dunmore Town, and the beach club.

McPhee pulled at the long worm, now a four-foot coil floating in the pan. He pinched the part closest to his foot and forced it out until the end emerged. A spot of blood flowed out of the hole, ran down his foot, and spread into the water. He dropped the worm and tweezers. From the leather case, he took out the syringe and needle, which he pointed to the ceiling. He flicked the syringe with his index finger, moved the bubbles upward, and pressed the plunger until fluid rose up through the point. He lifted a rubber tube from the chair and wrapped it around his left arm until the vein below the bicep bulged. When the needle entered, he could feel the first drop of phenobarbital. He pushed the needle in to its full length, leaned back, and depressed the plunger.

XIV

Randall Cay, Northern Bahamas

The Scarab moved in the dark at fifteen knots over high swells to Randall Cay on the west side of Abaco, one hundred miles east of Palm Beach. The automatic piloting system controlled the boat and pointed it to the island. Martel and the Guatemalan had locked themselves into two pilot chairs with four-point seatbelts. Their shoulders and hips were secure; if the Scarab soared over a wave—even if it flipped—they were strapped in and would remain attached to the boat. Both men had their hands on the chair handles and rode the boat over ocean chop that rose to ten feet. From motion sickness, the Guatemalan had vomited forward onto the console and then fainted and revived. Dehydrated and sick, he fainted again and sat motionless, his chin on his chest, and the remains of a meal on his lap. With no ambient light or stars, Martel relied on the guidance system, which he watched from the pilot's chair. Flawlessly, it brought the Scarab to the calm water on the western side, protected from the Atlantic swells and winds that came from the southeast. When the boat approached Randall Cay, it accelerated to the glow of floodlights two miles in the distance.

The Blue Hole faced east. Its buildings spread for three hundred feet along a bulkhead at the water. There was a stone veranda with an outdoor dance floor, cabanas, and a swimming pool. In the tourist season, rock and roll played past midnight with a steel drum, slide guitar, and trumpet. In the August heat, the entire expanse was empty, except for men who used rubber mallets to slam aluminum braces into the sides of hurricane shutters to seal them from the wind. Beyond the veranda was Victoria Pond, a bay connected to the inlet between Randall Cay and Abaco. Even in the rising wind, the water on the pond was calm. The Scarab cruised without a wake toward the floodlights that lit the men who worked on the shutters.

Two hundred yards from the bulkhead, Martel dropped the anchor from an electric winch in the bow. He retrieved an inflatable launch and fifteen-horsepower motor from the cabin below. With air canisters, he inflated the launch and lifted it over the transom into the water. The Guatemalan stepped in with the outboard motor and a coil of rope. Martel followed, attached the motor to the stern, and pulled. The engine started with a chug and pushed the launch to the shoreline and shallow water. At the Blue Hole, Martel turned west past businesses, private homes, and docks. The men began to count the docks—the seventh was their destination—and they moved at five knots to a long, twisted silhouette on tilted pilings that stuck out from a beach.

The dock was one mile past the Blue Hole where the rocky coast of Randall Cay had flattened out into a sandy bank filled with short pines, sea grapes, and weeds. The land sloped into the water to mangroves surrounded by algae. It stunk of decay, as if a septic tank had leaked, and the residents had decided to live with the smell. Boards were missing along the dock, and the entire structure listed to the left, ready to fall. Boats were moored to floats with ropes and chains. Abandoned and permanently beached among the weeds, a small wooden cabin cruiser lay in the sand, a hole in its hull. Martel turned off the motor and let the launch glide to the float at the base of the dock's ladder.

They waited in the dark. Except for the faint glow from the Blue Hole, there was no light. Randall Cay was abandoned. Every home was shuttered black against a wind that blew in, disappeared, and then came back in bursts. It bent the pines and rattled the sea grapes, a premonition of what would come. The feral cats had fled to crawl spaces under homes and into holes within the scrub forest of the interior. They weren't coming out. The birds had flown away, some for hundreds of miles, refugees who might not return for years.

From the darkness under the pilings, the men heard the scrape of steel against steel. A man in a wooden skiff had pulled back the hammer of a shotgun. With a soft, low snap, the spring-controlled mechanism moved into place, locked, and kept the hammer back, ready to fire. Martel and the Guatemalan looked toward the sound. Their eyes had adjusted and found the figure along the black outline of the dock's pilings and boards. They could see him against the moving trees. He was sitting in the skiff, positioned behind a piling, his head partly in view and lowered to the sights of the shotgun. The barrel was steady and rested on a board perpendicular to the piling. Twenty feet away, Martel could see the end of the barrel and imagined a flash, no sound. The pellets wouldn't disperse. They'd hit Martel before he heard the blast. The second discharge would kill the Guatemalan. They'd fall overboard and bleed out into the water, where they'd float beneath the surface, blown about in the storm and then ripped to pieces by sharks.

The man spoke from behind the piling. "Who did you come to see?" He pressed the stock of the shotgun against his shoulder and adjusted the barrel on the board.

"Christ," said Martel.

"Private property, man."

"Christ, God of all," Martel responded. His voice was louder, and he said the code correctly. "Christ, God of all, for fuel."

"Who sent you?"

"Asheville."

"How much?"

"Two skiffs."

"How much?"

"Five hundred gallons."

"Of what?"

"Diesel. One hundred of gasoline."

"Who pays?"

"We do."

"Put the money on the float."

The Guatemalan had stuffed into the waistband of his pants three stacks he'd taken from the aluminum briefcase. They were wrapped in paper sheaths; each stack was $10,000. He pulled them from his waistband and held them out front. "Thirty thousand," he said.

A pinpoint beam lit up from behind the piling. Attached to the gun barrel, the light locked on the Guatemalan's head; then it moved right to left, from two stacks in the right hand to one in the left. The beam returned to the Guatemalan's face, where it stopped. "Put them on the dock," the voice said, "and the board on top." The beam left the Guatemalan's head and shone on a small piece of lumber lying on the float. The Guatemalan stepped out of the launch and arranged the stacks in a row on the float; he set the board on top. When he returned to the launch, the beam followed him.

With his foot, the man guided a skiff forward from behind the pilings and pushed it to the outside of the float, where Martel could reach out and grab it. It was twenty feet long, aluminum, and far bigger than the launch. Loaded with three hundred gallons of diesel fuel, all in five-gallon plastic cans, it rode barely above the waterline. A second skiff floated out behind the first, attached by a tow rope. It rode low and carried the rest of the diesel and gasoline.

"Take it," the voice said. He returned to his position behind the piling and lit the Guatemalan's head with the halogen beam.

Martel tied a rope to the first skiff's bow and dragged it to the stern of the launch, where he tied the other end to a cleat. The voice spoke again and told Martel not to move, not even his head, and to keep his hands on the cleat. The man pushed off from the post and glided to the float. Martel held the cleat. The beam moved to Martel and then quickly back to the Guatemalan, who held his hands out front, palms open. Twelve feet away, they could hear the man breathe and step onto the float. The beam moved again, from the Guatemalan to Martel and then back, blinding them, as the man opened the wrapped packets of money, checked them, and stuffed them into a cloth bag. Not until he was back in the skiff on the other side of the float and among the pilings did he tell them to leave.

"Go," he said, and the halogen beam disappeared.

Martel drew his hands back from the cleat and moved them to the cord on the motor. He pulled it once to start the engine and felt relief that he didn't have to pull twice. He turned the launch away from the float into a black night and steered to the Blue Hole, slowly with two skiffs in tow, one mile at two knots, and across Victoria Pond to the Scarab, which rocked in the darkness.

At the Scarab, they sorted through the second skiff, separated out the five-gallon cans of gasoline, all twenty of them, and loaded them into the forward hull of the Scarab. Martel pushed them up against the point of the bow and secured them with netting and a pattern of ropes that would keep them pressed tightly against the front. He pushed padding and plastic boat bumpers in between them so they wouldn't collide during the voyage.

The Guatemalan transferred the diesel fuel cans into the open hull of the Scarab until it was crowded. He emptied some of the fuel into the Scarab's extra fuel tanks, topped them off, and then lined the gunwales with the rest in a web of braided rope to keep them from moving. He filled the empty cans with seawater, dropped them over the side, and turned over the two skiffs. The cans disappeared; the skiffs, filled with water, floated, their hulls barely breaking the surface.

Martel sat in the forward compartment with the gasoline and turned on the Bahamas Telecom satellite phone he had purchased in Great Exuma. He called the Four Seasons in Hamilton, Bermuda, identified himself as Señor Emilio Chavez, and asked for docking privileges at the marina. He provided a credit card number from a slip of paper, thanked the front desk, ended the call, and turned off the phone.

When Martel came up on deck, the Guatemalan was strapped in. He had turned the key on the Scarab, which brought the engines to life. The navigation system pointed the bow to the north. Martel stood over the pilot's console and set the navigation coordinates to N 33 30' W 77 35'. He checked the distance—five hundred and twenty miles of ocean—and then set the speed for twenty-four knots. He engaged the automatic piloting system, which would guide the Scarab to the destination, and held his hands back from the wheel. The boat moved out of Victoria Pond. When it arrived in the open ocean, it accelerated north on a direct course to Frying Pan Shoals.

XV

Manhattan

Peyton sat at her desk in the dark apartment and scrolled through Rachael's motion for a directed verdict. White, yellow, and blue light from the computer screen moved across her face. Through her window, the roof of the Museum of Natural History sprawled from Seventy-Seventh Street to Seventy-Ninth. It was surrounded by the tops of trees and lit by the line of lights on Central Park West. She corrected and redrafted the motion, inserted additions in blue and deletions in red, opened the cases Rachael had sent as attachments, and read them on the screen. They were better than expected. She closed out of the cases and forwarded the edited motion to Rachael.

The next e-mail, titled "Iberia," was from Dennis Upton. She opened it and found three attachments.

Peyton: We have a thin file. Iberia existed from 1975 until 2002. The formation and dissolution documents are attached. Boyle should not be allowed to argue that Iberia had anything to do with a loss in stock value of a company in 2007 and 2008, five and six years after Iberia was dissolved. It's irrelevant. Good luck. Dennis.

Simple, like the phone call. Dennis gave her only as much as he wanted her to know.

Peyton clicked on the first attachment, a certificate of dissolution dated August 2, 2002. Iberia had dissolved months before Maynard pumped loans into CIT and long before the stock price rose and fell. That was the argument: too remote in time and inadmissible as trial evidence to prove anything. She heard herself say it as she handed the certificate of dissolution to Judge Stapleton, hoping for agreement. Then Boyle's voice rose behind her, and she felt sick. Of course Iberia was linked with CIT, he would say, because it was an ongoing crime operating in a new business form. He demanded discovery rights and justice, more time, more of everything, her deposition, because she was actively involved. Then Stapleton agreed with Boyle, and Peyton felt weak. The judge opened the box marked "Iberia" and read the documents from the bench, asked her questions, ordered George Harwood into the courtroom as a trial witness, and reopened discovery.

Peyton sat up and looked at the certificate of dissolution. It bore a preprinted legend, an embossed stamp of the Bermuda Bureau of Corporations, and the signature of George Harwood. She read it on the screen:

> Under the laws of Bermuda, Iberia Company is hereby dissolved.

Peyton opened the second attachment, a letter of transmittal from Shirley Bates, George's secretary, enclosing the certificate of dissolution. The letter was addressed to a lawyer in Bermuda named Michael Bland, who worked for the Severington Law Firm. The letter stated,

Dear Mr. Bland:

Enclosed is an executed certificate of dissolution. Please have the document stamped and filed.

Shirley had signed George's name in legible ovals and loops. Peyton leaned back in the chair and turned on her phone. She scrolled to George's number and pressed the call button. His photo appeared on her screen; it was from years ago, in black and white, when he was sixty. Now, he was old, seventy-seven, like her father, but infirm. He had grown up with Edmund Sorel, moved to the Northeast for a career, and found gold in Maynard. George had done exceptionally well, first in the accounting department, later in finance, and then as chief financial officer and treasurer at the age of forty-one. Maynard was small at that time, a real estate company with development subsidiaries, but George made it grow. He transformed it into an international holding company with farmland, malls, office buildings, and hotels in twenty countries. It was a cash machine in good times and bad with guaranteed long-term leases that generated millions of dollars per day.

He had left the company in 2002 and officially retired in 2005, before the CIT liquidation, but remained the company historian and knew everything on the financial side. He owned homes in London and the Caribbean and had led a solitary existence since his wife had died. He had one son who'd moved away and few relations, so he traveled if his health permitted and spent his fortune.

Years ago, George came to Manhattan regularly to negotiate with banks and to see Peyton. He took her to dinner and invited her and Paul to his home in Greenwich on weekends. Eight years later, he made sure she received internal credit at Stewart & Stevens for bringing Maynard's litigation business to the firm. At first, it was modest, but the work expanded. By the time George had retired, Maynard generated tens of millions of dollars in legal work annually, and Stewart & Stevens was its national counsel. All litigation flowed through Peyton's corner office on the forty-fourth floor of the Park Avenue tower. There were lawyers her age as talented, but few had her trial experience, and none controlled the business of a major international client.

George's phone rang and went to voice mail. The voice was George, to the point, identifying only the number dialed, and then there was a beep. Peyton started with a pleasantry, told him she had some questions, and asked him to call back. She left her cell phone number and ended the call.

In an e-mail, she replied to Dennis in the shortest way possible. "Received," she typed, and pressed send.

Peyton scrolled to the next e-mail; it was from Rachael and was titled "New Paltz." In Arthur Konigsberg's personal files, Rachael had found one manila folder with the word "Iberia" written in script on the front. It contained two documents, both of which were attached to the e-mail. Peyton clicked on the first attachment. An unlined piece of paper with a handwritten triangle appeared on the screen. At the top of the triangle were the words "Bermuda Company." At the lower left corner were the letters "ECG," and at the lower right corner the words "McPhee/NGO." Below the triangle were words in handwriting:

Price to tea and coffee.

The notes ended there. The schematic was typical, all in George's handwriting. She left the document and clicked on the second attachment, a three-page handwritten list of entries that designated parcels of land by value. Next to each entry was the value in millions. Combined, the entries represented nearly one billion dollars. Peyton kept her eyes on the screen and rocked forward in the chair. At the top of the document were the capital letters "I/A," and the same letters were in lowercase next to each entry on all three pages.

She left the documents and replied to Rachael:

That's a lot of money. What does "I/A" mean?
Tomorrow, have someone identify where each parcel of land is by longitude and latitude and the acreage.
Please go to bed.

Peyton sent the e-mail and received a reply from Rachael in seconds:

I/A = International Agreement???
BTW—Marilyn Huff was in New Paltz at 2:00 p.m. She took two boxes, identified by serial number only.
Don't know what they are.

Marilyn was Dennis Upton's administrative assistant. Peyton typed a few words and hit reply.

Thanks. I'll speak with Dennis. See you tomorrow.

She turned off the computer and swiveled her desk chair. Across the living room, Paul's face, three times life size, hung on the wall above a table. It was an image painted in flesh tones, green, blue, yellow, and gray, with light in his eyes. He had painted it as a younger man, before he and Peyton had married, and she'd watched him do it. He had found every plane, color, and nuance of his own face. Years later, the painting seemed three dimensional and alive. Paul's lips were parted. Resting on his nose were broken horn-rimmed glasses, repaired in the middle with white medical tape. He had painted the light within the rims and caught the distortion in the lenses. The face looked straight at Peyton; his long hair was parted off center and pulled behind the ears. The eyes had light throughout, just enough pieces of yellow, black, and light-blue paint that merged in the distance to form the pupil and iris. He looked at her from years ago without speaking, an innocent, clean face, blue eyes, and jet-black hair. In the half light, she stood up and walked across the room. With the tips of her fingers, she traced the paint that formed the forehead and moved over the highlights along the rim of the glasses. She descended to the bridge of the nose, across the lips and along the jaw. He was vivid and young. Except for the glasses, he was indistinguishable from Ben.

Peyton left the living room and walked to the hallway. The only light in the apartment was from the blue radiant plugins along the baseboards and the ambient glow from the roof of the museum. She could hear the breathing of the boys in their sleep and other sounds—the clicks and whirs of the ventilation system and noises from the street that accompanied her at night when she completed her work. Unless she brought it home, the boys would see her only once per day or sometimes not at all. It had become a benchmark: end the day together, under the same roof, as best as she could. When they slept, so would she.

She walked to her bedroom and moved in the dark by memory, took off her clothes, and stood naked in front of the closet. Cold air from the vent swept down. She folded her arms and walked in, brushing her body and face against the jackets and shirts, which hung high on dowels. She moved through them like a forest of wool and cotton, soft and clean. She put her hands in the pockets of Paul's work shirts, as if she might find a receipt, button, or change, something to spark her memory, a place, a night, somewhere they had been with the boys or by themselves. She pressed her head and torso into the wool to smell him. Like leaves in a thicket, the clothing surrounded her, and she walked deeper into the dark, where she ran her hands over shoes, sandals, boots, and sneakers arranged on racks.

She had come for the red flannel shirt and found it by touch and smell. He was still there, no matter how much she had worn or washed it. Under the arms and on the shoulders, the smell brought him back in images that were hers alone and couldn't be found in the photographs, film clips, or computer files of the Mount Hood Park Authority. The park rangers and police had reported the fall in a detail that made her numb. Paul was on the Eliot Glacier with a climbing party of nine others, roped together at intervals of sixty feet. He had fallen through new snow over a section of the glacier that had pulled away and created a crevasse. He landed on an ice shelf fifty feet off the glacier. Ninety minutes later a helicopter evacuated him, and he died in the Gresham

Medical Center. Internal bleeding was the cause of death. The fall had been recorded on a video camera mounted on Paul's helmet. The date and time were on each frame as he fell through the snow; then the image went white.

She pulled the shirt against her face and breathed in. She had washed and sewn it after the medical technicians had cut it off of his torso and prepared him for surgery. Its effect was immediate. He came back and pressed up against her, naked in the closet. She put her arms around him, kissed him, and said his name out loud. Paul turned over—morning on the mountain. Her fingers brushed his face. They were bound in the sleeping bag, covered by a tent, breathing and moving together. She could smell him in the wool; he was in every thread. She should have been on Mount Hood but wasn't.

When he fell, she had been in a conference room in Boston taking depositions in a different case for Maynard. It was against the Internal Revenue Service and was settled weeks later. In tears, she had sat in the Gresham surgery center and looked at the video of the fall. From the time and date counter, she knew the questions she had been asking in Boston when the snow fell out from under him on the mountain—something about the tax treatment of international businesses—and then rage set in. She had begun to cry uncontrollably and dropped the laptop. The nurses had come to her and asked to help; she had stood up and demanded to see Paul. They had held her hands, asked her to sit, and told her he was in the morgue. She had pulled away and pressed her back against the tile wall of the surgery center. Her lungs had moved up and down, her breath hitching and stopping as she tried to contain the tears. The nurses had explained that the surgery hadn't helped, that he'd lost too much blood. One of the women had called for other nurses to help. Peyton had watched their mouths tell her there was nothing they could do, and then they were silent, as if the audio portion of her memory didn't function.

Six hours later, Peyton woke up in bed and heard the pulse in her neck. The sheets were wet with sweat and had taken on the smell of the shirt. Awake, the images hadn't left her. She could still see the nurses mouthing words about death in rhythm to her heartbeat. She thanked them and threw off the sheet, walked to the closet, and stepped in. The nurses disappeared. With her toes, Peyton pulled out one of Paul's boots and slid a foot inside. She stood three inches higher and reached up. Her warm gray suit and white blouse hung on a wooden hangar. She removed the hangar and clothes, stepped down, and pulled out of the boot. She hung the suit on the closet door and crossed the hallway to the bathroom, where she flicked on the light switch and stepped into the shower.

Fully dressed, Peyton stood in the hallway. Her hair was wet from the shower. She faced the full-length mirror at the far end near the front door and held a shoe in each hand. The baseboard lights lit her feet. On either side, the doors to the bedrooms were open. She watched her silhouette in the mirror and listened to the breathing of the boys. In unison, they were a slow, soft metronome at five o'clock in the morning. She stepped toward her image and shortened her stride near the door, turned the deadbolt with a soft click, and moved out into the hallway to the elevator. As the two brass doors closed behind her, she slipped on her shoes and pressed the button for the ground floor.

XVI

Foley Square, Manhattan

On Friday morning, Peyton sat on a wooden bench along the sixth-floor hallway of the federal courthouse. Alone, she reviewed Rachael's motion for a directed verdict and read through the supporting cases. She never heard the elevator ring or footsteps on the marble. Only when the points of Rachael's black leather pumps appeared in her line of sight did Peyton raise her eyes from the papers.

"Good morning," Peyton said with a smile. "Are we going to have fun today?"

Rachael raised her shoulders and took a breath. The pencil line of her lips opened just enough to let air out, and her cheeks bulged. She handed Peyton a manila envelope with the word "Bermuda" scrawled on the front. Peyton pulled out a stack of photocopied documents. The first was a copy of the front of a frayed envelope with the word "CONFIDENTIAL" in block letters underneath the address of the Bermuda Bureau of Corporations and the name "Mr. Geoffrey Meacham." There was a postal stamp dated August 5, 2002, from Ramsey, in Bergen County, New Jersey. There was no return address. Rachael sat down. Like Peyton, she had shoulder-length brown hair tied in a knot behind her head. Her square shoulders and long legs made her look like a younger sister.

"I'm not sure," Rachael said. "Ted found those this morning at the Bureau of Corporations in Hamilton. Iberia was dissolved when the certificate says it was. But there are other things I'm not qualified to sort out. Take a look. Ted wants you to call him before we go into the courtroom."

Peyton set aside the photocopy of the envelope and looked at the certificate of dissolution, an official document, the same as the page Dennis had sent her by e-mail last night.

"According to Ted," Rachael continued, "Iberia was a holding company. It seems to have owned land internationally. It's on a schedule in the packet. Some of it is the standard Maynard-type holding: small shopping malls, commercial buildings, that sort of thing. But it also owned agricultural and forested land too, probably for future commercial development." Rachael forced a smile. She was running on little sleep.

Peyton turned to the schedule, which was the next document. It was a poorly faxed copy of three pages that bore the title "Schedule A" and was an attachment to another document. At the top was a fax information line dated 9:30 a.m., June 17, 2002, with the words "Severington—Jersey." Schedule A did not provide the value of any of the property, but it gave the longitude and latitude of immense tracts of land: 120,000 acres, 125,000 acres, and 95,000 acres.

Peyton read the numbers and looked up. "Iberia owned this?"

"It looks that way, but talk to Ted. I have no idea why these documents would be in the Bermuda Bureau of Corporations. Why would someone have mailed them from Ramsey, New

Jersey? Ted doesn't know either. They aren't the kinds of papers anyone would ever file with a government office. It's a draft transaction schedule; I think it's for the sale of the property."

The remaining documents were miscellaneous typewritten pages from a sales agreement, marked up and edited, and a single white sheet, folded twice, torn and taped together and then folded again. At each corner there were numbers: 65-2 in the upper left, 44 in the upper right, 18-2 in the lower left, and 55 in the lower right.

"Did Ted say what this means?" Peyton asked.

"Not to me. It might be longitude and latitude. Whatever it is, there is no reason for a government corporation bureau to have some cryptic slip of paper. He's waiting to talk to you. He has a theory about why this was faxed from Bermuda to Severington's office in Jersey."

Peyton pulled her mobile phone from her briefcase and dialed Ted. "Is he still in Bermuda?" Rachael nodded, and Peyton walked away to the end of the hall.

Ted answered his phone from the fourth green at the Fairmont Hamilton Hotel. "Hi," he said. "Have you seen the documents?"

"Yes. What do they mean?"

Ted waved to his golf partner and walked off the green to a cart. In his early years at the Internal Revenue Service, he had worked on a joint task force with the Department of Justice prosecuting financial fraud and organized crime. Now he worked the private side. His firm, Rockwell Inc., earned 30 percent of its annual revenue through work with Stewart & Stevens. He took off his cap, sat down in the golf cart, and gave Peyton his high-priced report.

"Offshore holdings, my dear." He laughed and made her wince. "Iberia held real estate Maynard acquired in South America. I had someone in the New York office look at the longitude and latitude. There are a few urban buildings, office parks, malls, that sort of thing. But the agricultural holding is unusually large. I'm guessing it's for timber, coffee, and tea, all in northern Ecuador. Though, you know, there are other cash crops in that region."

Peyton closed her eyes. Ted couldn't resist an opportunity to be impudent. His humor was dark, and his theory of the world, which he had shared with Peyton more often than she wanted, was that anything that could happen would, and the best she could do is to prepare for the worst. It would inevitably arrive, driven by money, greed, and human nature. Peyton would be prepared with Ted's guidance, while other less-able lawyers would spin out and crash like amateur drivers on a high-performance race track. Ted loved NASCAR. Peyton didn't understand the attraction. He laced his theories with references to roll cages and fire-protection suits. He was often right, and she knew it, but his amusement at danger that didn't directly threaten him was annoying. His tone signaled that he'd sorted out the puzzle with only a few pieces on the table. He was arrogant, delightfully so in the right circumstances, but not now. This was bad timing, on the other end of a cell phone outside Judge Stapleton's courtroom. She wanted facts, not cryptic self-confidence from a putting green.

"When did Maynard acquire this, and did you know about it?"

"I've never seen it until today," Ted said. "The schedule shows three hundred and forty thousand acres. That's approximately half the size of Rhode Island. It's the kind of thing I'd remember. You would too."

"I have to stand up in front of Stapleton in a few minutes and tell him that Iberia was dissolved in 2002 and none of this is relevant. Iberia is irrelevant—the company, its revenue, and all three hundred and forty thousand acres—that's my argument. How's that sound to you?"

"Well," he said. "Sure, you're probably right, if there's no criminal problem."

She muttered his name under her breath.

"Look, Peyton, I know Maynard. So do you. You are Maynard's principal trial lawyer. I do tons of work for them. How is it we don't know about this? Maynard owns huge tracts of land in Ecuador that you and I've never heard about. That's not an oversight. And the dissolution date is suspicious."

"Why?"

"The Holocaust litigation and Nine Eleven."

Peyton looked down the hallway to lawyers who were gathering outside the courtroom door. In the distance, Rachael watched her and waited. "I have to see Stapleton in less than ten minutes. Start talking. This better be good."

"You know the Holocaust litigation?"

"Don't patronize me."

"Okay, here it is." Ted left the golf cart and walked down the edge of the next fairway. "The civil cases started in the New Jersey federal courts and eventually got into New York. Once those cases got traction, offshore privacy havens started to re-think their laws. Eventually those cases were settled, but they terrified companies with things to hide. Then Nine Eleven hits. Bermuda, Switzerland, and Luxembourg start looking at legislation to repeal corporate privacy protections. The United States leaned hard on them. The havens didn't want to be seen as protecting terrorists, not even garden-variety money launderers. So when the legislation hits in 2002, companies and individuals start to move assets for greater secrecy. They reincorporated in places like Jersey in the Channel Islands, which are ironclad. Severington has an office there. Look at the fax line at the top of Schedule A. It says "Severington—Jersey." That went to the Channel Islands, not across the Hudson."

"So Iberia is dissolving, and they're using Severington's offices in Jersey to do it?"

"No. Severington's Jersey office sold the assets before Iberia dissolved. The sale was cloaked in greater privacy than it would have been in Bermuda. Later, they dissolved Iberia through the Bermuda Bureau of Corporations, when the company no longer had any assets. Look in the packet. It's a one-page filing with the bureau."

"So what?" Peyton pressed him. "If Iberia sold the property in 2002 and dissolved, how can that have anything to do with CIT in 2007 and 2008?"

"It was a one-time deal for three hundred and forty thousand acres of land in Ecuador. Maynard moved the transaction out of Bermuda and into a vault of privacy right when Bermuda considered repealing its privacy laws. What does that tell you?"

Peyton stopped walking. Mobile phones chirped in the hallway, and lawyers began to move into the courtroom. She locked eyes with Rachael, raised an index finger, and turned away. "It's not necessarily illegal."

"You're right. But the papers you're looking at are remnants of larger files. What if those files show that Maynard sold the property to a new Maynard entity incorporated in the

Channel Islands? That's what companies and individuals were doing in 2002: dissolving and reincorporating. If Maynard still owned the property in 2007, and the executives were taking unreported income, that's tax fraud and a securities violation. It's an ongoing crime. It might not be part of this case, but think about what Boyle will do with that if it's true."

"Ted," said Peyton. Impatience rose in her voice. "That's a pretty weak theory based on the documents I'm looking at."

"If what you have in front of you is all Boyle ever has, then you're right. And you're lucky. Boyle will have a hell of time convincing anyone it's relevant. But you told me that Boyle has other stuff in a box he showed the jury. What's that about? What the hell does he have? How did he get it? Is he bluffing? The man's an animal, and he employs an army of them. I've never seen the bastard bluff. What kind of fee is he looking for? Two hundred million? Three? He's invested a fortune in this case. You think he'll stop?"

"I have five minutes, Ted." Peyton could see Boyle and the other lawyers entering the courtroom at the end of the hallway. Dennis Upton walked toward her, and she waved him back. "Give me the details. How's the theory work?"

"The Holocaust litigation was first filed in US courts in New Jersey, and every case was dismissed."

"Get to the point."

"Later, in about 1996, other claims were filed in Manhattan, and the court wouldn't dismiss them. The judge allowed discovery, so the plaintiffs had their hammer. The defendants were insurance companies and banks; most were Swiss and German, some were French. Part of the case challenged the Swiss privacy laws. Suddenly, the plaintiffs were permitted to send out subpoenas through the US district court for documents relating to Swiss bank accounts dating back to the Nazi era. They were issuing subpoenas to Swiss and German executives to force them to testify. The subpoenas were upheld as valid. It caused panic. People went nuts in Zurich, Bermuda, and Luxembourg. If the Swiss banks weren't immune from discovery in the US courts, no one was."

"Okay. 1996. Companies moving assets. Connect it up."

Ted continued. "For anyone with anything to hide, the Holocaust litigation scared them. But when Nine Eleven hit, secrecy laws that had been impenetrable for generations were reconsidered and subject to repeal. That's exactly what happened in Bermuda. There was pending legislation in 2002, just when Maynard moved the Iberia transaction out of Bermuda to Jersey. Why? To keep the ownership secret? To hide a crime? Did they create a new company in Jersey to hold the assets? Did they accumulate four billion dollars in offshore cash through Iberia and funnel it as a loan to CIT? If I were Boyle, that's what I'd say."

He had already said it. She thought about what she could say to Stapleton. "Why not just a sale of assets and a dissolution?"

Ted had circled back to the golf cart and put both feet on the dashboard. "It wasn't routine. It's a one-time deal for an enormous amount of land. Boyle's not stupid. He'll do everything to peel it back. Whether this will interest Stapleton, I have no opinion."

"I'm going into the courtroom. I'll call you when we adjourn. Please check the flight schedule to the Channel Islands, and buy a ticket."

"Okay, but call Severington in advance. They won't open anything for anyone unless the client says so."

"Use your charm?"

"I have none, but you do. Fly over with me, and I'm sure they'll do as you ask. Me too." He wished he hadn't said it.

"Ted. This isn't the time."

"I apologize. I never said that."

Peyton flicked through the pages and came to the last one, the photocopy of the folded page, torn and taped together, with the numbers in each corner. "What about the numbers, Ted? I'm looking at the last page. What do they mean?"

Ted picked up the original file from the seat of the golf cart, pulled the papers out of the envelope, and turned to the last sheet. It was frayed, falling apart, and barely held together in the wind. "I don't know. They could be a series of locations or might match up with numbers on the schedules. But there's a bigger question here. Why would the bureau of corporations have these documents? They were mailed from Bergen County, New Jersey, just before the transaction closed. Who would do that?"

"Who's the guy on the envelope, Robert Meachem?" she asked.

"A functionary at the bureau. Retired long ago. No one could tell me where to find him. It looks like Meachem received the envelope, put it in the Iberia file, and forgot about it."

She thanked him and said good-bye. At the other end of the hallway Rachael, Dennis, and Eric saw her turn off the phone and put it in a briefcase. She waved to them, and they walked to her.

"This is the strategy," she said as they stood in front of her. "Iberia was substantial, but we know very little about it. It appears, for now, to be unconnected to this case, so we can go forward with our motion. However"—Peyton raised her hand and addressed Dennis—"there's more here than we first thought. Iberia owned tracts of land in South America, mostly agricultural, that probably translated into huge offshore profits for Maynard. The fact that we have only ten sheets of paper that refer to Iberia doesn't feel right. Boyle will pound that issue. He'll accuse us of purposefully hiding or destroying information about an offshore subsidiary that was a cash machine."

Olsen protested and shook his head. "We don't do that, Peyton."

She didn't believe him but offered a reassuring smile. "I know, but Boyle will use anything he can. If he calls you to the stand, tell the truth. Don't be evasive. Tell them what you know, which right now is still, I assume, nothing. But I'm not confident about Iberia. Even if Stapleton gives us the directed verdict, Boyle will pursue it. He won't give up."

"But if he loses, Peyton, he loses," said Dennis. "You win a verdict; all he has is an appeal."

She shook her head. "No. Within a year, he can bring in newly discovered evidence and reopen everything. He'll dig away at this. If he finds anything that suggests we misled the court, this will be a nightmare. Iberia may never go away. I can't predict what Stapleton will do. No one can predict Boyle."

Eric tapped a text message on his phone.

She watched him. "Maynard should do an internal assessment," she said. "You might tell them that." She purposefully avoided the term "investigation," but that was what she meant.

"How do we handle these new documents?" asked Dennis. His phone vibrated, and he rolled it over and around in his hand. "You know, the dissolution issue."

"Exactly as you suggested in last night's e-mail. The dissolution and sale of assets were four years before the stock liquidation. There's no evidence that Iberia had anything to do with the CIT stock price, ever. Eric's testimony was truthful yesterday, and it still is. Iberia was dissolved, and from what I know, Maynard had no involvement after that. Right now, we have no records or witnesses who would say otherwise. Boyle has brought this up on the last day of his case. It's irrelevant and too remote in time."

Eric looked at his phone and spoke. "My orders are to close it down. I've been directed to tell you that. Nothing comes out."

Peyton forced herself to be civil. "I'll do what I can, but we have obligations. If we make any inadvertent misstatements about Iberia, we're doing it under oath. Both of us. Any mistake, we'll have to correct it. There's no choice. Otherwise, Boyle digs up the truth, comes into court, and accuses us of perjury. That's not farfetched. It's the equation we're living with right now, and Joe knows it. He wasn't ready yesterday, but he is now."

Eric felt his stomach contract and the hamstrings tighten. Dennis stared at her as his phone vibrated, unanswered. They followed her into the courtroom.

Peyton stood at the defense table as the clerk said, "All rise." Judge Stapleton entered. Rachael stood beside Peyton, and Dennis and Eric were behind them at the first row of benches. The jury remained outside of the courtroom, sequestered. The judge and lawyers exchanged pleasant "good mornings." With sarcasm, Judge Stapleton asked Boyle whether he'd been preparing all night "some informative testimony the jury might believe."

"Let me explain, Your Honor, I—"

Judge Stapleton interrupted, "I wish you would."

Peyton looked straight ahead with her hands on the table. Stapleton's tone was a gift, more than she'd expected.

"Your Honor," Boyle said, unmoved by the remarks, "we have been up all night. We have no additional witness today, but we have a statement for the record and a request. There are materials we need to digest and other documents we think exist but do not currently possess. As a result, we would like to call Mr. Olsen Monday morning, issue a trial subpoena for George Harwood, and argue what I am certain will be Ms. Sorel's motion for a directed verdict. I recognize that this is unusual, but we have serious concerns about what the defendant has done in this case. We will be in a position to present evidence Monday."

Peyton steadied herself. Boyle had survival skills and a capacity to confuse courts she'd never seen in any other lawyer.

"I'd like to make the statement on the record," said Boyle, "so I want to be sure the court reporter is taking all of this down."

Stapleton wasn't impressed. "I'm sure he is. Please proceed."

"We took discovery, Your Honor, deposed fifty-five witnesses, participated in seven separate motions to compel discovery, and we won some of those arguments. Nowhere in any document or testimony did we ever see the word 'Iberia.' Now, on the last day of our case, by virtue of our own diligence, not Ms. Sorel's, we have discovered a secret offshore Maynard subsidiary that was an international real estate holding company. Iberia held, Your Honor—and I want to emphasize this—hundreds of thousands of acres in South America in 2002. Maynard's statements to the SEC don't mention this. May I approach the bench?"

The judge nodded and held out his hand.

"I am handing to the court today a set of documents that only recently came to our attention."

Simultaneously, Julian Smythe handed the documents to Peyton, who paged through them. They were parts of the 2002 sales agreement Peyton had never seen before and quarterly statements Maynard filed with the Securities Exchange Commission in 2001 and 2002.

"The critical fact of these documents is that they impeach Maynard"—he went after Peyton—"and its counsel. Mr. Olsen testified under oath that he had no knowledge of Iberia. Ms. Sorel said the same thing. As an officer of this court, she is under oath when she speaks. She and her client are either grossly uninformed, or they are not telling the truth. The chief financial officer of Maynard is in the business of knowing Maynard's corporate history. Ms. Sorel has been primary litigation counsel to Maynard for ten years. There's no legitimate reason for their alleged lack of knowledge." He held up the pages and shook them. "They are withholding this information for a reason."

Peyton was prepared to speak, but Boyle continued. Each time he mentioned her name, he said it with contempt. "Schedule A, Your Honor, is the seventh document in the stack we submitted. It shows that in 2002 Iberia owned a breathtaking amount of land in Ecuador. Maynard never reported this to the SEC or shareholders. Now, to our grave disappointment, Mr. Olsen and Ms. Sorel stood in front of this court and professed no knowledge at all of these assets. What possible explanation could they have? The value of this land must be staggering. And why, why would they have withheld information on Iberia during the discovery period? One answer, Your Honor. It would have revealed criminal conduct."

Boyle paused, and Peyton looked at him, her face flushed.

"Are you finished, Mr. Boyle?" said Judge Stapleton.

"Thank you, Your Honor. I would only add that under the circumstances, the trial should be adjourned, discovery re-opened, and a new case-management schedule set. Since Ms. Sorel has moved for a directed verdict, we request the opportunity to respond in writing."

"Ms. Sorel," said Judge Stapleton, "perhaps you have a response?"

Standing, she kept her fingers extended, always visible, and touching the table in front of her. "We deny everything Mr. Boyle has said."

"Naturally," said Stapleton.

"We request that Your Honor first focus on the documents Mr. Boyle has provided. We received them when Mr. Smythe handed them to me this morning. The SEC statements are dated five and six years before CIT stock began to lose value. They are dated five and six years before the filing of the Fund's Complaint." Peyton paged through the 2002 SEC quarterly statement to footnotes at the end. "At page seventeen, footnote six, the 2002 SEC statement specifically states that the income from all subsidiaries is set forth in the consolidated audited financial statements, which are attached. There are no attachments; Mr. Boyle didn't provide them. Although I have not read them, my understanding is that they are accurate and truthful. Even if they contain mistakes—and I have no reason to think they do—the statements are irrelevant to the purchase and sale of stock in a California company many years later."

Stapleton shrugged and wiped his glasses.

"The documents show"—Peyton continued and handed up the certificate of dissolution—"that whatever the assets and income of Iberia were, the company was dissolved in 2002. Mr. Olsen was hired after the sale. It's not unusual for a CFO who came to Maynard after a subsidiary was dissolved to know very little, possibly nothing, about the subsidiary or its assets."

Judge Stapleton thumbed through the ten pages Boyle had handed him and studied schedule A. Peyton continued.

"I don't know anything about Iberia other than what is now before the court. But one thing we do know is that the existence and dissolution of a subsidiary long before the events that gave rise to this lawsuit are irrelevant. There is nothing that shows misrepresentation by Maynard regarding the CIT stock sale. The Fund didn't sue Maynard about Iberia. It sued about CIT, long after Iberia dissolved. Mr. Boyle is acting to continue this trial, because he doesn't want to see a directed verdict."

Julian Smythe scanned Peyton. She stood slightly above Boyle in her plain off-white blouse and gray suit. He looked for a flaw: a long strand of silver hair, a subtle scar from plastic surgery, a discreet tattoo. The judge spoke, and Smythe snapped his head forward.

"I agree. Mr. Boyle has a problem," said Judge Stapleton. In her peripheral vision, Peyton could see Boyle exhale and

Smythe look up at the ceiling. "But so do you." He looked directly at Peyton. "I have no idea what these documents mean. I accept your word. You're an officer of this court. But it's inadequate for you to come in here and say you don't know anything about them. It's close enough in time to CIT that you should be able to clear it up. You've moved for a directed verdict, and I'm inclined to grant it. But I'm not inclined to grant anything unless you sort this out by Monday. It's either relevant, or it's not. Show me." Stapleton paged through the documents. "Who signed the documents?"

"George Harwood," said Boyle.

"Then bring him in here."

"Your Honor, may I speak to that?" asked Peyton.

"Please."

"Mr. Harwood is retired, and to my knowledge he's out of the country."

Judge Stapleton took off his glasses and pointed them at her. "Get someone else. I have a lot of discretion here. If I want it cleared up, that's what you'll do. I can't think of anyone who'll reverse me on this."

Peyton was contrite. "Yes, Your Honor."

The judge looked at Boyle. "Have your papers filed by Monday morning, but use your best judgment. We'll send the jury home today. If you have witnesses for Monday, put them on." He turned to Peyton. "Ms. Sorel, if the case goes forward Tuesday, you'll call your first witness." Judge Stapleton smiled at both of them. "Have a pleasant weekend, and don't bill your clients too much. It won't help." He rose from his chair and disappeared to his chambers, the robe floating in the air behind him.

Peyton walked to the defense table and spoke to Dennis, Rachael, and Eric. "Follow me back to the room outside, but say nothing here." They filed out silently from the courtroom into an adjacent room along the hallway with tables and chairs and stacks of boxes filled with Maynard's evidence binders.

Eric sat in a chair. Dennis leaned against a wall. Peyton spoke. "I'm on a flight today to Wilmington, North Carolina. I'll fly up Sunday to prepare for Monday morning." She looked at Dennis. "He wants an answer."

Dennis shook his head. "What I gave you last night is all we have. The files were destroyed seven years after the matter closed. That's what the document-retention policy requires." Dennis pulled from his inside pocket a single sheet of paper with his signature dated August 17, 2009, authorizing the destruction of all Iberia files.

Peyton read the page. Dennis had personally supervised the shredding of the files one year before the trial. It provided Boyle with another argument that Maynard had hid information, but this was even worse, because Stewart & Stevens was directly involved.

Dennis shrugged. "The guy never raised the issue until yesterday. We don't have to keep every Maynard file that predates the filing of the lawsuit. After seven years, they go to the shredder."

"You have nothing?" She looked at Eric.

"Nothing. We dealt with this a long time ago."

Peyton contained her rage. "Let's be in touch, then." She picked up her briefcase, walked out of the witness room, and headed down the long marble corridor to the elevators. She heard the tap of Rachael's shoes behind her and felt a hand on her shoulder. Peyton looked back and motioned for Rachael to keep walking. Rachael followed her into the elevator, leaned against the wall, and breathed out. The doors closed.

"Now what?" Rachael asked. "Tell me what I'm supposed to do."

Peyton watched the lights descend floor by floor. "Prepare for our side of the case. We put on our witnesses Tuesday. Your motion is good. It really is. But if we lose and have to try our side of the case, I'll kick his teeth in." She looked at Rachael and smiled. "It will be fun."

"Iberia?"

"I'll face it."

"You'll face three hundred and forty thousand agricultural acres in Ecuador? How do you do that?" Rachael's neck and cheeks were flushed red. In the brass-walled elevator, she glowed as if lit by the sun.

"That's a good question," Peyton said. "Right now, I don't have an answer."

Rachael put her hands over her face and wiped her eyes. "I've been at this for five years, and I'm not sure how long I'll last. How do you do it?"

Peyton watched the lights above the doors. "They pay me a fortune, and I'm really good at it."

Rachael shook her head. "You know that's not what I mean. Three hundred and forty thousand agricultural acres in Ecuador, and your partners won't tell you anything. How do they do that? Ethically, how? And how can you accept it?" Rachael leaned back against the brass wall, breathed in, and produced a nervous smile. She hitched in a breath and smiled again, tense and urgent. She stared at Peyton.

"We're professionals, Rachael."

"Mercenaries then?"

"No. We have ethical obligations." Peyton pointed to the sixth floor. "They may not recognize it, but I do."

"Do you?"

Peyton contemplated not answering her. But the request was brave and honest, a plea for assurance that things wouldn't explode in the young woman's face. Peyton took in a breath and looked at her. "Rachael, we are the product of the people who made us. I believe that. When I look in the mirror, I don't just see my own face. I see my mother, whose face I have, but mostly my father. The older I become, the more I see him. You know who he is. Do you think I could ever do the wrong thing and look in his eyes again? Do you think I could look in a mirror again? You know the answer; it's easy. And what about my boys? What good am I to Ben and Frank if I can't look at them and know I did the right thing? I'm all they have. *Trust me.* This case is not about the money, not any more. Eric may think it is. Boyle too. But it's not."

Rachael wiped her eyes and smiled. "Can you tell me how it ends?"

Peyton stepped across the elevator and hugged her. She whispered in Rachael's ear: "If I knew, I would tell you. But I don't."

The doors opened.

"I have to get out of here," Peyton said. She walked out of the elevator and then turned back. Her foot held open the door. "Do you think I'd cut out a piece of my heart for them?"

"No."

"Good."

Rachael ascended back to the sixth floor, where she packed documents in boxes and arranged them underneath the defense table for the evening.

As Peyton exited the courthouse, Joe Boyle stood at the top of the steps, his back against a white column, and faced Foley Square. He heard the sound of her shoes and turned.

"Have a good weekend," he said.

She never broke stride.

He persisted. "You're hanging around with guilty people."

"It's a civil case, Joe." They walked down the steps, Boyle behind her, keeping pace and talking.

"It's the right term, Peyton. This won't end well. There could be criminal charges. You want to be careful—you know, protect yourself."

She walked out in front to the sidewalk below. Out of professional habit, she forced herself to say good-bye and see you Monday, shake his hand, but her case was sound. How did he do it, she wondered. On the verge of defeat, he threw something into the case that stopped her. It was like a falling object moving at high speed, aimed right at her head. *Damn him!* At first, Iberia had seemed like a stunt, but it wasn't. Boyle had a whole box of documents and threatened to take her license, said people would go to jail—it would be worse than Louisiana, where the proceedings against the lawyer were for civil disbarment.

She walked down the line of taxis with Boyle one step behind, talking. When she reached the cab at the front, she took a step back. Julian Smythe appeared from behind her. His face almost touched hers, and his eyes ran across her skin like the legs of an insect. Inches away, he opened the cab door. She drew her head back and looked at him, unafraid. He smiled and kept his eyes on hers. She stepped into the cab and pulled the door shut before Smythe could close it.

As the taxi rallied through Foley Square, Peyton dialed her apartment. Ben answered at the other end. "I'll be home in twenty-five minutes. Please bring everything downstairs to the lobby. We're going straight to LaGuardia." Then her voice cracked, and she stopped speaking. Tears flowed over her eyelids and ran down her cheeks. She didn't wipe them away.

"Mom?"

She held her hand over the phone, breathed in, and looked at the traffic. She spoke into the phone. "We're catching the early flight." She put her hand back over the phone and let the air out of her lungs.

"You okay?"

"Yes," she said, "sort of. Let's try to be in the water by lunchtime. That's where I'd like to be."

Ben said they were packed and ready to go.

She thanked him, told him she loved him, and ended the call.

XVII

LaGuardia Airport

At 11:30 a.m., with knapsacks on their backs, Peyton and the boys stood in line to board a regional flight to Wilmington, North Carolina. Peyton scrolled on her phone and called Ted. In two rings, he picked up the call and began the conversation.

"I'm getting a plane to Heathrow. Then I'll board a jumper to Jersey. I've contacted Severington. There's a woman named Worthy who'll see me tomorrow. How'd it go?"

"Not well. Stapleton wants George on the witness stand, and Dennis and Eric can't give me a decent answer. They destroyed all the files after seven years. Apparently, Dennis counted down the days."

"It's a blessing."

"There's no blessing here. Boyle just threatened me with jail time. Get me what Severington has, and meet me at the office Sunday morning. I'll be at my father's house on the beach in about three hours, so call me there or on my cell phone."

"Peyton," said Ted, "you're going into a hurricane."

"I need a break, and it's too hot. The boys have to get out of Manhattan. You'll know more in twenty-four hours. If the case goes forward, I'll deal with it."

"I mean literally. A hurricane is heading up the East Coast. CNN predicts landfall at Cape Fear."

Peyton looked at a TV set suspended from the airport ceiling and a satellite image of Hurricane Chloe, five hundred miles from the Carolina coast. She read the scrolling text. "That's why I could get on this flight," she said aloud into the phone. "It looks like the storm is ten hours out. If the plane flies, we'll be fine. It's a ninety-minute flight. We'll stay at the plantation tonight while the storm passes. Let's talk tomorrow about what you find in the Channel Islands."

Ted said good-bye, and Peyton and the boys boarded the plane.

Part 2

August 6 and 7, 2010

XVIII

Cape Fear, North Carolina

Beyond the outer rings of Chloe, the sea swelled an extra six feet. The wind picked up the waves and threw them onto the North Carolina barrier islands, where they curled and broke for three hundred miles, south to north, and pounded the beaches. Surfers descended like birds. In old cars, windows wide open and boards lashed to the roofs, they passed the renters and home-owners who had packed up and traveled in the opposite direc-tion, west to shelters and Raleigh and as far inland as they could go to escape the wind and water that would arrive in the evening and cover the islands. The surfers parked and plunged into the water. They rode wave after wave, even as the rains came, until the beach patrol pulled them out of the water, threatened them with jail, and enforced the mandatory evacuation.

Figure Eight, Topsail, Wrightsville, and Carolina Beach shut down. The police went house to house, carried the elderly out of cottages, and cleared people off the islands, no excep-tions. With a predicted storm surge of fourteen feet, the is-lands would be underwater by midnight. All but a few of the homes would be damaged, some reduced to planks and glass in the sand.

Due east of South Carolina, the Scarab moved over waves that pushed the boat up, lofted it into the air, and slowed its approach. The Guatemalan had belted himself into the pilot's chair and kept the boat under twenty-two knots. The automatic piloting system pointed the bow on a straight line to Frying Pan Tower, which appeared on the global positioning system as a pulsating green dot at one the end of a ribbon. At the other end, the Scarab was a green arrow moving by millimeters to the target. Below deck, Martel stood in the hold, pressed his back against a bulkhead, and held onto a safety strap that hung from the ceiling. Surrounded by gasoline cans in the front of the bow, he put the Bahamas Telecom phone in one pocket and pulled from the other the Guatemalan's satellite phone, a unit issued in Venezuela with a memory card. He found a satellite signal and dialed.

The phone rang on the polished oak bar at the private men's lounge at Sutton Beach Golf Club. Hermann Locke sat on a wooden stool, sipped a short glass of Kentucky bourbon with ice, and watched the Weather Channel report wind speeds from Wrightsville Beach and Bald Head Island. He wore a white pullover with a Sutton Beach logo—a heron above the letters SB in elegant blue script—and had unfolded on the bar a nautical atlas of Cape Fear.

Located across from Wrightsville, Sutton Beach was a collection of forty mansions and a clubhouse on five hundred acres. Surrounded by walls twelve feet high and electronic gates operated by security personnel, Sutton Beach spanned a white stretch of sand on the inland waterway that gave it the name. Four of the five hundred acres were occupied by two golf courses manicured with magnolias, tall pines, and duck ponds. The compound was accessible to residents, carefully screened outside golf members, paid employees, and no one else. Hermann was an employee. He taught golf in the mornings and afternoons and met the immutable employment requirements of the club: consummate skill, polished good manners, and physical beauty.

With an angular face, athletic build, and confident stride, Hermann looked like he belonged, but he didn't. Sutton Beach was separated into one hundred wage-earning employees and forty owners whose wealth was measured by a combination of the market price for commercial real estate, stock in privately held companies, and the daily fortunes of the Dow Jones Industrial Average. Visually, the difference wasn't clear. By hiring practice, the employees were as beautiful as the owners, but everyone knew the distinction. A thick, invisible line prevented one from becoming the other. It might as well have been a wall. When Hermann walked through the gates at age twenty-six, the first subject of the first day was a long speech littered with gruesome examples of unnamed former employees terminated for a poor choice of words or a friendship with a daughter or son of an owner.

For Hermann, the training sessions were a preposterous dare, and he smirked at the threats. Sutton Beach was where the money was. *Why else was he there?* He looked like them, spoke and walked like them, played tennis and golf better than any of them. Images sparkled across his brain of the daughters and young wives of Sutton Beach. Athletic and unknowing, they were there to be had—by him, whenever he wanted. For a year, he had watched and waited and then stumbled across the line. It was unintended, simple, with a woman twenty years older, and it made him laugh—the ease with which he did it. She'd invited him off the ninth green, led him home, and put him on a regular diet of wine and sex in the mornings three days a week when she was certain her older husband was in Raleigh or airborne over an ocean. It made him happy, proud, and delusional. In bed, with her straddling him, he looked over her shoulders to the ceiling and a carved plaster medallion of white roses, twenty feet above. The medallion was painted, set off in pale-green leaves and off-white flower petals two shades warmer than the surrounding white plaster. Acquisition, he'd thought, couldn't be far off. As the woman rose and descended, her legs and hips shook. He held her upper thighs, wet with sweat, and pressed his fingers into her skin. His eyes followed the molding along the edge of the ceiling to the furniture, which he couldn't identify but thought was luxurious and expensive, perhaps pieces worthy of a museum. She closed her blue eyes to small slits and kissed him; they rolled back in their sockets. She shuddered, thrilled with him, her body moving as if over small waves on the water, endless and soothing. She wouldn't stop.

It would take time, he had thought, to take the roses for himself, the ceiling, walls, landscaped property, and two thousand feet of winding driveway. He imagined opening the heavy oak front door clothed in nothing but white boxer shorts and picking up a newspaper, dutifully delivered every morning by the staff in a plastic bag with a Sutton Beach logo. He closed the door and walked across the living room rug. He'd looked it up online; it was a large Persian masterpiece purchased at auction in London. He stepped onto the stone patio, just off the ninth fairway, an undulating cut lawn that looked like the woman's torso, painted green and lying on the bed. She appeared on the patio, naked and toned by the club's trainers, looking younger than her forty-six years, and kissed him full on the mouth, her tongue reaching into his throat. That was the future, he had thought: the woman, white roses, and green leaves.

Two years later, he thought he had her, not in the sense that he had her in bed, three days a week, sometimes three times a day, but because for months she'd gone limp and silent when he touched her, and then she leaned against him, even with others at Sutton Beach watching. When he walked through the clubhouse, he caught her looking up from bridge games, unable to keep her eyes on the cards. She wiped her mouth on a linen napkin, as if she'd salivated when she saw him.

At night in the men's lounge, Hermann decided to make a play for her. He was ready; she was too. He'd forgotten about the demarcation line, the one he crossed so easily, without trying. She had become so malleable, wet, and soft, so much a part of his days and weeks that he could not recall that a barrier separated her from him. She was with him, alone, seated at the bar. He was on the other side and served her a third vodka martini, straight, with two round olives that rested on the bottom of the V-shaped glass. It was medicinal, he had told her, to ease her unhappiness and frustration. She described her husband as heavy, distracted, and disinterested. He was like a mammal, she had said, but not quite, and laughed when she said it. He was cold to the touch, more like a reptile, and sometimes wet in the wrong places.

Hermann had met him; he smiled at the description. Inspired, he turned the conversation to an option that didn't include an older man in his early sixties, gray, slow moving, rarely at home, and always distracted. A trip together, perhaps, he suggested. When her husband was away for a week or more, they could fly to the Bahamas or Puerto Rico, into hot weather. She liked the idea, so Hermann moved closer to what he wanted. Living with her in the sprawling home was how he put it, a proposal for something more permanent, so sex would never stop. They both laughed, thinking of themselves walking naked through the hallways, eating, then locked together on top of the marble bar or rolling on the priceless rugs. He stopped speaking and stared at her, looked at her intoxicated eyes and searched the blue for a response. They widened when he spoke of rolling on the Persian rugs and then blinked hard when she understood what he wanted. Like an owl, her eyes closed and stayed shut, as if locked for a moment, and then opened to a position that seemed wider than before.

She looked at him in silence and breathed as she understood it was more than a suggestion. The bold, laughing curve of her mouth flattened to a line. That's how Hermann described it to himself days later. It was her response to the impudent suggestion that he might be more than a body invited into the house and then sent away. She was cold, without vulnerability, as she gathered the words to correct him. She slid an olive between her pink lips, pushed it into her mouth, and swallowed. "Don't ever," she whispered. There wouldn't be life without the man. Another whisper: "Never."

She looked past him to the liquor bottles arranged on glass shelves against the bar's mirror. Her reflected image was beautiful. Dressed in blue silk, hair brushed back in dark waves, she raised the glass to her lips and poured the third martini down her throat. Hermann watched her step away and walk out of the lounge. Not a word or glance back.

He saw her many times again. They continued to have sex in the mornings and on some days more often. He no longer looked at the white roses. He made sure in bed that she was to his liking and forced it on her. He stole from her when he could. From the house, he took linens, silver, and alcohol, things she would not miss and could easily replace. One day, she changed the locks and stopped speaking to him.

Hermann moved on to other women who wanted to play golf and have sex in the middle of the day. He held them from behind and showed them how to swivel their hips and move their weight to launch a drive. He happily went to bed with them and received polite postcoital tips: a new set of golf clubs he could pawn or a large Christmas check, the dollar value of which was the equivalent of a minor error in the woman's credit card statement. He would perform for women ten and twenty years older but not for the sagging members of the club. He had some dignity, he told himself, and avoided them.

Years later, Hermann had abandoned any thought of marrying into Sutton Beach. People discussed him on the fairways and at lunch tables. He'd seen them suddenly stop a conversation when he'd enter a room. Tips for sex had become meager, not nearly enough to pull him out of the bungalow he rented near the cemetery. To supplement his golf income, he'd taken an extra job as a poorly paid junior executive at a branch of the Cape Bank. Housed in a one-story building in the corner of a sprawling shopping mall west of Wilmington, the bank did almost nothing but mortgages and real estate development loans. At thirty-four years old, Hermann had the highest appearance rating in the branch, knew almost everyone in Wilmington, and had already taught half the region's developers how to use a driver and pitching wedge. Whenever those skills were needed, Hermann was summoned and dutifully appeared to provide the customer with all the instruction he would ever need.

For that, and occasionally selling simple mortgages to middle class families, he occupied a one-window office in the back of the building.

In Hermann's own mind, mortgages and golf made him respectable, but he also knew they would never make him rich. He needed an expression of hope that he would one day leave his rented bungalow and have the money to which he was entitled—or at least enough to allow him to live better. Gambling, cash only, was that expression of hope, on golf courses and Texas Hold'em tables along the Southeast coast. Hermann knew how to lose small bets, bring more money into the wager, and win the large ones. Against golf instructors and bank executives stupid enough to challenge him, Hermann had taken money so frequently that he had to move south and find games in other communities. On the weekends and holidays, he combed the clubs along the South Carolina coast from Myrtle Beach to Hilton Head and Kiawah Island. He had won money and stashed it in multiple numbered accounts at the bank. If the winnings grew too large, he stuffed the money behind the drywall of his home and pulled it out when he needed it. The games in South Carolina had become hard to find. He'd become well known, and lesser players excluded him from games. He continued south to Florida for different players, more money, and higher stakes. He thought of himself as a gambling nomad. If he couldn't find a profit on eighteen holes, he turned to expensive card games, wherever he could find them, sometimes in Palm Beach or in Miami, and often in the exclusive private clubs in the Bahamas, where the stakes were higher.

In cards, Hermann found good stakes at the Ocean Club on Paradise Island, but the best were in Hold'em games at the Guana Cay Bone Fishing Club sixty miles south of Nassau. A private island with its own landing strip, Guana Cay attracted a wealthy clientele that traveled with yachts and private planes: Brits from the Virgin Islands, Brazilians from Key Largo, and Russians from Fisher Island. Table stakes often exceeded $1 million in a single day, depending on the players. Most of the clientele brought cash and knew what they were doing. Only some were professional. It was a path to profit or debt, depending on the hand, the opposing players, and the cash Hermann could scrape together to stay in a game. Most of the Americans came from exclusive estates on Lyford Cay and Paradise Island. Some came from the Southern states along the Gulf of Mexico. The professionals were from Las Vegas, New York, Venezuela, and London, many of whom won with frightening consistency.

Hermann had lost and won and lost some more, so he appeared at Guana Cay only when he knew in advance who was scheduled to fly in and what the stakes would be. His information was good, and he paid for it. If the talent and stakes were too rich, he stayed away. If the game involved players Hermann had beaten before, he flew to Nassau, walked to a distant hangar, and paid cash for a private plane into the Guana Cay landing strip.

It was never cheap. Hermann could win or lose $100,000 in a day. The losses made him sick. More than once he'd excused himself from the felt table to vomit his lunch into a toilet. It made him take loans—always unauthorized—from the Cape Bank to enter the games. The first time he'd flown into Nassau with rolled wads of cash in his backpack, he'd felt cold and faint, but far worse when he'd left with less. In two years, he'd played almost exclusively against players whose skills he knew. He paid the assistant manager of the club, Pedro Martel, 5 percent of what he won if Martel kept him informed week to week about the players and stakes at Guana Cay.

XIX

Cape Fear, North Carolina

On August 6 at the Oak Bar at Sutton Beach, Hermann let the phone ring three times and watched the newsreader report on Chloe and the locations of shelters and evacuation centers. The news video showed lines of cars and headlights rolling bumper to bumper over causeway bridges and local roads to the interstate highways and beyond to Raleigh and Charlotte. In the corner of the screen, a black-and-white satellite loop showed Chloe turning three full circles like a wide white wheel in the south Atlantic. The storm was eight hundred miles across, and the eye was deep, a straight tube from the stratosphere to the surface of the ocean. Jet black and clean, uninterrupted by thin cotton-like traces of clouds, Chloe's eye formed sheer walls that circled at 135 miles per hour. It spun off tornadoes with higher speeds. The storm was far north of the Abacos and followed one of three projected paths, all of which crossed Cape Fear, the Carolina barrier islands, or Wilmington.

Hermann drained the bourbon into his throat, wiped his mouth, and picked up the phone. Out of habit, he said his name and informed the caller that he had reached the private men's lounge at Sutton Beach. He covered the receiver with his palm, listened, and exhaled. Over the roar of the engines, Martel spoke in English and asked if he'd called the right number. Hermann assured him he had and asked for the Scarab's speed.

"Twenty-two knots," Martel said and told him that it was as fast as the boat could travel in rising waves.

Hermann pressed the phone against his right ear, closed his left with his other hand, and read the nautical chart. "Three hours," he said. "You have three hours until you see the tower. Move in close, and drop the boxes after you pass it. Drop them on the north side, away from the waves, not in front. If they're out front, I won't be able to pick them up." Hermann gave Martel his mobile phone number and asked him to dial it once so that Martel's number was on his phone. Martel acknowledged the information and repeated Hermann's instruction to drop the cargo on the north side of the tower. He ended the call and dialed Hermann's number on the Guatemalan's phone. He waited a few seconds, pushed the send button, and Hermann answered his phone as he walked through the dining room at Sutton Beach. It was an open space with a ceiling eighteen feet high and tables set with silver, water glasses, and yellow tablecloths. He identified himself for Martel, uttered a pleasantry, and ended the call. The room was empty except for workmen, who hung plywood along the windows and doors. As the boards went up, the light disappeared, and the room went dark.

The parking lot at Sutton Beach's main building was as empty as the dining room, except for a few maintenance vehicles, one of which was a small pickup truck with the Sutton Beach logo on the driver's side door. Keys were on the seat. Hermann walked to the pickup, slid in, and drove to the front gate, where he waved to the guard. He exited onto a small private entry road lined with oaks that he followed to Eastwood Road. He turned west on Eastwood to Wilmington and then north to Barrett's Marina and Boat Building, a maze of docks, bulkheads, and boats that stuck out into the river. There were hundreds of slips. Larger boats were roped to the floating docks and locked down, their open sterns closed off with tarpaulins snapped and tied to gunwales. Rubber bumpers and tires hung over the sides and lined the docks. Smaller boats were up on ramps and trailers. The expensive ones were in the storage sheds. Others were lashed to hooks in concrete.

When he stepped onto the docks, Hermann felt the first few drops of rain. He walked through the maze to a fifty-foot fishing boat with a crane on the deck for raising and lowering a cage. It was a shark boat Barrett rented for trips along Frying Pan Shoals and into the Gulf Stream. It had a wide stern for deep-sea fishing and a small sealed cabin. It hadn't been painted in years, and there were small cracks in the cabin windows.

Hermann stepped into the boat and turned on the electrical system. He tested the engine, the spot lights along the hull, and the winch for the crane. By the time he had finished, he was not alone. A young Mexican with black hair and a mustache appeared on the dock and stated his first name, Rodrigo. Hermann motioned to the bow and asked him to release the line. The engine rumbled, and the boat shook. Hermann maneuvered the boat out of the small spaces and into the main channel of the river, which flowed south and east to the sea. He pointed the boat to Bald Head Island, forty miles away at the mouth of the river. From there, Frying Pan Tower was another thirty-eight miles east and stood at the edge of the shipping channel.

The boat moved under the steel span of the Cape Fear Memorial Bridge and past the Wilmington docks, the container facility, and the white cylindrical oil-storage tanks. Immediately east and south of the city, suburban development had replaced the old plantations. The land was littered with homes, shopping malls, neon signs, and every franchised restaurant, clothing store, and coffee bar American enterprise had invented. It was a swath of asphalt and concrete, car dealerships, and parking lots on a flat plain. Every few miles, patches of pine trees and cut green grass appeared in public parks named for the souls who had dedicated the land.

The western side was different. Brunswick County was forested. There were miles of state hunting lands and undivided rice plantations whose cultivated fields were set out on rectangular grids of earthen levees at the river's edge. As the rain fell, the water rose along the levees. In the distance, far past the rice fields, hunting lodges and plantation houses were flanked by live oaks and lawns. The owners hardly knew what they had. Few bothered to account for the thousands of acres of fields, forests, and ponds. A survey was expensive, so they relied on ancient maps and written physical descriptions, which were as valid today as they ever had been. Trespassers were generally hunters and of no concern. The clever ones knew their way in and out. The careless got lost. Hermann had heard stories of people who'd walked in circles and never found the narrow paths that had brought them in and could take them out. Every so often, police reported a disappearance in Brunswick County and combed the estates and hunting lands with helicopters and trucks. Sometimes people were found, but often as human remains.

Beyond the plantations were small settlements and the Brunswick County poor, of which there were many. They lived in modest bungalows or trailers and drank and shopped at roadhouses. Only the state roads were paved.

In fifty minutes, Hermann could see the top of the lighthouse on Bald Head Island and the docks of Southport. Rain sprinkled the windshield. The sky in the distance had turned black. He navigated with depth instruments, a GPS, and electronic maps on the dashboard. The shark boat moved at twenty-two knots across Southport Harbor into the channel.

Past the harbor, Hermann opened a lid on the pilot's console and tapped into a keypad the GPS coordinates for the north side of Frying Pan Tower. It stood in twenty feet of water at the end of the shoals in the Atlantic Ocean, far beyond any interest of the coast guard, which focused on boat traffic close to shore. The shoals were a long, low underwater bridge stretching out to sea. At dead low tide, the first few miles were only three feet deep, and a person could walk from the southeastern beaches of Bald Head Island until land was out of sight. Miles beyond, the shoals were unpredictably shallow. Fifteen miles out, parts of the shoals broke above the water, and then in another half mile, an unmarked channel descended fifty feet. All the way to Frying Pan Tower, the shoals rose and descended, sometimes above the water and then to shallow channels that shifted with the tide and storms. Hundreds of ships had run over them, broken up, and become reefs for scuba divers and shark hunters looking for trophies. Sixty feet east of the tower, the water was twenty feet deep. One hundred feet farther, the ocean floor sloped steeply to the edge of the continental shelf and then plunged thousands of feet into an abyss.

One month earlier, Martel had explained the method and identified the spot. It was routine, he had said, something he did almost every week in the Bahamas. He stood under the thatched roof on the dock at the Bone Fishing Club and cleaned a five-pound grouper with the fish knife. Hermann leaned against the railing and watched him slice the fish for a guest, pack it in ice, and seal it in a Styrofoam container. It was the way the business transported and hid cargo, Martel had told him. Hermann would be an important part of the transport method, just once, for a large shipment, and never again.

Hermann had suffered three unsuccessful days of Hold'em that had left him with nothing but a return ticket. He was willing to listen. At first on the dock and again as they had walked across the Guana Cay landing strip, Martel had proposed a one-and-done partnership. Cryptic at first, he spoke in hypothetical terms and metaphors. As Hermann showed interest, the metaphors became detailed and included concepts of value, volume, and payment. On the dock, Hermann had asked about where and when, and Martel had responded with questions about locations, rivers, the open ocean—places with which Hermann was familiar—and methods of transport. Hermann described Cape Fear and Bald Head Island, the rice plantations in Brunswick County, and places to drop a package underwater and out of view.

On the tarmac, Hermann had told Martel about the shoals, how Cape Fear had acquired its name, because of the wrecks that littered the shallow channels. Martel pushed a luggage cart to the back compartment of a private plane and listened. When Hermann described Frying Pan Tower, Martel stopped the cart. Metaphors and symbols were no longer part of the conversation. The boxes were sealed, airtight, he had said, and they could rest safely underwater. Someone would drive them north in the open ocean and drop them at the tower. He liked the tower. It was far out at sea, far from the coast guard. No one would be there. It was one large shipment for a premium price. Hermann would pick up the boxes with a local boat and transport them for storage. He would make more money in a single day than he could make in his lifetime.

Martel had talked about the rain. He wanted the job done in the rain with a fishing boat. The business had invented the method. A well-known fishing boat was best, with numbers and owners the authorities knew and trusted. It wouldn't draw suspicion. Hermann would take the cargo to designated docks, transfer it onto a truck, and drive it over two-lane state roads to Asheville. Martel wanted to do it in advance of a storm, any storm, but in advance of a hurricane would be best. The heavier the rain, the more havoc for the coast guard and local police. No one would stop a known fishing boat heading upriver to escape the outer edge of a storm. In front of a hurricane, the truck would be one of many vehicles heading inland as the rains came. Martel had agreed that Hermann would face hazards on the water, but he would send a man to help, and it would be easy once the boxes were at the docks and ready for the truck.

At first, Hermann wouldn't commit. Three boxes, nearly one thousand pounds each, were large for any boat. Pulling them out of a swelling sea near Frying Pan Tower could capsize the shark boat and end his life. Getting caught would mean prison for twenty years. He stood on the tarmac and asked Martel what was in the boxes. Martel laughed. He returned to speaking in metaphors and symbols and mentioned the need to do bold things. Smuggling contraband, he said, was as old as the sea itself. He had done it hundreds of times at designated spots along Andros and the Abacos. It was exhilarating. With the right boat and crane designed to haul in a great white shark, the work would be easy. Martel explained the payment, and Hermann stopped him. He stood on the landing strip as hot wind blew back his hair and asked Martel to repeat the number. "Two million," Martel had said. The payment was $2 million in cash, all in new bills and perfectly arranged in a locked aluminum briefcase. It would be there, in one of the boxes, when Hermann unloaded the cargo from the boat to the truck. Once the cargo was in Asheville, the briefcase was his. He could take some contraband as well. A few bags would give him another $500,000 in street value.

Hermann had thought about it on the tarmac. All he had from three days of Hold'em was a ticket home, overdrawn credit cards, and the memory of losing hands that would haunt him until he won again. If Martel's plan worked, he could live anywhere. He would launder the money through the bank, quit his job a month later, and move away. He could hold the money in his house and slowly deposit it in separate accounts. Forty accounts in different banks would avoid suspicion. He could teach golf anywhere. He might move to the Cayman Islands, the South Pacific, or Costa Rica. He could change his name. No matter the risk, the possibilities floated in his head as images that transformed his life into something he'd never considered, something winning bets on golf and Texas Hold'em could never do.

On the landing strip, Hermann agreed. He knew where to rent the shark boat, and he'd been to the end of the shoals. Timing was important. Martel had to deliver the boxes in daylight on a specific date.

One week later, Hermann sat in the pilot's chair and took the shark boat past Bald Head into persistent rain along the southern edge of the shoals. Rodrigo sat next to him and looked through field glasses.

Ten miles south, Martel watched the GPS monitor and the graphic green triangle of the Scarab as it approached the tower. Constructed of steel girders and covered in chipped paint, it stood like an immense Erector Set in a choppy sea. Like an offshore oil-drilling platform, it had a flat surface large enough to land a helicopter. A steel tower with a beacon at the top rose thirty feet off the platform. The beacon revolved, blinked, and spread a wide beam of light visible for miles.

As the Scarab approached the tower, Martel took off his seatbelt, switched seats with the Guatemalan, and increased the Scarab's speed. The Guatemalan sat down on the stern floor and slid over water back to the boxes, holding on to ropes, diesel-fuel cans, and handles as he went. Each box was now surrounded by three black inflatable tubes with attached yellow canisters of compressed air. He checked each tube and pressed test buttons on the canisters to be sure they were ready to operate. He went to either side of the stern, disengaged a series of metal clips that secured the transom, and released the cables that held the containers to the deck. The boxes slid over the rollers and collided with the transom. The Guatemalan stood up and steadied himself, his back against the boxes and hands on the cables. He faced Martel and waited.

At the pilot's console, Martel guided the Scarab to the platform at twenty knots. When the beacon was three hundred yards away, he turned west, and moments later, north, directly to the light and steel girders. Martel looked back at the Guatemalan, who was pressed against the boxes. He let go of the cables and signaled with both thumbs in the air. The waves had pushed the Scarab within thirty feet of the northeast leg, so close to the steel girders that Martel could see chipped red paint and the barnacles that had accumulated for decades. He turned north, away from the tower, and pushed the throttle forward again. He flipped a toggle switch under the pilot's console, and the transom began to flatten out in a slow mechanized descent. The Scarab lifted over a wave and slammed into a trough north of the tower. With the surge, the boxes flew against the transom, and the Guatemalan went with them, his head bouncing off the center box like a ball. He lay against the boxes as they pushed the transom flat and rolled off the back. In succession, they tumbled and disappeared into the water.

Every two seconds, the revolving beacon lit the Scarab in white light. In his peripheral vision, Martel sensed an empty deck and looked back. The beacon blinked. The Guatemalan was gone, deep in the center of the Scarab's gray wake. Nothing rose above the foam.

Martel unbuckled his belt and turned the Scarab east for a better view. Oncoming waves slammed the bow. They pitched him off the pilot's chair. Flat on the rain-soaked deck, he spun into the brackets that secured the rollers to the floor. The steel cut a six-inch gash in his shoulder. Blood flowed with the water around the white fiberglass deck. Swells from the south pounded the bow upward and crashed over the sides. The boat was ready to flip. Martel crawled along the diesel cans until he reached the steel pillar of the pilot's chair. He pulled up and threw the wheel to the left, as far as it would go, to point the bow north and away from the waves. He reached for the throttle and pushed it forward. The boat shot out on the crest of a wave and descended ahead of the break. It turned north and rode the swells, outrunning them as they rose behind. The Scarab's speed had increased to twenty-eight knots, and water ran over the flat transom.

When the boat was steady, Martel pulled himself into the pilot's chair and locked himself in with the belt. He turned to watch the last of the water run out of the stern and flipped the toggle switch under the console that brought the transom back up. He opened the panel for the navigation system and tapped into the keyboard the coordinates for the southern edge of the Outer Banks. He put the boat on autopilot at thirty knots directly to Ocracoke Island. The Scarab moved beyond Chloe's outer ring and into calmer sea.

XX

Frying Pan Tower
Cape Fear River

Hermann drew close to the tower and slowed the shark boat. The waves had grown to eight feet, and rain pelted the windshield. Rodrigo donned heavy rubber boots, a raincoat with a hood, and goggles. He stepped out of the sealed cabin into a flooded stern. Hermann remained in the cabin. He brought the boat behind the tower to the west and then to the north side; he pointed the bow into the waves. As the boat rode the swells, Hermann massaged the throttle, pushed the boat forward, and then let it drift backward to maintain a safe distance from the tower's steel legs.

Resting on the console was an electronic box with an antenna, switches, and lights. Hermann raised the antenna to its full height and flipped the first switch, which lit up. In the sand below, the red lights on the canisters moved to green, and the air tanks released. The rubber tubes inflated in seconds, and one box, nearly nine hundred pounds, wobbled and rose off the sand, moved with the current, and bobbed to the surface with a bright, flashing strobe light. Rodrigo pointed at the strobe, and Hermann lined up the bow with the container, a floating, translucent cube wrapped in inner tubes. It rode on the water thirty feet to the south.

The waves pushed the box forward to the boat, which Hermann maneuvered back and forth with a slow throttle until the box was along the port side, the inner tubes bumping the hull and rising with the water. Rodrigo swiveled the crane. He pulled the cable and hook to the side of the boat and leaned his full torso over the edge. Hermann inched the shark boat to port as Rodrigo reached the braided ropes and held on. Rodrigo slipped the hook under the web of ropes that surrounded the box, stood up, and rotated both hands in the air. Hermann started the winch. From the sea, the box slowly emerged, surrounded by three black rubber tubes. In the gray light, they dripped with water and looked like a coiled snake hugging the cargo. Rodrigo pulled the box over the stern, and Hermann lowered the winch. Rodrigo took a folding knife from his pocket and sliced open the tubes. Air released, and they collapsed around the box, making room in the stern for the next cube.

Hermann flipped the second switch on the black box, and another container floated to the surface with an incandescent strobe. He throttled the boat forward and back and pointed the bow into the waves, directly at the strobe, which rose and fell on the surface. Again, the cube floated to the port side of the boat, and Rodrigo leaned over the edge and attached the hook and steel cable to the braided ropes. The winch moved, and soon the container was at rest in the stern. With three cuts, the black tubes fell limp around the cube.

In twenty minutes, all three containers crowded the stern. Rodrigo cut off the deflated collars and wedged them in between the cubes as bumpers. Through translucent plastic, he could see the red and white packages wrapped in cellophane packing tape.

Soaked, and with his goggles resting on his forehead, Rodrigo returned to the sealed cabin, peeled off his raincoat, and opened a can of beer. He poured it down his throat and opened another for the trip upriver to the Memorial Bridge and Barrett Boat Building.

At Southport, Chloe's clouds surrounded them. Visibility was less than two hundred yards. The waves of the open ocean were gone, but the rain flew laterally and covered the windshield. Hermann could barely see the silhouettes of the riverbanks on either side. He traveled by GPS and monitored the water depth on the electronic sounding screen. He stayed in the middle and kept his eyes on the water to avoid trees and other boats the current had pulled off the banks and into the river.

Fourteen miles from Wilmington, the pines of Santee Island rose out of the river. Water covered their trunks. One hundred years earlier, cultivated rice fields and earthen levees lined Santee in neat rectangles. Now, bushes, reeds, and pines covered the island. Santee sat left of center. The channel to the right was large and deep for container and oil ships. The flow brought most things to the right channel, like floating trees and smaller boats that had slipped their moorings and hurtled downstream in the current. Hermann steered to the narrower channel and the Brunswick County side of the river. It was safer and less traveled. He moved along the outline of the forest two hundred feet from the bank. Past Santee, the river would open up, and he would use the electronic sounding screen,

GPS, and visual cues to guide the boat to the steel span of the bridge. From there, Barrett Boat Building was three miles north.

He pushed the throttle against the current at twenty knots. The river was high and wide, six feet above its normal height, and it rushed to the sea in a muddy flow. The winds of Chloe whipped the rain into foam that made the dark impressions of the forest and Santee disappear and merge into a cloud that covered the boat. Hermann saw nothing but his windshield. He followed the purple ribbon of the GPS that provided the path north to bridge, and he watched the electronic depth gauge to keep the boat in fifty feet of water.

Hermann first sensed something was wrong when his windshield darkened to a warm gray, as if the darker clouds had fully descended. He thought he might have made a mistake and reached out to wipe condensation off the windshield. The numbers on the depth gauge descended in seconds from fifty to ten and then five. With his hand on the windshield, he didn't see them drop. When the impact came, it reverberated up his legs and into his torso. The boat went into an old stone levee that had separated a rice field from the river. Hermann catapulted forward, and the windshield shattered around him. Rodrigo hit the console and fell back onto the floor. Hermann kept his grip on the pilot's wheel as he fell back and pulled it down. The boat veered with the wheel and crashed through the levee. The hull of the boat split open when it went across the wall, and water poured in. The boxes slid across the stern. Twenty-five hundred pounds hit the port gunwale and pushed the boat on its side, just enough for water to rush into the stern and pull it down. The boxes tumbled out into weeds, the remnants of fallow rice fields. One fell into a trough ten feet below the surface, its corner stuck in mud. The others rested on a mound seven feet under.

Water entered the cabin and covered the men. Hermann was dizzy. His head throbbed. Blood flowed into his eyes, and he let go of the wheel. Rodrigo had hit his back and head against the side of the cabin. He sprawled, semiconscious, underneath the second chair of the pilot's console. Water rose in the cabin and swirled, sucking Hermann into the lower hold of the boat. Rodrigo grabbed the collar of his windbreaker and pulled him back. The two men kept their heads above the surface and crawled to the cabin door, where they rested in water that rose around their necks. They pushed open the door, now sideways, and ducked through into the water. When they emerged into the air, rain whipped them like hail; suffocating foam entered their mouths.

They held onto the side of the boat, unable to see and barely able to breathe. For forty minutes, they rested as the water rose, until they could feel the boat lift off the bottom and float. The current swirled through the rice fields and pulled the boat into the flow of the river. They could feel the boat catch the current, spin, and move out into swift water that would take them back to Southport.

"Can you swim?" Rodrigo yelled to Hermann over the wind. "We can't stay with the boat."

Hermann said nothing. He pushed away and swam in a wounded breaststroke back to the rice field, Rodrigo close behind. When they arrived at the levee, they stood on the remnants of old masonry. They walked, slipped, and fell along the levee, with water at their chests, and then swam north on the inside, where the current was weak. Every so often, they stopped, stood, and rested. In a half a mile, they came to a new levee, smooth and well built, that barely breached the water's surface. They gripped it and rested without speaking. Hand over hand, they moved north along the top of the levee. As the water rose, they resumed the slow stroke in the river, next to the wall, stopping at times to rest, holding onto the top of the wall to keep from drowning.

At the end of the levee, they arrived at a creek overhung in an outline of trees. It led west to higher land. Rodrigo pushed ahead of Hermann into a lighter current. They paddled like dogs, their heads barely above the surface, sometimes going under and then bobbing back up for air. They choked and flailed in the water. As the creek became shallow, they stood on the sides of the channel and trudged in mud, covering their heads and faces from flying sticks, stopping and resting as the rain hit them. Blood streamed from Hermann's forehead, which had a three-inch gash.

At the end of the creek, the forest rose around them. They could see trees and a mud embankment that led up from the water at a sharp incline. A large aluminum tube four feet in diameter was embedded in the embankment and shot out a plume of water as if from a pressurized hose. The embankment was a dam, and the tube drained storm water from a pond on the other side. They had arrived at one of the working rice plantations Hermann had seen on the trip downriver. There would be shelter somewhere on the property, if they could find it: a barn, a storage shed, or a plantation house, anything that would take them out of the wind and water.

When the creek grew deeper, they resumed the tired breaststroke, their heads bobbing up and down, barely able to move the last twenty yards. Rodrigo pushed Hermann forward, to the right of the plume, and his own head went under. Hermann reached the embankment, crawled halfway up, and lay on his chest in the mud. He breathed in and covered his head with his hands to protect himself from the pellets of rain.

Rodrigo bobbed to the surface and began to swim. After a few strokes and within twenty feet of the mud bank, teeth locked around his leg. Like a mechanized industrial clamp, the jaws came together all at once with precision and weight and without a moment for Rodrigo to slip away. They were out of place in the storm, deep underwater, and away from Chloe's havoc and noise. When Rodrigo went under, the jaws cracked his femur, and he went limp. The creature began to roll. In a lateral pirouette, Rodrigo flipped below the surface, flew out of the water, and descended again. The force dislocated his hip and shredded the tendons of his upper leg. Hermann heard a cry behind him and turned to see Rodrigo's head and arms pinwheel out of the water and then slam below the surface. The alligator moved in quick flips. Over and again, it whipped him like loose meat without bones, his head and hands snapping in and out of the water as he flew above and crashed under. He careened back and forth until his spine snapped, and then he felt nothing. The last thing Rodrigo sensed was the roll, over and around, in the depth of the creek, and the feeling of his face pushed into cold silt at the bottom. When he lay still, unconscious and drowned, the alligator covered the body with its nine hundred pounds and pushed Rodrigo deeper into the mud. It waited for minutes. When it was ready, in the quiet water six feet below the surface, the reptile floated up, gripped a leg in its mouth, and pulled Rodrigo back down the creek toward the river. It wedged him into a pack of tree roots underwater, where it could protect the new catch. It would return to feed later and pick the body clean of muscles and tendons until it was of no further use.

Hermann watched the man disappear and the swirl of water from the alligator's tail. He crawled backward up the incline and looked at the base of the embankment where the water reached the mud. He kept his eyes on the water until he reached the top, where an unpaved road separated the creek from an interior pond filled with cypress trees.

The wind had strengthened. It swirled thick rain and blinded Hermann to the tree limbs that flew at him in the fading light. On his hands and knees, he crawled along the road and felt his way down parallel dirt tracks filled with water. He did not stand. The wind tore limbs from live oaks and blew sticks and branches in all directions. They hit his body and face, which were bruised and bloody, and he could hear the loud smack of pine trunks snapping in the wind.

For thirty minutes, he crawled until his head hit a cinder-block wall. He lost his balance and fell forward, crawled on his belly, and found a gap. He slid inside a crawl space, damp but safe from the wind and rain. Under a house, in the dark, Hermann curled into a nest of sand and sticks, away from flying limbs and falling trees, where he drifted in and out of sleep.

XXI
The Outer Banks, North Carolina

South of Ocracoke Island, the Scarab ran at twenty knots four miles out at sea. The boat's guidance system approached a pulsating mark on the pilot's computer screen that designated the longitude and latitude where the boat would turn ninety degrees to the east. As he approached the mark, Martel pulled back the throttle, brought the boat to idle, and let it float. He was one hundred miles beyond the storm and the waves that had broken over the boat.

At the pilot's console, Martel installed the Bahamas Telecom satellite phone he'd purchased in Georgetown, Great Exuma. He plugged it into an electrical box that charged and operated the phone on a timer. He had preset the phone to turn on intermittently, to make a second call to the Ritz Carlton in Hamilton, Bermuda, and then to turn off. Martel plugged the box into the console for power and checked the timer to make sure it was set. If it worked—and it should—the phone would make three brief calls to the Ritz as it crossed the Atlantic to Bermuda.

He removed the cans of diesel fuel strapped along the gunwales and emptied them into the Scarab's fuel tanks. Below deck, he tightened the netting and ropes that held the gasoline cans at the point of the bow. He brought up the inflatable launch, two extra cans of gasoline, and the outboard motor. He inflated the launch to its full size, threw it overboard, and tied it with a rope to a cleat. He stepped in and attached the outboard motor. With a quick pull on the cord, the motor sputtered to life and idled on the back of the launch.

Martel returned to the Scarab and sat in the pilot's chair. He set a direct course on the automatic piloting system to the longitude and latitude of Somerset Island on the southwestern side of Bermuda. The boat would accelerate to twenty-six knots and maintain the speed for thirteen hours. Within fifty miles of Somerset, it would accelerate again to thirty knots. He turned the Scarab east, activated the piloting system, and set the speed instructions on a timer.

Martel stepped back into the launch, released the rope from the cleat, and floated away. In seconds, the automatic piloting system brought the Scarab to life. The engine moved from the low rumble of an idle to a loud hum two octaves higher. The boat moved north and west in a slow, wide arc on the water. It circled the launch once, as if the program required the system to understand where it was, and then moved east, directly for Somerset, at a slow speed. One hundred yards from the launch, the engine erupted and churned the water. The Scarab leaped forward and accelerated toward the middle of the Atlantic with a long, wide wake.

In the darkness, Martel watched the lights of the boat until they were out of sight. When they were gone, he turned the throttle on the outboard motor to its maximum speed and headed west to Ocracoke Island and the inlet to Pamlico Sound.

XXII

Mexico City
Eleuthera, Central Bahamas

Gonzalez had reclined his chair and was asleep when the first ping sounded. A yellow light glowed and pulsated at the top of a computer monitor, which fed satellite information from the Bahamas Telecom number received Thursday and Friday evenings. It was the light that would tell him something had happened.

Ten minutes later, a phone vibrated in his chest pocket and woke him on schedule. He rubbed his face, exhaled, and put on his glasses. The monitor was the size of a window sash and lit up the office with colorful light from multiple programs operating together. Still in an olive-drab uniform, he looked at the monitor and saw the hit. The military satellite link filled half the screen and had automatically scrolled to the mobile phone's number highlighted in blue. With a few codes, Gonzalez accessed the site that contained tracking data and pinpointed the time and location of the phone when it was activated. The screen showed a satellite image of the United States' eastern seaboard. The program descended to a blue dot three hundred miles out at sea, east of Cape

Hatteras, and far from Chloe, which was over land and heading toward Raleigh.

Gonzalez shook his head at the location. He exited the program, waited, and watched the beating yellow light as the program reset. He began again, back through the site to the satellite image to see if he'd misapplied any of the codes. The eastern seaboard came back onto the screen, and he descended into the image, back to the blue dot, far out in the Atlantic. With two keystrokes, he entered a series of codes to access the phone's history. The calls north of Eleuthera were from Thursday afternoon, and the one from Abaco had lit up the monitor Thursday night. Each time the phone had called the same number: the Ritz Carlton in Hamilton, Bermuda. There was a third call to the same number on Friday in the open ocean, hundreds of miles west of the blue dot, moving east in a direct line to Bermuda. Gonzalez leaned back in the chair, pulled his satellite phone from his chest pocket, and pressed one button for Leandro.

At the Princess Hotel, the only sounds in the suite were snores from the bedroom and the soft movement of paper as Leandro sifted through Guana Cay documents retrieved from the sunken club boat. It was 2:00AM Saturday morning, and he sat on a sofa and sipped hot tea. The storm had made a direct hit on Eleuthera and kept him there through Friday. A laptop on the table in front of him showed damaged black-and-white video from security cameras at the Bone Fishing Club. The video came from one of the computer hard drives Martel had removed, thrown into the trash bag, and sunk with the club boat. It had been damaged by seawater; with the screwdriver, Martel had destroyed most of the hard drive. The parts of the video Sean had preserved jumped from one image to the next, stalled and stopped, and occasionally showed partial images of guests in the bar and main room, some playing cards, and others moving in and out of the entrance near the tarmac. The images were taken by one camera mounted behind the mirror over the bar and another mounted within the ceiling of the outside entrance.

Leandro paused the video. At the top of a stack of documents, he read phone records of outgoing and incoming calls to the business office. He moved them face down to a pile on his left, and read the next set of documents, which were credit card reports for the past month. He reviewed a list of customer names Sean had prepared and wrote notes on a writing pad embossed in script with the name and logo of the Princess Hotel.

Joseph and Sean lay on beds in an adjacent bedroom. They sounded like hospital patients on the brink of something serious or alcoholics recovering from a crawl. When the snores stopped, Leandro ceased reading and listened. When the breathing began again, he went back to the stack and leaned forward to a single page that showed credit card activity for the last seven days. There were names and credit card numbers used at the Bone Fishing Club. When matched against Sean's guest list, one name stood out: Cedric Peoples. Leandro made a handwritten entry on the writing pad.

The satellite phone rang and showed the number of the encrypted site on the screen. Leandro answered the call.

"That Bahamas Telecom phone," said Gonzalez. "If that's your man, he's on a boat to Bermuda. He made a call Thursday night from Abaco to a hotel in Hamilton. We got a hit Friday night from the same phone and again about seventy-five minutes ago. It's in the open ocean, three hundred miles east of North Carolina. The call was to the same hotel."

"Uplink the image to the site so I can see it," said Leandro. "Keep tracking the number. As soon as he makes another call, let me know. If the signal stays live, track it in real time, and stay with it."

Leandro logged into the encrypted site and watched the laptop load a satellite image of the Atlantic framed by Hatteras on the left and Bermuda on the right. A smaller inset displayed the blue dot that represented the Scarab and the number of the Bahamas Telecom phone.

"One other thing," Leandro said. "There's a name I want you to check on the site: Cedric Peoples. It's an alias. I'll wait for the answer."

As he waited, Leandro scrolled through the security video and stopped at the image of a bald man in a Madras shirt. He let it play, stopped it, rewound it, and played it again. As the video started and stopped, it showed the man waddle through the Bone Fishing Club, sit at the felt table with four other players, and place a cigar between his teeth. He had a three-day growth of beard and a comb-over that stuck to his head like wet toilet paper. At the table, he sucked in and blew out a thin stream of smoke. As he leaned back, the wet shirt clung to his belly.

Leandro rewound the video and held the phone to his ear. Gonzalez finished the search and responded. "Biloxi, Mississippi," he said. Leandro connected the image of Cedric Peoples with the Isle of Palms Casino near the Bay Bridge in Biloxi. "Is he your man?"

"No. But he was there. The name is on the guest log and some credit card receipts." Leandro played the video again. "He's on the security camera too. I'm looking at him."

On a separate ninety-inch monitor that spanned half the length of the workstation, Gonzalez dialed up a live satellite image of the easternmost point of Biloxi's Big Island, where Route 90 traveled over the Bay Bridge. The Isle of Palms was lit up in carousel lights at the eastern end of the main road. It faced the Gulf of Mexico. The live image showed streetlights that glowed along the bridge in the early morning. Traffic was constant, and people, lit by lights on the footpaths, walked through the casino's parking lots and hotel gardens. Some teetered, fell over, and lay on the lawns to recover; others sat on benches, wandered to the beach, or moved among cars and trucks in the parking lots to sleep or drive away. North of the beach, Biloxi was in total darkness, a grid of blocks, some with damaged homes and buildings and others wiped clean, now empty lots of cracked concrete, weeds, and cut brush.

"It's doing business," said Gonzalez, referring to the Isle of Palms.

"It should be thriving. We made sure he rebuilt first so the money could flow through. Send me all of his information from the database, and file a flight plan from Eleuthera to Hamilton. We'll need landing rights for the plane. Do you have all the information?"

"Yes." Gonzalez called up a program on a separate monitor for flight plans and landing rights.

"We'll be in Hamilton in about four hours. Once we're in the air, Sean will file the flight plan for Biloxi."

"How long should I track the number in the Atlantic?"

"Until I say otherwise. Contact the plane when that phone lights up again. I want to know where he is."

Leandro terminated the call and walked into the adjacent room. In the beds, Sean and Joseph lay on their backs with their mouths open, eyes closed. They sounded like dogs sleeping through a dream. He grabbed their bare feet in succession as he walked along the ends of the two beds. The snores changed to groans. Sean rolled out of a bed, held onto the walls in the dark room, and staggered to the bathroom, where he flipped on a light switch and cursed. Joseph raised his head, sat up, and blinked. He hacked phlegm up from his bronchial tubes and spit into the sheets.

Leandro returned to the main room of the suite, reviewed the remaining documents, and noted on the hotel stationery the names, credit card numbers, and home cities of every visitor to the Bone Fishing Club in the last four weeks. He scrolled through the video and stopped at frames where he could see the faces of the men who had visited the club in the last seven days. He downloaded still frames of the video onto his laptop and cropped and enlarged them to images of faces, some in full view, others at three-quarter or profile, and almost all taken by the camera behind the bar. Some of the images were at a distance, as the men sat around the felt table. Others were close-ups, taken when they sat or stood at the bar.

He saved multiple images of every man. Most were older. A few, like Cedric Peoples, were middle aged. His round face, lined with beads of sweat, filled the screen. Three of the men were younger. One wore a dark T-shirt with the words "Rice University" written in white script across the front. Another wore a golf shirt embroidered with red lettering Leandro could not read from a distance. The third was Hermann, who had been at the bar and the table for a week. Leandro enlarged the full face and opened up the video from the last two days. He hadn't yet combined the face with a name. The man was tall, young, and athletic, more physically imposing than the others. In the video, he was confident when he walked through the main room and ordered a drink at the bar.

Leandro scrolled back for several days on the video, sped it up, and watched for a private discussion between the tall man and Martel. On the second day, Hermann spoke to Martel across the bar, like any other customer who ordered a drink. A day later, they spoke when no one was in the main room, but the conversation was brief and appeared routine. Many of the other days' images had been destroyed. On the last day, the video was poor, but Sean had retrieved some of it. What existed halted in and out of partial images, stopped entirely, jumped to many minutes later, and then started again. Only once could Leandro see Hermann speak directly to Martel, and the image was at a distance, far from the bar, near the front entrance. It lacked clarity, but he could see them shake hands, and then Hermann pulled his hand away and slid it into his right pocket. Leandro rewound the video, enlarged it, and played it again. He stopped it just before the handshake and scrolled through the images frame by frame. The handshake was firm and a second too long. Leandro moved to the next frame, and the tall man's fingers began to curl. Ten frames later, his fingers were around an object within the palm. As Leandro moved through the enlarged images, the tall man pulled his hand away and slid it into his pocket. Then he removed his hand and rested it along the outside, as if to feel the object.

Leandro rewound the video and played it again. When he arrived at the handshake, he let the video play in slow motion. It was an exchange. Martel had given him something. The handshake lasted too long, and then the tall man pulled something away. The camera was too distant for Leandro to tell what the object was, but it was something. This time he let the video play out to the end. He watched Martel and Noah shake hands with the other guests as they left through the entry portico. The handshakes were perfunctory, quick, and casual.

Leandro stopped the video and closed the laptop. He packed up the documents, hard drives, and disks from the sunken hull and slid them into his leather briefcase. He walked to a bedroom on the other side of the suite and gathered his private belongings. By the time he was ready, Sean and Joseph stood in front of him. They had shaved and showered, wore clean clothes, and carried knapsacks on their backs. The three men left the Princess Hotel in the dark and met the driver Leandro had ordered at the front entrance.

Chloe had blown apart the hotel grounds. Downed trees had fallen across paths and access roads; some rested on the cracked roofs of bungalows whose shingles had been torn off by the wind. A small maintenance shed near the entrance had collapsed in pieces under the force of the storm. Water flooded every depression. It would be weeks before the hotel staff had cut up the trees and removed the trash that covered the property. Some of the outbuildings were destroyed, but the main building, where Leandro and the two men had stayed, was intact. Steel-reinforced cinderblock, an aluminum roof, and hurricane shutters sealed the structure and kept out the rain and wind.

Leandro, Sean, and Joseph stood under a wooden portico in the dark when the car arrived. They drove out of the hotel compound and heard the whine of multiple generators and the loud sound of chainsaws cutting through trunks of trees. Outside lights lit the driveway, which was partially clear. The car weaved through the downed trees like they were barricades and traveled west into north Eleuthera to the private airstrip where the Citation had landed. It was at the end of the tarmac and pointed north. Before first light, the plane took off for Bermuda.

XXIII

Winnabow Plantation, Cape Fear River

A breeze blew up the Cape Fear River under a cloudless sky. The water ran high with floating trees, dead animals, and the effluent from flooded pig farms. It all flowed to Southport and the sea, where the current took it to the Gulf Stream and dispersed it into the Atlantic. On a shoal at the southern tip of Santee Island, the shark boat lay below the surface like a carcass caught in an eddy. Recognizable as a boat only to those who plied the main channel for things lost in the storm, it was gone, disappeared in the swollen river, like any skiff that had broken loose, turned over, and drifted with the current. Water surged past the hull and formed whirlpools that spun inward. They pulled at the boat, which moved off the shoal into the center, where things flowed together as rapidly moving junk to the river's mouth.

Most of the trees on Santee had snapped high on their trunks, and the broken tops had fallen, one end on the ground and the other still attached to the trunk: right triangles, up and down the island, that would remain until they collapsed or someone came to cut them down.

Along the western bank, across from the northern end of Santee, the rice fields of Winnabow drained floodwater. They were surrounded by clay and stone levees—impoundments, they were called—which spread for a mile as a grid of red rectangles. The levees extended three hundred yards out to the water and served as access roads twenty feet wide for migrant workers, who harvested and moved the rice onto the solid ground four times a year. Along the levees, vehicles had cut ruts now filled with storm water that sparkled in the sun. Every two hundred feet, aluminum pipes shot water out of the impoundments and into the creeks and river.

To the south, the old impoundments were decayed, ruined, and infested with weeds. Floodwater swirled over them.

Winnabow was an approximate rectangle, six thousand acres of forest, fields, and cypress ponds. One long side spanned the western bank of the river for more than a mile; the other followed State Route 133 to Southport. It was a remnant of a larger tract, sold off piecemeal to the state; the other 7,000 acres to the south had become public hunting lands. There was no discernible border, and the two properties flowed together as one. Hunters often wandered north into Winnabow, where they encountered the roads, well-worn paths, and tall grass fields filled with pheasant and grouse.

North of the impoundments was high yellow grass. Horses wandered in pastures where the hay had been cut and rolled into bales. Between the river and the grass, a one-story white house was set apart from the trees. Surrounded by a scrub lawn and azaleas, it had a peaked blue steel roof attached with cables connected to aluminum beams. A covered porch supported by steel columns surrounded the house. The windows were floor to ceiling, tightly closed behind aluminum shutters covered in blue paint. The walls were reinforced cinderblock.

Peyton woke up to the sounds of the shutters pried open, folded back from the windows, and latched against the outside walls. Ben and Frank opened the house to the morning air, which circulated the smell of coffee into the bedroom. In green boxer shorts and a gray T-shirt, she rose and stepped out onto warm wood.

South across the lawn and down the main road, branches and trees littered the property. They covered the lawn and flagstone walkways that connected the house to the pastures and the double-track main road that ran along the impoundments to the dock and then west to the main gate. South of the house, two oaks had come down. The wind had blown the smaller of the two into several large pieces. The big one had fallen across the road onto an empty yellow bungalow, closed and boarded up years ago. The high part of the trunk had crushed the roof at its peak, entered the living room, and caved in the northern wall. The house was open to the air and showed peeling wallpaper, ruined furniture, and the broken edges of plywood covered by branches, leaves, and Spanish moss. The structure listed to one side, waiting for demolition. Peyton looked at the house and shook her head.

Beyond the field was Winnabow's largest black-water pond, where she had learned to sit in the brush and wait for ducks in November mornings. Thanksgiving 1992 was the last time she had discharged a shotgun. The pictures flipped through her mind like an old film that had been spliced and reassembled. At first, whole sections were missing, and then the narrative returned in the right order, with pictures that played like a digital loop in her mind. It moved from black and white to color, and the important parts were there, every time she returned to the plantation. Flocks of ducks descended from the air, flew across her retina, and fell from the sky. Three black dogs burst into the water and across the pond, swimming to the fallen birds. Paul was there, and he crouched at the edge of the water as she loaded the Browning .20-gauge shotgun with two shells. Every frame came back in silence. Then she snapped the weapon closed, smiled, and spoke to him. "Watch this," she said.

It was eighteen years ago. They had walked to the edge of the pond in the darkness to shoot ducks for Thanksgiving dinner. Paul was an instructor in painting at the Boston Museum School of Fine Arts, and Peyton was in law school. He had come to North Carolina to meet her family for the holiday. In the cool morning, mist rose off the water, and early light gave color to the forest. On one knee, she was motionless, dressed in a dark-green shooting coat, with gloves whose fingers had been cut away so she could feel the trigger. Her chestnut hair was behind her head and fell in curls along the back of the coat. Paul sat beside her, sipped coffee, and waited for the call of the birds. Three black dogs, Poppie, Tar, and Seamus, lay with muzzles on the ground, waiting for the sound that would make them rise and the command that would send them into the water. The ducks flew south in formation. Their calls pierced the air, and the dogs looked up. Peyton had removed two extra shells from her coat pocket and put them on the ground, one foot from her left boot. As the flock descended, she stood, shifted her weight, and braced her leg against a tree trunk. The bead at the end of the Browning led the formation by two feet when she discharged the barrels: the right one first, a one-second interval, and then the left. Two ducks fell, and the rest stopped the descent and veered upward to the west and away from the pond. The dogs were on their feet, ears up, with their eyes on the birds.

"Back," Peyton shouted, "Back."

Tar and Seamus flashed out of the brush and into the pond. They swam for the birds that had hit the water and now bobbed up, floating on their wings. Peyton never took her eyes off the formation. She opened the barrel of the weapon, pulled out the spent shells, and picked up the two on the ground. She loaded the shotgun, closed it, and pressed the stock into her shoulder. In the sights of the weapon, the formation rose above the tree line at the far side of the pond. Peyton discharged the barrels again in the same order: right one first, just above the birds, and then the left. The shot hit the back of the formation as it dispersed. One duck fell and hit the water. "Back," she said, and Poppie ran into the water.

Tar and Seamus swam to the first two ducks and brought them back. Poppie passed them in the pond for the third. Separately, each dog retrieved a duck for Paul, who stood at the edge of the pond and cradled them in his hands when the dogs arrived at the bank and shook themselves dry. The female, Poppie, paddled far behind and was the last to arrive. It was here that the loop grew more vivid and the colors exaggerated. Peyton could see Poppie's shining black nose and eyes barely above the water's surface, twenty yards from the shore, with a large duck, brown, green, and white, limp in her mouth. In her memory, everything else receded. Paul had dropped his coffee on the ground as the dogs had arrived. Shooting was new to him, and he moved carefully as he took the ducks from the dogs, arranged them on a tarp, and wrapped them up to prepare for cleaning.

It was then, as she watched Paul arrange the ducks along the tarp, that she heard the slap. The sound of a sharp, flat tail splitting the water was part of her memory, an alarm from childhood to stay away, move to higher ground, and climb a tree. She turned her head on instinct and pulled a shell from her coat pocket. Directly behind the dog, the water swirled as she loaded the Browning, and then Poppie's head went under. With the stock on her shoulder, Peyton aimed the barrel at the spot where the dog had gone down. Seconds went by. She stepped into the black water, her right eye trained on the bead at the end of the weapon. Paul said nothing; she could feel him walk into the water behind her, inches away, ready to pull her back or move ahead if the reptile came at them.

The dog's head suddenly broke the surface, the duck still in her mouth. Peyton raised the weapon above Poppie's head. The moment the alligator came up, she squeezed the trigger. At twenty yards, the pellets never dispersed. A three-inch hole formed in its skull; no blood, not in her memory, just a black hole. The alligator dropped below the surface and disappeared.

Poppie swam another ten yards and went under. Peyton threw the Browning to the ground, and she and Paul trudged deeper into the pond. Paul found the dog under the water, grabbed her collar, and pulled her back up, the duck still in her mouth. He carried her to solid ground, as blood flowed from a hind leg. The alligator had snapped it, ripped away the flesh, and taken the foot. What was left was covered in bright blood, as if it were the only color in the world, the only one that attracted light. She pulled off her coat and laid it on the ground. Paul set the dog on the coat, removed his sweatshirt, and cut it into strips with a field knife to make a tourniquet. She remembered him saying the words "We'll save her," as if he knew the chances of her survival and what he needed to do.

Peyton stood on the porch, looked south to the pond, and said the words out loud: "We'll save her." She saw Poppie blink as she lay on the blood-soaked coat.

Paul picked up the dog and walked through the forest to the sandy road where they had parked a small pickup truck. Peyton followed and carried the ducks, shotguns, and ammunition. They laid the dog in the bed of the truck, and Paul stayed with her, holding the leg and tourniquet tightly to his chest for the thirty-minute drive to Southport.

The tourniquet had worked. The veterinarian gave her an immediate infusion of blood and amputated the leg. Peyton could see the white-tiled operating room, lit by fluorescent lights, and the stainless instruments lined up on a cloth-covered tray. She stood and watched the veterinarian work until he picked up the saw. When the cutting began, she left the room, tears in her eyes, Paul behind her.

The entire loop in the vet's operating room was black and white, except for the red blood that stained the sterilized gauze and cloth. When they left the room, Paul disappeared. She was alone in the medical examiner's vault in Gresham, Oregon, sixteen years later. It had the same white walls and steel tables as the Southport operating room, but no instruments. The room smelled of alcohol and formaldehyde. Paul was lying on a long steel table, covered to his shoulders by a sheet. His face was cold, and his features had lost their shape from swelling. He was gray and white, bruised, barely different in color from the scrubbed walls. At the edge of his mouth, the blood had been wiped away. It was her last memory of him, a dry, stiff, colorless recollection that made her ache.

"Save who?" Ben asked. He had walked up behind her and held a broom he used to sweep the porch.

"Poppie," Peyton said. "A dog that lived here. We saved her, your father and I, before you were born." Peyton looked at him through a film of tears and smiled. "She lost her leg to an alligator but survived, hopped around here on three legs, even had some litters. She died when you were about six years old."

Ben studied her face. "I remember Poppie, Mom. No one could forget her." He watched her wipe her eyes. "There's breakfast if you want it."

XXIV

Somerset Island, Bermuda

The Citation descended onto the runway at Bermuda International Airport at ten o'clock on Saturday morning and taxied to an aviation hangar reserved for corporate jets. A rental car Joseph had leased through the bank under a false name was waiting at the hangar.

Leandro left the plane and slid into the backseat of the car. His satellite phone showed a received call; he answered it, and Gonzalez described the picture on the sixty-inch monitor.

"I'm looking at a live image of a boat moving at, say, thirty to thirty-five knots. Its trajectory is straight for Somerset Island on the southwest side of Bermuda. It is sixty-one miles out. Approximate arrival time is less than two hours."

"Same phone from Abaco?"

"Yes. Ten minutes ago. He made another call to the Ritz. It was live long enough to pinpoint the boat. The satellite is in position to track it all the way to Bermuda. Is that him?"

"Yes."

On the screen, Gonzalez watched the Scarab cut through the sea, occasionally leap on a wave, and leave a long white wake. He explained to Leandro the mathematical calculations that predicted the Scarab's course to Somerset, with an arrival at cliffs near Ely's Harbor.

In little more than an hour, Joseph pulled off the main road and parked the car under sea pines at Ely's on the edge of a calm bay. Leandro left the car, walked out onto a plateau thirty feet high, and scanned the horizon with field glasses. Water lapped at the base of the rocks along a short beach. Beyond Somerset, the Atlantic stretched out to Cape Hatteras hundreds of miles away. The satellite phone rang, and Leandro answered.

"He's nineteen minutes out, same speed, same path." Gonzalez calculated the distance against the curvature of the earth and estimated six minutes before the Scarab hit the horizon. "You should see him soon. If he never changes course, he'll anchor at your feet."

Leandro surveyed the rocks in front. "He'll move," he said. "He'll turn north or south, and you call me when he does. He has a place in mind."

"I'll call in seven minutes."

Joseph and Sean left the car and stood among the pines. Leandro made short calls to Venezuela, the eastern Caribbean, and Mexico City. He stood on the rocks with a clear view of the horizon. Gonzalez called back, reported that the boat was on the same course at the same speed, and asked Leandro to find it through the field glasses. The boat appeared as a dot at the horizon, like an insect crossing a line. In seconds, Leandro distinguished the white wake from the painted blue bow. As he looked through the glasses, Joseph and Sean knelt among the trees.

"This is it," Leandro said to the men. "He's a few minutes out."

Gonzalez called back and explained what he saw on the screen. The boat had increased its speed over calm water. The

Scarab was a silhouette against deep blue, moving in a direct line on the same course and covering five hundred meters of water every fifteen seconds, a speed that would bring the boat to Somerset in minutes. Leandro backed up behind a large pine and kept the Scarab within the lenses. It kept coming. Gonzalez described the path to Somerset, a yellow line on the monitor measured in meters per second. If Martel stayed on the line, he would dock the boat at the cliff in Ely's Harbour.

The angle of the boat's path suggested a turn north. Leandro asked Gonzalez about docks and marinas along Somerset that would be logical landings with an anchorage and facilities to remove cargo. Gonzalez reviewed the Somerset coastline of villages, docks, and homes perched above the water.

"There are many places north of your position," Gonzalez said.

"If he turns north, you tell me right away, because he's moving faster over the water than we can move along these roads."

"Right now, he's on course."

Leandro looked at the coastline beyond the rocks to the large white, blue, and pink homes that faced west over acres of lawns, hedges, and fruit trees. It was wealthy and crowded, tightly packed with tourists, property owners, and constables on narrow roads, with no obvious open space to transport and hide two and half thousand pounds of Amy. Dense, high-end civilization, hundreds of miles into the Atlantic; it didn't make sense. Leandro had wondered why Martel had chosen Bermuda and had followed the reverse logic. The American coastline was an obvious destination, so Martel chose the opposite, a place so remote and unexpected that his pursuer wouldn't think of it. Martel would store the material in Bermuda, perhaps in a cave or below the water line, and retrieve it with a pleasure craft after Leandro had given up.

When the Scarab was one mile from the coast, Leandro told Joseph and Sean to be ready with the car so they could follow the boat when it turned. The flatter the water, the faster the Scarab moved, and in the last half mile, the speed increased again. Gonzalez spoke into the satellite phone and had Leandro's attention.

"It's not turning."

The speed was alarming. Bermuda made no sense at all, not for what Martel had stolen.

"How far above the boat are you?"

"Three thousand meters," said Gonzalez.

"Get a larger image. Go lower."

"Why?"

"See if anyone is in the boat."

Gonzalez enlarged the image and descended to the Scarab, which had increased its speed to forty knots. The picture blurred from the distance and speed.

"I can't tell."

"How about in the back? Do you see any boxes? Anything on the deck floor, under tarps, anything?"

Gonzalez looked in the stern. It was empty. "There's nothing," he said. "Could it be under the bow?"

Leandro didn't respond. He lowered the field glasses, and his eyes widened as the boat rushed into the bay. He watched the Scarab disappear among the rocks and into the cliff. When it hit, the cans of gasoline against the bow compressed, and the boat exploded in a fireball that flashed white, yellow, and red. The impact and force of the blast split the Scarab down the center and splintered every part of the hull into pieces no larger than a twelve-inch shard. The diesel engines and fuel tanks never lost speed and collided at the rocks with as much force as the bow. They exploded in a flash, a fraction of a second after the first. The blast wave took off blossoms, bark, leaves, small branches, and pine needles. It snapped two trees, which nearly landed on Joseph. It churned up dirt for two hundred yards, tore up immaculately laid lawns, and leveled sculpted topiary hedges. Flowerpots fell into swimming pools, and windows shattered in homes along the bay. A woman walking a dog was thrown across the road, and a boys' soccer team in an adjacent field fell flat. A black cloud mushroomed four hundred feet into the air. Pieces of the Scarab flew like shrapnel, severed small tree limbs, and lodged into the walls of homes like nails shot from a cannon.

The three men closed their eyes, dove behind trees, and covered their heads as pieces of fiberglass, rock, and metal flew overhead and clattered around them. Part of the blast wave hit Sean, who fell before he reached cover, and a shard penetrated his calf. He groaned in pain at the impact and pulled himself behind a tree trunk. He sat up and looked at the pant leg. Fiberglass stuck in like a blade. His blood trickled out and spread across the fabric. He left it in place and brushed pieces of fiberglass from his hair.

When the noise of falling objects gave way to silence, splintered remains of the boat floated in the water and covered the rocks. Large sections of the cliff had disappeared into a fine dust that covered homes, grass, trees, and parked cars.

Leandro moved out from behind a tree and walked along the plateau to the edge of the rocks. Pieces of the Scarab floated on the water for four hundred yards. Below the surface, the engine block, split open and black, lay on the sand. Leandro

looked for human remains and parts of the plastic containers. He stepped over pieces of the Scarab on the plateau and
took pictures with his phone. When he turned back, Sean and
Joseph were standing and pulling flecks of rock and fiberglass
from their hair and clothing. He waved them to the car and
walked with his head down, eyes searching the ground. He
passed Joseph and followed Sean to the car, its hood dimpled
with dents. A thin crack ran along the windshield. He slid into
the back seat and looked at Sean's leg, the shard still in place.

"Don't take it out; we'll treat it on the plane," Leandro said.
He dialed Gonzalez.

Joseph turned the car onto the main road of Somerset and
saw flashing lights. A siren rose in the air. He turned into a side
street, and the three men watched as the police car passed.

"Drive slowly," Leandro said as he brushed dust from his
hair. Joseph turned back to the main road and drove south to
a stone bridge and the large island.

XXV

Winnabow Plantation

In the main room of the house, Judge Edmund Sorel sat at a wooden table before a plate of eggs and a stack of binders. Above him, the ceiling was eighteen feet to the peak of the roof, which was connected to walls and rafters by steel cables that kept it from blowing away. The floors were yellow pine. The windows and doors on both sides of the house were open, so the eastern breeze blew across the table.

The main room had an open kitchen with a Formica countertop that ran along the eastern wall of the house. At a stove, a lean, elderly man with black skin and close-cropped white hair worked at a griddle and broke open some eggs that popped and crackled on the stove. He turned his head when he saw Peyton on the porch. She walked into the room, patted the top of her father's head, and kissed him on the cheek. Edmund had short, uncombed white hair and a hawklike nose that pulled him forward over the table and plate. His neck and shoulders were thick. He wore a white cotton shirt and paint-splattered khaki pants. The face was clean shaven and lined, set with a square jaw and high cheekbones. He tapped a finger on a set of black binders.

"Those are for you."

"Financials?"

He nodded. "Our first year without a loss."

She gave him a weak smile.

The man at the stove looked back at them and sipped a cup of coffee. Linus Pendleton was Winnabow's manager of all things, long-limbed, and not a pound of fat. He smiled and flipped a fried egg.

"Peyton, my dear, tell me what you want to know," said Linus. He slid two eggs onto a plate and offered them to her. "You can start with the binder on top."

Peyton poured herself a cup of coffee, picked up the first binder, and opened it. The Winnabow financial statements listed gross revenue of $2 million, $1.5 million in expenses, and $450,000 held for contingent matters, including taxes. The net distribution to shareholders was $50,000, $10,000 of which went to Peyton, a 20 percent shareholder. Linus looked over her shoulder and turned the page. His long black finger moved down the right side until it reached the item titled "Volume per cultivated acre." It read, "Seven tons as per three mos."

Linus had increased the output per acre fourfold. Six years earlier, he had started to rebuild the impoundments north of the dock and install a drainage system. He deferred work on the dilapidated impoundments to the south. He would rebuild them only if the new ones worked. Peyton had contributed half of her savings to help finance the project and buy stock in the company. After Paul had died, she had stopped contributing capital.

"It worked," she said with a smile and looked up at Linus, who nodded.

"Some profit; no losses," Linus said.

Peyton continued to read. The new dikes had modern valves to control the water level, the critical part of the system. At its optimum height in every season, the water killed the weeds, and the rice grew to its maximum capacity. With the new system, the impoundments were never too wet during the rainy season or too dry in the winter. Now, the yield exceeded expectations. If prices stayed stable, the new fields would pay off the debt and provide a profit.

"How good can this get?" she asked.

"It's about the water level," Linus said. "If we keep the weeds out, the yield could be three, maybe four times what it was this year. And then it might double again. That's a lot of rice."

Linus reached over Peyton's shoulder and turned the page. His fingers moved over a schematic drawing of the drainage system and a graphic of aluminum tubes and valves embedded in the impoundment walls. He explained how the water level rose and fell naturally from rain, absorption into the soil, and evaporation. The valves kept the water line at an optimum height in the impoundments to kill weeds and keep the rice plants soaked. Whenever the water level dropped below the optimum, the valves opened, and water flowed in from the black-water cypress ponds. If the water rose too high, drainage valves discharged the excess into the river and creeks. During Chloe, the water had risen fifteen feet and spilled over the levees, so the valves stayed open, and the water drained as the river subsided. The older impoundments were different. For them, there was no drainage system. But for breaks in the old levees, they'd retain the floodwater for weeks even as the level on the river dropped.

"If the yield keeps going up, we'll rebuild the old impoundments, maybe in a year or two," Linus said. "Then, it becomes a real business. Right now, it's a little better than breaking even."

"You know, if you expand, I might not have the money for it—at least for now," she said.

"No worries," said Linus. "We have an investor."

Peyton looked at her father. "Who?"

"George," said Edmund, as he ate the last of his eggs. He looked up and grinned. "He's the richest friend I have, and I'm selling him some of my shares."

Peyton's scalp tingled at the name. She watched Edmund consume the food. "How many?" she asked.

"Shares?"

"Yes."

"A third of what I own."

Peyton felt like grabbing his arm but kept her hands on the table.

"Actually, Dad, you might not need George."

Linus and Edmund looked at her.

"Why not hold off?" she asked. "Give me a few weeks. I think I'll have the money. I'll buy the shares you've offered George. That keeps it in the family."

The two men stared at her in silence, and then her father spoke. "That might be more of a risk than you want."

"Is it less than ten million?"

Linus rested the spatula on the edge of the stove. "Damn, yes—much less."

"Give me a week or two."

Edmund sat back in his chair.

She smiled at him. "I mean, I might be able to do it. And you won't have to go to George. Give me some time. You can do that, can't you?" The two men nodded in silence, and she changed the subject. "Then, Dad, you can retire." She knew how to distract him and saw his face change.

"Retire?" He said in a booming voice and shook his head.

She saw the smirk and knew what was coming.

"There are many benefits, my dear, from having a job for life. One is that it keeps me out of trouble. I'm safely on the bench and out of harm's way. If I left the court"—he looked up at Linus—"what do you think would happen?"

Linus turned back to the stove and said, "Tell her."

"I'd start eating lunch at the Downtown Club in Wilmington, what with all those landowners from upriver."

"Yes, you would," said Linus.

"Can you imagine them sitting around a table and talking to me in conspiratorial tones."

"I can see it now." Linus shook his head and cracked two eggs on the stove.

"Oh yes," said the judge, and he raised a long finger. "They'd talk me into a concentrated hog operation right here on the property. And they'd call me 'Judge' and offer to pay me a fortune in rent to start something down here." Edmund pointed his fork to the screen door and beyond to the yellow grass. "A few acres right there, a big shed, and one thousand pigs reproducing every four months: hogs, sows, and piglets everywhere. Those hog farmers would do all the work and pay us rent. I'd also get a percentage. 'No problem, Judge,' they'd say. 'You're not on the bench anymore.' And they'd wink when they'd say it and pass me a drink. Since they care little for all that regulatory nonsense, the pig effluent goes unaccounted for. And what happens next? It seeps into the groundwater, flows into the cypress ponds, and makes its way into the impoundments. The water contaminates the rice with E. coli, and the unsuspecting Linus Pendleton sells the rice to relief organizations."

"Uh-oh," Linus groaned as he flipped the eggs. Peyton stared at her father.

"The *New York Times* reports that small children in Haiti are poisoned. The UN high commissioner on refugees investigates, traces the E. coli to rice, and names Winnabow in the investigation. When the news media finds out I'm a retired federal judge and you're a partner in a big Manhattan law firm, our photos are on the opening screen of every Internet news site in the world with the word "SHAME" underneath in block letters. The words 'E. coli,' 'contamination,' and 'small children' will be linked to us forever. It will be in our obituaries. And God forbid a child dies. We can't sell rice or hogs, Winnabow files for bankruptcy, and Linus moves back to South Carolina to take care of his older sisters, who drive him to drink, illness, and an early death." He paused and took a breath.

Linus put the eggs on a plate.

"Think about it. I retire and Linus meets an early death. Can't have that. No way. Not going to happen."

Peyton smiled at Linus, who looked at the judge and laughed. "I'll never say the word again," she said.

Linus winked at her. "I talked him out of the hogs last year."

"Are you going to finish those eggs?" Edmund asked.

Peyton pushed her plate across the table. Linus sat down with a plate of his own.

Ben and Frank stepped onto the porch carrying hand saws. They left the tools on the porch floor and walked into the main room.

"Ready," they said.

Linus wished them good morning and gave them instructions over his shoulder. They were to start with the main road and clear limbs they could lift. It would take time. The main road ran along the impoundments for more than a mile to the dock and storage sheds. It turned west, away from the river, to the gates of the plantation at Route 133. Linus pointed the boys to two sets of heavy work gloves near the sink. Any limb too large to move was to remain, he explained, and he would follow in his truck, cut them up with the chainsaws, and pull them off the road. The boys were to ignore the crushed house. He would wrap a steel cable around the oak and pull it off. Boards and branches would fly around when the tree began to move. They were to stay away. When they came to the end of the main road and arrived at the dock, they were to check for broken boards and walk around the storage sheds and offices to look for damage to the walls and windows. Then the chapel, one mile from the main gate, was next, a small white building surrounded by azaleas. It had been painted, and the roof was new. Linus wanted to know whether a tree had crushed it.

The last task was the slave house in the forest west of the largest cypress pond at the edge of the hunting lands. On high ground, Linus had finished it in the spring. It was surrounded by pines and uncut camellias. The original house had a stone foundation four feet deep and a chimney. It had been destroyed in 1896 after the Wilmington riot, when all the buildings at Winnabow had burned, and the freedmen, who had received the property from the Union army, had quit Wilmington and moved north. Forty years later, the Sorel family had bought the property at auction, and the slave house was forgotten. What was left rotted away and fell into the foundation. In later years, hunters discovered the ruins and sat around the chimney in autumn, drank, and told stories.

Linus and Edmund had rebuilt it for history. It was the oldest remaining structure on the property and dated from a time and event most people intentionally forgot. It wasn't right, Linus had told Edmund. The slave house was the only thing left that said anything about the people who had lived there for three hundred years and built the plantation. For $20,000, Winnabow rebuilt it and used the new structure as a camp at the edge of the hunting lands. Like the chapel, dock, and storage shed, it was a line item in the Winnabow budget. Linus hired a local historian as a consultant and rebuilt it as closely to the original as he could.

The boys tugged on their gloves and walked out onto the porch with Linus behind them. He pointed south to the crushed house, beyond it to where the road turned east to the river and then continued straight past the impoundments to the docks and storage sheds. Linus clapped his hands and urged them on. They jumped on bicycles and rode south under the limbs of live oaks.

From her bedroom, Peyton's mobile phone called to her, and she stepped out of the kitchen and along the porch. The phone's screen showed a British number.

"Ted?" she answered.

"Yep. It's me."

"What do you have?"

"It's complicated."

"Can you give me a bottom line?"

"How about a theory?"

Another theory. "Give it to me."

Ted described what Severington provided based on the fact that Maynard was the client, verified by a call from Rachael.

"There's not much: two and a half boxes of files that are exclusively Maynard's. They involve a 2002 transaction whereby Iberia sold all of its assets to ECG—Ecuadorian Coffee Growers—but there's a not-for-profit corporation, a foundation, involved too, called Children's Bay Cay Foundation. It's registered in the Bahamas. The money went directly to Iberia, which was then dissolved. It's not clear how the foundation is involved other than the fact that it received a fee or contribution as part of the deal, but we don't know how much. How Maynard and Iberia handled the taxation is not part of the files."

"What was the sale price?"

"Two hundred and fifty million."

Peyton sat down on the bed. "What were the assets?"

"The land in Ecuador, some of it, possibly all of it—the same properties on Schedule A, the one Rachael found in New Paltz, same as on the handwritten list from Bermuda."

"Are there any documents that explain how the transaction worked?"

"There's an agreement I haven't read yet. The triangle, the one from the handwritten notes Rachael found—that's in here. There are lots of references to McPhee, who was involved with the foundation. All the money came from ECG, which bought the property and financed the deal. Chances are ECG has some connection to the foundation. I'm not sure what it is, but it appears that the foundation acted like a broker and received an investment banker's fee disguised as a charitable contribution. I've never seen that before. We're having our investigators run down the identities of the people involved, what they did in the past, that sort of thing. I'll have more tomorrow."

"What about McPhee?"

"He was the deal maker, the principal of the foundation. He signed the agreement for ECG, and so did a lawyer. On the agreement, McPhee's address is a post office box in Nassau. I Googled him—found nothing."

"Nothing?"

"Nada. And nothing for the foundation, which is weird. Charities are registered. Any charity involved in a transaction of this size usually shows up somewhere, like on a blog or a public document."

"Who at Maynard did the deal?"

Ted sat on the edge of a bed in his hotel room. His window faced east to the coast of France. He flipped through pages on his lap. "George Harwood. He's the only Maynard name I recognize on the documents. Maynard got the sales price, but it's not clear who paid the foundation."

Peyton focused on the trial. "Two hundred and fifty million in cash goes to Maynard in one transaction in 2002, and Eric knows nothing."

"Peyton..." Ted's voice trailed off.

"What?"

"Two hundred and fifty million is pretty cheap for half of Rhode Island. And let's face it, Maynard buried corporate history with the last treasurer. That's pretty common practice. It makes Eric a perfect witness. When he says he doesn't know, he's telling the truth. He's a great-looking stone wall. But from what you tell me, Stapleton doesn't like it, and that's a problem. For you."

Peyton's face flushed. "Is there anything else?"

"Bottom line, it's an inside deal, like ECG and Maynard are agreeing on a price for the land, which is allegedly coffee property in Ecuador. It's back-of-the-napkin stuff and doesn't make commercial sense, not to me anyway."

"You've lost me."

Ted flipped through the pages on his lap and held a document up to the light of the hotel window. "Here's an example. In the actual transaction documents, a twenty-thousand-acre tract in Ecuador is valued in 2002 at two hundred dollars an acre. That's on schedule A. So it's a four-million-dollar purchase price. But if you compare the handwritten list Rachael found in New Paltz and the version of schedule A I found in Bermuda, the same property has a value at twenty times that number—eighty million."

"Maynard made a mistake and undersold the asset."

"By a factor of twenty? Not a chance."

"Okay, then it can't be the final deal."

"It's the final deal. That's what I'm reading from. The documents are signed and dated."

"Could it be a valuation mistake?"

"They agreed on a price."

"What about a decrease in land value?"

"Peyton."

"They received something else in return?"

"How about four billion dollars, untaxed and laundered through real estate operations over twenty years?"

"Ted, stick to the point. Why would Maynard sell a piece of land for two hundred dollars an acre when a different schedule says the price is four thousand per acre?"

"We're in Northern Ecuador."

"Another transaction for other assets we don't know about?"

"It's the center of the coca universe. The mountains are filled with the stuff."

"I know, but George Harwood cannot be part of that business. It's not possible." Peyton fell back on the bed, held the phone to her ear, and watched the ceiling fan spin. The warm air descended across her face. Before Rockworth, Ted had twenty years of experience with the Internal Revenue Service. He saw things other people didn't. His theories weren't always provable, but they were logical and based on behavior he'd seen before. In earlier years, Peyton had wondered if Ted saw imaginary things in income statements, general ledgers, and balance sheets. He didn't. He was right, and he proved it to her again and again. Peyton's job was to question him, doubt him, and make him prove his case before she brought it to a judge or jury. If he could convince her, she could convince almost anyone, and she pushed back.

"It's a theory you can't prove."

"Very few at Maynard knew about this. Those who did are dead or retired. For years, Iberia operated offshore and then disappeared. And the transaction? They moved it to Jersey for secrecy. They're valuing rural mountainous land in Ecuador at coffee prices, but coffee is not the region's most valuable export. That, Peyton, is a great cover."

Peyton felt her cheeks grow numb. "And you think Boyle has some of these documents."

"He knows the name of the company. So the theory goes like this. Somehow, Boyle got his hands on Iberia documents. He doesn't intend to use them, because he doesn't understand them. Then, his case splinters in front of Stapleton, so he pulls them out to see what happens. If I'm right, Boyle has already analyzed whatever he has and is thinking what I'm thinking. He may have enough evidence to make Stapleton open up discovery. If not, maybe he has enough to interest the US Attorney and the IRS. Either way, how much will Maynard pay to get those documents back? Boyle's demand will be astronomical. And by the way, how come George Harwood spends most of his retirement offshore?"

"It's too old, Ted."

"I'm just saying…"

"The year 2002 is too old to have anything to do with this case. It's not relevant. I bet I can keep it out."

"Out of the courtroom? Yes. You're right. But good luck keeping it away from the authorities. If Maynard doesn't settle this with Boyle, you don't want to think about what could happen. If Boyle finds Children's Bay Cay Foundation and Tracy McPhee, that's a deposition you don't want. You don't want George's deposition either. I don't care where he is. Boyle can track him down. If I'm Maynard, I'm telling him to stay out of the country forever."

"I'll fly up first thing tomorrow. When will you be in New York?"

"Nine o'clock."

"Can we meet at the Park Avenue office?"

"Yep. And one more thing. Arthur Konigsberg is all over this. He designed it, did the deal, and signed papers. If Boyle gets traction with this, he'll come after Stewart and Stevens too. It's not just Maynard."

His words washed across her body like anesthesia. She was suddenly numb and grateful she was lying down. Ted continued.

"You might want to find out whether Arthur squirreled something away at home. Hopefully, he shredded everything, and you won't have anything to hand over."

"Ted, I'll be in tomorrow. I have to make another call."

"Peyton, you know what I'm talking about."

"I do, Ted. I really appreciate it." Peyton thanked him, ended the call, and hit a speed-dial number for Rachael, who sat at her desk on the forty-fourth floor of the Park Avenue tower. Peyton offered a minor pleasantry and went to the point. "We have a problem. Can you track down Arthur Konigsberg's wife? Let me tell you why." Peyton explained that Konigsberg had designed the entire transaction and signed the asset purchase agreement for Maynard. He had died soon after the transaction, a suicide with a grieving widow, confused relations, and stunned partners. On the chance that he took some files home or shipped them off to a self-storage unit, they needed the address of his widow, and Rachael would have to go through whatever data still existed from his computer, which the firm retained on disks and stored in the library archives. One piece of evidence at a time was the only way to sort this out, she explained, and the first step was retrieving anything that traced Konigsberg to Iberia.

"Ted is bringing two and a half boxes of documents from the Channel Islands tomorrow. I'll fly up in the morning, and we'll go through them. Let's see if Konigsberg's computer still exists on disks and whether we can find his widow."

"When did he die?" Rachael asked.

"In 2002. Also, we need to know whether the firm ever represented Children's Bay Cay Foundation and anyone named Tracy McPhee. Run a search through the client archives. Arthur was part of it. His name should be in there."

"Could Boyle know the information we're looking for?"

"I don't know. But whatever he has, he'll use it Monday."

"Peyton?"

"Yes."

"Do you mind if I throw up first?"

"Go right ahead. I'm about to do the same thing."

Peyton ended the call, looked at the ceiling, and closed her eyes.

XXVI

Winnabow Plantation

The lower joists of the clapboard house had cracked and bowed when the oak fell across the living room. The weight had pushed the middle joists six inches lower. From the wet sand, Hermann looked up at the underside of the floor and saw it coming. Covered in damp spider webs, it smelled of rot, and the wood groaned as the trunk pressed down. Cracked beams with nails a foot from Hermann's face strained under the weight, ready to fall. The house and tree would flatten him so fast that he couldn't breathe before he was gone. Beneath, he shimmied across the sand, sticks, and pinecones to the cinderblock wall. When he heard the clicks of bicycle gears and the shouts of boys, Hermann stopped.

Ben and Frank circled the house, parked their bikes on the road, and walked to the roots of the tree, exposed and upright at the front porch. They spoke as if the house were a dead animal, lying on its side, rotting in the sun. Frank leaped onto the trunk and skipped over limbs to the top. Ben followed. Both stood at the farthest part of the trunk and looked into the exposed living room filled with limbs, Spanish moss, broken shingles, beams, crumbled drywall, and old furniture.

Through gaps in the floorboards, Hermann saw the boys move around the limbs. The tree shifted, and a tremor hit the joists. The north wall caved in, and the tree dropped a foot as the joists broke and descended onto the sand next to Hermann. He felt some boards hit his back.

The boys held on. Ben grabbed Frank by the waist and gripped the tree. The boys turned down the trunk and jumped to the ground.

Parts of the fallen joists had ripped away Hermann's shirt and cut his shoulders. He pushed himself against the cinderblock wall and moved to the gap he'd crawled through the night before. He waited, pressed against the wall, until he saw the boys pedal south along the road through mud and rainwater. They stopped to clear away whatever they could move and continued on. In a half a mile, the road turned east to the impoundments and dipped into a trough. The boys made the turn and disappeared.

Hermann pulled himself past the fallen joists and floorboards and crawled through the gap in the cinderblock wall. He stood and ran. A short path took him into the high yellow grass that spread out behind the ruined house for hundreds of yards. His clothes were covered in gray and black sand. The shirt had bloodstains from the cut on his forehead, which was purple and swollen. His left eye was puffy and shut. Small cuts covered his face from branches and sticks that had hit him in the wind as he had crawled along the road.

Seated in the high grass, Hermann pulled out his mobile phone from a buttoned breast pocket, turned it on, and received nothing. Like everything else, it had gone underwater. He removed the battery and memory card and blew on them.

With the driest part of his shirt, Hermann rubbed the exposed open back of the phone to remove the moisture, replaced the battery and memory card, and returned the phone to his pocket.

Within the grass, Hermann crouched and kept his head low. He walked south and parallel to the road for two hundred yards, sat, and listened. Behind him, he could hear Linus's truck. With one end of a steel cable around the trunk and other attached to the hitch, Linus pulled at the tree. The engine revved, and the tires spun in the wet sand. Hermann looked through the grass at the road. He had followed it the night before in rain and wind. If he followed it again and stayed within the grass, it would take him back to the creek where Rodrigo had disappeared. He walked parallel to the road through the grass and into pockets of forest, where he stepped over downed tree limbs and fell into soft holes. In the distance, the black cypress pond covered half a mile to the west, past the trough in the road where the boys had turned away and disappeared.

Hermann walked through the forest to the pond, listened for movement, and stepped out onto the road where it divided the pond from the impoundments and creek. The aluminum tube still poured water in a white surge.

Tied to a cypress tree was a gift—a swamped aluminum rowboat with oars in metal brackets. Hermann turned over the boat to drain the water and check for damage to the hull. It was solid, and he pulled it across the road and down the embankment to the creek. He sat on the middle bench, dipped the oars into the water, and pulled east to the river. The levee was five feet above the waterline, rust red, and twenty feet across. Dense forest lined the other side of the creek, and tree limbs hung over the water in a canopy that blocked the sun. Hermann pulled hard under the branches.

When the rowboat arrived at the end of the creek, it emerged into light. Hermann raised the right oar out of the water, and the river's current turned the boat. In a swift glide for half a mile along the levee, he floated to the rocks of the old impoundment, just below the water's surface. Hermann turned into the impoundment and scraped across the rocks. The rowboat spun in swirling water. He scanned the banks and looked out to the middle of the river. The shark boat was gone. It had broken free of the shoal at the end of Santee and floated in the current to Southport. All he could see was brown water pushing trees and piles of things to the sea.

The rowboat moved in eddies and struck a container. Just below the waterline, it rested in mud. Next to it was the second, tilted on its side. The third had disappeared into a trough and rested at the bottom of the impoundment. Hermann stepped out of the rowboat up to his waist. He slipped into the trough next to the first container and splashed away the mud, sticks, and grass. Through the translucent top, the red-and-white bags were sealed, dry, and wrapped in clear plastic. They bore a printed white profile of a knight on horseback against a red background. The words in large block letters read "White Knight Flour" and in smaller letters "Brattleboro, Vermont." Along the side of the bags were approval stamps in blue ink from the US Food and Drug Administration, nutrition facts, the ingredients listed according to the percentage of the fat and protein content, and a short history of the oldest flour company in New England.

Hermann stood in the mud and moved his hands in the water until he made contact with the second container. It was one foot below the surface, slightly at an angle, and surrounded by mud and weeds. He wiped the weeds from the top. The aluminum briefcase lay just beneath the translucent lid. With a pocketknife, he worked with the screws that attached the lid to the container. In ten minutes, six screws were out, and Hermann pulled back the lid and let water flow in. He squeezed the briefcase out of the box, threw it in the rowboat, and removed four bags. He pushed the lid back down onto the box until it caught tight against the gasket and remained in place.

Back in the rowboat, he sat up and put the oars in the water. East across the narrows to Santee, he pulled hard. The current jostled the boat as it moved across the river and south to the bottom of Santee, where the current bifurcated in whirlpools on the shoals. He turned into the island and pulled until he reached the mud and brought the boat ashore. In the sun, he rested and looked north to the span of the bridge. A few miles beyond were the Barrett docks where he had left the truck.

In his chest pocket, he felt for the phone, removed it, and pressed the button. It lit up. He laughed as he looked at the glowing numbers and letters. He pressed the speed number for Darla Knowles and listened. She answered, and the interrogation began. Where had he been, she asked, and what had happened? She asked if he had been with another woman. She thought he was dead, which would be a lucky fate if he'd been sleeping with anyone else. And they had to be at the bank this morning. What was he thinking? The auditors came on Monday. Everything they'd done for the last two years would be for nothing if they didn't fix the accounts. They had two hours ahead of them just to work on the accounts and then thirty minutes to reset the system. She had to adjust seventy-five accounts and lines of credit. He knew that, so where was he, and where was the money?

As Darla spoke, Hermann pulled the briefcase onto his lap and felt for the key around his neck. Martel had tied it to a string and handed it to Hermann when he'd left the Bone Fishing Club. They had exchanged it in a handshake, one palm to the other, and Hermann had pocketed the key before he left. On the plane to Nassau, he'd put the string around his neck. Since then, he'd never taken it off. He inserted the key into the lock and turned to the left. The top opened on immaculate stacks of money in sheathes of tan paper. The money filled the case. Except for the $30,000 Martel had taken to buy the fuel and another $10,000 each man had removed for expenses, it was all there. He described it, and Darla stopped talking. She asked him how much, and he told her.

"Maybe you should close that up and bring it to where it belongs."

"I need help. I'm on the river."

"Give me the address."

He was too exhausted to smile. "There is no address. I'm in the mud on Santee Island."

Darla took in the information. "If you're on Santee, where'd you sleep last night?"

"You don't want to know. But remember, whatever I tell you, that's the story. That's all you ever know."

"What's the story?"

"I don't know yet." He breathed heavily, tired from rowing. "I need you to drive to South College Road as far as it goes and get over to River Road. Look out to the river, and you'll see me. I'm in a rowboat, floating south. Call me. I'll bring it in through one of the creeks to the walking path. I look terrible. Be there when I pull up on the other side."

"Are you hurt?"

"Nothing permanent."

XXVII

Wrightsville Beach, North Carolina

Chloe's storm surge had covered Wrightsville Beach, collapsed old cottages, and pushed two hundred thousand cubic yards of sand offshore. It all moved south across the inlet to Masonboro Island, an eight-and-half-mile nature preserve donated two generations earlier by a woman who thought at least one barrier island should be for the birds. With no roads or structures of any kind, Masonboro was accessible only by water. It was covered in forests and dunes that rolled to a beach wide enough to land an airplane. In the early morning low tide, the waves formed tubes that curled north to south in a steady progression.

The Guatemalan came in on a breaking wave that pounded him into the sand. The rising water deposited the body in a tidal pool, where he lay, bloated, missing a leg, an arm, and the top of his skull. Coast guard lieutenant Hugh Ayers discovered him during a patrol for destroyed or unmanned boats. For three years, Ayers had worked at the coast guard station at the southern end of Wrightsville. After storms, he took a launch along the beaches to search for wreckage and fatalities. He spotted the body through field glasses. From offshore, it looked like rags and driftwood, and he dismissed it until gulls descended in flocks and pecked. Ayers turned into the beach and expected the carcass of an animal. When he saw the leg and foot, he brought out a body bag, shooed the gulls away, and rolled the remains into the bag. He brought them to the coast guard station along the inland waterway at Wrightsville.

On a stainless steel table in the examination room, the body lay under a fluorescent light; the skin was chalk white, having lost its copper color from time in the sea. The lieutenant was inclined to designate the cause of death an "accidental drowning" but changed his mind when he lined up the contents of the Guatemalan's pockets on an adjacent table. He assembled them in a neat row and wrote the word "suspicious" on the preprinted form. For the man's identity, he wrote the word "aliases," and on the line for "vocation," the word "courier."

Innumerable Mexican farm workers traveled through North Carolina in the summer and fall, but very few drowned. Those who died in the water were usually found in swimming pools located behind the walls of private estates where they worked on lawns and gardens. These were clear cases of accidental drowning, and the victims were farm workers who couldn't swim. None were fishermen, and they didn't own boats along the lower North Carolina coast, where docking fees cost more than a modest home.

Lieutenant Ayers called the FBI office in Raleigh, and the phone system put him on hold. Music played until the call was routed to Robert Sandhurst's cell phone, which was attached to his belt. He cut up a tree that had fallen across his driveway on Rankin Street in downtown Wilmington, and the roar of the chainsaw drowned out the ring of the phone. The call moved to voice mail. Ayers hung up and tried again. Deep into the tree trunk, the blade of the saw stopped when it hit the hard wood, and the machine shut down. Sandhurst heard the ring on Ayers's second call and picked up the phone. He stood over cut logs and listened to the lieutenant describe the partially dismembered man and the contents of his pockets: one Israeli-made shell casing with defaced identification numbers; a Bahamas Telecom phone card; two laminated drivers licenses, one for Florida and one for Venezuela, both with identical photographs of the dead man but bearing different names; a smeared phone number with the Wilmington area code written on a receipt from a hotel in Georgetown, Great Exuma; one hundred wet US bills, one-hundred-dollar denomination; and a nonfunctioning satellite phone with a data card issued in Venezuela.

Sandhurst walked into his garage and put the saw on a workbench. Inside his house, he searched through a closet, where he found a flowered shirt, a black suit jacket, and some pressed tan pants. He pulled on the pants with the phone cradled between his shoulder and cheek as Ayers described where he had found the body and held the Florida driver's license photograph up to the dead man's bloated face to check for a visual match.

Thirty minutes later, Sandhurst arrived at the coast guard station at the southern end of Wrightsville. The Station had a dock with hoists and its own hangar to store boats and equipment. It faced west over Banks Channel, which was filled with swamped boats, some floating barely above the waterline and a few stranded in the marshes to the west, turned on their sides and masts bent or broken. Every dock was damaged, and the ones south of the station, closest to Masonboro, were gone.

Sandhurst walked along the bulkhead to the station, let himself in, and entered an open room filled with desks and computers. Covering half the far wall was a touchscreen electronic map of the region. Lit like a computer monitor, the screen showed the islands, waterways, and shipping channels in a high-definition satellite image from one thousand feet. Every dock and boat was there. In blue light on the left, a legend reported water depth at various tide heights. On the right, a list displayed the height of the previous night's storm surge from Topsail Island in the north to Baldhead in the south. Circles of red light on the map designated locations where boats and ships had sunk or disappeared. The nautical identification number for a missing craft was within each red circle. One touch on the number filled the screen with photographs, video clips, imaged documents, and written text from the investigation.

Lieutenant Ayers sat at a terminal and finished his reports from the morning search. Most were initial assessments of storm damage, swamped watercraft, listing piers, and the massive erosion of sand that made Wrightsville 10 percent smaller. The body was one of many, but the only human remains. When Sandhurst entered, Ayers stood up. The agent was taller, ten years older than Ayers, with pale skin and sandy-red hair. He had a broad nose and hadn't shaved. His long arms and thick shoulders fit tightly in the black jacket, and his flowered shirt was tucked around a hard waist that belied middle age. The lieutenant shook Sandhurst's hand and felt the grip.

Ayers and Sandhurst walked down a hallway to the makeshift morgue, where the Guatemalan lay in the bag. The lieutenant opened the door to a windowless room. The scent of the dead body penetrated their noses, eyes, and mouth, and Sandhurst stepped back. The lieutenant handed him a jar of cream. Both men wiped two stripes of Vick's Vapo-Rub under their nostrils to overwhelm the olfactory nerve. They entered the room and closed the door.

Fluorescent lights lit the bag. It was zipped up and closed on a steel table waist high to Sandhurst. Along the wall was a wooden desk, stacks of paper files, and a computer workstation. The Guatemalan's possessions were neatly arranged on the desk. Ayers had set notecards with typed descriptions next to each item. Sandhurst walked to the wooden desk and settled reading glasses at the end of his nose.

"I have a theory about the deceased," Ayers said.

"False Florida driver's licenses," Sandhurst said out loud. "Numbered bullet casing, numbers removed, cash, onshore contact number." He opened the satellite phone, removed the data card, and examined it. He muttered the word "Venezuela" and then looked directly at the lieutenant. "Your theory?" Sandhurst removed a camera and dictation machine from a leather case.

"He's not the only dead body," said Ayers. "We've had interdictions this far north—I've been involved in one. The stuff in his pockets shows he's a runner. But then there's the bullet casing. Why would he pick up an empty casing and keep it? There's probably another body somewhere with a hole in it. Maybe here in New Hanover County, maybe somewhere else."

Sandhurst took off his jacket and hung it on the back of the door. He walked to the body bag and unzipped it to the foot of the corpse. He closed his eyes at the stench. "Maybe he's the body. Someone killed him and put the casing in his pocket. Are there any entry wounds?"

The lieutenant shook his head. "There are missing parts, but what you see is clean."

"How long do you think he's been in the water?"

"No more that twenty-four hours. After thirty-six, they bloat and are unrecognizable. Even without the top of his head, this guy still looks like the license photos."

Sandhurst folded the bag flat against the table and wedged it under the body. He pressed the Dictaphone and began his report. He noted tattoos on the neck and remaining arm. He described the missing limbs, open cranium, and general state of decay. He picked up the driver's licenses and compared the photographs to the Guatemalan's face, which was intact. The face matched the photos.

The lieutenant handed Sandhurst the evidence envelope filled with the cash, and Sandhurst stopped dictating. He thumbed through the bills, which were wet.

"Ten thousand?"

"Exactly."

Sandhurst stated the sum into the Dictaphone and picked up a digital camera. He thought about the hundreds of evidence photographs saved in a file on his computer. He knew all of them. They lingered and helped fill his hard drive with cold cases where progress had stopped, the case grew stale, but the file wasn't closed. Weeks from now, he'd return to the file and look at the photographs of the body, the shell casings, hundred-dollar bills, and false licenses for something that would make the case move; but it never would, not with a dead criminal, not unless Sandhurst made progress quickly.

Otherwise, there'd be nothing. There was no identifiable victim, no one would claim the body, and whatever crime had occurred, no one would report it.

As Sandhurst took close-up shots of the body, the lieutenant asked him whether the tattoos meant anything, showed an association with a gang or a cartel.

Sandhurst shook his head. "I don't know. We'll run the images through a database and have an expert look at them. If there's something there—a match, similarities, symbols—we'll find them." He walked to the table and took photographs of the back and front of the satellite phone. He turned over the card and took multiple shots. "This is what I came for. It should get us probable cause."

His cell phone rang, and Sandhurst put down the camera. He answered with a quick hello. Assistant US Attorney Agnes Pembroke was at the other end. Sandhurst provided a short description of the dead man, the contents of his pockets, and his theory of why Agnes should obtain a warrant. It should be for the records of all transmissions to and from offshore satellite-enabled units in the last thirty-six hours. He offered Agnes a view of the body, but she declined.

"Probable cause," said Agnes, who stood on her front porch in downtown Wilmington and watched a street crew carve up a downed tree. "On a morning after a hurricane, you have to convince me there's probable cause and an emergency. If you can't convince me, I can't convince the judge, not this one."

"It's the phone, Agnes. It's from Venezuela and a high-powered satellite device. There can't be many of those operating in this county or offshore. Ninety percent of the cocaine and methamphetamine coming into the Southeast is transported out of Venezuela. It follows a path due north and comes into the United States in a hundred different ways. I can give a judge all he needs to know about that. Also, this guy is not a courier; he's a transporter, and there's a difference. Transporters are behind the scenes and don't make exchanges. They stay on the boats and the planes, and they don't try to disguise themselves. This guy's not hiding anything, because he doesn't expect to encounter anyone but the couriers. He brings the stuff north and delivers it to them. They work for him. He contacts them for delivery. That phone will tell us who they are." Sandhurst looked at Lieutenant Ayers. "Also, the Coast Guard has a theory about the bullet casing. The deceased had it in his pocket. Maybe he fired a pistol, killed someone, and picked up the casing so no one would find it. If the officer's right, the dead man could have called it in; that's a phone number we'd want."

"Why is he offshore in a hurricane?" asked Agnes.

"I haven't figured that out. But I still have probable cause for data mining and a trace on the phone. Why he ended up on the beach doesn't matter."

"And the emergency?"

"The body's been in the water no more than twenty-four hours, so he's been out of communication for a full day. His contacts will freeze up, and they'll throw away their phones if they think he's been caught. If we don't act, the case goes cold in hours."

"Is there anything you can do with the phone?" asked Agnes.

Sandhurst turned the data card over in his hand. "It has the letters 'VZ' for Venezuela." Sandhurst inserted the card into the phone. "It doesn't work, but we have some people who can pull some codes out of the card. It won't be the actual phone number, but it will be stuff we can link to the number, if it shows up from data mining."

"Get it all together, but be prepared. The emergency judge is a real civil-liberties type. He may tell you to work the data card for a while and come back Monday."

"Shit, Agnes, we have to work the lead now. If we wait until Monday, the case freezes, and we all go home."

"Then be clear about what the data card can and cannot give you. This guy doesn't like invading people's privacy unless he has to."

"What?" Sandhurst's voice rose. "I have a dead Venezuelan from the current hub of cocaine exports with a false Florida identification, a satellite phone, a spent bullet casing, and ten thousand dollars in cash. He washes up on a playground for North Carolina's blue bloods, and I don't have probable cause to find out who he's been calling? Where is the Patriot Act when I need it?"

Agnes held the phone six inches away from her ear. "I'll quote you."

"You won't need to; I'll be there. I'm going to bag up this stuff and bring it to your evidence locker. I've already taken photos of the dead man, and I'll bring them to the court on a DVD. I'll identify them, and you mark the DVD as evidence. You sure you don't want to see him?"

"I'll rely on the photos. Meet me at the courthouse."

Agnes called the federal courthouse emergency number. An operator identified the Honorable Edmund Sorel as the emergency judge for criminal warrants and transferred Agnes to the judge's mobile phone. Edmund sat across the kitchen table from Peyton and looked out over the porch to the road where Linus pulled the fallen tree off the house. Edmund and Peyton heard the sounds of the tree separating from the house, tearing at the walls and floors, and collapsing the foundation. Edmund answered the phone by speaking his name.

"This is Agnes Pembroke calling, Your Honor, assistant US attorney." Her voice was a mellifluous alto filled with professional courtesy. She went to the point. "I'm seeking an application today for a warrant involving phone transmissions in the region. It involves suspected narcotics trafficking. There is an emergency nature to the warrant, and I will bring with me an FBI agent to verify what we need and why time is of the essence. Otherwise, we would not be bothering the court on such a day."

"How are your mother and father, Agnes?"

She was pleased by the response. "Quite well, Your Honor, and you?"

"Fine, Agnes. Can you give me about ninety minutes? I'm out at the plantation, and we have trees across the road. If I run late, I'll let you know. My dear, in advance, would you kindly tell me what it's all about."

"Of course," said Agnes. Her index finger slowly moved down the notes she had taken during the call with Sandhurst. She described the dead body, where it was found, and the contents of the pockets. "The FBI and my office will request a warrant for data-mining transmissions to see if we can identify the phone's Venezuelan numerical code. We think he called people onshore. If we fail to act now, his contacts on shore will disappear. We have a short window of time."

"I'll see you in ninety minutes," Edmund said. He ended the call with a pleasantry. He looked at his daughter and pushed away from the table. His long limbs unfolded as he rose.

"Dad, can't younger judges do the emergency work?"

"Yes," he told her, "but I enjoy it." His tone was light as he spoke. Warrant applications had to be addressed right away. It wasn't just a matter of fulfilling his oath as a federal judge, though that was as good a reason as any. People who appeared in front of him relied on him to know the law, apply it properly, and make the right decision. Lives changed in his courtroom, sometimes permanently. And it meant to him what it meant to them: getting it right was his life. As long as he could make his way into the federal building on North Water Street, that is where he would be and where she could find him.

"And, truly, I don't know what else I'd do," he said with a laugh. "Being called off this hot plantation to uphold the law is not so bad at seventy-seven years old. It's better than golf."

"What's the emergency?"

"Same as always. The methods are different, but the crimes are the same. You go back one hundred, two hundred years around here, and you see the same things: smuggling, piracy, sometimes murder. It's the river and the port. Everything's more sophisticated now, but the crimes never change much."

Edmund's face contracted at the pain in his knees. He walked out of the main room and gathered his belongings for the trip to Wilmington.

XXVIII

US District Court, Wilmington, North Carolina

There wasn't any need for a courtroom. Judge Sorel conducted private hearings for warrants in his chambers. Edmund opened the door and welcomed Agnes and Sandhurst into his office. His old khaki pants had lost their crease and bore traces of faded yellow paint. His white tennis shirt was thin from bleach. He wore old sneakers on his feet. Agnes shook his hand and introduced Sandhurst, still in his flowered shirt and black jacket, who expressed gratitude for the hearing on short notice.

"Your Honor," said Agnes as she chose a chair, "this is an easy one." Sandhurst sat next to her with a cardboard box of evidence at his feet. He watched the judge walk to his desk. Edmund's head was out front and pulled his body into the chair.

As he sat, Edmund raised his hand and motioned to the court reporter to begin. The reporter nodded, and Edmund spoke. "They're never easy, Ms. Pembroke, but let's see what you have." He reached across the desk and received from Agnes a five-page memorandum she'd written that described the "probable cause" to support the warrant to data mine the Venezuelan satellite phone transmissions within a one-hundred-mile radius of Masonboro Island. Sandhurst had helped her write it over the phone. He wanted the numbers the dead man had called in the last forty-eight hours and the calls those numbers had made and would make over a four-day period. Sandhurst had convinced Agnes to seek an expansive warrant. The FBI would segregate the information. Access would be limited to Sandhurst, Agnes, and the FBI information technology staff. Drug trafficking and targeted murder had become a national security issue. The suspects were skilled, disciplined, and well financed. They were experts at evading detection. Sandhurst wanted as much information as possible. He sat patiently waiting to testify.

Edmund turned the pages of the memorandum and read every word. When he finished, he looked at Agnes, who had hoped that the papers would suffice. They didn't.

"Please proceed," Edmund said.

"Would Your Honor like me to present Mr. Sandhurst as a witness, or would you like to ask questions yourself?"

"He's your witness."

The court reporter asked Sandhurst to raise his right hand and recite the oath. Agnes began by asking Sandhurst to explain his background in a joint FBI-DEA prosecution task force. Sandhurst testified that Venezuela had become the starting point for the import of cocaine and methamphetamine from Latin America to the United States and Canada. He stood up, planted his computer on the judge's desk so Edmund could see the screen, and opened up the file with the photos of the body. Agnes asked him questions about the photographs, who took them and when, what they identified, and where the body had been found. Sandhurst moved to the evidence found in the dead man's pockets and picked up the cardboard box. He handed the judge the two driver's licenses and showed him photos of them, enlarged and side by side on the computer screen. Edmund saw two different names and the same face. He interrupted Sandhurst.

"Is there any evidence that the deceased has ever been convicted of a crime in this country or any other?"

Agnes intervened. "Your Honor, it's not necessary."

"I didn't ask him whether it was necessary. I asked him whether he had evidence."

Agnes sat up and took a different approach. "Your Honor, under the Patriot Act, the probable cause standard for a warrant is no different from the normal standard: whether law enforcement has enough evidence to form a reasonable belief that a crime may have been committed."

"I know the standard. Please answer the question."

"We have no information about the deceased, Your Honor," said Sandhurst, "other than what we are presenting today. We don't know his real name or his criminal history, but we do know this: the names on both of those Florida driver's licenses are false. That's a crime right there, falsification of government-issued identifications. Our database in Virginia searched the names on both licenses. They appeared on deaths notices in Miami for children who had died in the 1980s. I know that alone is not probable cause that the crime of narcotics trafficking is being committed, but it is evidence that the deceased stole identities, and that's a crime. Coupled with the other evidence, it allows us to form a reasonable belief that the deceased was engaged in recent ongoing and substantial criminal activity in this region—probably narcotics trafficking and possibly murder."

"Please continue."

Agnes asked Sandhurst to remove the satellite phone and data card from the box and identify them. He stood up, showed them to Judge Sorel, and scrolled through the enlarged photographs on the computer screen. He explained that the information on the back of the data card showed that the phone had been issued in Venezuela and operated with a Venezuelan carrier. FBI forensics could retrieve basic information from the data card and internal codes that would help identify the card's phone number. It was probably the only Venezuelan phone operating in the region, which would allow a targeted search.

Judge Sorel asked Sandhurst to take his seat and made his ruling.

"The court finds that the evidence presented and Mr. Sandhurst's testimony gives rise to probable cause that a crime has been committed and, in one form or another, is ongoing. The court also finds that the evidence shows that the deceased was most likely involved in the organized transportation of illegal narcotics into this country. The false identifications are a felony. Combined with the cash, spent bullet casing, the phone, and the time and location of where the deceased was found, there is a reasonable probability that the deceased had contact with others for the purposes of criminal activity."

Judge Sorel paused and turned the data card over in his hands. "However, the warrant application is too broad. It's for four days and is unlimited in scope as to real-time monitoring of persons who called or received a call from the deceased." The judge paused again and flipped through a thick casebook. He read aloud from a reported case that limited the breadth of warrants, until the US attorney presented some evidence that the people who actually owned those other phones were engaged in probable criminal conduct.

Sandhurst looked down at his shoes, held his hands together, and tightened his knuckles.

Judge Sorel referred to constitutional protections under the Fourth Amendment against unreasonable searches and seizures. He cited cases in Texas that limited the use of trap and trace devices unless the FBI had established probable cause for each individual phone subject to the warrant.

"Ms. Pembroke and Mr. Sandhurst," Edmund said. "The court grants the warrant, but only for offshore transmissions during the past forty-eight-hour time period. A sealed order will follow. There won't be any tracking of the phones with which he had contact. If you develop evidence for an expanded warrant for other phones, the court will hear the request for real-time monitoring on an emergency basis."

Agnes put her hand on Sandhurst's arm to prevent him from speaking. She thanked the judge and assured him she would be back. Sandhurst shook the judge's hand, picked up the evidence and laptop, and left the chambers.

When the elevator doors closed, Sandhurst looked at his reflection in the polished steel and started slowly. Did the judge not read the news? Was he unfamiliar with investigations? What was wrong with him? Wasn't he supposed to give the FBI leeway to gather evidence on a confidential basis, never to be seen or heard by anyone but the people designated by the warrant application? If the information was worthless, it never went anywhere; if it supported probable cause to monitor other phones, it could be used to protect the public. He'd narrowed the request beautifully, he said, and there was no risk to the people whose phones he might identify through the dead man, unless they had worked with him. He turned to Agnes with a red face.

"Whose side is that motherfucker on?"

"He's really strict about this," said Agnes. "If the dead man calls a wrong number by accident and leaves an incriminating message, what happens then? You go monitor the cell phone and find out the owner, who has nothing to do with the dead man, is engaged in garden-variety tax fraud. You forward that information to the IRS, which prosecutes him because you had an expanded warrant to listen to private calls. The whole thing turns into wild litigation, he challenges the validity of the warrant, and he wins. I look stupid, and Judge Sorel gets reversed for writing an order that violates the Fourth Amendment."

"That's lawyer talk, Agnes. He doesn't have skin in the game. If he did, he'd be helping us. He wouldn't fall in love with ideas and wonder about how I might invade the privacy of some tax cheat." Sandhurst stared at Agnes's image in the elevator doors. "How about this one: Sorel doesn't give us a big enough warrant, and this guy's buddies kill people on their way out of town."

"He doesn't want to get it wrong."

"Remind me, who's the Fourth Amendment supposed to protect when dead guys like that wash up on Masonboro?"

"I'll get you a copy."

"I've memorized it; it's part of my job."

The elevator doors opened, and they walked through the lobby and out onto North Water Street.

XXIX

Biloxi, Mississippi

A few blocks from the Bay Bridge in Biloxi, Mississippi, the Isle of Palms Casino had come back. Rebuilt on the beach side of Route 90 and reopened before any other resort, it lay on six acres. There were two full floors for gambling laid out in large rooms the size of airplane hangars. Fans in the ceilings pulled air up through vents in the roof and out into the summer sky. A tower of seven hundred rooms stood next to the casino and faced south to the water at the eastern end of Biloxi's Big Island. Lawns and gardens surrounded the buildings, and rows of coconut trees stretched to the edge of the beach, where people covered in lotion lay in the sun or under cabanas.

August was a heavy month, and $12 million flowed across the gaming tables every day. Caleb Parrish and his accountants kept a live running subtotal on the upper-right-hand corner of their computer screens. From the executive offices, they watched the numbers move every second, like the Dow Jones Industrial Average, but better. It was cash: real money and real profit in real time. Like charts that track the Dow, a green triangle pointed up when revenue rose. It was never off, not since the Isle of Palms rebuilt. Green numbers in a legend below the running totals showed an upward progression for the day against the monthly average. Saturday morning in mid-August beat the trend. By noon, Parrish expected $13 million in activity for the day and $6 million in pure profit for the first week of August. He sat at his desk and watched the numbers when his assistant, Eliza Swift, called and asked him to look at the security monitor for the executive suites. Parrish hit a few keys, and the black-and-white images from the cameras came onto his computer screen. A man sat on a couch in the anteroom. According to Eliza, he had identified himself as a friend of the casino; his name was Robert Erwin, and he was looking for a man named Cedric Peoples. Eliza had searched the casino database and told Caleb that she had found neither Erwin nor Peoples in the Isle of Palms records. The man insisted that the President of the resort would know him.

Caleb leaned forward in his large leather desk chair and adjusted an unlit cigar between his teeth. He looked at Leandro Dufau, who sat on a brightly colored striped sofa under artificial ceiling light. He wore pressed summer-weight khaki slacks, polished slip-on brown shoes, a blue blazer, and a modest print tie. He read the Money and Investing section of the *Wall Street Journal.*

"Where did he say he was from?"

"He didn't," said Eliza. "He said you would know him."

Caleb recognized the face. He knew there was a representative of the business, focused and quiet, a solver of problems known only to a few, who carried with him the fixer's air of finality. He had moved in and out of meetings Caleb had attended outside of Mexico City in the mountains. He spoke to very few, gave whispered reports, and disappeared. This was the man, most likely the fixer, and Parrish could not turn him away. "Show him in," he said.

Eliza walked out of her locked office and into the foyer. She introduced herself to Leandro. He rose, shook her hand, and introduced himself as if he had been visiting the area on business and had stopped by to see an acquaintance. His unhurried smile and good manners made her comfortable. She sized him up as athletic and well bred, perhaps Texan, and supremely wealthy, which explained the elegant, understated clothes and quiet anonymity. They walked down a hallway to the door of the president's office, and Eliza knocked—she had no entry card. Parrish let them in by pressing a button under the edge of his desk. Leandro nodded, shook Eliza's hand, and wished her a pleasant weekend.

After Eliza left, Parrish began to speak. Leandro held up his hand and shook his head for silence. He closed the door and mouthed the words "turn off the video." Parrish sat in his chair and turned to the computer screen as Leandro crossed the room. He logged into the office functions until he arrived at the sound and camera systems. Parrish turned the monitor toward Leandro so he could watch him disable the system that recorded every word spoken in the executive offices.

"And the cameras," said Leandro.

Parrish disabled the security cameras as well.

"Now erase the last thirty minutes."

Parrish did as instructed—it would be a jump in the record—and offered a chair to Leandro, who declined.

Leandro began by stating that "Cedric Peoples" had signed the guest log at the Guana Cay Bone Fishing Club this past week and ran up charges on a credit card under the same name. Was he at the Bone Fishing Club, asked Leandro, and did he use that credit card and sign the name? Leandro knew the answer, which was the expected yes but with an explanation. The Bone Fishing Club, Caleb told him, had become a private gambling venue for three years. Word of mouth attracted wealthy players who liked to fish and were willing to play for good stakes. The heat and storms in summer kept families away and left the Club to the players. There were five or six who were constant, and he was one of them. He admitted that he used the alias but with a reason. He didn't want disgruntled small-timers following him back to the Isle of Palms after they'd lost a retirement account. It was unseemly, said Parrish, and dangerous. He never gave out his real name at poker games where amateurs could lose a fortune.

"Would you?"

Leandro didn't answer him. "What else did you do at the Bone Fishing Club?"

Parrish rolled the unlit cigar from one side of his mouth to the other and thought about the question. In the Bahamas, he said, he fished for wahoo, tuna, and bonefish. The answer came out of his mouth too quickly, curt, through teeth clenched on the cigar. When he heard it in the air, he regretted it. It sounded like a clever retort, not an answer. He looked at Leandro to see if it had registered in the wrong way. It had. The younger man's eyes focused a moment too long to be inquisitive. As Leandro stepped around the desk, Parrish grew still. His teeth lost their grip on the cigar. Leandro rested one leg on the edge of the desk and watched the cigar drop into Parrish's lap. He opened the desk drawer, which was empty except for a gold-plated lighter, a collection of expensive pens, and a few business cards interspersed with a carved ivory letter opener. Leandro picked up the lighter, opened it, and flicked the wheel against the flint. It produced a long flame and the smell of butane.

"Pick up the cigar," Leandro said.

Parrish took the cigar off his lap and put it in the flame. He sucked in the fire. In a few puffs, smoke surrounded the middle of the desk; he began to relax. Parrish rocked back in his chair and looked up at Leandro.

"I'm telling the truth," he said.

"We'll see."

"May I ask a question?"

"Yes."

"Why would the business be interested in a poker game at the Bone Fishing Club?"

"It belongs to us, like you do."

"I didn't know that."

"You're not supposed to know."

"I fish and play poker there—that's it, nothing else."

Leandro tested him. "You were there on Thursday?"

"Yes." Right answer.

"How did you leave?"

"Private plane." Right again. The club's records showed the arrival and departure times of the plane.

"Who was there in the last week? Give me the names, every one."

Parrish was an excellent money launderer and a good and practiced liar. Leandro had reread the Guana Cay business records on the Citation before it had landed in Biloxi. He had committed to memory every face and name from the past seven days of video and credit card charges. Parrish began by naming the players around the table—five, including himself—and then named three others who had left the island before Thursday. He adjusted himself in his chair, raised an eyebrow, and nodded to Leandro as if to say the list was complete.

"You forgot Noah."

"Sure, the Manager. Of course Noah was there."

"And Martel?"

"Pedro? Sure, he's always there."

"Was Martel there when you left?"

"Yes."

"Anyone else?"

"With Martel?"

"Yes."

"Noah and the kid. You know, Cartwright. He was there too." Parrish blew a stream of smoke through his lips. "We left because of the storm. They were closing the place down. They were worried about a high storm surge coming into the buildings. Something happened after that, right? After I left. That's why you're here."

The top of the desk was inlaid in dark wood and heavily laminated. Under the lamination, a deck of cards was embedded, spread face up in an arc in the center of the desk. Through the plume of smoke, Leandro examined the cards and found the duplicates: two aces of spades and two queens of hearts camouflaged by many cards in a deck of fifty-four.

Parrish watched Leandro scan the arc. He rocked lightly in his chair. "It's a joke. Casino humor. Nothing wicked." He let more smoke swirl out of his mouth.

"Shall I have someone come in here and examine your accounting—make sure none of our money is missing?"

"You're welcome to," said Parrish. "It's all on the underlying system, fully encrypted. We can account for every penny."

"Martel went off island without our authority," said Leandro. "Everything we had stored there went with him. I want it back. You were there." Leandro looked at the ivory letter opener. "This can be a long conversation or a short one."

"Nothing happened while I was there. I left on a private plane, and so did everyone else. Noah, Cartwright, and Martel were alone when we left."

"He didn't do this alone. Who helped him?"

Parrish shook his head and puffed on the cigar. His brain scrolled through the faces at the club. There were many earlier in the week, but only five when Martel began to close the place for the storm.

"How about men Martel's age? People he might have talked to privately. Any of those?"

Parrish thought of the younger men. "There is someone you might want to talk to. He plays there now and then, knows Martel pretty well, better than most."

"Name?"

"Hermann Locke. We overlapped for a few days."

"North Carolina?" From the credit card information, Leandro had already matched every name with a home location.

"I suppose. I know little about him, except..."

"Except what?"

"He plays Texas Hold'em like a dumb college student."

"Which means?"

"He plays his own cards, and that's it. He doesn't follow the other players. You know, follow their bets and raises, assess their weaknesses and when they're bluffing. I don't see Hermann ever doing that. He just plays the cards. Good, he's in; bad, he's out. It sounds like a conservative approach, but it's not. It makes him easy to read. I sorted him out a long time ago." Caleb smiled. "You want to know my theory about him?"

"Yes."

"He's a fine-looking guy and probably has women all the time. The cards he draws—they're like women to him, so he focuses on them and not the other players. If he thinks they're ugly, he doesn't play them—not well anyway, because he thinks they'll make him lose. If they're beautiful, he falls in love with them." Parrish clamped the cigar between his teeth. "He's predictable that way, and he comes with money. So, you know, he's always welcome. We like players like that."

"Does he work? Or is he just a traveler? Game to game."

"Not sure."

"Is he reckless?"

Parrish shook his head. "I don't know."

"He makes mistakes?"

Parrish puffed on the cigar. "All the time."

"You'd recognize him?"

"Anywhere."

Leandro took a disk from the inside pocket of his jacket and slipped it into Parrish's computer. He scrolled through the black-and-white images from the Guana Cay security cameras. Parrish saw his own face on the screen. He leaned forward and took the cigar out of his mouth. When Leandro reached an image of the tall blond man, he stopped and clicked through three pictures. The first showed Hermann at the bar. The second was a profile, and the third was Hermann's full face as he looked directly into the camera behind the mirror.

"That's him," said Parrish.

Leandro took out the disk, shut off the computer, and told Parrish to pack a bag.

Part 3

August 7, 2010

XXX

Cape Fear River

The ringtone for Hermann on Darla Knowles's mobile phone bounced out the sound of a Caribbean steel drum, went silent, and jumped again. With her left hand on the steering wheel, Darla drove along the east side of the river. With her right hand, she emptied her handbag onto the passenger seat and found the phone amid the scattered contents. Darla answered it with an impatient plea for help on Hermann's location and what the rowboat looked like. The wind blew through the car and her black curly hair as she looked out of the passenger window at the east side of the river. The rowboat floated among the marshes. Hermann described the location—four miles past Santee at the entrance to a creek. There was a small footbridge that was part of a running and bicycle path. He held the left oar in the water and pulled the rowboat into the creek, listening to Darla all the way to the footbridge and assuring her that there was no one on the path, and, yes, he could manage his way up through the marshes, but no, he wouldn't wait until she found the path.

"Just be there," he said. "Look for the footbridge."

Hermann guided the boat under the bridge and into the mud and reeds. He stepped out into water and sank in the silt. It was knee deep, black, and cool. With the sacks of White Knight flour pressed against his chest and the briefcase in his hand, he trudged up the bank to the path, sat down, and called Darla, who walked along the running path and answered the phone. Hermann lay on the grass and turned his head to see her walking in a light skirt and cotton shirt that was frayed and barely buttoned. His thoughts turned to gratitude and sex as he watched her move, imagined her body through the clothing, and thought about the warmth that he'd missed the night before. She started to run when she saw him.

Hermann's face hurt. The cuts were covered in dried blood, and the bruises were large. The golf-ball sized bump on his forehead had subsided but was purple and yellow and still bore the cut from the windshield. Darla dropped to her knees, looked at him, and started to cry. She kissed him on the mouth and ran her hands along his head, neck, and chest. He told her he was all right—just tired—and that he needed to go to the bank and then to his house to clean up. He gripped the handle of the briefcase and raised it slightly off the ground. It was the money, he told her, and he started to laugh. Her mouth was barely touching his when he spoke, and amid the tears she laughed, kissed him again, and let her hands run across the rippled aluminum of the briefcase. She helped him off the ground, and he sat on the grass. She walked to the river and soaked her shirttails in water. With the wet ends of the shirt, she wiped away the streaks of blood, sand, and dirt from his face. He pulled back in pain when she wiped his forehead.

"What happened to you?" she asked.

Hermann ignored the question, stood up, and admired the bright day. He began to walk north along the footpath to the car. She followed him and held the packages of flour in her hands. They had flattened out from packing and were heavily wrapped in plastic and tape, so she could see only the white-and-red coloring and large print. A question formed in her mouth, but she held it back and reminded herself there was information she didn't want to know.

"A piece of flying plywood did that," she said. "Right? Plywood. You were boarding up a window just as the storm hit, and the thing went funny in the wind, flew off, and hit you. That's terrible, Hermann. And then you fell from the ladder. You landed in those rose bushes next to the house, and look what happened. That's the story, and it's a shame." She curled an arm around his waist. "You could have lost an eye."

Hermann nodded. He slid into the passenger seat of the car, reclined the seat, and told her to drive to the bank.

The main branch of the Cape Bank was located at the northern end of a mall that spanned one full mile on Oleander Avenue. It housed offices for the executives and information technology personnel. A turf putting green on the flat roof was where Hermann and the managers spent time practicing their short game. They exchanged bets and discussed how to generate more fee income for the bank, write down bad loans, and attract large-borrowing developers, many of whom had already dug up all the land on the east side of the river and paved it with malls, parking lots, and low-rise residential developments.

Darla parked the car south of the bank and looked down at Hermann, asleep in the reclined seat. She'd met him three years before when he'd come to the bank as a mortgage broker. That summer on the roof, she decided that he would belong to her. She was marking bets during a putting competition among the managers. Hermann had interrupted with a shy confidence and something about getting in on a game that wasn't too rich. He lost several times and found himself in a $5,000 hole, so he took bets on a thirty-foot putt. Everyone laughed and shook their heads as he shined the ball on his shirt. He had a wide mouth and a curl to his lip that for Darla made him look like a blond Elvis—shy, beautiful, and with a future. He positioned the ball on the turf, looked at her and smiled. He struck it on a curved line to the right and never looked up until it hit the bottom of the cup. His employers—all six of them—were immediately obligated for $5,000 each. Darla, one silky knee resting on the other, felt the air compress on the roof, looked down at the spreadsheet, and marked $30,000 owed to Hermann. He had hustled his new employers for half his annual salary. For Darla, he was charming but stupid, a short timer who'd risked his job on a golf bet. And then he spoke. He told everyone that he taught golf at Sutton Beach on the weekends and wouldn't take their money—his conscience wouldn't let him. He received what he wanted: smiles and nods, a clean slate with no debt, and respect. The second misdirection was more skillful than the first. Darla had found someone with whom she could work.

In the car, she shook him awake. It was time for her to readjust the accounts and for him to take a shower. He pulled himself up and out of the seat. They walked along the periphery of the surveillance cameras to the back door, which Darla opened with a security key. Hermann entered a private shower near the executive offices, and Darla went to her office in the information technology department, where she set the aluminum briefcase on her desk and logged into the security system. When Hermann reappeared, he had showered and shaved. Other than the cuts and discoloration, his face was unchanged. He had high, sharp cheekbones and long limbs, square shoulders, and a lean build. He wore a clean shirt he kept in his office and held a bag of ice on his forehead, which still throbbed. He had combed his wet blond hair flat against the scalp. As he sat next to Darla at the carrel, she could smell him like a taste in her mouth. She loved everything about him and told him so. As the bank's security system opened up on the screen in front of her, he kissed her on the neck, unbuttoned the two remaining buttons, and removed her shirt. He put his hands on her breasts and reminded her of the times they'd had sex in the bank vault.

She pushed his hands away and sweetly admonished him to pay attention to the money. As vice president for information technology, Darla had access to every account, the entire electronic security system, and the mandatory software installed by government regulators that prompted automatic warning e-mails if cash deposits, withdrawals, or transfers among accounts occurred in sums of $10,000 or more. The system was designed to detect money laundering and other illegal transactions, including tax evasion, blackmail, and fraud. The warning e-mails always went to Darla first, and she forwarded the warnings to the vice president for regulatory compliance, who reviewed and decided whether to send them to law enforcement. What Darla never sent, no one ever saw. As she typed, Hermann pulled the cord from around his neck and showed her the key. He unlocked the aluminum valise and turned it in her direction. She stopped, naked from the waist up, and took her hands off the keyboard. The bills were crisp and new, surrounded by tan-colored paper sleeves.

"In three days. You won that in three days? That's what I'm supposed to say?"

"It's a rich game."

"How much?"

"Two million, minus fifty thousand."

She put her hands on her chest. "Where..."

"Don't ask."

The amount gave her vertigo; she leaned back in her chair. "Lucky man," she said. She reached out, stroked his hair, and kissed his mouth. She gently rolled her chair to him. Keeping her mouth on his, she put her hands on the sides of his face and kissed him as deeply as she could. When they parted, she was one inch from his face and stared into his eyes.

"Better lucky than good," he said.

"Why's that?"

"Lucky means you win. Anyone can be good."

"Not anyone. That's why you have me." Darla patted the side of his face and turned back to the computer. The security system allowed her to enter a general ledger, an account for a real estate developer based on a line of credit provided by the bank. The general ledger was for a building project, a running record of hundreds of transactions per week—checks written for labor, architects, materials, scaffolding, cranes, financing, legal expense, deposits, and transfers from bank loans. On any day, $1 million in withdrawals and deposits flowed through the general ledger for the project. Darla scrolled back in time, exactly seven days, to a week of activity that showed 608 transactions in five business days. She selected one entry, an extra finance charge of $2,000, a relatively small expense buried within the credits and debits on an $80 million building project. She deleted the charge as if it had never happened.

"Gone?" Asked Hermann.

"Almost." Darla went deeper into a backup program, where the transaction was recorded a second time. The date and time of the transaction was recorded alongside Darla's initials, which identified her as the person who had entered the transaction in the first place and all the subsequent modifications to the general ledger. She deleted her initials and the data that showed what she had done and when she had done it. In a few keystrokes, the numbers, dates, and letters disappeared. In the cash ledger for the project, she balanced the account by adding back $2,000. She then modified and deleted the computer data as if the $2,000 had never been removed from the account seven days earlier.

"For that one, we're done." Through the security system, Darla entered into seventy-five different commercial accounts at the bank, all of which had lines of credit, mortgages, and loans. Each one regularly paid finance charges. Seven days earlier she had registered to each account a bank financing charge between $1,000 and $3,000. The accounts had substantial weekly activity—some recorded one thousand individual transactions in short periods of time—so the finance charges were buried within a maze of entries in general ledgers and checking accounts.

She had transferred the money to Hermann in a numbered account, which gave him $150,000 in poker money—a one-week unauthorized loan he had to pay back. Today, Hermann paid it back, and Darla reversed the process. She entered every general ledger and account, deleted the finance charge, and restored the proper cash balance in the account. She removed any trace that she had been there or that the charge had ever occurred. In all, she moved $150,000 in small sums back to where the money had been seven days earlier and readjusted the accounts. During the process, her security e-mail system operated on the lower-right-hand corner of the computer screen. She could see whether her activity triggered the security program that would send a warning that she alone would receive. Nothing happened.

She went into Hermann's twenty-six numbered accounts, which showed small sums, recently withdrawn, that together added up to $150,000. If anyone had examined the accounts during the seven-day period, the activity report would have shown twenty-six healthy long-term savings accounts with a relatively insignificant withdrawal for that week. Darla had embedded in the accounts a security program that showed whether anyone had attempted to monitor them in the last seven days. She checked the program. Satisfied that that there had been no entry, she swept clean the activity data within the account and removed all the underlying data within the backup program.

After she altered the records, Darla reset the bank's overall computer program for account activity and allowed it to run. It readjusted the seventy-five commercial accounts, Hermann's twenty-six numbered accounts, and the cash on hand at the bank. When it finished—the program took approximately seven minutes to make the adjustments—the bank's overall account ledger showed an additional $150,000 in cash in the bank's vault, the same amount she had given Hermann seven days earlier.

Darla closed the briefcase, stood up, and walked into the vault. She and Hermann removed the paper sleeves and unloaded $150,000 into the vault's cash boxes, mixing the new cash with the old. Darla walked to a section of the vault for safety deposit boxes. Two keys on cords around her wrist swung as she cruised through the hallway. At her safety deposit box, she inserted the keys, and Hermann stopped her. He held the briefcase flat, opened it, and showed her the remaining money: $1.8 million.

"Fifty-fifty this time," he said.

Darla's standard cut was 10 percent of whatever Hermann won. She looked at him and didn't smile. "Why?" she asked.

"This is it; after today, we don't do it anymore."

"Why stop now? Did you clean them out?"

He shook his head. Exhaustion twitched his eyelids. "I slept under a house last night in the hurricane. Maybe I'll change my mind tomorrow..." He thought about retrieving the boxes and transporting them to Asheville. "But, no, I won't." He handed her the briefcase. "Keep it. Send it to that account you have in Tahiti."

"Cook Islands."

"What?"

"The account is in the Cook Islands."

"How much do you have?"

"Six hundred thousand."

"Now you have $2.4 million. With my accounts, we'll have more."

"Hermann, we've made that in only a few years. If you're winning like this..."

He stopped her. "Today," he said. "You have to do it today, as soon as possible. Use the bank's next-day service for secured packages, with instructions for the custodian not to open it until you arrive. It won't get scanned, and it won't go through customs."

Hermann didn't do anything with urgency, and he didn't crack, but that's what she saw, like a straight line on a tooth, as if he had clamped onto something too hard. One more bite and things would separate into pieces. It moved down his face and neck and across his chest. Watching it made her legs weak. She leaned against the safety deposit boxes and asked questions. They tumbled out slowly—what had he done, who else was involved, had he stolen the money, why, and what were the red-and-white packages. She didn't look at him as she asked the questions. He didn't answer. He shook his head as he told her that he needed a boat and she needed a one-way ticket to the South Pacific. Darla slid down along the wall of safety deposit boxes until she reached the floor. She looked at the aluminum briefcase on her lap and then at Hermann, whose face had lost its color.

"A boat?" She asked.

"Thirty to forty feet."

"When?"

"Tonight."

"And the flight?"

"Tomorrow, early morning."

XXXI

The Mansion, Wilmington, North Carolina

Miller Street shimmered in the sun one block south of Oakdale cemetery in downtown Wilmington. In the height of summer, the live oaks spanned the roadway and covered the neighborhood in shade. Just inside the gates of the cemetery, men and women in dark suits and dresses attended a burial amid faded marble and granite headstones packed together in tight rows. Limousines and cars were parked outside the gates, partially on the grass. Among the limousines, a rented sedan faced away from the cemetery. In the front seat, Leandro had a perfect view of 323 Miller Street, a clapboard-and-brick bungalow with a cut lawn, rose bushes, and a front porch.

At five o'clock, Darla and Hermann left the house. They entered Darla's car, drove south to Market Street, and turned to the river. The sedan moved out of the cemetery and followed. Ten minutes later, it came to a stop and pointed downhill on Market Street opposite Saint James Church, where a crowd in bright dresses and smart suits gathered on the sidewalk.

Hermann walked up the hill with Darla and crossed the street to the church.

"You're certain that's him?"

"Yes," Caleb Parrish responded from the backseat.

"The woman?"

Parrish paused before he spoke. He cleared an edge in his throat and said, "I have no idea."

Leandro turned to Sean, who sat behind the steering wheel. "Find out."

Sean nodded.

When the sidewalk in front of the church was empty, Leandro stepped out of the car, unlocked the trunk, and removed the blazer and tie he had worn to the Isle of Palms. He closed the trunk, told Sean to leave, and crossed the street. As he walked up the steps of the church, the sedan made a U-turn on Market Street and retraced its path back to Miller. It turned into the modest driveway of 323 and came to a stop. Sean and Joseph left the car and walked behind the house.

In the vestibule of the church, a party of women congregated around a bride in a colossal white dress. An organ played softly. Leandro smiled, quickened his pace past the women, tied his tie in a Windsor knot, and added an American flag pin to the buttonhole of his lapel. He walked up the right side of the church and scanned the pews for Hermann's head, which he found in the sixth pew from the front. Leandro sat in the transept with a good view.

At 5:30 p.m., three hundred friends and relations poured onto the church steps for photographs, and then spilled onto Market Street. They began a four-block procession to the Mansion, a three-story brick-faced antebellum home surrounded by a whitewashed wall and azalea gardens that occupied half a city block. Leandro walked out onto the street and followed the back of Hermann's prominent blond head within the crowd. He watched Darla and Hermann stay to Market and pass the small colonial side streets that formed a maze of cobblestone alleyways. Darla held Hermann's hand, and they moved quickly up to the Mansion, scanning faces, exchanging smiles and greetings, and occasionally stopping to speak to friends. Leandro stayed in the distance.

The Mansion was the largest antebellum home in the state. Now a museum, it was built at the highest spot in central Wilmington on a brick foundation twelve feet off the ground. Covered porches supported by wide columns surrounded the house. Floor-to-ceiling windows twenty feet high were open and pushed back against the exterior walls. Guests circulated through the windows and doors and out onto the covered porches. The building's red-brick facing was lightly washed with white paint and glowed pale rust in the late afternoon. Tables with white cloths and candles were set on the porch and throughout the gardens, where thick, sculpted azaleas formed green globes along lawns and paths that connected the Mansion to restored slave quarters and carriage houses. Leandro stood in a line at the front gate and watched Darla and Hermann climb the main steps. A woman in a hoop gown offered him a white carnation, which he accepted. She pinned it on his lapel.

At the top of the steps, Peyton Sorel and the judge stood on the porch among extended relations who moved in and out of the doorway and touched Peyton on the shoulder, kissed her, told her how pleased they were to see her. She had melted into this crowd all her life. They instantly revived the cadence in her speech that made her unmistakably native to the region, as if she'd never left, as if litigation was the suit she took off and left behind in the apartment. She was no longer like them—not in a courtroom on Foley Square or in her Manhattan office tower—but she was of them and felt an easy kinship with Carolina low country people. They had taught her to set crab pots, water-ski, sail, drive a truck along dusty roads, and ride Masonboro's long curls on a short board. From the outside, they appeared to be preoccupied with marriages, births, deaths, card games, cocktail parties, and golf outings. But they were more than that. They operated businesses, supported churches and synagogues, ran for public office, fought in foreign wars, healed the sick, passed legislation, and tended to their own. They didn't talk much about it—polite society didn't do that—but it was all there, and Peyton knew it. In a second, she shed her acquired cold northern manner for the warmth of people who loved her unconditionally and whose kindness felt like the tide in summer.

She moved into the crowd and put her arm around Aunt Ellen Hawthorne, the judge's cousin, a stout woman of seventy-five who had applied her considerable mathematical skills to investments and the game of bridge with equal success. Without a word, Peyton kissed Aunt Ellen on the cheek and elicited a murmur in the crowd as Ellen turned to Peyton, whom she'd not seen in three years. Ellen clasped her hands on Peyton's cheeks and in a whisper thanked heaven she had returned. The crowd closed around them as hands reached out to touch Peyton's shoulders and arms. People kissed and hugged her, told her how much they'd missed her, and asked her about the boys. It was unrestrained goodwill. They were always there, welcomed her back, and remembered her as a small child and teenager, even if in her own memory she could not recall every face and name.

Ellen pulled Peyton and the judge into the building to meet the bride, a distant cousin from Raleigh whom Peyton hadn't seen in ten years. Caryn Jones stood in the main hallway in front of a wide staircase that swept up to an intermediate landing and then split in opposite directions to the second floor. Large fireplaces of carved granite on either side of the hall framed Caryn as if she were a life-sized ornament. Peyton went through the receiving line and smiled at faces she knew she knew but forgot some of the names, and now and then nodded at a gentle reminder from the judge, who whispered over her shoulder.

Darla stood on the main staircase behind the receiving line and walked up to the landing. She pressed her mobile phone against her ear and turned toward the crowd to find Hermann, who moved through the hallway into a front parlor, looking for the contact who would give him the key to the boat he'd use later in the darkness. She listened to the ring—six times until the voice mail kicked in—and dialed again.

Leandro stood on the stone apron of a fireplace, sipped a glass of champagne, and watched Hermann navigate through the people. Always within eyesight, Leandro followed him onto the porch. He kept the champagne glass at his lips, moved with a purpose to prevent people from talking to him, and kept to the porch railing, where he could admire the gardens from above and turn away if Hermann reversed course through women in flowered dresses and broad hats.

The camellias had bloomed again in the late summer and formed a meandering red line in and out of the lawns and shrubs, among the trimmed beds of flowers and boxwoods, mulched with crushed white oyster shells from the beach. A hand touched his shoulder, and Leandro turned from his view of the garden to two women, one dressed in a lime-green floral print and the other in a strapless black cocktail dress. They were holding champagne glasses and smiling through lipstick. He pleasantly asked if he could help them.

"Do I know you?" asked the lime.

He wondered what she'd taste like, but stayed to his role, which he had practiced in the pew. He was from out of town, looking at real estate to develop, he said—wasn't everyone— and they all laughed. Yes, the accent was from Texas, the Gulf Coast, where he worked with his father, first cattle and now land, but no, he was certain they had never met.

"Who are you with?" The black dress was amusing. She had a large, inviting smile, clean white teeth, and a perfect nose. An elderly friend of his father was the answer. He tipped his glass to the back parlor and pointed to people seated at tables near a long wooden bar and a line of men waiting for service. They couldn't see him, but the older man was there, seated; it was difficult for him to walk, so he remained at the table. No, he didn't know the connection between the bride's family and his host, but he would find out. The diversion was lasting too long.

Over the shoulder of the black dress and along the railing, the porch had emptied out, and Hermann had disappeared. Leandro motioned to a waiter with a tray, asked the women to drink up, and exchanged his empty champagne glass for two full glasses, which he handed to them with compliments and a partial bow. He excused himself, and their eyes followed him across the exterior wall of the Mansion, through an open floor-to-ceiling window, and into the front of the house. Without stopping, he selected another glass of champagne from a waiter's tray and picked out the back of Hermann's head. He was looking slightly downward, talking to someone, and moving through the back parlor to the hallway.

The crowd was thick near the bar. Leandro parted people and walked to the left near the tables. Seated against the open window, his cane hooked over an adjacent chair, the old man sat facing two visitors and stopped Leandro with his eyes. Leandro wanted to move on, as if it had never happened, but the two people speaking with George Harwood stood in his way and saw the exchange. Peyton looked to George for an introduction, but he hesitated, his lips parted, and then Leandro held out his hand to Peyton and introduced himself.

"Robert," he said. "Robert Erwin. From Texas. I'm visiting George."

He looked at her in a slipover dress painted in strokes of bright red, blue, green, and white. It was tight and clean, as if taken from a late-in-life canvas by Henri Matisse and cut into an hourglass shape. In two-inch white leather pumps, she was slightly shorter than he and wore pink lipstick. Her brown hair was pulled back in a tight French braid still wet from a shower; it emphasized her cheekbones and almond-shaped eyes that looked at him without blinking. She wasn't anything like the lime or black cocktail dress. The exact words Leandro needed with which to walk away weren't there—they wouldn't rise in his mind—so he stayed, did what he could, and used her for cover to avoid an involved introduction to anyone else. He looked over her shoulder to Hermann, who was in the hallway and spoke to a man in a tan suit. Hermann received a set of keys, nodded, and returned to the back parlor. He passed Leandro's shoulder, stood in line for a drink, and kept his eyes straight ahead at his own image in an ornate mirror over the bar.

A drink—Leandro offered to get her one—and Peyton walked with him to the bar. They stood behind Hermann and Darla, and Leandro talked with her in the simple role he had practiced. He asked her about herself, and she answered. Hermann played with his cell phone as he waited for the barman, rolled it in his hand, and tapped out a text message until he ordered two drinks—a cosmopolitan and a beer. He brought the first to Darla, who had walked back to the porch and looked out to the lawn of white tablecloths and candles that glowed in the fading light. The porch rested on stone pillars linked together by a short brick wall that was low to the ground. Below, children walked along the wall like a balance beam. From the railing, Darla and Hermann had an aerial view of immaculately dressed girls and boys who raced through the gardens and around tables, slowing down when chided by an adult and then sprinting again.

Hermann's phone rang, and an unknown number appeared on the screen.

At a pay phone in a motel parking lot in Asheville, Martel spoke to Hermann in soft, controlled tones. He sought answers. Why were the boxes not in Asheville? He was paid only if he delivered the boxes. Did he remember that?

Hermann walked down the porch with the phone at his ear and lightly skimmed a Corinthian column with his hand. Darla followed.

"They're in the marshes along the river," he said. "No. Not like that."

Hermann stopped speaking and listened. Martel threatened him and yelled into the phone.

"The boat went over," Hermann said. "Stop and listen." He stood alone in the corner of the porch and motioned for Darla to go back. He kept his voice low and explained to Martel what had happened—that the boat had broken over an old levee, and the boxes had fallen off the boat when it turned over in a rice field—but they were safe, below the water line, and he planned to return to the rice field at night in a boat he'd just borrowed from someone Darla knew.

Martel wanted to know exactly where they were, and Hermann described Winnabow, identified the entrance along route 133, parallel to the river, and explained the checkerboard system of levees. He told him the address, about the break in the levee directly across from Santee Island, and how he'd cut the rubber rings long before the boat had turned over. They were there, he said, among the weeds, and he'd have to enter the water to retrieve everything. But he could find them under the moon, because they shimmered white in the water.

"The river's receding," Hermann said. "They'll be exposed tonight. I'll open them up, put everything in a boat, and meet you tomorrow. Bring a truck. We'll load it up."

"I'll call you on this number tonight," Martel said. "Two in the morning. Make sure we have everything. If you don't..." Martel's voice grew quiet in the last few words. Hermann terminated the call.

At the phone booth in Asheville, Martel wrote the description of Winnabow on the front of a North Carolina road atlas and then looked at the receiver as the dial tone sounded. He returned to his truck, a large ranch vehicle with a flat bed, and opened the road atlas to the map from Asheville to Wilmington. He pressed it against the dashboard and used his index finger to trace I-40, a straight drive from Asheville to Durham and then south to Wilmington—six hours, if the highways weren't damaged from the storm. From there, he found Memorial Bridge, the river, and route 133. His finger stopped when he identified Santee. Martel started the truck with a rumble. He drove out of the parking lot, kicked up asphalt, and headed onto the Blue Ridge Parkway east.

Hermann turned back to Darla, clinked his beer bottle against her martini glass, and told her to enjoy herself. He'd wait until the sun went down and start late, in total darkness, when river traffic was gone. He imagined her in the boat shining a flashlight on him, waist deep in water, pulling out the paper sacks and heaving them into the stern of the boat. He brushed a few fingers across her cheek.

The mirror over the bar was large enough to reflect parts of the porch. It caught the reflections of Hermann and Darla as they looked out from the railing and spoke. Leandro saw them over the barman's shoulder. He handed a glass of wine to Peyton, who was relaxed and well scrubbed. They walked to George, who sat alone at the table, sipped whiskey, and listened to a live orchestra that had begun to play on the other side of the Mansion. Leandro pulled out a chair near the open window for Peyton and looked directly at George as if to say that he was returning her safely. She thanked him, and he excused himself to respond to a phone call he had missed—it was a client, important, not a man to leave waiting. He held out his hand and told her it was a pleasure to meet her, a surprise, and memorable. She liked the thought and the way he expressed it; she nodded and said nothing. Leandro turned away and walked toward the music and into the crowd.

XXXII

The Mansion

George had watched the performance. The accent was seamless, as if the persona had lived elsewhere for a time—perhaps in the northeast of the United States or the West Coast—and lost the vowels and cadence of Texas speech but reacquired them when he had returned home. It was artful and acute. Leandro had heard the same traces in Peyton's speech. He'd mimicked and mixed them with his own idea of understated elegance. Then he blended into the reception as if he were one of them, a Southerner, but from the West.

"Running with the younger generation these days?" Peyton smiled.

George threw his head back and laughed. He glanced at the hallway where Leandro had disappeared and shook his head. "First time I've met him." He lied and changed the subject. "How about you, my dear? And what are you up to?"

The question made for an easy transition. Had he received her voice mail, she asked, and George responded with a puzzled look.

"Cell phone?" he asked. His voice was filled with the speech pattern of the deep South. Years in New York and Connecticut hadn't squeezed it out of him.

"Yes."

"I've misplaced it. It's somewhere in the house. The battery's bound to have run out, so people will think I'm gone forever. I'm rarely in these parts anymore."

Perfect litigation strategy—he'd disappeared—but what brought him back? "I know," she said. "I'm surprised to see you."

"What's on your mind?"

"CIT. We need some help with corporate history."

George looked away. "If I can."

During the day, Peyton had thought about how to approach him. The Iberia transaction was eight years old, and George was seventy-seven. He might not remember the details, but he was still sharper than most of the people with whom she worked. If Ted was right, George would remember everything, not just the broad strokes. She trusted Ted's instincts, but he'd dissected so many schemes of fraud, tax evasion, and money laundering that he tended to see crime in the interstices of a sloppy transaction. Most of the time he was right, but sometimes he wasn't. Perhaps he was wrong this time, and it went like this: George had handed the transaction to Arthur Konigsberg, paid little or no attention to it, and then signed off on whatever Arthur had put in front of him. But Arthur was older, had done a poor job, and had pushed it through with a lower-level lawyer, who didn't understand the deal or document it well. It was unlikely, not like Arthur. The value of the property was reported to be so large on the handwritten document that it was implausible that a lower-level lawyer would have primary responsibility for the deal. But it was possible. Out of respect and loyalty, she wanted the possible to be true. George and Arthur weren't young in 2002. Arthur was six years older than George and would be eighty-three if he were alive today. He could have made mistakes; he had in the past. George deserved the right touch, her most respectful one. But she had to ask the question.

"It involves an offshore subsidiary that held land in South America."

His eyes stayed with her. Peyton saw the effort. He kept them still, and then an eyelid shifted, like a twitch from too much coffee. She waited for something that would open up the subject or postpone it until the reception was over, but he said nothing. He looked at her, frozen, as if the question had hit him in the forehead. There was nothing; he couldn't find a response. He tried to control his eyes, but he blinked, looked down at her colorful dress, and glided his hand across the ironed white tablecloth as if it had a wrinkle.

"There were many subsidiaries," he said. "Usually, they were for, you know, special-purpose projects." He was telling her what she already knew. "We used them, dissolved them, and moved on." He turned the question back on her. "What's this about?"

"Joe Boyle says the subsidiary has something to do with CIT. He's wrong, but he has the judge's attention. There's a ton of money connected to the subsidiary."

"What's that have to do with CIT?"

"Nothing, the sub was dissolved in 2002, long before. But Joe's good. He raised it Thursday out of nowhere. We know almost nothing about it."

She expected him to ask the name of the subsidiary, but he didn't. He looked off to the people in the hallway. She watched him and waited. He didn't have to ask; he knew it all. She leaned forward and put her hand on his. "Iberia," she said. George turned back and looked at her blue eyes. He was silent, frozen in a spot light. She'd ask him nothing more.

He looked away. "I love Cole Porter," he said. "Stories with great melody. People don't write songs like that anymore. Was it an operating company?"

"Probably not. It looks like a holding company. But we can't find any internal files. Maynard and the firm destroyed everything after seven years."

His face relaxed; she could see it in his profile.

"But Boyle has some documents from Bermuda, where the company was incorporated, and he used them in court on Friday."

George watched the men and women glide and spin across the floor. The women's dresses fanned out in summer colors, and the volume of the orchestra rose into something from Bennie Goodman, full of brass and movement, a round sound that pumped through the Mansion.

"They won't let it go, George. They'll cause trouble with this," she said.

He watched the dancers and did not react.

"If things develop in the wrong way, and we can't control it, they'll take your deposition. Boyle demanded it Thursday."

George closed his eyes and adjusted a hearing aid. He told her the music was loud and that he couldn't hear very well. Would she be kind enough to help him to the porch and front gate? He took his cane from the adjacent chair and slowly stood up, one hand on the table and the other on the cane. She stood with him, and they walked onto the back porch, her hand on his elbow. Together they wound through the crowd to the front porch and down the steps to the gate. On his left leg was a large removable boot that extended above the knee and stayed in place with Velcro straps. It had become a permanent fixture. He ignored the pain and remarked how the gardens were well tended and how rare it was for the flowers to bloom in August. He walked along the porch with one hand on the railing and one on the cane and asked about the boys. She told him they were somewhere on the grounds of the Mansion; he looked for them on the lawns without success.

She helped him down the front stairs and accompanied him to the gate, where she kissed him on the cheek and told him she would see him later. She would find him if she needed him. His car was waiting. As they approached the curb, George looked back to her. Over her shoulder, Leandro stood at the top of the steps and watched. Peyton held George's arm. The uniformed driver came around from behind and opened the car door. George threw his cane into the backseat and turned to her. He was no longer inquiring and forgetful. He stood straight and gripped her forearm.

"There won't be a deposition." His eyes strayed to Leandro on the porch and then back to Peyton. "Get rid of it. It won't end well. Not for me, not for you. Not for anyone."

He released her forearm and turned away. He sat on the backseat, pulled his legs in, and told the driver to head home. Peyton closed the door. The car rolled down Market Street to the river. The evening had set in, and she watched the taillights move past Saint James, turn on Dock Street, and disappear.

On the front porch, Leandro stood next to a column and watched Peyton walk through the gate and along the path to the steps. When she reached the top step, he held out his hand and asked her to dance. She accepted to escape the moment.

What she needed was time alone to think about George and Iberia, the next twenty-four hours, Ted's theory, and what she would say on Monday morning when Judge Stapleton asked her to explain what Boyle was ranting about. George's parting words were fatal. Iberia was a disease. Remove it now. That was the message: cut it out, and move on. That's what good lawyers did—find the solution. But if Ted was right, Iberia wouldn't disappear. And she wouldn't make it disappear, not for George or anyone else.

She took Leandro's hand with a polite smile and walked into the cavernous front hallway, where the orchestra had stopped, and a young woman in a pink dress adjusted the height of a microphone. The last light in the sky shone through the windows on the landing and reflected off brass instruments that leaned against stools and amplifiers. Two men, one with a guitar and another with a tall African drum, stood on either side of the woman, who tapped on the microphone to assure herself that the sound was right. As Leandro and Peyton walked across the floor, the first measures of "Moon River" rolled off the strings of the guitar. The drum provided a barely audible rhythm. In an effortless mezzo-soprano, the woman's voice soared through the room and filled every inch of the hallway in an upper register Peyton could feel along her back. It was personal, as if the song belonged to the woman alone and had been written that day. She told the story to everyone, and they listened, attentive in silence, particularly Peyton, who thought about dancing with Paul to the same song years ago in the darkness of the New York apartment. Leandro held Peyton's right hand, put his arm around her waist, and drew her in; his face almost touched hers. He had shaved and showered before the wedding, and his skin was smooth and clean, without a trace of sweat from the August heat. She rested her hand on his shoulder and smelled the soap that mixed with his own scent. She thought about what it would be like to be with a man again.

He knew how to lead. She followed him within the rhythm, as they spun around the floor, until the voice and the sight of them moving in tandem inspired others. His mouth to her ear, he asked her how she knew George.

She whispered back. "Family friend."

"Do you see him often?"

"He lives in the Caribbean."

"Have you been there?"

"Not in years."

That was all he needed. He splayed his fingers and placed his full hand on her back, said he admired her dress and the beautiful way she danced, which elicited a smile. Gratuitous flattery—she knew it, liked it, and accepted it graciously. She whispered in his ear that he knew how to dance as well. He laughed with her and used the compliment as an excuse to hold her closer, press her against his chest, and brush the side of his face against her cheek. She didn't resist. He smelled good and moved well. The entire dance evoked memories of Paul and of other men before him. When the singer's voice moved up half an octave in a crescendo, pleaded to the river, and prayed for the future, Peyton let go. She let her cheek rest against his face as images of Paul came out of the distance in late August, dancing in a dark apartment, swimming na-ked in the Masonboro surf, and lying on sweat-soaked sheets. It was all in the song, his square shoulders, the smell of his clean skin and starched collar. There were no tears. The mem-ories were vivid and exciting and made her ready to become someone other than a woman in mourning. Leandro moved his face in front of hers, and his lips brushed across her mouth. Instinctively, she kissed him, gently pulled back, and pressed her cheek against his. A small smile crossed her lips.

When the song was over, applause erupted around them. Peyton parted from Leandro, clapped her hands, and looked at the singer, who smiled, nodded, and thanked the audience. Peyton turned back to Leandro. He stood inches away, folded a business card into her hand, and told her that he had to make a call. Did George know how to contact her, he asked, and then he offered that he saw George frequently, that he was an old friend, and perhaps they could meet again. It all tumbled out in the light Texas lilt, and Peyton nodded with a smile.

XXXIII
The Mansion

Leandro walked onto the front porch and pulled a cell phone from his pocket. Beyond the porch, Hermann and Darla moved through the front gate and onto the sidewalk. Darla stood under two gas lamps, had a brief exchange with Hermann, and then watched him turn away and begin the walk along Market Street to her car, three blocks farther than Saint James. She wore spiked high-heeled shoes, unsuitable for walking, and patiently waited at the illuminated gate.

Across the street and one block away, Sean and Joseph sat in the sedan and watched Hermann. Sean pulled the car out from the curb and rolled down Market Street toward the church. They passed him once. In the backseat, Joseph turned and kept his eyes on the target. They found Darla's car and parked behind it. Three blocks away, Hermann was alone and walked briskly downhill on the dark street, lit only by the lights in distant windows and passing cars.

Leandro passed through the front gate of the Mansion, looked at Darla, and smiled. He nodded and said good evening. She smiled back, said good night, and watched him cross the street. He turned left and walked toward the oldest section of the town, to the dark warren of colonial cobblestone streets, row homes, and mews, two square miles in the middle of the town where streets unexpectedly changed their names and the only lighting was over the front doors. The streets were narrow—only one car could pass—and lined with thick trees that had grown up toward the sky and spread their leaves among the second and third floors of the houses, which had been renovated and restored long ago. The original cast iron hitching posts, painted black, were still embedded in the sidewalks.

In the dark, Leandro walked, checked a text message on his phone from Sean, and arrived directly across from 84 Summit Mews. He slid into a walkway between two homes, lit a cigarette, and waited.

———

Joseph sat on Hermann, who lay face down in the well of the backseat. He had punched Hermann several times in the back of the head until he bled and had bound his hands behind him with a plastic cable tie. Pieces of silver duct tape were across his eyes and mouth. With a stiletto, Joseph cut a two-inch gash through the back of the blue blazer, pushed the point into a lateral muscle, and twisted it to hold the prisoner's attention. Hermann shook from pain. Every so often Joseph gave him a warning that the knife would go deeper if he moved.

Sean drove down Market, continued to Dock Street, and made several turns and a sharp descent into a basement garage, where the car stopped, lights went on, and an automated garage door closed with a motorized hum.

"Let's patch him up and clean up the backseat," Sean said, as he opened the driver's door. "How much do you think he weighs?"

"One eighty," said Joseph. "maybe one ninety."

Sean took an aluminum tube from his pants pocket, removed a needle and syringe, and held it up to the light. He pressed the plunger and let some of the liquid flow out of the needle until it reached the correct level in the syringe. Joseph pressed down on Hermann's face, and Sean opened the passenger door. He administered a light dose of sodium pentothal into an exposed part of Hermann's neck to keep him pliable. They pulled him out of the car, laid him on the concrete floor, and held him down until the anesthetic brought on a stupor and slow breathing. Joseph wiped the stiletto clean with a rag and slipped it back into the scabbard strapped to his ankle. Both men crawled into the backseat with rags and fluid to clean the blood off the leather and carpet.

When they had finished, Joseph and Sean picked up Hermann and walked him across the garage, down a flight of stairs to a subbasement, and through a steel door. He staggered, barely conscious, and his knees buckled. They laid him face down on a cold steel table.

———

At the gate, Darla paced. Hermann had left ten minutes earlier and hadn't answered his phone. She walked half a block downhill on Market Street, turned back, and struggled, walking on tip-toes back up the hill to the Mansion. She looked at her phone and dialed him again: nothing, just an immediate voice mail greeting. She considered removing the shoes and walking to her car but abandoned the idea. Hermann had the car keys. If he wasn't at the Mansion's gate, then he was somewhere else, with the keys and the car, and he had forgotten her. Or was it intentional? She wondered whether he had left to protect her from what he would do with the boat, where he would go, and what he would pick up. He kept secrets to keep her safe—he told her that. And still, she had the money. Half was his, and he had to come to her. She would return home and follow his instructions: drive to Charlotte and find a flight to the West Coast. In Charlotte, she'd use a secure overnight bank box and characterize the shipment as private documents. The briefcase would arrive in the Cook Islands under her authority without being scanned or opened. She'd pick it up at the Cook Islands Trust Bank when she arrived. Hermann knew where to find her.

Darla inhaled. She didn't want to think that something had happened to him, but she couldn't explain his absence; it wasn't the plan. Someone could have come for him. The thought repeated in her mind. Her mouth went dry, and sweat beaded up under her arms and ran down her ribs. Behind the locked door of her house was where she wanted to be. From the inside, she'd think about what to do—perhaps rent a car and drive to Charlotte that night.

Darla stepped out of her shoes and looked down Market Street for any sign of the car. The street was empty. She stuffed the shoes in her handbag and in bare feet ran across Market, leaped onto the sidewalk, and began the walk home. It was a quick trip. She would walk two blocks along Market and turn right on Anderson Lane. Two more blocks took her to the mews, where her home was eight houses in. From the other side of Market, she looked back at the Mansion. The porches were filled with people. Laughter and brass sounds wafted from the house.

She walked two blocks to Anderson and looked back again. The dark sidewalk behind her was lined with small buildings,

which were once houses and now served as offices for lawyers, doctors, and dentists. Small lawns spread out like aprons
in front of the buildings, and the old-growth trees provided
a canopy over the sidewalks that partially blocked the light
from the streetlamps. Among the trees she saw the outline of
a man's head and shoulders. He stood in front of a Victorian
home. She couldn't tell whether he was looking at her or facing away, until he moved into the leaves and continued to
watch her.

Blood pumped in her chest, and the muscles in her thighs
tightened. Two blocks down Anderson was all she needed. A
sprint in the dark, the turn onto the mews, and at the eighth
door, she'd be in the house. She kept her eyes on the image
within the trees, backed up to the corner, and turned down the
street. She started out at a brisk pace, skipped, and then broke
into a steady trot. At the cross street, she stopped, looked back,
and saw nothing. The light of Market Street illuminated an
empty corner. Halfway down the second block, she turned and
saw him. He had arrived at the corner of Anderson and Market,
closer than before, and stopped. He turned and looked at her.
She felt cold but strong enough to run. She sprinted the rest of
the way down Anderson, crossed over to the left at the mews,
and ran along the cobblestones. Her skin tingled, and she kept
her eyes on the light over her front door. She veered onto the
sidewalk, hit a cast iron hitching post with her thigh, and fell
forward. Her handbag flew out in front of her and unloaded
the shoes, keys, phone, money, and credit cards onto the sidewalk. She landed on her elbows and knees, scraped them, and
jumped to her feet. In a crouch, she pulled the possessions into
her handbag and looked behind her. Holding her breath, she
listened for the sounds of footfalls along Anderson. Her neck

and scalp were wet, cold, and tight, and she felt a scream roll up her throat. She held a hand over her mouth to catch it.

In the darkness, a voice startled her. Part of her scream leapt out. She fell back on the sidewalk and dropped the handbag. She peered into the darkness in front of her at the glowing red embers of a cigarette and a man walking slowly toward her in the middle of the street. Her lungs heaved, and she stood up, holding the handbag against her chest. Into the dim light, Leandro emerged, the same man from the wedding reception who had pleasantly said good night to her fifteen minutes ago. He stopped about twenty feet away and asked whether she was injured and needed help. In a navy-blue jacket and green tie, he was a relief; the calm, low voice was courteous. In silence, she tried to discern why he was there and accepted his quick explanation—an evening walk with a cigarette. She told him that someone was following her, a man on Anderson Street, who would arrive any minute. She backed up against the wall of a home, and pointed to the corner. Leandro asked what the man looked like, and she told him that she didn't know and had only seen a dark outline in the distance near Market. He offered her a cigarette, for which she thanked him, and he lit it with a match. He walked to the corner of Anderson and Summit Mews, looked both ways, and returned.

"Nothing," he said and shook his head. "There's no one."

The tobacco made her feel better. Her body shook as she inhaled. He offered to walk her to her door, and she accepted, holding the cigarette in her lips and searching through her handbag for house keys. At 84 Summit Mews, Darla slid the key into the lock and opened the door. She turned back to thank him, and he was too close, inches away. He wrapped his arm under hers, put his hand on her mouth, and lifted her off the floor. He pushed the door open and glided inside. His hand covered her entire face. She could neither scream nor pry her body away. In the darkness, he closed the door with his foot and locked the bolt with his free hand.

XXXIV
Wilmington

On Market Street, Leandro walked past the Mansion and headed downhill. The music played sweetly, and people milled about on the lawns and porches. They produced a distant happy hum of conversation, shouts, cries, and laughter. From the elevation, Leandro could see the river, the dark forests of Brunswick County, and the stars in the southern sky. He enjoyed the warm night as he walked to Dock Street, turned east, and continued a few blocks to a stone mansion on a steep rise with gardens that descended to the river. The front of Highland House had three lawns. They were terraced with retaining walls and divided by a walkway that Leandro bounded up, two steps at a time. He arrived at a well-lighted columned portico with stained glass windows on either side of a door painted black. He put a key into the lock, entered, and closed the door behind him. He turned the bolt and shut down the house for the night.

Highland House had a large center hallway with a winding staircase that ascended three flights and circumnavigated an elevator that rose to the top of the house in an ornate column of steel and art deco brass. It dated from the early twentieth century and had been updated many times with new cables and machinery but retained its antique design and metal-mesh gates. Paintings of ancestors lined the walls of the hallway. On the left were a living room and library; on the right, a dining room and gallery. The ceilings were twenty feet high.

In the dining room, Caleb Parrish sat alone at a table that could seat thirty people. His shirt was covered with a white cloth napkin tied like a bib; he leaned over a plate of fried chicken and ate it with his fingers. With food in his mouth, he looked at Leandro, who walked through the room into a well-lit kitchen where George Harwood sat on a chair, his leg still in the removable straight brace. The housekeeper, Luisa, in a black uniform with a white lace apron, stood next to the marble table in the center of the kitchen. She asked Leandro if he would like some food: fried chicken, green beans, and rice. Leandro took a beer bottle from the refrigerator, opened it, and drained half into his mouth. He asked Luisa to retire for the evening so he and the gentleman could speak. She looked to George.

"It's all right," said George. "We'll see you in the morning."

She bowed and left the kitchen. The metal-mesh gate opened and closed. With a hum, the elevator took Luisa to her rooms on the third floor. Leandro closed the kitchen door.

"Tell me," Leandro said with grin. "What do I call you here?"

"George will do."

Leandro picked up a thigh, devoured it, and used a linen napkin Luisa had folded for him on the kitchen table to wipe his mouth. He remarked that she was a good cook and then turned the conversation to Peyton.

"The woman in the bright dress, with the colors, dark hair—you spoke with her when you left. What was that about?"

"A private matter."

He pointed the chicken bone at George. "There's nothing private while I'm here. Tell me what you said to her."

"It was nothing."

Leandro threw the chicken bone in the sink. "What does she do?"

"She's a lawyer, not a prosecutor. She does civil litigation and is always defending. She asked me some questions about a case she's trying in New York for the company."

Leandro picked up another thigh and measured George with his eyes. "What's it about?"

"Securities. There's some background information she thought I knew. I don't."

"Did she ask about me?"

"Not a word."

Leandro finished the thigh, wiped his hands on the napkin, and left at the opposite end of the kitchen. He walked down into the garage, where Sean sat at a table. With a thin black cable connected to a desk computer, Sean downloaded the contents of Hermann's cell phone into a laptop. Hermann's other possessions lay on the table. Joseph sat on the floor of the garage at the back of the sedan, removed the license plate, and installed a new one.

"How long will he be out?"

Sean looked up. "Another hour."

"I want you to pick something up," said Leandro.

"What is it?"

"It's a cargo trunk covered by a blanket." Both men stopped what they were doing and looked at Leandro.

"Where?" asked Sean.

"Eighty-Four Summit Mews, a couple blocks from the Mansion." He tossed Darla's keys to Sean. "You'll find it in the front hallway. Pick it up, and bring it back. We'll find a permanent location later."

XXXV

Highland House, Wilmington

When Hermann awoke, he was immobilized. His forearms, hands, and feet were wrapped with duct tape to the arms and legs of a wooden chair, and his head was taped to a board that had been bolted to the back. The tape was tight over the gash in his forehead. All he could see was a bright spotlight and the shadows of men who walked along the walls to the back of the room.

"Hermann. That's your name, isn't it?" Leandro stood along the wall and beyond Hermann's view.

"Yes."

"Will you be making us an offer?"

Hermann looked straight ahead. "No."

"Do you believe in redemption?"

"I work in a bank."

The men laughed.

"Tonight, we will help you find some redemption, and you will help us find what we are looking for."

"You've made a mistake," said Hermann. He tried to shake his head but couldn't.

"Redemption is never a mistake." Leandro leaned against the cinderblock wall out of Hermann's view. "And right now, it's your only option."

"I don't know what you're talking about."

"One hundred million dollars says you do."

Hermann was silent.

"A brand-new life?" asked Leandro. "Where? Europe? California? Asia?"

"Whoever you are looking for, it's not me."

"I'm talking about one hundred million dollars in pure, uncut, expertly processed cocaine. The best in the world. From Ecuador. You stole it." Leandro lit a cigarette, inhaled, and let the smoke flow out of his mouth. He walked around the chair, stopped at the back, and leaned forward over Hermann's shoulder. Tobacco smoke floated across Hermann's face.

"The equation is simple," he said. "You tell me where I can find the packages, and I won't hurt you. If you don't tell me, I'll do what I do, and you'll wish you were dead. You'll beg me to kill you."

Hermann persisted. "I didn't steal anything. I couldn't steal a car!"

"Where are they?"

"What?"

"Where is Martel?"

Hermann hesitated and stared into the darkness. Leandro looked at Sean, who typed and looked up from the laptop at the other end of the room.

Leandro took a guess. "Does Asheville have the shipment?"

Hermann was silent.

"I'll pay you twice what they offered."

Hermann's face changed, and Sean stopped typing. He looked at Leandro, who stood behind Hermann and whispered in his ear. "Was Arnold involved?"

"Arnold?"

"Arnold Glass?"

"I don't know who you're talking about."

"Other than you and Martel, who did this?"

"I don't know what you're talking about."

"Who is your contact in Asheville?"

"I can't help you."

"Where is the boat?"

"What boat?"

Leandro extended his hand over Hermann's shoulder. Attached to a miniature red-and-white buoy, the boat key dangled from Leandro's index finger. Hermann was silent. Sean continued to type.

"McPhee? Do you know McPhee?"

"No."

Leandro walked around the chair. All Hermann could see in the light was Leandro's silver belt buckle and dark pressed pants.

"I don't know who you are or what you're doing," Hermann said. "You've got the wrong person."

Leandro snapped his fingers. Sean wheeled the stainless steel table directly in front of Hermann. Leandro picked up an object along the wall and landed it on the table with a loud metallic slap. Hermann's breathing came to a halt. He closed his eyes as nausea crept up his throat, and he felt like he was falling. He tensed his muscles to absorb an impact, and then he spat and opened his eyes.

The aluminum briefcase lay on the table in the spotlight. Leandro opened it. Nearly $2 million were arranged in the case, all in paper sleeves.

"You know where I found it." It wasn't a question.

Hermann didn't respond.

"Shall we count it? Some is missing. But I suppose that's the least of your problems."

Leandro stepped forward and leaned in toward Hermann. He pulled up the lid of the right eye. Before Hermann could blink, he cut a small slice from the cornea with a scalpel and took a slice from the left eye too. With the nerves exposed, Hermann felt the pain explode, as if long needles had penetrated his eyes. The pain built into an enormous scream that started below Hermann's waist and cascaded up his throat and out of his mouth. The noise reverberated through the room. His heart beat faster, and his neck widened as blood raced up the carotid arteries and through the capillaries of the eyes. It pulsated against the exposed nerves and expanded as if the blood were magma. With every heartbeat, the pain swelled, subsided for a second, and swelled again.

Hermann's eyes were covered in tears; he shut them to avoid the light. His lungs were the only part of his body that moved, and they heaved up and down. He clenched his jaw to avoid any movement. In between breaths he gurgled out a question. "What do you want?"

Leandro slapped him on the face and sent pain through his eyes. Hermann screamed and clenched his jaw again to contain the pain. Tears streamed down his face, and he licked the moisture.

"He might be ready," Sean said from the back of the room. Leandro took a small plastic bottle from a shirt pocket and pulled open Hermann's right eyelid. He applied three drops of fluid to the right eye and then to the left. The effect of the anesthetic was instantaneous. The pain disappeared, and Hermann's breathing subsided. He opened his eyes to the spotlight and could see the silhouettes along the walls of the room.

"Feels good, doesn't it?"

"Yes." Hermann's voice was normal. The anesthetic had worked. He felt no pain in his eyes, only the mild ache of the cut on his forehead and the wound in his back. He wondered whether he was on a missing-persons list and whether anyone had seen the men pull him into the sedan. Based on the time he had been in the car, he was somewhere in the middle of Wilmington.

"It wears off in ten minutes," Leandro told him. "Ten minutes. All that pain is coming right back, worse than before, and it will be with you for a long time. All I do is wait. So think carefully about how you want the rest of this evening to proceed. It's up to you. I want to know about the packages, who stole them, and where they are."

"I work in a bank. I teach a little golf." It was a plea for mercy.

"I'll see you in ten minutes." Leandro walked through the steel door and closed it. Sean and Joseph remained.

In the kitchen, George sat in the same chair. "Do you have everything you need?"

"We're fine. Get some sleep. I'll need you tomorrow." George stood up from the kitchen table. With the cane, he walked out and motioned for Leandro to follow. Together, they walked to the elevator.

"What will you do with him?" George spoke in a whisper.

"When I have what I want, I'll dispose of him."

"Don't be reckless. This is a small town; everyone knows him. You can't just throw him in the river or a vacant lot. Take him far away." George stepped into the elevator, turned back to Leandro, and handed him an envelope. "I've marked how to get there. Have your people drive inland and dispose of him in the Swamps. It's a hunting preserve near the South Carolina border. The wildlife will tear the body apart and carry it away. He'll never be found, not even pieces of him." Leandro closed the metal-mesh gate. "Do it tonight," said George. "Don't wait." He pressed the button for the second floor and rose out of sight.

Leandro returned to the kitchen and took another beer out of the refrigerator. As he walked back down the stairs to the garage, he drained half the bottle. Inside the room, Hermann had begun to groan as the anesthetic wore off.

"Want a sip?"

"What?" said Hermann. He was disoriented and barely able to speak.

"Beer," said Leandro. "Do you want a sip of beer?"

"Okay, yes," Hermann said, hyperventilating, trying to remain still.

Leandro touched the bottle to Hermann's lips and let him take a short swallow.

"Good?"

"Yes." Beer ran down Hermann's chin.

Leandro poured the rest of the beer on Hermann's head. As the liquid descended over his eyelids, Hermann blinked, and the alcohol entered his eyes and washed over the exposed nerve endings. Hermann's chest heaved. The more he tried to move his arms and head, the worse the pain became. The faster the blood flowed through the capillaries, the deeper the needles penetrated, and a scream flew up out of his mouth in a long howl.

"That's beer, Hermann. Imagine what isopropyl alcohol does. Shall I show you?"

"No, no. No, please, no. Give me the anesthetic, please."

"I thought you'd be friendly," said Leandro. "I give anesthetic to friends. What you're doing is not what friends do."

"I'm a friend; I promise. Give me the anesthetic."

Leandro went to Hermann's side and put one hand on his forehead, poised to pry open one of his eyes to insert liquid. "This is a test, Hermann. Where is Martel?"

"I don't know." Hermann answered truthfully. "I swear I don't know. I haven't seen him."

"But you know who he is, don't you?"

"Yes, yes. I'm telling you the truth."

"Does he know where the shipment is?"

"No."

Leandro pulled open Hermann's right eyelid and squeezed out a few drops of isopropyl alcohol from a small bottle. The nerve endings erupted. Against his restraints, Hermann squirmed and tried to move. He screamed repeatedly, and his chest pumped up and down. The chair, which was bolted to the concrete floor, wobbled as a bolt came loose under the pressure of Hermann's movement. Exhausted, he sobbed and groaned unintelligibly.

"You must not lie to me. I'm the only one who can give you the anesthetic." Leandro held Hermann's mobile phone in his hand. He turned it on and looked through the numbers that designated the recent calls made and received. "I have your phone. Which calls are from Martel?"

"Last one," mumbled Hermann.

"Received?"

"Yes."

"When did you receive it?"

"Tonight."

"Where is he?"

"A motel on I-40."

"Which one?"

"I don't know; he didn't say."

"Hermann." Leandro's voice held a warning.

"I promise. He didn't tell me." Hermann could barely articulate the words.

"Are you planning to meet him?"

"Tomorrow."

"Where?"

"He said he'd call me on the phone."

"When?"

"In the morning."

Leandro held Hermann's right eye open and applied three drops of the anesthetic; he did the same to the left eye. Instantly, the pain disappeared.

Hermann opened his eyes. He saw the floodlight and shapes of men along the wall.

"Hermann, you shouldn't be in this business."

"I know."

"And your choice of friends could improve."

Hermann looked at the small bottle on the steel table. "Please keep the anesthetic nearby."

"We have a lot of it, Hermann. Sit here for a moment and relax. When I return, I want to talk to you about where the shipment is. Do you understand?"

"Yes."

Leandro gave him a pat on the side of his face, turned, and walked out. He went to the first floor, dialed Gonzalez in Mexico City, and read him the number of the last call received in Hermann's cell phone. "From the number, I think it's a public pay phone, but if it's not, track and trace it all night. I want to know where he is and where he's moving."

"Yes, sir," said Gonzalez. "Do you need anyone else to fly in?"

"Yes. This will be over soon. I'll tell you where to land later."

Leandro returned to the room in the subbasement. The pain had returned and welled up into the capillaries, which swelled with Hermann's heartbeat and pushed against the nerve endings.

"I need more," Hermann pleaded.

"I need more too."

"Please, I will tell you whatever you want. Just give me the anesthetic. The pain is coming on again. Please."

"The way this works is you tell me what I want, and then I give you a reward. No information, no reward. False information, you get the alcohol. Got it?"

"Yes."

"Good."

Hermann heard the steel door open. Sean entered and gave Leandro a report from Gonzalez on the location of Martel's call. "No progress, but it appears you've been truthful," said Leandro. "You get one drop in one eye. That's five minutes, so we have to work quickly, understand?"

"Yes. Please help me."

Leandro put one drop of anesthetic into Hermann's left eye, and the pain disappeared. Only the right eye felt the needles. "Now, where are the packages?"

"In the mud."

The answer was imprecise, and Leandro smacked him hard across the face.

"Don't lie."

Hermann was surprised by the response. He screamed in pain as the slap brought blood through the capillaries and into the nerve endings of his right eye. "No, no." He screamed. "It was an accident. They're in the mud. In the river."

Leandro yelled at him for the first time. "How in the name of the Mother of God did my cargo end up in a river?"

"No, it's on the bank of the river...in marshes. You can get them. It's easy. You just need a boat. Please, please, give me the medicine. I'll tell you everything."

"Not until you tell me where they are."

"Winnabow," he screamed. They're at Winnabow."

"What is Winnabow?" Leandro's voice was suddenly calm and quiet.

"Winnabow. The plantation. The boxes went overboard. They're in the rice fields."

Leandro looked into the darkness to Sean. "Are you getting this?" he asked. He received an acknowledgment from Sean, who typed on the laptop.

Leandro turned back to Hermann. "Where in the rice fields?"

"Get me a map. I'll show you."

Leandro applied anesthetic to the right eye, and the pain disappeared. Hermann's voice returned to its normal tone, and his body relaxed.

"You have a few minutes. We will set a map in front of you, and you will pinpoint for me exactly where the cargo is. Do you understand?"

"I do."

The map arrived in the form of a road atlas. Joseph brought it to Leandro, who opened it up on the rolling steel table in front of Hermann. It showed the Cape Fear River from Wilmington to Bald Head Island and everything in between.

"Listen carefully. You will start by identifying large landmarks that are closest to the product, and we'll get more specific from there."

"Yes, sir."

"Where is it, east side or west side of the river?"

"West."

"South or north of the bridge?"

"South."

"Near an island?"

"Yes."

"Where?"

"Santee, about ten miles south of Wilmington."

Leandro pointed the tip of a pen to Santee Island. "There?"

"Yes. Then go west—to the left—they're in the mud on the river bank just west of Santee."

"What do you mean by 'they,' Hermann? Be specific."

"The containers. Big plastic containers. They're full of packages. I have no idea how much they weigh, but they're big, maybe one thousand pounds each."

"I need more than that. You tell me exactly where they are."

Hermann had expected him to be easy as the information came out, but Leandro grew agitated. "If you take me there, I can show you."

"No. You will be precise. Where did you put them?"

"It was an accident."

Leandro slapped him across the face. "Don't lie."

"I'm telling you the truth. I ran the boat aground in the storm. It flipped into a rice field on the bank of the river. It's an old plantation."

"How many rice fields are there?"

"Too many to count, but this one's easy to find. The boat went over just south of the new levees. You'll find them. They're just inside the broken wall. They are there. I swear to you. You can take me there now."

Leandro pulled back the lids of Hermann's eyes, squeezed one more drop of anesthetic onto each, and left the room.

When he reached the first floor of Highland House, Leandro dialed Gonzalez. "I need the most recent satellite images of the Cape Fear River at Santee Island," he said. "Focus on the western bank. Confirm that there are rice fields and a system of dikes, levees, that sort of thing. I need them now, ultrahigh clarity, multiple recent images from various distances, the latest ones from today. Send them electronically to the site."

"Calling them up now."

Gonzalez logged onto the satellite website and typed in a series of codes that allowed an uplink of the last seven days of worldwide satellite photographs of the planet. The satellites covered every inch of inhabited land and most of the oceans. He accessed images from the last twelve hours and narrowed his search to the last six hours of daylight in the Cape Fear region. Santee Island instantly appeared on the screen. Along the western side of the river, the picture was unobstructed and sharp. He could see ripples on the water and the ruddy hue of clay roads along the levees. He downloaded two dozen images of the impoundments across from Santee, forwarded the files to the encrypted website, and called Leandro.

"They're coming now," he said. "The longitude and latitude are included."

Leandro tapped his way into the website on a laptop at the dining room table, retrieved the images, and closed the computer. Caleb Parrish watched from the other end of the table and slurped a glass of red wine filled to the rim.

Leandro returned through the steel door in the subbasement with the laptop. Hermann breathed heavily.

"I need it," he moaned. "Please help me."

"At your service," Leandro said and stationed the laptop on the steel table. He picked up the bottle of anesthetic and applied two drops to each of Hermann's eyes.

"Better?" he asked.

"Yes. Tell me what you need."

Leandro rolled the steel table in front of Hermann. The screen of the laptop was eighteen inches from Hermann's face and showed a perfect digital image of Santee Island and the Winnabow rice fields from one thousand feet. Hermann's mouth opened slightly as he took in the image's clarity.

"Recognize it?"

"Sure. That's Santee. And those are the rice fields."

"Which field, Hermann?"

He hesitated. He wasn't sure. Terrified, he wanted to be correct. "Can you get closer?"

Leandro brought the image to five hundred feet. The clarity was so perfect that Hermann could see on the top of the new levees the tread marks from all-terrain vehicles used to transport the rice. Then he found his landmark. "It's south of the creek," he said.

Leandro pointed the tip of a pen at a section of the satellite image. "That creek?"

"Yes. The boat went over in the older fields south of the levees. They're filled with weeds. The boxes are underwater. After we went over, I swam upriver and turned at that creek."

Hermann followed the levee south and found the old impoundment. Just below the green river water, the translucent tops of the containers shone as light squares, framed by weeds and mud.

"Bring it closer," Hermann said.

Leandro enlarged the image to within two hundred feet.

"There," said Hermann. "You can see the boxes."

Leandro pivoted the steel table and looked at the enlarged image. He picked up a magnifying glass and traced the levees with his eyes, north to south, until he saw the containers in outline under the water, twenty feet inside the broken levee wall. The satellite image was dated that day, photographed at 7:27 p.m. He rolled the steel table back in front of Hermann and, with the tip of a pen, pointed to the containers.

"These?"

"Those."

Leandro rolled the table back against the wall, tapped on the laptop, and sent the image to his satellite phone, along with the longitude and latitude of the old impoundment. He turned back to Hermann and crouched down. For the first time, Hermann saw his face and understood what had happened. He was the man in the transept of the church. He had been outside on the sidewalk near Saint James and later stood behind him at the bar, like a guest, like anyone else, a cousin of the bride or groom, as if he'd been invited. At the reception, he had disappeared and reappeared in the crowd, from the porch to the large rooms and back again, admiring the gardens, talking to women, introducing himself. Then he'd suddenly been a presence on the porch and the front steps as they left, dialing on a phone to the men in the car to pick him up, tape his face, and push him down in the well of the car with a knife in his back. Hermann had been clumsy, like a small animal tramping through the underbrush, making noise, easy to locate from above. He looked into Leandro's green eyes and wondered how he had done it, how he had found him so quickly and worked his way into a coveted wedding reception for a daughter of the Wilmington elite.

Leandro held up the keys to the boat. "Where is it?"

The nautical float rocked back and forth in front of Hermann like a red-and-white pendulum. He was exhausted. "Would you give me something in return?"

"You're not in bargaining position."

"Let her go."

Leandro nodded. "We will. Where's the boat?"

"Seapath Marina, on the access road to Wrightsville Beach."

"What's it look like?"

"Large. Thirty-six feet with a fisherman's deck and transom."

"Name?"

"*Starlight.*"

Leandro stood up, walked to the steel door, and whispered to Sean. "Do the standard procedure. He's strong, so give him more than one injection. I'll be back in thirty minutes." Leandro left and closed the steel door behind him.

Inside, Sean opened the small black case of vials and syringes, color coded in blue, orange, and pink. He picked out the blue syringe Leandro had prepared in advance. Joseph held Hermann's right hand, and Sean guided the needle into a bulging vein on the top of the hand. The solution worked quickly, and Hermann's eyes fluttered and closed. Sean pinched Hermann's cheek for a reaction and found none. He unwound the duct tape on the board, and Hermann's head pitched forward.

Part 4

August 8 and 9, 2010

XXXVI

Mannion, North Carolina

North Carolina State Route 177 cuts through the town of Mannion and across a geological anomaly that straddles the South Carolina state line. The water rises up from underground streams that have flowed from the mountains of western North Carolina for thousands of years and stops short of the Atlantic coast, where it hits granite and sandstone deposited when the continent formed. The water percolates up through the rock into eighty square miles of uninhabited bayou, sixty miles inland from the sea and unconnected to any estuary, river, or lake. Extraction companies have known that minerals are there, but never bothered to dig. They left the territory to local people, who claimed it as their own and cleared miles of roads and dirt paths to blackwater cypress ponds, forests, and fields.

Most of the soil around Mannion is black, rich, and well irrigated, a direct result of the underground water that feeds the Swamps, the name the farm families use for their coveted hunting park. Soybean and alfalfa fields spread to the edge of the territory and surround it on both sides of the state line. Almost every farm has a smokehouse. In most seasons, they're filled with open masonry pits, smoldering ash, and the pink remains of skinned bobcats and deer nailed to rafters and cut in strips. Featherless turkey and pheasant, heads cut off, sometimes plucked, hang upside down on hooks over wooden floors caked in black blood and salt.

At four o'clock in the morning on August 8, Route 177 was a narrow canyon covered in kudzu. Joseph and Sean relied on George's map—the GPS on the dashboard was worthless without an address to locate—and it took them west and south to the town of Saint Thomas in South Carolina. They turned north at Saint Thomas and drove Route 177 to a marker four miles south of Mannion. An entry point to the territory was marked by benches and a small wooden sign that designated the Swamps as a game reserve and part of the North Carolina state hunting lands. Joseph and Sean missed the sign twice, turned back, and found it at the beginning of a double-track dirt road grown high with weeds. The car's headlights bounced through potholes and brown water that splashed along the doors and onto the windshield. On either side, the forest was impenetrable, thicker as they descended in a straight line, past branches that whipped across the hood of the car. Their destination was a pond a mile wide filled with lily pads and black cypress. It was deep into the territory, three miles from the benches and wooden sign.

Sean held the map, read the instructions, and described a clearing where walking paths fanned out in all directions. They would take the center path and walk three hundred yards from the clearing to the pond. That's where they'd sink the cargo trunk and float the body. They discussed their preference to drag Hermann and the trunk into the forest, but the brush was too thick, so they drove to the spot George had designated. Short of the clearing, a fallen pine across the road made them stop. The remainder of the road was filled with brush blown about by the storm.

Sean turned off the car, left the driver's seat, and opened a back door. He grabbed a leather handle and slid the trunk across the seat. Joseph gripped the handle on the opposite side of the box. With flashlights, they traveled three hundred yards in the darkness, stepping around fallen branches, tripping and falling, and breaking open the side of the cargo trunk when they dropped it over a downed tree.

When they arrived, a quarter-moon lit the pond. They could see a bank of mud at the edge of wide water that spread out like shining black oil under silhouettes of cypress. Sean and Joseph dropped the trunk. Ten yards along the bank, a hollow rotten tree had collapsed onto hard ground. It lay open among the weeds like a masonry pipe that had cracked down the center and fallen apart. In the moonlight, alligators had congregated near the tree. A large one had crawled into it, as if to claim territory. It faced them. Quiet and stationary, the reptile's eyes reflected the beams of the flashlights. It blinked, and the eyes went to black. They opened again, and lit up like tiny lamps within the head. Sean stood over the trunk, kept his beam on the alligator, and watched for movement. Joseph shined his flashlight on the cargo trunk and kicked in the side that had cracked. It opened up. Darla's white skin lit up in the beam. With a screwdriver, Joseph punched holes in the trunk's top and sides, until he developed a mist across his brow and sweat along the back of his shirt. With fifty holes in the box and the side caved in, he floated the trunk into the pond and pushed. It glided twenty feet across the water, rolled, and tilted, first on one side and then the other. Water rushed in through the openings. One end went down, and it sank until it stopped and bobbed up and down with a corner above the surface. When the water filled the air space, the box disappeared.

The men returned to the clearing, over the pine, and then to the car. Joseph opened the car's trunk and pulled out the body, which tumbled headfirst onto the ground. Sean turned Hermann over and splayed out his arms and legs. He checked the pockets. Credit cards, a driver's license, and slips of paper that could identify him—Sean removed them all and threw them into the trunk of the car. He felt each finger for a ring and ran his hand over the body's wrists and chest for bracelets and a necklace. He removed the belt, wrapped it in a coil, and threw it in with the other items. Joseph removed the shoes and socks and dumped them next to the belt.

They picked up Hermann and in single file, each with a section of the body over a shoulder, carried him to the pond. He was still dressed in the blue blazer with brass buttons that flickered in the moonlight. They entered the clearing and dropped the body. Hermann was face up in the mud, bait at the edge of the pond. Sean shined a flashlight on the hollow tree. The reptiles were gone, possibly in the water, attracted to the smell of Darla's body within the box. With Hermann at their feet, the men scanned their flashlights over the water. Nothing moved. Sean and Joseph dragged Hermann to the weeds where the alligators had congregated and rolled him into the open hollow log, his head flung back, mouth open, and teeth visible in the beam of Sean's flashlight. The big alligator would return to its place, tear him to pieces, and take the body parts into the water, where it would feed. Satisfied, Sean and Joseph backed away from the hollow tree and returned to the path that led to the car.

XXXVII

Mannion, North Carolina
Saint Thomas, South Carolina

The alligator had returned to claim its territory. It was next to its catch when two hunters discovered Hermann at approximately five thirty in the morning. "Luck" was how Jack Parsons described the encounter to the police in Saint Thomas's Hospital Emergency Room. Had they arrived any later, the body would have been gone, dismembered in the black water.

Jack and his father Roy had entered the Swamps on an unmarked road from the south and walked to the pond. They had moved along the tree line where hard ground gave their boots a purchase. Their destination was always the same: fields north of the pond where pheasant and grouse build nests and hatch eggs. Jack and Roy had planned to flush the flocks into the air as the sun rose and shoot six birds before the heat set in. Jack had a small flashlight attached to the side of his hunting cap that illuminated the water. They had walked along the edge of the pond and seen remnants of the cargo trunk in the water, ripped apart. A section of the trunk with a brass hinge had lodged within roots of a cypress tree. Jack's light caught the brass, and he stopped. On the surface of the pond, leather, cloth, and wood floated, as if a piece of furniture had exploded. The interior cloth of the cargo trunk had a striped pattern—Jack could see it on a large section that had come to rest on the mud.

Alligators swam among the debris. The reptiles' black bodies were an inch above the surface, like knotted floating wood but with legs and tails that propelled them through the water. It had been a frenzied attack. Some still tore at sections of the cargo trunk. Others snapped and fought over small pieces of pink meat. They twitched their tails and cruised through the pond, scooping up whatever they hadn't devoured at the beginning. In seconds, the creatures could be up the bank and at the men before they could take a step.

Jack and Roy backed away and walked north. They stopped when Jack's light lit up Hermann's white shirt at the hollow log. He was as Sean and Joseph had left him: head back, mouth open. Alligators had gathered on the grass. Some were small, not more than five or six feet, and at a distance from the body. The large one had returned. Its tail was to Hermann, and its head and jaws faced the lesser ones that slid within the grass and looked for an opening to grab an arm or foot. The big one opened its mouth. When it saw the beam of light, it turned at Jack and hissed. It made a quick move at the hunters and then turned back to ward off the other alligators impudent enough to attack.

Roy estimated the large alligator at fourteen feet from snout to tail and approximately eight hundred pounds. He opened his double-barrel shotgun, loaded two cartridges, and handed it forward to his son. Jack took aim and waited. The light on the side of his cap illuminated the reptile, which turned to face the hunters. He fired twice. Lead pellets split the alligator's head down the middle and tore out its eyes. The smaller lizards fled into the water and disappeared.

In the green tiled hallway of St. Thomas's Emergency Room, Jack and Roy sat on metal folding chairs and sipped coffee. An older police officer sat in between. He held a recorder in his hand and took Jack's statement. A younger man with a trainee badge sat across from the three men and wrote on a notepad. Jack and Roy explained that the body was near dead when they found him. Hermann didn't have any broken bones or bruises, not that they could find, and no bite marks from the alligators.

The police officers told them they had become witnesses; Roy was happy to oblige. He lived six miles to the north and had never left the territory. He raised five children on his own after his wife had died, and every one of them had moved away to find jobs. His eldest son Jack was a US Marine Corps firearms instructor at Parris Island and made regular visits to Mannion to prevent the older man from hunting alone. Everyone knew that people disappeared in the Swamps. Four miles deep in the forest, a snake bite, a heart attack, or a stroke would kill a man. Like carrion, his body would be picked apart and carried off by the wildlife. For years, Jack's brothers and sisters pleaded with their father not to hunt alone. Roy assured them he would do as they asked, but did as he pleased. So Jack drove north and hunted with his father on the weekends.

Jack had arrived the day before and stayed with his father in the family house, a wood-frame bungalow that hadn't received a coat of paint in thirty years. The police included the rural deposit address on the report, with a map Jack had drawn for the officers. He had arrived after the hurricane to check on his father and make sure the bungalow was still standing. Wind and water had ransacked the region. He had spent the day repairing the roof, patching a few windows, and reinforcing the main beams that had begun to sag. The two men went to bed early, rose before dawn Sunday morning, and packed boots, provisions, and shotguns into the pickup truck for the five-mile drive to the southern entry point on Route 177.

In the morning darkness, they had arrived at the unmarked road and drove until sticks and limbs blocked the path. Jack and his father had collected shotguns and knapsacks from the flatbed. They walked the rest of the way in the dark, detouring around broken trees and tramping through boggy soil that swallowed one of Jack's legs and oozed up over the top of the rubber boot.

With the alligator dead and its head split in half, Jack and Roy had pulled Hermann off the log and dragged him onto the grass. Jack explained to the officers that he moved his hands up the arms and legs and felt for puncture wounds, blood, and broken bones. The man had straight white teeth and gold fillings, thin blond hair, and features like smooth shale assembled as a face. The skin was tan and splotched where it had peeled, burned, and peeled again. His neck was thick. The fingernails were manicured. He wasn't from Mannion; most likely, he was from the South Carolina Sea Islands, Charleston, Bald Head Island, Wilmington, or places in between, all more than one hundred miles away in either direction, where dinner jackets are required and half of the fairways had a view of the water.

Jack had sat him upright at the pond. With the torso over his shoulder, he stood up and balanced a tall man, more than six feet. He adjusted the weight and moved forward over the downed limbs and through puddles of rainwater.

Roy had gathered the knapsacks and shotguns and followed. The two men walked back along the path to the truck, where Jack laid the man on a tarpaulin in the pickup's bed. He checked for signs of life and listened for a breath or a heartbeat he could not find.

In the hospital hallway, Roy tapped a pack of cigarettes. "God bless him," he said. "I saw one six years ago, mostly bones and clothes. It was farther in, on the other side of the pond. The alligators had ripped it apart. The face was gone, and there wasn't much left of the body. He could have been a hunter, but I never heard of anyone missing, not then. I reported it, but nothing happened. No posters, nothing from the local police." Jack shrugged. The officers nodded.

In the Swamps, Jack had inserted the key in the truck and started the engine. He maneuvered backward to a place in the road where he could turn around and then drove out of the forest and up an incline to the state road. The truck had pounded over potholes in the macadam. Roy watched from the rear window and saw the body flop around in the bed. The man moved, reached out an arm to the side of the truck, and slapped his hand down on the bed.

"He's alive," Roy had said and told Jack to stop.

The truck swerved across the midline, veered back into the southbound lane, and came to a skidding stop on the grass embankment.

Jack stepped out and walked to the side of the truck. Hermann lay on his back on the pickup's bed. He opened his eyes to the morning sky. Jack climbed into the flatbed, kneeled next to him, and turned on the light attached to his hunting cap. Hermann didn't blink. White pupils rolled back in his head, reappeared, suddenly still, and then moved again. The eyeballs were swollen, soft, and bulging. Etched lines covered the corneas and cut across the pupils. Roy watched through the back window of the cab.

"Who are you?" Jack had asked. "Tell me your name."

Hermann's mouth was open. He moved his lips. From his throat came a sound that gurgled up into his mouth. It became a moan and then trailed off into silence. Jack asked him again, and there was no response. Tears covered the white globes and spilled out over the skin. They tracked a path down the side of his face and dropped onto the chipped steel bed of the truck.

Jack slid a tarp under Hermann's head, flipped open his phone, and searched for a signal. He notified Saint Thomas's Hospital that he'd be in the Emergency Room in twenty minutes.

At 6:00 a.m. on Sunday, Jack and Roy had stood on the asphalt parking lot of the Emergency Room as nurses removed Hermann from the back of the truck, loaded him onto a stretcher, and wheeled him into the hospital. On the stretcher, Hermann was barely breathing. The medical staff hooked him up to an intravenous drip and injected a painkiller. They took his blood pressure and stuck nodes on his chest for an electrocardiogram. By the time Dr. Georgia Brownlee arrived in the room, Hermann had stopped breathing. They wheeled in a heart-lung machine and hooked him up. It whirred and beeped with each induced breath.

Dr. Brownlee examined the patient and then walked to the two police officers, seated in the hallway with Roy and Jack. She wore a white lab coat. Her short blond hair was secured with clips on the side of her head. She interrupted the interview and addressed the police. "Have you ever seen anything like this?"

Before they could answer, Jack spoke. "I've heard of it, but never seen it."

Dr. Brownlee addressed Jack. "What did you hear?"

"Pull back his eyelids. Look at the swelling and cuts."

"I already did."

"At the pond, I thought he was dead. When I tried to speak to him in the flatbed, he couldn't respond, not a word."

"Alcohol?" a police officer asked.

Jack shook his head. "He wasn't drunk."

"Heard about what?" Dr. Brownlee asked.

Jack scanned the faces. "It's a theory."

"What is it? I'm the treating physician."

"I've been in the corps since I was eighteen, ma'am; that's twenty-six years. We hear things—stuff that comes out over beer and pool tables. What you're looking at"—Jack pointed to the examination room where Hermann lay attached to machines—"that's rendition, but an extreme form of it."

"What are you talking about?"

"That man didn't know who he is or where he was. He was conscious but couldn't speak. He couldn't even form a sentence. He couldn't see. His eyes have been sliced up. Otherwise, he didn't have a mark on him. No head injury. No nothing. How does that happen? Why do that?"

"I've never seen it before."

"Neither have I, but I've heard about it. Some of the people in the Agency, I teach them marksmanship now and then. They've described it. I'm not saying they do it, but they've heard about it, maybe even seen the results. Interrogators use it when they want to leave a subject unable to function: no memory, eyesight, or speech. Then they turn him out into the streets. Even if he doesn't die, he's brain damaged and can't provide information. He can't say or do anything. His people either take care of him, or he dies in a ditch."

Dr. Brownlee motioned to Jack to come into the room where Hermann lay with tubes in his mouth and arms. The police officers followed. She leaned over Hermann and pulled back the lid of one eye. With an examination scope, she looked at Hermann's eyes and then swabbed the inside of the lower lid. She put the swab in a plastic bag and then into the pocket of her white coat.

"This is torture?"

"Yes, with a second step."

Dr. Brownlee gave Jack a confused look.

"When I spoke to him in the back of my truck, he couldn't respond. He couldn't tell me anything. He couldn't understand what I was saying. He's blind. He may not be able to hear. That's not water boarding; it's not pulling someone's fingernails out. It's not even electrocution with a car battery." Jack looked at Hermann's face. "Look at him. There are no marks on him. No one hit him, beat his head in, or burned him. But they dumped him in the Swamps where they knew he'd be eaten. They knew he was disabled."

"How would that happen?"

"Chemistry—brain damage by chemistry."

Dr. Brownlee opened the door and spoke to her assistant. She handed him the plastic bag with the cotton swab and told him it would go to the laboratory for testing. She instructed him to draw three test tubes of blood. "I'll give you the list for the lab in a moment."

She closed the door and turned to Jack. "He's an unusual ER patient; that's obvious. I'll look at the medical databases for these sorts of conditions, but if it's based on drugs used in military rendition, it won't be reported. Not in any literature I've ever seen. Whatever was put into him, I wouldn't even know what to call it. I wouldn't know what to ask our lab to test for."

Jack opened a drawer of the bedside table and took out a pen and pad of paper. He wrote on the pad and handed it to Dr. Brownlee. "Try that."

XXXVIII

Manhattan

Peyton took the regularly scheduled morning flight from New Hanover County Airport and arrived at LaGuardia at 8:45 a.m. By 9:30 a.m., she had crossed the Tri-Borough Bridge to Manhattan and directed the taxi to the Stewart & Stevens offices on Park Avenue. Twenty minutes later, she was in the elevator lobby on the quiet forty-fourth floor of the glass-and-steel tower. She pressed her palm and fingers against the electronic hand reader and waved an entry card across a scanner. Her name and digital image appeared on a screen, and she typed in a pass code. The door opened electronically with a thump.

She entered her office, a corner suite of glass, and greeted Ted Heilman, who stood at the side of her desk wearing a baseball cap and reviewing pages in an open folder. Three boxes of documents rested on the corner; they bore the word "Severington" in scrawled black marker. Ted looked up and smiled as she walked in.

"You ready to camp out?" he said. It was Ted-speak for what was ahead: hours of reading documents, drinking bad coffee, and making sense of a puzzle with missing pieces.

Peyton cast her briefcase on a couch. "Two and half boxes won't take long."

He looked up from the folder. "It's the missing documents I'm concerned about. Severington didn't have much, but I know how and why this was done. And we really need to talk about Arthur Konigsberg."

"What do you want to know?"

"Is he the partner who died?"

"Yes, a long time ago. It was sad. He was about to retire."

"Was he the suicide?"

"Yes."

"How did he die?"

Peyton paused and thought about the question. "Why?"

"I'm interested. Tell me what you know."

"My knowledge is secondhand, things people told me or I read in the newspaper. I was a junior partner when it happened."

"Give me some details."

"He was found at home. Death was ruled a suicide. No note. He injected himself with potassium ferro cyanide. It's a chemical people used to be able buy in retail stores for lots of applications, like developing photographs. No one can buy it now, because of the threat of terrorism. Apparently, Arthur dissolved it in a solution and injected it."

"How do you know all this?"

"George told me."

"What else did George tell you?"

"Are you cross-examining me?"

"I'm trying to figure something out."

"He told me the solution worked so quickly that death was instantaneous, as if the cyanide froze Arthur, with his eyes open and the needle still in his arm. I'd never heard of a life ending that way, so I remember it. No one understood why he did it."

"How did George know Arthur died with the needle in his arm and his eyes open?"

Peyton paused and thought about it. "I don't know, but there's probably a reasonable explanation."

"Like what?"

"Maybe he saw a police report."

"He wouldn't have access to that."

Peyton shook her head. "Maybe Mrs. Konigsberg told him."

"Was there a criminal investigation?"

"There could have been, but if there was, it was wrapped up quickly. The death was considered a suicide. That's what everyone at the memorial service thought."

"If Mrs. Konigsberg is still alive, I'd make an appointment for today. She may know things you'll want to find out before tomorrow. I'll bet she's rich, really rich, and she might have Arthur's missing files squirreled away."

"Rachael gave me the number yesterday." As she spoke, Peyton tapped on her phone and called up the phone number and address of Helen Konigsberg. She stood in front of the couch and watched Ted select documents out of the boxes. He placed them in the order in which he would show them to Peyton. The notion that Arthur's death was anything but self-inflicted was far-fetched. The case, if there was one, had been opened and closed quickly. He died without any suggestion of wrongdoing. In her memory, there was nothing with which to pursue an investigation, no fact, no accusation, just sadness and shock in the Stewart & Stevens offices and a grieving family. George was devastated, no different from anyone else. If she suspected something, wouldn't Mrs. Konigsberg have made an accusation or pushed the police to investigate? Ted pulled the selected documents and spoke.

"Let's start with the parties to the transaction. One thing we know is that Iberia sold the assets to another company named ECG, Ecuadoran Coffee Growers. Take a look at the letter from ECG's lawyer. It was in Severington's files." Ted handed Peyton a letter from a Columbia law firm based in Bogotá.

Peyton read the letter and held it up to Ted. "So call him."

Ted shook his head. "The law firm doesn't exist. We called and looked him up on the Internet. I had some Spanish-speaking associates in my office run searches on other databases that give us access to international tax filings, birth and death certificates, passport registrations, credit card use—that kind of thing. There is only one record. The law firm appears to have been established the same year as the transaction and dissolved six months later. It paid no taxes, just six months of rent and some telephone bills at the address on the letterhead. Otherwise, it never existed, not before, not after. And here's the real kicker…"

Peyton looked up from the letter.

"The lawyer who signed the letter—Señor Pavio Ignacitis—he died in 2000, two years before the transaction. Whoever created the temporary law firm used his name and identity as a transactional lawyer in Bogotá."

Peyton sat down on the couch.

Ted picked up some markers and walked to a white board in her office. "Unless we are completely wrong about that—and I doubt we're wrong—the law firm was created and dissolved in the same year to make the deal look legitimate to

Severington, the law firm in Bermuda and Jersey that represented Iberia in the transaction."

"Keep talking."

"Remember the schematic, the drawing of a triangle from Arthur's archives?" Ted drew a triangle on the board with a black marker. "It had words at each corner of the triangle."

Peyton nodded and watched.

"At the left corner were the words 'NGO/McPhee'—nongovernmental organization, right?" Ted drew the words in red.

"The NGO is Children's Bay Cay Foundation, located in the Bahamas. Think of the NGO as the broker of the deal. It received a big fee for this, which means McPhee received a fortune." He pulled a folder of documents out of a box and handed it to Peyton. "McPhee operates the foundation out of a post office box in Nassau. There is no record of the guy anywhere, except for records related to the foundation and an Irish passport issued in 2002, same year as the deal. We looked in every database we have—we scoured them—and we found evidence of only one grant given by the foundation: one million dollars every two years to an orphanage in Nassau. The grant is always named in honor of the prime minister of the Bahamas, whoever holds the office. It's been happening since 2002. Other than that grant, there's no activity at all and no information on McPhee anywhere."

In her hands, Peyton held a two-page document stating that Children's Bay Cay Foundation was a registered foundation under the laws of the Bahamas, with Tracy McPhee as the sole director. She looked up at the marker board.

"At the top of the triangle," said Ted, "are the words Bermuda Company, which has to mean Iberia." Ted wrote the words "Bermuda Co." at the top of the triangle in blue marker. "And at the lower right corner is ECG." Ted drew the remaining letters on the board in green.

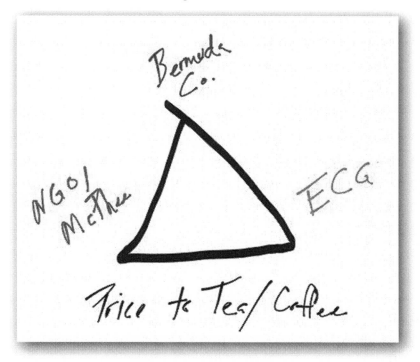

Ted handed Peyton a document the size of a telephone book. It was titled "Asset Purchase Agreement" and had forty tabs along the right-hand side. "You don't have to read it," said Ted. "I'll tell you what it says. This is the final transactional document. Look at the signature pages."

Peyton flipped to the last three pages, just in front of the tabs.

"You'll see that George and the Severington law firm signed it for Iberia. The deceased Señor Ignacitis rose up from the grave and signed it for ECG. So did McPhee. If you look at the first tab, you'll see schedule A, which lists all the same property you saw on the list from Bermuda and the handwritten list in Arthur Konigsberg's personal files. Actually, this is where things get weird."

She turned to the first tab and began at the top of the schedule. It was the clean typed schedule with all 340,000 acres. This time, each tract of land had dollar values. She let her finger slowly move down the page as Ted spoke, and she found the sum total: $250 million, the sales price.

"We checked the databases for the values of agricultural coffee property in that part of Ecuador for 2002. For some of it, the numbers are reasonable."

Ted took another document from the folder on the desk.

"Now, look at the handwritten list of property Rachael found in Arthur's archives." He handed Peyton a copy of the document she had reviewed in her apartment Thursday night; it was the three-page document from Arthur's files that had listed the property at wildly higher prices. In handwriting, the pages recorded the size and location of each piece of property; next to each entry was a dollar figure and the letters "I/A." The same letters appeared in uppercase at the top of each page. The numbers added up to nearly $1 billion.

Ted continued. "What's Arthur Konigsberg doing with a handwritten schedule of the same property priced at four times the sales price? And look at the handwriting. Compare it to Arthur's signature on the agreement. Arthur wrote that schedule. Why?"

He reached into the box and pulled out another thick document. "And what's Severington doing with a draft of the agreement that tracks the numbers on Arthur's handwritten document and states a billion-dollar sales price? Look at schedule A. The numbers are the same as the ones on Arthur's handwritten list."

Peyton looked at the draft and turned to the page with the sales price of $950 million. The number 9 had a line through it and was replaced in handwriting with the number 2. The word "wrong" was written on the margin. She turned to schedule A, the list of property. All three pages of the schedule had large handwritten lines through them from top to bottom. At the top of the first page, she read the word "No." Next to her on the couch was Arthur's handwritten document. The first entry was a notation for a large piece of agricultural property—fifteen thousand acres—on the border of Columbia and Ecuador. The number forty million and a dollar sign had been written to the right of the entry and, again, the letters "I/A." With the draft agreement on her lap, Peyton looked at the first entry of schedule A. It was the same property with the same value: $40 million. She picked up the final agreement and flipped to schedule A. Iberia was selling the same property for $9 million. Peyton looked up at Ted.

"Why would they sell all of this at a loss? What am I'm looking at?"

"I was wondering the same thing. Why do Arthur's handwritten notes list exponentially greater values for the land than in the actual agreement? And then someone marks and corrects a draft and reduces the purchase price. Why does this handwritten list exist in the first place?"

Ted handed her another folder. She opened it and found a 2002 appraisal written in Spanish that valued one tract of acreage in Ecuador at $7 million. "They had one appraisal for one piece of land," he said. "There are no other appraisals in the files."

Peyton thumbed through the appraisal. "So why do they need only one appraisal, and how does Arthur make such a mistake with the numbers?"

Ted went back to the marker board. "Remember the triangle and the notes Rachael found in Arthur's files." Ted wrote the words on the marker board: "Price to Tea/Coffee." He said, "I kept looking at Arthur's list and wondering about that sentence. There's no question that they valued the land at prices for tea and coffee growing property. But there's also no mistake on Arthur's list. Those aren't land values."

Peyton looked at the handwritten list again and compared it, side by side, to schedule A. She pulled in a breath, put her hand on her chest, and looked up at him. "It's revenue."

"Yes. I/A means Ingresos Anuales—annual revenue. It's the total amount of money they were making on the land every year. Nine hundred and fifty million dollars. Coffee doesn't generate revenue like that."

"Coca does."

"Maynard's unloading the land at appraisal prices for coffee-growing property; they only needed one appraisal for that. For twenty years they held it, owned it by title, and probably collected payoffs from ECG as an ownership front. That's how I read this. Arthur knew it; he helped create it. He had that revenue schedule in his files. My bet is he compiled it over time. Then he and George had a dispute—a bad one—over money. Arthur wanted a bigger buyout from ECG, say one year's annual revenue, but George said no, so Arthur showed him the annual revenue schedule as a threat. He demanded a higher payoff to get the deal done."

"And then he died."

"Hard to believe these people weren't involved in Arthur's death. That's how my monkey mind works. I'll lay down a bet right now."

"How could they have ever become involved in this?"

"Originally? Maynard was probably a legitimate purchaser. The company uses Iberia to buy agricultural land in Ecuador in the 1970s with the idea they'd flip it as coffee prices go up. They find themselves collecting rent from coffee growers who will pay twice, three, then ten times the price, because they're not growing coffee. The large growers don't want to buy out Maynard, because ownership by an absentee Bermuda company is a great cover—it makes it look like a European or American business owns the land, so it must be for coffee. George likes the money, looks the other way, and receives a revenue stream. Twenty-five years later, George realizes Maynard should get out, so he does a deal that makes it look like Iberia is selling coffee-growing property at the market price. Maynard reports the income and dissolves Iberia, and everyone forgets about it. That's the 'I got out, and I'm not really complicit' version; you know, something he'd say to his lawyers or to the US attorney to bargain for immunity."

"Do you think that's what happened?"

"No."

"What really happened?"

"George is smart and knows what he's doing. As Iberia starts to receive very high rents, he exploits that end of the business. Why? Because the 1970s and early 1980s are an economic disaster for real estate, and Maynard is teetering toward insolvency. The South American revenue saves the company when every other real estate concern is filing for bankruptcy. In light of the profits, Iberia takes title to more land in Ecuador, and the coca property blends in with legitimate coffee-growing property. That little offshore company becomes a profit center for Maynard, which turns into a national and then international conglomerate. Iberia fuels Maynard's expansion, but Maynard can't report the revenue. So George underreports the Iberia income to the IRS, funnels the excess money to other Maynard operations, and overreports revenue from other parts of Maynard's business, laundering the money through Maynard's shopping centers, office and apartment buildings. At the end of every tax year, all the revenue is accounted for, and Maynard pays its corporate taxes. And if he's laundering Maynard's Iberia revenue, he's probably laundering other money too, for whoever operates the coca business. He was treasurer and chief financial officer for thirty years. He could have done it. I think he did do it."

"And that's why Maynard has four billion dollars in cash in 2002?"

"Probably from offshore, and much more than that. With Nine Eleven and the Patriot Act, everyone gets nervous. George orchestrates the transaction with Arthur's help. They use Severington as the offshore lawyers, so all this stuff stays out of Bermuda and out of the Stewart and Stevens files. But it's Arthur's last gig and, of course, he's greedy. He blackmails George. To protect himself, he keeps personal files. The documents are nothing by themselves. But you line up the revenue schedule with the numbers in the agreement and then add in the location of the property, the deceased Señor Ignacitis, and the timing of it all, and you have an amazing scheme. It's better than Madoff, far smarter. They pulled it off for a long time, generated billions in cash for the company, wrapped it up, and retired. How Boyle ever learned about Iberia is your next big question."

Peyton was still on the couch. "I saw George last night at a wedding reception." Ted looked back at her in silence. "He lied to me; he said he couldn't recall the company."

Ted looked at the ceiling and hooted. "This was pure genius."

"But then I walked with him to the street, and he said something. He told me to get rid of it, in those words. 'Get rid of it,' he said. And then he warned me that if it stayed around, it wouldn't end well for anyone."

"Do you need more confirmation than that?"

"No." She pictured in her mind Robert Erwin. "He lied to me about something else too."

"How's George look?"

"Not well. He needs a knee replaced."

"He's really wealthy, isn't he?"

"Exceptionally. We thought he made a fortune on his stock options and invested well."

"He did." Ted laughed. Peyton didn't.

"How does the foundation fit into this?"

Ted went back to the diagram on the marker board. "Iberia got its two hundred and fifty-five million, and ECG made a donation to the Children's Bay Cay Foundation. The asset purchase agreement mentions the donation in a side agreement, so it's part of the deal. The value of the donation isn't mentioned, and the side agreement is not in the files. We don't know what the foundation received."

"Can you think of any legitimate reason for the donation— like a tax break, anything?"

Ted shrugged. "My best guess is that McPhee orchestrated the deal from the ECG side, and the donation was a payoff, an investment banker's fee, something like that, but it was never taxed, because it went to a foundation. If you find McPhee and put him on a witness stand, he'd have some explanation. But within the context of this deal, it was a personal payoff to get it done, bury it, and keep his mouth shut. That's what they paid him for."

"How does this affect what I'm doing tomorrow?"

Ted shook his head. "None of it's good. If I'm Boyle, I argue it's an ongoing crime. The four billion in cash came from Iberia, and everything flowed from that. Iberia affected every aspect of how Maynard did business and how it treated its stockholders. That's his best speech."

"But from what we know now, the property was sold, and Iberia was dissolved in 2002. Nothing proves otherwise. Fair statement?"

"Yes. I know what they did, but I can't prove it in a courtroom, not with what's here. If we can't prove it, then maybe Boyle can't prove it either."

"Unless there's something in the box."

Ted adjusted the cap on his head. "You'd think that if he had a weapon, he'd have used it on Friday."

Peyton scrolled on her handheld screen, found Rachael's e-mail from the day before, and dialed Helen Konigsberg. A woman answered the phone with a soft cadence that floated through the receiver; she informed Peyton she had reached the Konigsberg residence.

"This is Peyton Sorel, ma'am, calling for Helen Konigsberg. I'm a partner in the law firm of Stewart and Stevens, the firm where Arthur Konigsberg once worked. May I speak to Mrs. Konigsberg?"

The woman asked her to spell her name and then put her on hold. Peyton sat on the couch, one leg over the other, in pressed khaki pants and a powder-blue work shirt. The office faced west, and cool morning light filled the room. After sixty seconds, a voice scratched by years of nicotine spoke into the phone.

"Ms. Sorel, this is Helen Konigsberg. Can I help you?" The voice was weak and slow, but direct.

"Hello, Mrs. Konigsberg." Peyton spoke with a soothing sound. "Please forgive me for interrupting you. My firm is looking into a business deal from many years ago. Your husband provided legal advice about the transaction just before he died. We are looking for Mr. Konigsberg's archived files for the transaction, and we can't find them. We were wondering if he had brought files home. If so, perhaps some are from the transaction we are reviewing."

"Who do you work for?"

Peyton identified the firm a second time. She spoke slowly and told Mrs. Konigsberg that her husband Arthur had been a partner at Stewart & Stevens his entire career and possibly had kept files at home. There was silence on the phone, and Peyton heard the labored breathing of a habitual smoker.

Mrs. Konigsberg spoke. "You better come now. I haven't much time for this business, and I want to be rid of it."

"Thank you," said Peyton. "We'll be there. We understand how painful this—"

Helen interrupted. "I won't speak about these matters on the phone. Come today, but not after two o'clock."

"Thank you," said Peyton. "I'll be there right away."

"Eleven Fifty-Six Loch Haven Drive in Upper Saddle River. Ring at the gate; Maddie will let you in." Helen Konigsberg ended the call without saying good-bye.

Peyton looked up at Ted. "We need a driver to Upper Saddle River right now."

"That's Bergen County."

Peyton stood up from the couch and went to her desk. She moved the boxes and turned over paper and documents piled together across the surface. She found the envelope from the corporations bureau in Hamilton, Bermuda, with a postal stamp from Ramsey, New Jersey, in Bergen County. It was dated August 5, 2002.

"It came from Arthur," she said.

"Who else? He did the Bermuda filings for dissolution. He mailed it to the bureau so he could use it in the future. When did he die—the exact date?"

Peyton went on the computer and typed in Arthur's name and the word "obituary." She clicked on the news item from the Bergen County Record and found a black-and-white photo of Arthur Konigsberg, white hair, glasses, no smile, and the full column notice of his death.

She stared at the screen. "August 7, two days later."

XXXIX

Wrightsville Beach

Leandro held a hose at the docks of the Seapath Marina and sprayed away mud that had splashed along the sedan. He picked Hermann's cell phone out of his pocket, turned it on, looked for a message or missed calls, and found nothing. He turned off the phone and looked at Joseph and Sean asleep in the car, eyes closed, mouths open. He tapped on the window, and Sean moved.

"I have the boat," Leandro said.

Sean pressed a button on the door and opened the window. His eyes were slits in the sunlight, and his hair was a thatched mess. "Big?"

"Big enough."

Beyond the car was a series of floating docks in the inland waterway that formed slips for boats too large for a private dock. It was a small city of deep-sea fishing rigs, all with cabins, trolling polls, and observation platforms.

Leandro opened the trunk of the car, removed his briefcase, and walked to the docks. By the time he reached the *Starlight*, Sean and Joseph were sitting upright and sipping cups of coffee. They could hear the *Starlight*'s inboard diesel rumble along the docks and churn up water, a sign they had to move. When they stepped onto the stern, Leandro stood next to the pilot's chair with the open briefcase, which contained the Herstal, his laptop computer, and a stack of color satellite photos of the plantation with longitude and latitude marked on a grid across the images. He entered the coordinates for the southernmost levee into an onboard navigation system and patiently waited for the program to set the course. A thin yellow line appeared on the screen and traced a path along the inland waterway, through a shipping canal, and up the river. Sean walked into the cabin, sat in the pilot's chair, and watched Leandro complete the program. When the navigation path appeared on the screen, Leandro closed the briefcase and asked Sean to move the boat out of the slip. Joseph untied the bow and stern lines, and Sean guided the *Starlight* into the waterway. Telephone poles stuck deep in silt marked the boat channel south past Sutton Beach and adjacent estates that dominated the waterway for miles.

The tide was high and the water flat. The boat moved alone and wound like a snake through the islands that were covered in forest and moss, thick and green from the heavy rain and filled with birds perched on oaks and magnolias. Pelicans flew past the *Starlight*'s bow, skimmed their beaks on the water, and dove for fish.

Sean headed for the shipping canal, which cut through the barrier islands at Carolina Beach and the lower part of Cape Fear directly to the river. It had been built wide and deep for the container ships that approached from the north and provided a route to Wilmington that avoided Frying Pan Shoals and the extended trip south to Bald Head Island and the mouth of the river.

At the canal, the waterway opened up, and Sean pushed the throttle forward. The *Starlight* increased its speed gradually to twenty knots and turned west. Without a container ship in sight, the boat moved easily up the passage and emerged into the river, where it turned north to the faint sliver of Santee Island in the distance. Leandro told Sean to follow the navigation system. He climbed the ladder to the observation deck, where he braced himself against the aluminum bars and looked north through field glasses.

Winnabow's docking facility was at the end of Moore's Creek, a stream that ran into the river along the southern side of the plantation. Linus had widened and dredged the creek so that Moore's now resembled a half-moon cove one hundred yards wide and deep enough for large boats and small ships. The dock was formed of thick wooden beams on steel girders and pilings set into concrete deep in mud. It was sixty feet wide and stuck out into the river like a tongue. At shipping time, tractors, trucks, and cranes rolled from storage sheds onto the dock to load the bulk rice onto the transfer ships that would take it north to the Wilmington cargo terminal. A cantilevered crane painted dark green was at rest on the southern side of the dock, ready to swivel and transfer containers to the smaller ships that came to collect the rice in September.

The *Starlight* was one mile from Santee when a twenty-eight foot boat with a canopy and twin outboard engines moved out of Moore's and crossed the *Starlight*'s bow three hundred yards to the north. As it accelerated across the river, Leandro held up the field glasses and found the boat in the lenses. At first it was a blur, a powder-blue object moving quickly on the river. It came into focus as Leandro adjusted the lenses. When it was halfway across, Leandro read the name on the hull—*Broad*

Jumper—and saw two figures at the pilot's console. The boat's speed increased, turned south, and carved a path through the water on the eastern side of the river. Through the field glasses, Leandro followed the *Broad Jumper* to the mouth of the shipping canal until it became a speck in the distance, alone, heading for the inland waterway.

Sean moved to the western side of the river and stayed on course. The impoundments and levees first appeared half a mile south of Santee. Leandro kept his eyes on the levees as the *Starlight* passed the southern tip of the island and followed the yellow navigation path north to the longitude and latitude of the old impoundment. One-quarter mile later, the three translucent boxes were above the waterline, exactly where Hermann had said. Sean arrived at the broken wall in a slow crawl. From the observation deck, Leandro saw the problem.

"Pull closer," he called to Sean, who moved the boat alongside the impoundment and reduced the engine to an idle. The boat floated silently downriver, as Leandro looked through the field glasses. Sean throttled the engine forward past the impoundments, put it in idle, and let the boat float again on the current. The tops of the boxes had been removed and stood upright, wedged in the mud and weeds, now partly exposed by the receding water. Leandro left the platform and descended the ladder.

"I want you in the water." Leandro pointed to Joseph. "Swim in there. Tell me if anything's left."

As Leandro stepped onto the bow, Joseph looked at Sean, muttered under his breath, and shook his head. He took off his shirt and shoes and asked Sean to keep the boat as close to the impoundment as possible without striking the bottom. He dove off the stern and started swimming. When he reached the old impoundment, he stood in mud. Through waist-high water, he trudged to the boxes. He grabbed the first box and looked in. It was empty. At the bottom of the translucent box, he could see the outlines of crushed weeds and moving water. He walked to the other two boxes; both were empty. He looked at Leandro and howled the word "No."

XL
Winnabow Plantation

At Winnabow's main dock, Leandro pulled the Herstal from his briefcase and stuffed it in the back of his waistband. He was first off the stern and followed a roadbed of hard earth and crushed stone, which led into the forest and storage sheds at a four-acre clearing surrounded by pines and brush. The sheds were two stories of cinderblock, painted green, with peaked cedar roofs. There was a constant hum from a ventilation system that blew hot air from vents in the roof to remove moisture and heat and keep the temperature of the rice at its optimum level throughout the summer. Security cameras monitored the doors to each shed. Entry was through a keypad and alarm system. Leandro stopped at the edge of the clearing and waited for Joseph and Sean, who walked to him and stopped.

"Not here," he said. "The building is probably connected to the local police department."

They backed away, walked to the main road, and turned north. On both sides, the forest was thin for the first twenty feet off the road and then thickened with dense green brush, smaller young pines, and bushes that made it impenetrable.

The men headed east to the river and the levee near the old impoundments. The surface was damp, and ruts from a wheelbarrow were fresh in the soil. They stood on the levee and looked down at the empty boxes.

"He was here," said Leandro. "He took it out of here in wheelbarrows." He pointed to the ruts in the levees and told Sean and Joseph to find anything that looked like wheel tracks, red clay, or footprints, anything that showed recent travel along the main road or into the forest. "Follow the road south, and call me if you find anything."

Sean and Joseph walked out to the main road and along paths that took them south. Leandro turned north and looked at his feet. There were no impressions in the sand and grass. If a wheelbarrow had ever been there, the path had been swept clean. He turned the sandy soil over in his hands for the remnants of wet clay from the impoundments but found nothing. He turned west into the forest, where the paths branched out in forks and narrow trails. He walked as far as he could until the forest forced him back. He stopped and listened, surrounded by thick green walls of vines and brush. Heat built on his neck and scalp like a new rash.

Martel could be there, somewhere in the forest. If he'd emptied the boxes, he could be waiting for them to return to the boat. After risking so much, he wouldn't leave Amy behind. Leandro scanned the canopy above him for a figure hiding in the limbs and then below to the forest floor. He walked back to the main road, looked for movement among the limbs, and occasionally stepped through the brush and peeled back the vines on either side of the path. He found nothing and kept moving.

At the road, he walked north and found the hurricane house. The front door was unlocked. Inside were large white rooms, immaculately swept, with a few pieces of wooden furniture. The windows were open to the air, and a breeze blew across the kitchen. Leandro touched the cold stove. The refrigerator contained a bottle of wine, butter, and a carton of eggs. He walked through every room and opened empty closets and drawers. With his feet, he pressed the floorboards for an entry point below the house. He left by the front door and circled the house along the porch and again on the ground. There was nothing—no entry point below the floor and no track of a wheelbarrow.

Beyond the house to the west were mown fields, a fenced paddock for horses, and a barn with a tractor. Leandro walked to the barn and moved around the building to the back. Parked at the paddock was a blue Ford F-150, unlocked with the windows down. He reached in and pulled a map from the passenger seat; it bore a red line that traced I-40 from the Blue Ridge Mountains to Wilmington and across the river at the Memorial Bridge. In the well of the front passenger seat was a duffel bag. Leandro picked it up, unzipped it, and found clothes, a stack of money, and a loaded semiautomatic .45-caliber pistol. He zipped up the bag, removed it from the truck, and stuffed it into the crawl space under the barn.

Leandro pulled the Herstal from his waistband and tightened the suppressor. He entered the barn from the back and walked up an incline to a hallway of wooden planks built above ground. On either side were stalls. Five were empty and swept clean; the other three were filled with hay. He entered the three filled with hay, pushed away the mess with his feet, found nothing, and moved on to the closets, where he found saddles, boots, helmets, and bridles.

A hayloft was on the second floor with wrapped bales stacked in threes and arranged in rows. On the staircase, Leandro raised the Herstal and aimed it as he walked up to the bales. He stopped and listened and then mounted the last few steps to the loft in a crouch. He walked along the rows, alone except for two calico cats that lay on the bales and watched the deliberate search down one row and up the other.

Leandro descended the stairs, returned to the back of the barn, and circled west. He stood behind a tractor and looked south across the yellow grass to the forest that rose up at the edge of the fields. The grass was high and thick; it separated the paddock from the forest. He looked to the tree line for movement. He walked out to the front of the barn, paced, and waited. In plain sight, he returned to the main road and walked south until he came to a set of trees covered with kudzu, where he dropped to a crouch and disappeared. On his knees, he crawled through a path in the yellow grass marked by wild azaleas, found an open spot, sat, and listened. He heard nothing in the pasture around him. He removed small field glasses from his front pocket and, in a crouch, looked across the top of the grass to the tree line. He waited, flicked away flying insects, pinched flat those that dared to land, and focused on the forest, where all color and light merged into gray, brown, and green shapes among the trees. If Martel moved, Leandro would find him, and he did, after twenty minutes.

Martel walked out from behind a tree where the forest met the yellow grass. At first he was low to the ground; the only movement Leandro could see was within the leaves. When

Martel rose, his black hair formed a moving dot above the top of the grass. He came forward into the first ten feet of grass and retreated back into the forest. In the lenses, Leandro saw a shadow and then, in focus, a distinct figure in a dark shirt, moving, craning his head upward to see the main road.

At the edge of the forest, Martel climbed up a pine and looked out onto the field and then to the road. His whole body leaned from the tree to find a view. He descended, and Leandro's eyes followed him as he disappeared into the brush.

From his back pocket, Leandro pulled out his satellite phone and contacted Sean, who had walked south into the hunting lands, west of the storage building and dock, and beyond the borders of the plantation. He told him to turn back to the main road and walk without speaking along the river to the place where they had parted and then to the first path west that Leandro had followed. Martel was on the property, he explained, and was moving through the forest, looking for them but keeping some distance.

Leandro turned off the phone, crawled out to the road, and started running south with his head low, below the top of the grass. He passed the crushed house and, two hundred yards later, found the path he had inspected first. He turned west, ran for another quarter mile, and stopped. He stepped into a thicket on the right side of the path, lay flat on his stomach on the forest floor, and listened. His pulse throbbed. From the main road, the path was straight west and then turned, where it branched into hunting trails. Lying in the brush, Leandro felt for the Herstal in the back of his waistband. It was gone. He looked back along the path and saw it, a black object on white sand sixty feet away. Along the path, there was an uninterrupted view for four hundred yards to the impoundments. If Martel came out of the forest, he would have a view to the river and the black object lying in the sand. Leandro listened for sounds in the forest, and they came as soft footfalls on sticks and leaves. He raised his head and looked through the field glasses.

Fifty yards away, Martel walked among the trees and stepped over a trunk and around a mass of limbs and vines that had come down with the hurricane and made travel outside of the paths slow. He stepped to the edge of the forest from behind a tree and looked east. He took one step onto the path, over branches and brush that gave way under his shoes, and he leaned forward for a better view. Leandro saw his head enter into sunlight. Martel barely breathed. He stood and listened.

Martel had grown. He was bigger and healthy, now deep in his twenties, with an extra forty pounds, but the same young man from the stern of the fishing boat with a mop of hair, Mayan cheekbones, and black eyes. He moved onto the path and had a full view of the impoundments. In the middle of the path, he looked at the river and then crossed into the trees on the other side. He walked east inside the tree line, fifty yards to Leandro, who lay in deep grass on the other side. Martel stopped, leaned out into the path, and then returned to the tree line, where he stepped through the brush.

Thirty yards closer, he came out and walked at the edge of the forest, his eyes straight ahead. The morning sun rose in front of him, and he shaded his eyes with his hand. He passed Leandro.

When he was twenty feet farther, Martel stopped and saw the Herstal. It was ahead of him, the black shape unmistakable on the ground. Martel looked behind him and then into the trees. When he looked at the Herstal again, Leandro rose and ran. He came from the other side of the path and kept his eyes on Martel's hands and waistband for a weapon, intent on hitting him, knocking him to the ground, and disabling him at once. Martel heard the sound behind him and turned away from the oncoming rush. He drew the fish knife from a pocket, faced Leandro, and swung it in a short arc. The blade missed Leandro's raised hand but hit the front of his shirt. Leandro felt the blade graze his collarbone. He spoke in Spanish and told Martel that Hermann was dead, and the boxes were empty. He tried to distract him by asking questions about where he had put Amy and made an offer to pay him more if he handed over the shipment.

In a flat expression, Martel's eyes stayed on Leandro. Blood spread across the older man's shirt. He threatened with the knife, moved it in and out in thrusts to the sides and midsection to catch flesh again, and then drew back as Leandro parried with his hands. He came close to Martel's eyes with erect fingers to gouge and disable.

Martel stepped back, relaxed, and circled to the right. He shifted the knife to his left hand, parried twice, shifted it back to his right, and stepped forward. He lunged with an overhand thrust aimed at Leandro's neck and face, hoping to make contact. It was an amateur's mistake, too eager from early success. Leandro saw it coming and moved in the direction of the swing; he rolled under it in a crouch. The blade missed him by an inch. He came up on Martel's right shoulder, grabbed the right wrist, and brought his left forearm around Martel's neck. He rammed his left knee into the smaller man's back, pulled upward, and picked him up off the ground. He twisted Martel's wrist backward, and the forearm followed. With a dull snap, Leandro dislocated the ulna at the elbow. The fish knife dropped, and he heaved Martel onto the sand.

Martel was unable to breathe. He lay flat and still as Leandro picked up the fish knife, stood over him, and pushed his left knee onto the man's chest. He placed his right knee on Martel's left arm and wrapped his hand around his neck. With the fish knife, he stabbed the neck, just enough to bring blood onto the blade. Martel's dislocated right arm lay helpless on the ground.

"Where is it?" Leandro asked.

Martel looked up without a flicker of light in the iris. "I don't know." He choked in the grip.

Leandro pushed the knife and drew more blood. "If this goes in, it hits the artery. Where is it?"

"I don't know."

"Where did you take it?"

"I'm the same as you; I'm looking for it. Some boys took it."

Leandro leaned over him and blocked the sun. He eased his knee up from Martel's chest, enough to allow him to breathe, and pulled the knife from the neck. The blood from Leandro's chest dripped onto Martel. Leandro kept his hand clamped around the younger man's throat and looked into his eyes, dark and solid, to find something that would betray a lie.

Leandro took a deep breath, and Martel felt the opening. He slid his left arm under the knee and threw sand in a fistful he had gripped when he landed. The older man was in darkness, and Martel twisted to the right to throw Leandro off. As the knife came down, Martel raised his left hand and caught Leandro's wrist; he held it firm, far above his own chest. He tried to raise his right arm off the ground to reach for Leandro's eyes, but it was immobilized, the ulna out of the socket.

Leandro compressed his grip on Martel's throat, kept his balance, and pressed his knee onto the chest. He pushed his right hand downward, moving by centimeters as Martel's one good arm pushed up.

Martel spit at him. He could barely breathe. The weight of the larger man pushed down, and Martel's grip collapsed. Leandro bypassed the front of his chest for the side. In one quick movement, he flicked the tip of the blade along the second and third ribs and jammed it hard into the chest cavity up to the hilt. The blade hit the heart, and the blood began to drain. Martel's hand fell away. When he stopped breathing, his black eyes were open, indifferent, the same as they had been that first day on Arnold's boat.

Sean and Joseph were one hundred yards away and running. Leandro sat on the sand with his head down. When they arrived, he stood up. Blood covered his chest. He told them to search the pockets, take everything, and bury Martel deep in the forest where he would never be found.

"Drag him into the trees," Leandro said, wiping blood onto his pants. "Dig a hole. He was never here."

In Martel's pockets, Sean found money wrapped in a rubber band, unrolled it, and formed it in the shape of a Japanese fan: all dollars, hundreds, twenties, and ones. He handed the money to Leandro, who wrapped it up and put it in his pocket. The remaining contents of Martel's pockets were a false driver's license, loose coins, miscellaneous papers with indecipherable writing, and keys to the F-150 pickup behind the barn. Sean showed them to Leandro, who picked up the keys and turned them over in his hand.

Sean handed Leandro the Herstal, which he had picked up on the path. Leandro put the weapon back in his waistband and walked to the dock.

Sean and Joseph picked up Martel and carried him into the forest. They dug a shallow grave with their hands, rolled him in, and covered him with sand, leaves, and fallen limbs.

When they came back onto the path, Leandro was out of view, far ahead on the main road, walking to the dock, where he would wash his face and hands in water and clean the fish knife. He picked the satellite phone out of his pocket and made a call. At Highland House, the phone rang until Luisa picked it up. She announced in her efficient sing-song Portuguese that the caller had reached Mr. George's home and that she was available to help.

"Mr. Harwood, please. Wake him if necessary."

George Harwood sat at the kitchen table, his right leg wrapped in the brace. He received the phone, said hello, and asked Luisa to leave him, his hand positioned over the receiver.

Leandro was direct. "You know the people who own the rice plantation, don't you?"

George was silent.

"You know them," Leandro repeated.

"And if I do?"

"They have what I came for. It's here."

"If they have what you came for, you've lost it. The owner of that land is a federal judge. The woman you met last night is his daughter. If they have your shipment, the police will be there in minutes. Get out of there. There's nothing more to do."

Leandro stood on the dock and watched the river. "Listen to me carefully. Hermann Locke dropped thousands of pounds of our best product in a rice field. It was in three plastic containers. They are now empty. Just before we arrived, a boat named *Broad Jumper* came out of the dock and crossed the river. There were two figures in it. I found the thief on the property, and he told me he was looking for the missing shipment, just like I am. You know what he said?"

"No?"

"That two boys had taken it."

"You believed him?"

Leandro ignored the derision. "Who are they?"

"The judge's grandsons. They didn't remove more than a ton of cocaine from boxes sunk in rice fields. Your thief lied to you. Ask him again. Be persuasive this time."

George's contempt focused him. "The shipment is still on this property, whether or not Martel removed it. I know it's here. I want to talk to those boys, and I want them now."

"You don't need them."

"I want someone who knows this property."

George closed his eyes and rested his forehead in his hand. He imagined himself on the third floor with the spiral staircase and brass rail winding below around the elevator. It was high; the view was dizzying. Luisa would explain that he was infirm and had missed his grip on the railing, which was low and designed generations ago for shorter people. He was nearly eighty, lost his balance frequently, and suffered from a leg condition. He dragged it behind and caught it on the edges of steps and carpets, which made him pitch forward. He'd fallen in the past, sometimes badly, but this one would be the last. He'd hit the first floor, and that would be the end. Leandro would have no recourse, no one to talk to, no place to stay as Highland House turned into a funerary spectacle. He would fly home and write off the losses.

"I won't let you near them," George said.

Laughter rose in Leandro's throat. "This is simple. I have one day left, possibly less. I will leave here with as many packages as I can locate. If you don't bring me the boys, I'll find them myself. And when I leave, I'll take them with me. At five thousand feet, I'll drop them in the sea. Now, tell me you understand."

"I understand."

"Let's start this again. The packages are on this property. What are you going to do about that?"

"Come to Highland House," said George. "We'll discuss it."

XLI
Wilmington, North Carolina

Sandhurst walked into a pharmacy on the corner of Front and Market Streets, where he bought a cup of inexpensive coffee. When he walked back out, he stood on the street corner, and his mobile phone rang. He juggled the cup, and hot liquid spilled onto his hand. He opened the phone with a shout and saw a text message. By code, it directed him to his section of an FBI website. He walked two blocks south to the river, almost a mile wide at Memorial Bridge, and turned down a small cobblestone alley to Margaret's Bookstore, which offered better coffee, wireless Internet, and terminals. Sandhurst dumped the old cup in a trash can and bought a large coffee with hot milk—no latte or cappuccino, just "coffee with hot milk"—which is what Margaret sold.

At a terminal in a semiprivate carrel, he logged onto the FBI's encrypted website for remote transmissions to field agents. He entered his password-protected folder and called up the results of the satellite phone search. According to the file, the Venezuelan had called two onshore numbers Friday evening at 4:04 p.m. and 4:08 p.m. respectively. The first call came approximately forty miles south of Frying Pan Tower to a line at the

Sutton Beach Golf Club. He clicked on the word "detail" and found the specifics of the call. It had been transmitted from a location thirty-eight and two-tenths of a mile southeast of the tower to the phone line at the men's bar. It had lasted sixty-five seconds. The second call came from approximately the same location to a mobile phone registered to Sutton Beach. It lasted five seconds. He scrolled deeper into the file and found a list of Sutton Beach employees who had club-issued mobile phones. One was Hermann Locke; the others were women. Hermann's address was listed as 323 Miller Street, ten blocks away.

Sandhurst walked out of Margaret's to Market Street, uphill and away from the river, turned left on Eighth Street, and walked two miles to the cemetery. The house on Miller Street had a well-kept lawn, some rose bushes, and two small outbuildings: a one-car garage and a work shed. The house was built two feet above the ground on cinderblocks with brick facing. It had a modest covered porch with a swing. Live oaks framed the house on either side with enough shade to keep the sun off the front yard in the later hours of the day. Weeds had grown up in the flowerbeds. The front door was open behind an aluminum screen door.

He walked up the concrete path to the steps, stopped, and adjusted a standard-issue .45-caliber automatic in a holster strapped on the back of his belt. He flicked the safety latch to the off position, flattened his jacket, and walked onto the porch. Agnes Pembroke was on the other side of the screen door. She stood in the middle of piles of books, broken lamps, ripped curtains, and wood. She spoke with two City of Wilmington police detectives.

"FBI," Sandhurst said from the porch. "It's Bob, Agnes, Bob Sandhurst."

He showed his hands, palms up, with his FBI identification in his right. The detectives looked through the screen and then to Agnes.

Agnes waved Sandhurst into the house. "We have a person of interest, Bob."

Sandhurst opened the screen door and stepped over a couch that was flipped on its side; the springs and stuffing had been torn out and strewn on the floor. Chairs had been turned over, cut open, and searched. DVD cases and paperback books were on the floor in piles. A small brick patio on the other side of two sliding glass doors had been pulled up; every brick had been thrown onto the lawn and the underlying sand probed and poked with a shovel that lay across the pile of discarded bricks. Sandhurst was silent as he looked around the room.

"Every room looks like this," a detective said in response, waving his arm in a semicircle. Agnes introduced Sandhurst to the detectives and suggested that they search the garage and outbuildings while she explained the evidence so far. The detectives left by the back door and headed to the garage. Agnes handed Sandhurst a folder. As he opened it, she explained.

"This came into every police department in the region this morning by fax and e-mail. When he arrived in the emergency room, he was little better than how you see him in the photos. He's dead now. Two hunters found him in the Swamps near the South Carolina border. He was miles in, lying by a pond and barely alive. No entry or exit wounds, except for a shallow slice in his back from a knife wound someone had stitched up. The hunters thought he was dead, but he was alive enough to open his eyes. According to the police reports, he was seconds from becoming alligator meat."

Sandhurst looked through medical photographs of Hermann Locke taken at Saint Thomas's Hospital. In the first ones, his eyes were closed and skin pale. Some of the photos were images of Hermann's eyes with the lids pried open that showed the clouded irises and swollen corneas with slices and divots. Sandhurst recoiled and whistled. He looked at Agnes for an explanation.

"He was left for dead, Bob, in a blazer and pressed pants, no shoes or identification. According to the people who found him, he couldn't speak, even say his name. He couldn't see—his eyes, you can see what they look like."

Sandhurst flipped through the medical reports. "Any drugs or alcohol?"

"They tested him: negative for barbiturates and recreational drugs, positive for alcohol, but very minor—trace amounts, like he'd had a few beers. So they tested him for something else." She handed him a laboratory chart that showed the results of blood tests. At the bottom in handwriting was a description of the results. "It's called hypoprofen," she said. "Have you heard of it?"

Sandhurst shook his head. The handwritten notes of the treating physician were a one-paragraph diagnosis, barely legible in a scrawl that required Sandhurst to guess at letters and words. He recited what he read: "Patient presents as aphasic—trouble speaking—no comprehension or comprehensible speech. Very low heart rate, blood pressure. Severe respiratory depression. Low oxygen levels. Positive blood test for rare combination of benzodiazepine-based hallucinogenic compound that results in arterial atrophy in frontal cortex and reduced blood flow. Result from MRI shows extreme atrophy and multiple lesions, one hundred or more. Eyes severely damaged from external application of low-force trauma by cuts and abrasions and introduction of pharmaceutical that eroded, weakened, and permanently clouded cornea—most likely excessive and repeated doses of oxybuprocaine over many hours."

He looked at Agnes. "Are you telling me this came out of Saint Thomas' Hospital ER?"

"I'd like to meet the doc," Agnes said. "She worked it up in less than an hour."

"How'd she know to test for this—this benzodiazepine-based hallucinogenic compound?"

"I don't know. It's not in the file. I've never heard of it." Agnes handed him a second folder. "After the test for hypoprofen, they did a brain scan. Take a look."

Sandhurst opened the folder to a set of full-color MRI scans of Hermann's brain, all in perfect color and three dimensions, modulated in shadow and light.

Agnes pointed to the lesions. "They're specks throughout the frontal lobe, scattered randomly, where speech and memory occur. And they're in the area that controls the diaphragm. According to the doc, the normal result is asphyxiation. He was alive when he came into the ER, but he died soon after. Stopped breathing."

Sandhurst looked at seven printed color photographs from the brain scan. They were vivid and showed gray-and-black spotting throughout the frontal cortex. "Was there any penetration of the skull?"

"No."

"So it's a chemical lobotomy?"

"Yes. The body's still at New Hanover General. There'll be a forensic autopsy later today. Whoever did this must have a medical background. I've never seen anything like it. Have you?"

Sandhurst surveyed the room. Every framed picture had been removed from the walls and lay on the floor among shattered glass. Holes had been cut in the drywall, which was ripped out so the wooden studs and brick were exposed. "No," Sandhurst said quietly, mostly to himself. "He's not medical."

On the desk in the living room were loose wires and cables and an empty computer mouse pad. The computer was gone. Sandhurst looked back at Agnes. "When Hermann came into the emergency room, did he have anything with him, any personal property, identification, wallet, cell phone?"

She shook her head. "Nothing but his pants, a shirt, and a jacket. He was unidentifiable when the hunters found him. We recognized him from the photograph the local police circulated."

Sandhurst handed Agnes the file. "Whoever did this might have his phone, and he thinks Hermann has disappeared. If he uses it or searches for information on it, we can find him. The man we're looking for..." He tapped on the files. "He's an interrogator."

Agnes straightened her back. "Bob, how did you know to come to this house?"

"Hermann's our guy, Agnes. The dead Venezuelan called two numbers the day of the hurricane. One was the phone at the bar in the men's locker room at Sutton Beach. The other was a cell phone assigned to an unidentified Sutton Beach employee. Three employees have assigned cell phones. Two are women; Hermann's the third. With what we have so far, we'll trace that phone and get real-time transmissions—if they ever turn it on."

She pulled her phone out of her pocket. "The judge will see us now."

Sandhurst waved her off. "I expanded the warrant on my own. We're tracking Hermann's phone right now. If it lights up, we'll get the hit."

Agnes put her phone away. "Bob, you could at least have the decency not to tell me that."

Sandhurst shrugged. "It's the Patriot Act at work. I need results. Waiting for that judge means the case goes cold. The best chance we have is right now."

Agnes put the medical folder in her briefcase. "I never heard this," she muttered to herself.

Sandhurst walked out onto what remained of the patio. Across the backyard, the Wilmington detectives had opened the doors of the shed and were pulling equipment out onto the lawn. They rolled out a lawnmower, grass catcher, and weed whacker and dumped a wheelbarrow filled with rags and cans of turpentine, motor oil, paints, solvents, and brushes. They wheeled out through the double doors of the shed an old 1959 Chevrolet Corvette, opened the trunk and hood, and inspected every compartment. They dismantled the interior of the garage and produced the sounds of cracking wood and prying hammers. Neighbors gathered on the sidewalk to watch the detectives pull out boards, nails, and lawn equipment and lay them on the grass. At the back of the garage, they found an empty paint can. Wedged in the bottom was an empty paper sack of White Knight Flour. The detectives laid it on the hood of the Corvette. One detective cut open the white-and-cherry-red paper with a pocketknife and scraped deposits of powder onto the blade. He wiped the blade on the inside of a plastic bag, which he marked with a pen. The other took photographs of the evidence.

Sandhurst joined the two men and toured the property. They moved through the garage and shed, ripped out drywall, and threw it on the back lawn. They looked for false walls and hidden interior spaces in the outbuilding: the perfect places to hide kilogram packages of cocaine until Hermann was ready to move them. They sifted through storage bins and trashcans. They stamped around the backyard and looked for loose sod or signs of a freshly dug hole. They turned over every flagstone that led from the shed to the garden and thoroughly checked for turned soil and something buried.

Agnes called Judge Sorel. At 10:00 a.m., on his back porch at Wrightsville Beach, Edmund rocked in a wicker chair, sipped tea, and listened to Agnes. In the distance, the two boys stood at the end of the dock at high tide loading the *Broad Jumper* with bait, lunch provisions purchased at Robert's Grocery on Lumina Avenue, and a large cooler for fish and crabs. Ben and Frank stepped in and out of the stern and arranged rods and reels on the racks under the gunwales and a long pole with a hook for pulling up crab pots in the marshes. Edmund patiently listened.

"Your Honor, there are emergency circumstances to expand the warrant. They involve murder. The victim is Hermann Locke. It looks like he's involved in the transportation of cocaine, amphetamines, stuff like that. We were hoping you're available now—today—to expand the warrant."

He cut her off. "What happened to Hermann?"

"He was found in the Swamps on the South Carolina border, left for dead. He was blind and brain damaged when hunters brought him to a local hospital. He died earlier this morning. The treating physicians say he was tortured and injected with chemicals that cause brain damage and death."

"How is he connected to the warrant?"

"The dead man on Masonboro called him twice Friday night. I'm standing in Hermann's house right now. It's been torn apart—not by us."

The judge considered the answers. "What kind of expansion are you looking for?"

"We want to track and tap Hermann's cell phone—it's missing. Someone might have it. If they turn it on, we'll find them. We also want to track and tap anyone who communicated with Hermann in the last forty-eight hours."

"Meet me at the courthouse," Edmund said. "Twenty minutes."

Edmund stood up from his chair and stepped onto the dock. His knees creaked and popped as he walked forward. He wore the same khaki pants from three days before with flecks of paint and a long-sleeve cotton polo shirt to protect his arms from the sun. A breeze blew through his hair, and gulls hovered above.

"Ben," Edmund called to the older boy as he reached the end of the dock. "I'm headed out for a while to the courthouse. I may stay in chambers for the day to get some things done, so you may not find me when you come back. If you need me"— Edmund waved his mobile phone in the air—"it's charged."

Edmund turned back, and the boys watched him maneuver up the stairs onto the porch and disappear into the house.

At Miller Street, Agnes wound her way through the bungalow, entered rooms, and opened closets. She stopped in the doorway of Hermann's bedroom. The bed was in place, but the mattress had been cut down the middle. Padding and springs were around the room. All the drywall had been ripped out and lay in piles. Ductwork had been pried loose and pulled out of the ceiling. Broken drawers were on the floor. Sliding doors to the closet had been torn off.

Agnes stepped over the piles to the far side of the bedroom and an empty chest of drawers. A half-length mirror in a large wooden frame sat on a chest and listed precariously to one side, on the verge of collapse. Agnes held the frame in both hands and gently tugged at it to encourage the chest in its final movement to the floor. The mitered joints buckled, the chest collapsed, and the mirror fell forward. Agnes lost her grip on the mirror, backed away, and fell over the corner of the bed and onto the carpet. The mirror fell forward and shattered on the floor. The wooden frame splintered at her feet, and shards of glass flew into her face.

At the back of the broken mirror, two sacks of White Knight Flour were pressed flat, wedged between the mirror and frame. Agnes sat on the floor and removed pieces of glass from her hair and clothing.

From the backyard, Sandhurst called out, asked her what the noise was, and walked into the house. In the bedroom, Agnes sat on the floor and slipped the sacks of White Knight Flour into plastic evidence bags. She looked up when he entered the room.

"This is what we're looking for, Bob. Whoever tore this place apart wanted these."

Sandhurst picked up one of the bags and examined the packaging. He held up his phone and showed her a text message from the FBI tracking station. "Hermann Locke's phone lit up for fourteen seconds at 6:08 a.m. at the Seapath Marina."

XLII

Upper Saddle River, New Jersey

In mid-August, Upper Saddle River, New Jersey, was abandoned. The roads were empty, except for polished blue flatbed trucks that transported lawn and garden equipment from one estate to another to keep them pruned, mowed, and blooming through September when the owners returned from summer travels. The German sedans had been tucked away side by side with collectible sports cars in immaculate temperature-controlled garages to keep the paint and leather in perfect condition. The houses were set back on large tracts among trees, far from the roads and locked gates; neither Peyton nor Ted could see the buildings connected with the addresses.

When their car turned onto the private road to Mrs. Konigsberg's estate, it entered a half-mile approach bordered on either side by sycamore trees that reached up one hundred and twenty feet. They covered the road like the ceiling of a cathedral. Rain had come the night before and fell in a mist that cleaned dust off the windshield.

Peyton stepped out of the car in front of Helen Konigsberg's estate and looked up the driveway to the distant portico of a mansion built of gray and copper-colored stone from eastern Pennsylvania quarries. Black steel gates were attached to two stone columns twelve feet high. From the columns, an eight-foot spiked fence ran the length of the private road and surrounded the property. The letter "K" in sculpted bronze was in the center of the gates.

Peyton pressed an intercom button on a column and waited. Maddie, Helen Konigsberg's maid, answered professionally and exchanged a pleasantry with Peyton. The two gates swung open to let the car roll onto the grounds and up the driveway.

Under the shade of the portico, the driver stopped. Peyton and Ted left the car and walked up the stone steps. Peyton pressed the lighted button of the doorbell, and they waited until Maddie opened the door and welcomed them into the house.

The home had forty rooms. Every doorway was arched to a stone gothic peak, and the doors themselves were carved mahogany three inches thick. The entry hall was two stories high. Stone covered the first ten feet of the walls, and then cream-colored plaster flowed up to ribbed vaulted arches in the ceiling above. A medieval French tapestry of a boar hunt hung on the wall just above the stone. It depicted the moment when dogs had cornered the wild pig in a clearing, and men on horseback with spears descended to complete the hunt. On the other side of the hallway, a large painting in oil eight feet long and five feet high hung on the wall. It was an English landscape of a wooden waterwheel at a stream, a copse of large trees, farm animals, and billowing clouds against a blue sky. The frame was ornately carved wood covered in gold leaf. An oval set into the base bore the painter's name in script: "Thos.

Gainsborough." Peyton looked at the painting and then to
Ted, who stared at the ceiling, his mouth slightly open.

Maddie asked for their business cards and collected them.
"I will find Madame," she said with a bow. Peyton and Ted
thanked her, and she turned down the hallway to a back room.

"I don't know anything about tapestries," Peyton said as she
looked at the boar hunt and then to the Gainsborough, "but
that painting, at auction—it could be worth as much as some
of the homes around here."

"Not this one."

"No," said Peyton. "Not this one."

Ted looked at the landscape. He shook his head and remained silent. Peyton walked along the central hallway and
peered into adjacent rooms. They were filled with paintings.
Not one was less than a testament to perfect taste, as if Arthur
had engaged an expert in western European painting for an
extended spending spree at Sotheby's under a directive to buy
only the best work of the last four hundred years and nothing
painted after 1914. The paintings were by Monet and Seurat.
She had drawings by Raphael and portraits by Whistler and
Sargent. Whoever had accumulated Helen Konigsberg's collection knew the work well—only the best would do—and had
amassed a fortune in paintings alone.

Ted and Peyton were interrupted by the sounds of an
elevator and then the electric motor of a wheelchair. Helen
Konigsberg rolled into the hall through the double doors of
a library.

"The lawyers, I presume?" The words spilled out of
Madame's mouth like pits of cherries deposited onto a napkin. She had the raspy voice of a woman who suffered from

emphysema and exhaustion. Her face was lined by years of tobacco use. Her hair was frosted white, swept back, and held in place by spray fixative. Attached to the wheelchair was a small tank of compressed oxygen. A light plastic tube traveled from the tank to a mask she held in her right hand and every so often brought up to her mouth and nose. She wore a bright-white shirt clipped at the neck with a gold pin and had a light blanket over her legs. She moved her left hand in the air to punctuate her words, which she spoke with an English accent that faded in and out.

"Please," she said without a smile, "you're Miss Sorel, aren't you?" She held Peyton's business card up to the light and read it through half glasses attached to a gold chain around her neck.

Peyton could not place her accent but suspected Connecticut, a Swiss boarding school, and European cousins. She held out her hand, and Madame locked her eyes on Peyton's face. She dropped the glasses to her chest and shook Peyton's right hand with part of her left. Peyton could feel the cold flesh.

"Yes. Peyton Sorel, Madame." Peyton explained the nature of the visit, introduced Ted, and reminded Madame Konigsberg of the telephone conversation earlier in the morning. Her purpose was the files the late Mr. Konigsberg may have brought home. She flattered him and described him as a brilliant partner who had worked on a myriad of transactions others could not do as well. Helen's face never changed.

"I'm dying, Ms. Sorel, but I'm not stupid. I know a lawyer's answer when I hear one. Be specific. Why do you want his old files? Your answer will be important."

Peyton was surprised by the question. The files belonged to Maynard and Stewart & Stevens, not Arthur Konigsberg and certainly not Helen. Whatever files Arthur had, he'd taken them without authorization years ago. Now he was dead, and dead people owned nothing. His widow had no right to files related to Iberia.

"Some ancient transactions, ma'am. Buying and selling assets, that sort of thing." Peyton shrugged as if it were nothing. "The company doesn't have any records of what it bought and sold a long time ago and the prices paid and received. We thought the files Mr. Konigsberg had brought home might shed some light on that. He worked on many transactions for the company."

"That could not have waited until Monday?" Helen watched Peyton's eyes.

Peyton opened her palms and held out her hands. "We're in the middle of a trial, which compresses everything into a short time period. If we could have waited, I assure you, we would have."

Helen held Peyton with a gaze, pressed the breathing mask to her mouth, and took some oxygen. Her arms were like spindles. The blanket that covered her legs barely concealed limbs withered to bone.

"There's something else, Miss Sorel, isn't there?" Cross-examination from a dying woman surprised Peyton. "I was married to the man for fifty years. I didn't know what Arthur did, but I knew he did something. It was something that allowed him to bid millions at auction for priceless paintings and to buy this estate for cash. You can't do that, can you? None of your partners can either. Why could Arthur?" She took a breath of oxygen as she moved her eyes around the hallway.

"Now someone is scratching away at what Arthur did long ago, and you're on an errand to find out what it is. Have I guessed well?"

"It doesn't sound like a guess, Madame." Peyton crouched and looked at the woman face to face. "Would you tell me what you know?"

"You're not the first lawyer who's been to see me."

The Gainsborough had distracted Ted, but the last remark made him turn his head to the old woman.

"Who?" Peyton asked. "Who came to see you?"

"My trust and estate lawyer, Christopher Holland. Used him for years. I wanted to make an adjustment in my estate. There are no heirs, Miss Sorel, just charities. All of this wealth will go to a foundation, and I want to spread it as best I can, make it useful. He came to review some files and advise me on tax issues. All of the files are in boxes in a basement workroom. We met and discussed what I wanted, and he went to the work-room to review the files, some of which he took with him. He had an assistant with him, a young man I'd never met. He introduced himself and said he worked with Mr. Holland."

"What was his name?"

"I can't recall, but Maddie knows. He gave us a business card. She wrote it down."

Maddie handed over a note pad, and Helen read the name. "Julian Smythe. Charming in a cheap way, he was. I thought nothing of him, went for a nap, and spoke with Mr. Holland a few days later. But something happened in the basement, and I suppose you know what it was."

"Please continue."

"The foundation files were gone, because Mr. Holland was allowed to take them. I had him sign for them. But one week later, Maddie noticed that an entire shelf was empty where Arthur's old files used to be. Three or four boxes were missing. Other boxes had been opened. I called Mr. Holland, and he professed ignorance." She smiled. "I find it amusing when a lawyer says he doesn't know something. It's so unlikely. Then I called the general number of his firm and asked for Mr. Smythe. No such person works at the Holland firm. Do you find that suspicious?"

"I do. Have you fired Mr. Holland?"

"Not yet. And then you come calling about Arthur's old files. Tell me, Miss Sorel, why are you digging in my garden?"

"There were things—transactions—things about transactions Mr. Konigsberg orchestrated. They were for a real estate company. That company is a defendant in a case I'm trying in federal court in Manhattan, and the trial's almost over. Mr. Smythe—your Mr. Smythe—works for the opposing lawyer. We know almost nothing of the transactions; they were eight years ago. But Mr. Smythe and his colleague have already made accusations about them at the trial, some of which, if true, have criminal implications. That's why I want to see those files."

"For whom does Mr. Smythe work?"

"Joseph Boyle. Boyle and Price. He's my opponent."

Recognition swept across Helen's face, and her lips parted. She nodded, looked up at Maddie who stood next to her, and said, "The Polo Club."

Peyton said nothing and waited.

Helen Konigsberg dug under the blanket that covered her legs, pulled out a key, and held it up to Peyton. "Take it. You'll find a locked door in the basement. Maddie will show you. This is bad business. I have lived handsomely on it for decades and pretended it wasn't there. What do you lawyers call it, when a person looks the other way as a crime is committed?"

"Willful blindness."

"Wonderful term. Do people go to jail for that?"

"Yes."

"Marvelous! All those people in the financial district—willfully blind to crimes around them. Perhaps I was too, but not anymore."

Peyton took the key and looked at Ted who had walked across the hallway and stood next to her. He held in his hand the envelope from the Bermuda Bureau of Corporations. She handed him the key and took the envelope. She bent down on one knee in front of Madame Konigsberg and removed the documents.

"Is this Bergen County, Mrs. Konigsberg?"

"It is."

"Do you use the post office in Ramsey?"

"We do."

Peyton showed Helen the schedules of property and asked her if she recognized anything, but she didn't. When Peyton came to the frayed piece of paper with the four sets of numbers, she handed it to Helen, who read them and then looked up at Peyton and back to the sheet. "That's Arthur's handwriting."

"Do you know what they mean?"

"I don't know what the duplicitous Mr. Smythe took from me, but whatever he found in the basement, it wasn't what Arthur had put in the safe." She handed Peyton the slip of paper. "That's the combination. Arthur knew it. I didn't. Or perhaps I didn't want to know it. The safe is in the back basement and hasn't been opened in years, not even after he died.

No one knew about it but me, and the combination went with him. Maddie will show you."

Peyton read the series of numbers as Helen Konigsberg took a breath of oxygen. She was more than Peyton expected. Haughty, abrupt, and arrogant—Helen Konigsberg was all that. But she was brutally candid and deserved the same. Peyton spoke plainly. "Would you like to consult a lawyer before you allow me access to the safe? A lawyer would advise you about protecting your own interests. If, as you imply, Mr. Konigsberg acquired any part of his wealth improperly, that could affect you and your estate." She looked around the hallway. "What comes out of that safe could affect your ownership of these assets. I'm not your lawyer, and I cannot promise that I will protect your interests. My duty is to my firm and to my client. It's up to you."

Helen looked up at Peyton and for the first time showed a trace of kindness. "I'm not an accomplice, Miss Sorel. Not today, not anymore." Helen turned the electric wheelchair away and rolled into the library through double doors, which Maddie closed behind her.

Maddie bowed to Peyton and Ted and asked them to follow. She walked to a door under the staircase, which led down to a well-lit series of corridors and rooms and the constant hum of dehumidifiers. In the back of the basement, Peyton handed Maddie the key, and she led them through a door to a room with thirty cardboard archive file boxes on metal shelves against a stone wall painted white. All had lids. Yellowed packing tape had been stripped away and the tops removed. Some of the boxes were half-empty, and Peyton and Ted flipped through the files, all of which related to the day-to-day operations of Iberia. There were check registers, partial tax filings from many years ago, miscellaneous correspondence with accountants in Spanish and English, by-laws, and charts and printouts with numbers that neither Ted nor Peyton understood.

Deeper into the basement, Maddie flipped on light switches along white-washed stone walls and brought them to a room filled with dusty trunks, boxes, and things from a different life. There were buckets of rags, a cracked wooden rudder from a sailboat, boots, empty wine bottles, piles of abandoned shoes, and a bench strewn with woodworking tools. Covering one wall was a map of the world printed on a canvas the size of a bedsheet. It hung on a dowel mounted on the ceiling. Maddie pulled back the map and revealed the door of the safe. It was jet black, inset into the wall, and seven feet high. As Peyton and Ted looked in silence, Maddie told them they could find her upstairs if they needed assistance. Peyton thanked her, and Maddie left.

The safe had a traditional combination lock with a numbered dial in the center of the door and a large wheel to the left that spun clockwise to pull open the steel rods that locked the vault. Peyton stepped forward with the slip of paper in her left hand and pushed it flat against the black steel. With her right hand, she spun the numbered dial three times to the right until the zero appeared at the top of the dial. She spun the dial to the left two revolutions to the number 65, then right to 44. She spun it left two revolutions to 18 and then right to 55. She backed away and turned the large wheel to the right. Peyton pulled, and the door opened. A puff of stale air floated into the room. A fluorescent light automatically went on inside the safe. Shelves lined the three walls and surrounded a table in the center. Peyton walked in. On the shelves were stacks of bearer bonds, each worth $25,000;

velvet cases with jewelry; years of correspondence from Arthur Konigsberg's early life; boxes of old photographs; wrapped stacks of one-hundred-dollar bills; gold bars in padded cloth; and three archive boxes of documents with no markings.

Peyton lifted a box from the shelf and handed it to Ted, who rested it on the table and began to thumb through the contents, a collection of tightly packed files in manila folders with metal clips.

Peyton opened a box on the shelf, removed the first few folders, stacked them up, and started to read. "Anything that looks like the transactional papers, okay? We want to confirm they're here. It sounds like we can take all of this stuff with us, but let's be sure it's what we came for."

Ted agreed with a low grunt as he pulled the files and opened folders.

In the first set of files, Peyton found schedules of land valuations and the name "Iberia" written somewhere on every document. There were letters from Señor Ignacitis to George Harwood, Arthur Konigsberg, and Tracy McPhee. There was a thick binder of transactional documents with an index and tabs, which she handed to Ted without a word, and aerial photographs in black and white of hills and fields planted with coffee. In silver marker on the photographs, handwriting designated tracts of land by number and, in the margins, described the property, all in Spanish. Formal written appraisals of land were in separate binders in both English and Spanish.

The file was not unusual. In many respects, it was perfect in its normal, professional craftsmanship. It was well documented and properly put together to build a record of the deal but not so perfect as to feel fabricated. Peyton read the letters. Evidently, the deceased Señor Ignacitis and George had a dispute over pricing and a mistake, later resolved, about tracts of land that were not for sale but inadvertently included in the papers. Later, they had agreed to remove the parcels from the transaction. There was an adjustment in the purchase price, negotiated in letters. It was a staged disagreement, a scam to deceive Severington.

In the third folder, Peyton found the incorporation documents. Arthur had prepared them for George in 1976, signed them, and filed them in Bermuda. He had been there at the beginning.

In the last folder in her stack, she found an expired British passport, an attached birth certificate, and miscellaneous papers. The birth certificate was for Tracy McPhee, who had been born in Cork, Ireland, on November 22, 1929. The miscellaneous papers were a death notice and a page from the registry of a church in Cork that announced McPhee's death as an infant on December 7, fifteen days later. She opened the passport to the first page and read the name Tracy McPhee, a British citizen. The passport had been issued in 2002. She looked into the photograph and saw the face of a man with oversized black-rimmed glasses, his eyes obscured by lenses and the glare of light. He had a white beard, a receding hairline, and thin lips he held tightly together for the photographer. His skin seemed pale, as if he had been sick, and he hunched down as if intentionally lower in the frame. He wore a brown tweed jacket and a pale-blue tennis shirt buttoned at the neck. With the glasses, beard, and hunch, he looked like a college professor, innocuous, unrecognizable to many, sufficiently different to be someone else in South America or the Channel Islands for a moment in time. But everything else was there—the brow, chin, and countenance from eight years ago. She recognized him.

Ted heard her breathe in, and he looked up from the table. She shook and held the edge of the shelf. She felt his gaze and handed him the passport and papers. He looked at the photograph and turned it over to see the birth certificate, death notice, and page from the church registry.

"It's him." Ted said.

"Yes." Peyton closed her eyes and gripped the shelf.

Ted was inclined to smile, even to laugh and express admiration for the dark mind that had done it. One of his professional pleasures was unraveling the complex frauds of outwardly upright people who could not resist the temptation of diverting money to themselves and descending into impossibly complicated schemes. At first, they were like mathematical puzzles only the creator could untangle. But when Ted understood the basic elements, the schemes were simple. He loved to pick them apart with the cooperative mastermind, safely in police custody, who alternately boasted of his work and bemoaned his downfall, but invariably asserted that his methods had been sound. Maintaining a scheme was always troublesome. The economy would conspire against the plan. Loans would be called. Redemptions demanded. A sudden unexpected need for cash would arise that required alterations of accounting records and implausible explanations. Ted had interviewed dozens of men and women who had defrauded purchasers of almost anything that could be represented on a sheet of paper or a computer screen: securities, mortgages, certificates of deposit, cars, land, buildings, commodities,

funeral homes, marriages to foreigners, and, the worst, children for adoption. Except for the women from Oklahoma
who ran an adoption website like modern-day Fagins, he liked
every criminal he had met. Once caught, they were polite,
intelligent, nonviolent, and completely candid. In police custody, they had limitless free time and were always pleased to
see Ted, because he was interested in their work, which—but
for the elements that were illegal—were in their own minds
profitable and stimulating businesses. On the surface, their
schemes were legitimate; underneath, they were false corporations that engaged in sham transactions that siphoned money
from customers who were unlucky and careless, sometimes de-
luded and greedy.

The passport made it different. Never had Ted encountered anyone who had created a fictitious person to help exe-
cute the crime. A person who moved from country to country
and masqueraded as a separate party in a three-way transaction with an outside lawyer who himself was dead. And he
did it to cover up the details of a twenty-five year crime. Tracy
McPhee was George Harwood, and George was Tracy McPhee.
How did he keep it straight? Ted wanted to talk to him for
days over coffee and unwind the scheme. He looked at the
face on the passport and imagined George explaining how
simple and brilliant the plan had been. The confession would
take days of video to explain the deception with its elements
of drama, comedy, and tragedy. FBI investigators would jock-
ey for position behind the one-way mirror as the elderly Mr.
Harwood would explain how it started, developed, expanded,
and then disappeared, all without a trace. And then it unraveled when a trust and estate lawyer stumbled across boxes in

Arthur Konigsberg's basement, rifled through them, and told his friend Joe Boyle at the Upper Saddle River Polo Club that Helen Konigsberg had a bomb in her basement.

Ted stopped the confession when the face in the passport said, "And no one got hurt." It wasn't true. It was never true. McPhee's passport said otherwise. It was tucked away in the safe owned by the coconspirator. Arthur had been in the scheme from the beginning, designed the transactions and fraudulent tax returns, and then mysteriously committed suicide days after Iberia was dissolved. He had the documents. He had McPhee's passport. He had George. Whatever Arthur had wanted, he could have demanded. His death was designated a suicide by a local suburban police department that knew nothing of the buried corporate history, the offshore company, and the criminal business that looked legitimate, even routine. The scheme was too sinister for Ted to admire, now or ever.

Peyton exhaled and shuddered as she spoke. "Shall we take all three?"

Ted handed her the passport and birth certificate and slid both boxes across the table. "Yes. And all the boxes in the first room."

"We'll talk in the car." Peyton packed up the box on the shelf, picked it up in her arms, and left the safe.

Ted took the other two boxes, and they walked through the basement corridors to the stairs and the main floor. At the top of the stairs, Maddie sat in a chair. She nodded as Peyton and Ted entered the hallway and arranged the three boxes at the front door. They returned to the basement and brought up the other twenty that contained Iberia's operational records. When they had finished, Peyton and Ted carried the first three boxes to the car, and Ted dialed a courier service to pick up the remaining twenty. Peyton asked Maddie to tell Madame Konigsberg that they were leaving and that they would take three boxes with them but would send a courier for the others. She handed Maddie a second business card, thanked her, and left.

XLIII

Wrightsville Beach

At four o'clock, Ben and Frank ran the *Broad Jumper* past the northern end of Masonboro and entered Banks Channel at thirty knots. The boat was filled with buckets of snapping crabs the boys had retrieved along the Masonboro marshes and inland waterway. Ben pulled back on the throttle as he reached the docks at the southern end of Wrightsville. Built on pilings, the docks extended 150 feet into the channel. Almost every dock had a storm-damaged gazebo at the end and floating platforms to moor boats. The hurricane had torn off the roofs and scattered shingles onto the water. Whole docks were missing, and pieces of lumber lay in the marsh grass to the west on the other side of Banks Channel. One dock with a double-deck gazebo listed to one side; warning signs were posted on all four sides, and yellow police tape cordoned off the front. Some motorboats were swamped. Others lay on Waynick Boulevard with flooded cars, shingles, bicycles, laundry, and broken furniture.

Ben maneuvered the *Broad Jumper* to his grandfather's dock, the fourth one north of the Coast Guard station, and Frank manned the bow with the boat pole to push away floating pieces of wood. When they arrived at the dock, Frank walked like a cat along the gunwale to the stern and leaped to the dock. They tied up the boat and began to unload.

When they finished, they climbed the steps to the gazebo and dumped their life jackets in a long fiberglass footlocker for boating equipment. They walked down the dock to the porch and up the steps to the front door, rested rods and reels across the arms of the green wooden rocking chair, and took off their damp shoes. They left the cooler with crabs on the back porch.

When they entered the house, Frank went upstairs to the shower, and Ben walked through the downstairs rooms, careful not to call out to his grandfather, who at this time of day often slept on the living room couch and snored. Except for the rhythm of his feet on the floor, the house was silent. In the living room, the couch was empty; Edmund hadn't returned. Its long, orange feather-filled cushion held the indentation of the judge's back, head, and legs from years of naps. Ben spoke out loud as if Edmund were there. He asked him questions about what it was like when he was sixteen and hurricanes hit the beach. Since the judge was absent, Ben answered for him and provided a now-memorized speech about an unnamed storm years ago that had put boats in backyards, torn up trees, and brought a twenty-foot storm surge over the island. Ben mimicked his grandfather as he walked through the rooms. He nodded in agreement with the judge and said out loud, "Yes, Your Honor," to Edmund's speech. It was so embedded in Ben's memory that word for word he repeated it and imagined his grandfather, "the sitting federal judge," sitting upright on the old orange couch, bleary-eyed from a nap, his shirt partially unbuttoned, and his white hair tossed about on his head.

Ben bounded up the stairs three steps at time to the sunlit room he shared with Frank and began to undress. The house phone rang, and he returned to the first floor and answered it. The voice was old, like his grandfather's, with a cadence that he'd heard before.

"It's George Harwood, Ben, your Uncle George."

Ben stood in the kitchen, said hello, and tried to connect the voice to a face. The image of his mother's godfather came to him—George—a respected peripheral presence in the family. He'd seen him from a distance at the wedding reception. Ben politely told him that his mother was in New York and the judge at the courthouse.

"Then perhaps you can help me," said George. "I'm on the porch of the yacht club. Would you be willing to come down and sit a spell?"

George sat in a wooden rocking chair on the covered front porch of the Carolina Yacht Club, a collection of buildings that stretched from the beach on the east to Banks Channel on the west, where hundreds of small sailboats were moored in the water or stored on trailers along the docks and bulkheads. He looked west over a parking lot, where Leandro's white rental car was parked, and then out to the endless masts and occasional flapping sails on boats about to be launched. The yacht club itself had survived the storm, but the waterline had left a mark three feet above the porch floor and eight feet above ground level. Men and women with sponges and rags washed the walls to clean away the waterline like a ring on a bathtub. Every so often, a metal sound of a hammer rang out as it struck a nail.

In his hand, George held an open folder with a stack of high-resolution satellite photographs and held the phone to his ear. "I have some questions about Winnabow. There are some police officers here looking for something that was lost along the banks of the plantation. You might be able to help answer questions. Would you be so kind?"

"You mean the boxes. This is about the boxes, isn't it?"

George was silent at first and then spoke. "Are they large boxes?"

"Yes, plastic. They're in an old impoundment in the weeds."

"Ben! That's good. That's very good. You must have found them. The police officers are looking for what was lost. Can you tell them anything?"

"Well—the boxes—they're empty," said Ben. "We looked at them this morning when we went to get some crab pots at Winnabow. We hadn't noticed them before, because the water was so high. But there was nothing there, so we just...we thought they were storm junk. You know, stuff the river swept in. And we were going to tell Linus about it later."

Leandro wandered inside an open room next to the porch, a dance hall, where he browsed the glass cases of sailing trophies, signal flags, and historical photographs of races, dances, and ceremonies that went as far back as 1856, when the original yacht club had been built. When he heard the conversation, he appeared on the porch, and George looked up into the man's eyes. Leandro pointed to the floor and mouthed the word "here." George shook his head and reached into his pocket. He removed a small box of pills and put a nitroglycerine tablet between his gum and lip to relieve the angina in his chest. He swallowed it and rocked until the pressure disappeared.

"Ben, I have a police officer here who would like to speak with you. Can you come down to the yacht club?" George put his hand over the mouthpiece and asked to see the Interpol identification. Leandro handed it to him. It was an official Interpol card with a contemporary photograph of Leandro's face. George read from the card. "His name is Nicolas Jackson, and he is an investigator. It won't take long."

It was four thirty. Dinner wasn't for three hours, and knowing the judge, it would be the late buffet at the Surf Club on North Lumina Avenue, where everyone wore jackets and ties. He agreed and told George he'd take a bicycle and be there in ten minutes. Ben walked out of the front door and chose an old red bike from under the house. He pedaled north along the narrow path that was South Lumina, barely an alley, past palmetto and pear trees, small well-tended lawns, croquet sets, and baskets of flowers that hung from back porches. Every fifty feet, he wove around speed bumps that kept the cars to a slow crawl. Two blocks from the yacht club, a sign set into the ground showed the levels of the storm surge during past hurricanes. Floyd, a category three, brought a storm surge of twelve feet. At the top of the sign was writing that noted the storm of 1961 and the famous surge of twenty feet, an educated guess based on the fact that almost every home on the southern end of Wrightsville had been destroyed or carried away.

At the yacht club, Ben leaned his bike against a fence and walked up the main path to the porch, where George rocked in the shade. He skipped up the stairs, saw the familiar face, and smiled. He held out his hand, gave George's hand a brisk shake, and sat down in an adjacent rocking chair. The old man smiled back and thanked him for coming.

George held the folder of satellite photographs on his lap. He shifted them to Ben. On top was the close-up image of the old impoundment and the translucent boxes, one above the water and two slightly below. The image was radiant, with

more detail than Ben had ever seen in a photograph. The boxes were clear and crisp, but they were sealed, not as Ben and
Frank had found them—empty, with the tops removed and
wedged in the mud. Along the dikes, the rainwater and tracks
left from all-terrain vehicles were in the same clear focus.
Ben turned to the next photograph, which showed sunlight
reflecting off the large pond and the tails and manes of the
horses—the chestnut and a bay that grazed on the green-and-
yellow grass north of the pond. He looked at the next photograph, and his lips parted in silence. The pillars and gates of
Winnabow's main entrance were in such a fine detail that Ben
could distinguish the head and tail of the bobcat that sat atop
one pillar and the wings of the eagle that sat on the other.

"Where did you get these?"

George finessed the answer. This was a police investigation, he said, and the police, like the military, used satellites.

"Has the judge seen them?" Ben asked.

George's cheeks fell flat against his face, and his eyes
looked away momentarily. He recovered and spoke. "The police will show him everything." George measured Ben's face.
"They'll speak with him."

Leandro walked out of the dance hall and onto the porch.
His sunglasses were perched on top of his head. "You must be
the man who knows Winnabow." His white teeth were exposed
in a smile. Ben stood up, and Leandro extended his hand. He
was six feet tall, three inches taller than Ben, who reached out
and shook the older man's hand.

"Are you the police officer?"

Leandro pulled a wallet out of his back pocket, opened
it, and handed it to Ben, who looked at the Interpol identification card. "I'm an investigator. Interpol is an international

police agency. We're looking for what I think you may have found."

The card identified Leandro as Nicolas Jackson, an "investigator" and "officer" with a business office in Caracas, Venezuela, and Paris, France.

Ben handed back the wallet. "Actually, I didn't find anything—just some empty boxes."

Leandro moved quickly. "Okay," he said. "Maybe you can help us anyway. Let's say we've caught the person who is responsible for taking what was in those boxes, but he's not talking. Do you think you can help us find where he put it at Winnabow? We suspect it's still there."

"Maybe."

Leandro was patient. "Tell me what 'maybe' means."

"Whatever you're looking for—it could be anywhere."

"Do you know the plantation?"

"Yes."

"Well or not so well?"

"I know everything about it."

"Then you're our man. If the person we have in custody emptied the cargo out of those boxes, where would he put it?"

"Winnabow is big, sir."

"But it won't be just anywhere. It will be well hidden, in a place he'd return to later. Then he'd transport it out of the plantation."

Ben thought about the puzzle. "Then it wouldn't be in a place people use."

"Such as?"

"The hurricane house, at the end of the main road; it's white with a porch all the way around. The manager lives there during the harvest. Same with the barn—the horses live there. And the rice sheds—no one can get in, because they're locked."

"Okay. Where would you hide it?"

"I didn't."

"I know." Leandro smiled. "The question's hypothetical."

"Do you mind me asking what 'it' is?" asked Ben. "What are we talking about?"

Leandro was blunt. "Cocaine."

The answer shocked George, who fell limp at the candor.

"In all three boxes?" Ben asked.

Leandro nodded. "I've been chasing the people involved. The good news is I caught them. Right now, finding this stuff should be the easy part."

It was a good recovery, and George saw some satisfaction on Ben's face. The boy nodded. "You'd want to find that."

"I don't want it lying around where innocent people could stumble over it. We're trying to clean things up at this point."

Ben was impressed. "It could be in the old chapel," he said. "At the edge of the big pond. It's hard to find, and it's a long way from the impoundments."

"Okay, where else?"

"The slave house. It's deep in the forest. There are paths if you know where to find them. They connect to the hunting lands south of Winnabow. If he stumbled across the paths, he could have found it. It's a good place. I mean, you know, it's possible."

Leandro liked the leads. "Is that all? Can you think of anywhere else?"

Ben shrugged. "The sand pits. They're in the forest, closer to the impoundments. That's a good location. He could hide them there and then drive a truck to the main road and pick them up. It's funny, actually. They're sand dunes. You go through this really thick forest, down a trail, and then suddenly, like, they're there, in a clearing, all these sand dunes, twenty feet high. That's where I'd put the stuff."

George hadn't been to Winnabow in years. He knew the chapel but not the slave house or sandpits. He couldn't find his way through the trails. George thanked Ben and asked him whether he could identify the places on the aerial photographs.

Ben paged through the images on his lap. There were forty satellite photographs, and most of them displayed the summer canopy of trees that covered the paths and roads. Markers Ben knew on sight were hidden. He shook his head, and George urged him on with a pen, asked him to locate the slave house, chapel, and sandpits in the photographs. He couldn't, he explained, because the photographs were too similar, covered by the trees. In isolation, they were meaningless. Like pieces of a puzzle, he would have to spread them out onto the porch floor and fit them together until they made sense. Even then, he might not be able to create a reliable map.

Ben took the pen from George, turned over a photograph, and began to sketch the property. Ben's father had taught him to draw, and the boy filled the map with all the details he knew. He started with the river and Santee and then moved west to route 133. He filled in the main road and hunting trails, drew boxes for the chapel and slave house, and showed the system of levees, ponds, and creeks that made the property a real enterprise. He identified the forests in a cross-hatch pattern and used an arrow to point south to the hunting lands. In the last two years, he'd hunted deer and wild turkey with his mother

along the trails to the south, so he knew them well and counted them as part of the plantation.

George and Leandro watched the drawing develop. Ben
placed the point of the pen on the creek that led from the
pond to the river and explained that it split the new impoundments into two equal sections. Then he moved the pen south
along the map to the broken levee. He drew a circle around
where he and Frank had found the boxes. Ben sketched in the
final two elements, a nautical compass in the lower left that
pointed north and the legend in script, "Winnabow, by the
hand of Ben Sorel, 2010."

He showed it to George and asked him what he thought.

"Extraordinary," said George. He held the map in hand
and scanned it. Ben had shown the main trails with hyphen-
ated marks and the roads in thick dark lines.

Ben rocked back and forth and smiled.

George held the map up to Leandro, who took it and admired the craft. In free hand, Ben had showed him the complete property. He studied the image of Santee Island and the
rice impoundments, identified in a schematic image of dots
and lines. He crouched next to Ben and pointed to the old
levees across from Santee. "This is where you saw the boxes?"

Ben looked up and nodded.

Leandro pointed to the barn, fences, and paddock Ben
had drawn on the north side of the map, the place where
Leandro had found the pickup truck. "That's the barn?" He
asked.

Ben said yes.

"You certainly know the place, don't you?"

"I do."

"I have a car in the lot. I'll introduce you to my colleagues, and we'll drive out there. Let's see what we can find." He looked at George. "What would that take, one hour?"

"One hour," said George, as he put the photographs back into the file folder and struggled to his feet.

The three walked off the porch. Ben held the map and stood next to George, who rested a hand on the boy's shoulder as they maneuvered down the steps. They walked the main path of the yacht club and arrived at the white rental car. Leandro introduced George and Ben to Sean and Joseph, who were now shaved and well dressed in light-colored shirts and trousers. They shook hands. Neither said a word. Leandro opened the back door, and Ben slid into the middle of the backseat. George followed. Leandro entered the backseat on the other side. He thanked George and Ben for helping and directed Joseph out of the parking lot to Waynick Boulevard, the causeway and bridges, and up Market Street, a straight drive into Wilmington past malls and shopping centers that stretched in every direction for miles.

Ben felt safe with George, a family friend and his mother's uncle, in a small city where people knew each other. It was different from New York, where no one knew anyone outside of school or work. In Wilmington and Wrightsville, men and women he was sure he'd never met stopped him and spoke to him in supermarkets, restaurants, and on the beach, as if they'd known him all his life, because they did know him. Often, they were related by blood. The men shook his hand, and the women kissed him, asked him how his mother and grandfather were doing, and told him how much he had grown and looked like his father. People loved him, because they loved his mother and grandfather, and they wanted him to do well for himself, for them, and for the region. There were no strangers in Cape Fear, only affection and identity, which gave him comfort and confidence. Ben would treat Nicolas Jackson graciously, as his grandfather would any police officer on official business.

"You're an honorable man," said Leandro.

"Aren't we all?" Ben smiled.

George looked out of the window and held the photographs against his chest.

At Fifth Street, Leandro instructed Sean to turn left for Highland House. They needed a truck, he explained, and it would take only a few moments. In the parking area, just outside of the garage, Sean came to a stop, and Leandro left the sedan. The garage door opened to the blue Ford F-150, which Leandro backed out of the garage.

Above the parking area, Luisa stood at the kitchen sink washing dishes. She looked out of the window as the truck came into view. Leandro left the truck, walked to the sedan, and opened the passenger door. He helped George out of the car and positioned him in the parking area, leaning on his cane. In the sedan, Ben craned forward to speak, and Luisa saw him. Leandro leaned in and took the map from Ben. He put his hand on Ben's forehead, and pushed him back. He slammed the car door, and the electronic locks snapped shut. The sedan did a U-turn in the parking area and moved up onto Dock Street. In a mile, they were headed north and west to the bridge.

XLIV

Winnabow Plantation

In the sedan, Ben fell against the seat back as Sean pressed the accelerator and the car surged out of the parking area. Sean looked into the rearview mirror, jutted out his lower jaw as he considered the young face, and spoke.

"We'll drive to Route 133. You tell us from there."

Ben's throat tightened; he looked at Sean's eyes in the rearview mirror. He turned back to George in the parking area, where Leandro took the old man's arm, turned him around, and led him into the garage. Heat rose in Ben's neck and face as the antebellum streets of Wilmington raced by. Nicolas Jackson seemed like all of the professional people who worked with his mother and grandfather: honest, direct, and motivated. He was shaven, nice looking with good clothes, and he spoke well. But he'd separated Ben from George and hadn't done what he said he would do. Without explanation, he'd taken George and pushed Ben back into the car. Ben was about to speak and felt Jackson's palm and fingers on his forehead. The hand was large. He'd pushed hard, as if Ben were an object, stolen and locked in the backseat. He had fooled him. Like an actor who had perfected role play, Jackson had the veneer of a good voice and stories, an identification card, and a background he presented with confidence.

Ben coughed to hide the swelling in his throat.

Sean waited for an answer.

"Fine," Ben said. "Let me know when you need me."

The white sedan moved over the Cape Fear Memorial Bridge, where the expanse of the river spread out to the south, a harbor of container ships and fishing vessels. As they quit the bridge and turned south on Route 133 for the fifteen-minute journey parallel to the river, Ben was ready to speak. He asked Sean and Joseph if they knew anything about shipping on the river and the history of rice in the region. They didn't. He chose to be conversational and told them about both. He described the rice operation at Winnabow, the chapel, the slave house and other places to hide things as they drove him deeper into Brunswick County and farther from his grandfather.

"How long have you been in the police business?" He said it with a casual tone.

"About ten years," Sean said.

"It's dangerous, isn't it?"

"How do you mean?"

"You're under pressure," said Ben.

"Yes," said Sean.

"And you have to do the right thing, don't you?"

Sean found Ben's face in the mirror and asked him what he meant.

"You're the law," said Ben. "The law has to do the right thing. You have to follow the rules even when you don't want to—you know, if bad people threaten you. Maybe they even kill you. That has to be a hard part of police work, right?"

There was a solemnity to the question. Joseph wanted to reach back, grab the boy, and hit him, but Sean raised his hand and spoke. "There's good and bad in this business," he said philosophically. "When you do what we do, you never really see any good. There's no profit in treating them fairly." Sean looked in the mirror. "You know what an end game is?"

Ben shook his head. "No."

"We're the end game. You know, finish stuff off, make things final. We don't negotiate." Joseph laughed and looked at Sean.

They had no veneer.

"That's harsh," said Ben.

"It is," said Joseph.

Ben sat back and looked at the forest.

The entrance to Winnabow was a dirt road that appeared fifteen miles south of the bridge on the left-hand side. Two masonry columns marked it at the edge of Route 133. For miles on either side of the entrance, there was not a roadhouse, home, trailer, or driveway. As the car traveled closer, Ben stared at the forest and occasionally his bare feet. Joseph watched him from the front seat. From the sounds of the tires and the curve of the road, the boy knew where he was. He had traveled Route 133 to Winnabow so often he could lie in the backseat with his eyes closed, count the curves, listen for the sound of loose stones, and predict within seconds when his mother or grandfather would slow down and make the left-hand turn. When the car rolled over the short wooden bridges that took Route 133 over creeks that flowed into the river, the sound of the tires changed for a second and signaled where they were. After the third bridge, Ben waited until he heard a patch of gravel under the tires. Without looking up, he announced that the entrance was around the next bend on the left, over a rise in the road, about four hundred yards away.

"You'll see some stone columns on the left side," he said. "Some oaks line the access road. Turn in there. You'll see a gate."

Joseph looked at the boy. Ben turned his face to the window as the forest sped by. Four hundred yards later, the columns and oak trees appeared. Sean turned the sedan over a driveway of crushed stone and dirt, under branches that stretched across the road, and past the columns that marked the entrance.

At the gate, Sean pulled the car up to a keypad on a black stanchion. He sat back, turned around in the front seat, and asked Ben for the numbers. Without looking up, Ben recited the code: "PP92 pound"—Peyton and Paul and the year they were married. Sean tapped them into the keypad, and the black steel gates swung open on a dirt road that went straight for a few hundred yards and then snaked through a forest of pine, oaks, and magnolias dotted with flowers that had bloomed in late summer and punctuated the road with red and white.

Sean drove and weaved in and out of the puddles and mud holes left by the storm. Brown water flashed up along the sides of the car and dotted the windshield. Limbs and trees Ben and Frank had pulled away Saturday morning lay on the side of the road. They narrowed the passage, scraped the side of the car, and left long brown scars along the doors and fenders.

The main road was at the southern edge of the plantation, near the state hunting lands. It went past an access path to the chapel and then turned north near the dock and storage sheds, along the impoundments to the last stop: the hurricane house, fields, and barn on the northern side. After a mile, Ben asked them to slow down and move to the right onto a bank of grass near a carved stone mile marker. Sean pulled onto the grass, and both men looked back at Ben.

"It's the chapel," Ben said. "You know, he wanted me to show you the chapel. It's a place where the people might have hidden what you're looking for."

Sean and Joseph exchanged a glance, left the car, and looked around. Ben knocked on the inside of the window and asked to be let out of the car. Joseph opened the rear passenger door, and Ben stepped out. He walked along a path south of the mile marker and into the forest to a well-tended clearing of green grass. At one end, a small white building and a perfect lawn dominated the clearing. Ben and Frank had inspected the chapel early Saturday morning, removed the limbs and branches, and reported to Linus that the clearing and chapel were in good condition. The chapel was painted white with a peaked roof and cedar shingles. Three steps led to the only door, which Ben opened to a room with eight benches and an altar under a wooden cross fixed to the wall. The room was empty.

Sean stamped on the floorboards. "What's beneath the boards?"

"The ground," said Ben.

They walked out, inspected the crawl space, and found nothing. Sean stayed with Ben while Joseph moved around the perimeter of the clearing and peered into the forest. There was nothing, just a tight thicket of vines, bushes, and trees.

"The slave house," said Joseph. "There's a slave house out here we're supposed to see." Ben motioned with his head, and the three moved back up the path to the car. "Drive another mile," Ben told Sean and pointed east to the river. "You'll turn left this time, to the north, onto a small road, and we'll go a few hundred yards. From there we'll have to walk."

Sean drove along the main road and at Ben's signal turned left at a double-track path that ran along the large cypress pond one mile across. The road narrowed as it moved away from the water and into the forest. Ben looked up at the dashboard of the car.

"Are you interested in the time?" Joseph asked.

"My grandfather expects me to be home. He's a federal judge. He doesn't like to wait."

Sean and Joseph were silent.

The car moved down a straight part of the road. On either side, oaks and magnolias had grown together with weeds and vines to form a long canopy of leaves, limbs, and moss that blocked the sunlight. The car bounced along the road, which turned and followed the curve of the pond. In a half-mile, it straightened out again and moved into the forest. The road ended in a small clearing, where two horse trails branched out on either side. One was barely identifiable as a path; the other was clear and worn.

Sean stopped the car and turned to Ben. "Is this it?"

Ben nodded from the backseat. "We walk from here."

The three walked to the narrow path along sandy wet ground. On the bottoms of his feet, Ben felt the sticks and burrs he would have to avoid to outrun them on the path and into the forest. He thought about how fast his feet would go, the burn in his thighs, the sound of the men behind him, how he would never stop, and where he would turn, about two hundred yards ahead, where the path forked. If he went to the left, he'd head back south to the hunting lands; right and west would take them to the slave house. He would tell Sean and Joseph that the slave house was at the right fork and through trails that zig-zagged up a short rise in the land, the only hill on the property. He would sprint to the left fork and hope that Sean and Joseph would abandon him and follow the trail to the slave house. He was faster than Sean—he was sure of it— but not Joseph, who was young and big with strong limbs that could sustain a sprint for a long time.

Ben walked ahead, feigned a smile, and asked if they were coming. Sean said yes and kept walking with a slight limp from the shard that had penetrated his leg on Somerset Island. Ben explained where they were going, to the right fork ahead, and the two men were silent. He said it again, looked back to them, and added that the slave house was to the right where they'd see winding paths up a hill to the clearing. It was the only elevation on the land, he explained. As long as they kept moving upward on the trails, they would find it. The two men kept pace.

When he approached a bend in the path, Ben shot out ahead and accelerated as fast as he could. The men shouted in Spanish, and Ben heard footfalls behind him. It was another one hundred yards to the fork, and he ran with his eyes on the left hunting trail that had not been cleared. It was thick with branches and vines, and he planned to move quickly over the fallen trees and make his way through the dense underbrush. It didn't matter if he cut his feet and knees in the forest; he would crawl if he had to through sticks and thorns to convince Joseph that the chase wasn't worth it.

Fifty feet from the fork, Ben felt a hand grab his shoulder and shirt, and he pulled away. He ran up the left side of the fork with Joseph reaching out behind him. He felt the grip on his shirt thirty feet onto the path and the man pull him to the right. Joseph hurled him into a pine tree. At full speed, Ben's head bounced off the trunk, and he fell backward onto the sand. His eyes were open, and the sky spun before him. Joseph looked down and cursed the boy in Spanish. He picked up Ben by the shirt, held him upright, and faced him back down the path. Ben's forehead and nose bled. He felt dizzy, and his knees buckled. He fell forward. On all fours, he looked down at the sand until his head cleared. Sean walked up the path, pulled out a short length of clothesline from a back pocket, tied a slipknot in one end, and pulled the line through the knot. He slid the rope over Ben's head and around his neck, pulled it snug, and whispered in his ear.

"Do that again, and I'll choke you to death. Get this done, and you can go home." Joseph pulled Ben off the ground. He held his shoulders and pushed him ahead. Soon, they were into the right fork and then onto a narrower path. They took lefts and rights up small trails covered by the forest canopy, and the land rose as they walked. They moved through the brush, walked up a short rise, and entered a clearing. Two feet above the ground on a cinderblock platform, the slave house was a trim pine cabin with a stone chimney, a single door, and one window in each wall. Linus had dug a short basement another two feet below grade and laid a concrete pad. The cabin was surrounded by wild azaleas, but without a lawn and in deep shade. With Sean behind him, Ben walked up the steps and into the house. Blood flowed from his forehead, and he wiped it away with his shirt. Joseph remained outside and circled the clearing, walked down trails and back again, looking for any disturbance or evidence that Martel had been there. From the hill, he could see the light glitter off the large pond half a mile away.

Ben stepped into one room. Swept clean, it had a table, two chairs, and a stone fireplace. It was open to the air, the result of Ben's and Frank's work around the property the morning before. Otherwise, it was empty. He walked to the corner of the room and stuck his finger in a small knothole in a plank of the floor. He pulled and opened a trapdoor on hinges.

Ben pulled at the rope around his neck. "I'll have to look in the crawl space. Would you take this off?"

Sean shook his head. "Get in the hole, and see what's there."

Ben sat down. Sean let out the rope, and the boy slid through the opening to the concrete floor. He took his time as he looked in the darkness along the walls. Through the trapdoor and gaps in the floorboards, light from the room partially lit the space. Ben felt lightheaded, and his forehead hurt from the collision. Blood from his forehead and nose spotted his mouth and chin. The crawl space was broom clean, just like Linus liked it, without a package, sack, box, or container.

"Your man hasn't been here." Ben shook his head as he spoke.

Sean stood above and looked at Ben seated below. "What's the problem?"

"There's nothing here. Nothing's ever been here." He looked up at Sean, who lay flat on the floor with his head through the hole. He looked into the corners and along the walls in the dim light. Upside down, he cursed in Spanish and then leapt to his feet and tugged on the rope. Ben moved quickly out of the hole as the slipknot tightened around his neck. Sean guided him to the table and sat him in the chair. He tightened the slipknot, wrapped the rope around Ben's right hand, and pulled it behind the back of the chair. In between the wooden slats, he guided the rope up the back of the chair and tightened it in a bowline to keep Ben's right hand in place and to prevent the boy from standing. The slipknot burned Ben's neck; he slumped slightly in the chair. Sean picked up the chair from the other side of the table, positioned it in front of Ben, and sat down. He snapped his fingers twice and grabbed Ben's face with his left hand.

"Look at me." He growled at the boy. "We'll play a memory game. Ever done that? Nod your head if you understand me."

Ben nodded. His tongue stuck to his palate.

"I'm going to find out how much you know. After it's over, I'll know what you know, and we'll be on our way."

Ben's face contorted. He told Sean that he knew nothing about the missing cocaine, had never seen it, and was trying to help. Sean reached behind the chair, brought out the loose end of the rope, and tied it tightly around Ben's left bicep. He pulled the boy's arm onto the table and with his fingers palpated the large vein at the joint. He reached into his back pocket, took out a shiny aluminum tube, and laid it on the table.

"What are you doing?"

Sean pulled a buck knife from a sheath at the back of his belt, held it up to the boy, and let the light from the windows bounce off the blade. "Don't move," he said and set the knife behind him, far from the boy at the edge of the table. He tightened his grip on Ben's left arm and opened the tube. He removed a syringe with a needle and put it on the table. Ben sat back and shook his head. Sean grabbed him by the jaw and tightened the rope around his neck. With one large index finger, he warned the boy and glared at him over the tip of the finger. Ben stared back without blinking. Sean's left hand came hard across his face, and blood began to flow again from his nose, across his lip, and into his mouth.

Sean worked quickly. He removed a plastic cap from the needle and pushed up the plunger until liquid flowed from the tip of the needle. He returned the syringe to the table and looked at Ben, who recoiled, pulled back his left arm, and struggled to free his right hand tied behind the chair. Sean slammed the boy's left arm against the table, cracked the elbow, and held the arm flat. He tightened the rope around Ben's neck and pressed a boot down on the boy's right foot.

Ben cried in pain, choked, and lowered his head. He narrowed his right hand within the rope, twisted it, and then pulled; it slipped out of the knot. He relaxed, breathed and looked down. Blood from his nose dripped onto his pants.

Sean took it as defeat; the boy had accepted the process. He ran his fingers over a vein on the forearm and tightened his grip on Ben's left wrist. He looked up at the boy, ready to administer the dose. Ben raised his head, and their eyes met. For that moment, Sean stopped, and the boy brought his right hand from behind the chair and reached across his body. He picked up the syringe. In one fluid arc, Ben brought it back and slammed the needle into Sean's right eye. He leaned forward, pushed, and screamed in horror as he felt the needle scrape the bone of the orbit and sink into soft tissue. He strained forward against the rope and pushed the plunger down. The full dose of sodium pentothal shot through the back of Sean's retina and into his brain. Sean released Ben's arm and exhaled with a dull groan. He threw his head back, grabbed at the eye, and tipped the chair. Ben lifted his feet, pushed, and sent Sean and the chair backward. The man's head hit the floor, and the syringe bounced out of the eye and rolled away. Ocular fluid spurted up in a short plume, followed by blood that welled up in the eye and flowed down the side of his face.

XLV

Winnabow Plantation

Sean's head throbbed from the impact. As the first stage of delirium set in, he felt for the phone in his pocket, pulled it out, and pushed a button. In slurred speech, he called Leandro over the phone, told him that the boy had stabbed and tried to kill him. He mumbled something incomprehensible about rope.

Traveling south on Route 133, Leandro looked at his mobile phone squawk on the passenger seat of the truck, picked it up, and asked what had happened. Sean's voice was garbled and wounded. All he could say was the pass code to the front gate and a few unintelligible sounds. His hand fell back to the floor as the sodium pentothal washed through his brain and along his scalp, jaw, and neck.

Joseph had combed the paths that led down the hill to the pond for any sign of the cargo. He had entered the forest, circled north, and reentered the clearing when he saw Ben break out of the slave house and sprint south to the hunting lands. Joseph ran to the cabin and stood in the doorway. Sean was flat on his back, quiet and still. Blood flowed in a small stream down the side of his face and onto the floor. Joseph flew down the path after Ben, who was fifty yards out in front.

Ben heard the man behind him and stayed to the path that took him to the main road, which he crossed east of the chapel. He sprinted into narrower trails that lead to the hunting lands, past the chapel, and deep into dark forest covered by tall pines and thick deciduous trees that thrived in the southern heat. Joseph crossed the road behind Ben. He had gained ground in the sprint along the wide path. One hundred yards into the hunting lands, Ben could hear Joseph behind him, closing the distance and moving freely and quickly on worn, flat paths.

Ben turned east along a narrow track full of fallen limbs. He leapt over a tree and turned off the trail into the forest over sticks, pine cones, and thorns that cut his feet. He ducked under low limbs and wound his way into the densest parts of the hunting lands, hoping to lose Joseph in the brush.

Joseph turned into the forest after Ben, stumbled over fallen limbs, crashed through thickets, and cursed the boy. Thorns jabbed at his eyes and forced him to run with his hands out in front to protect his face. His pace slowed against the tangle of vines, trees, and chaos left by the storm. In minutes, Ben had regained some separation as Joseph slowed his pace and lost track of the boy. He stopped, listened, and peered into the forest in front of him. He couldn't see Ben but could hear the distant cracks of sticks broken by feet moving quickly through the underbrush. Joseph pushed through limbs and tripped in the holes and pockets of the sandy soil. He shouted in Spanish what he would do to the boy when he caught him.

Ben's feet had started to bleed. Blood flowed in a stream from cuts along the toes and arches, and one of his heels had opened up when he stepped onto thorns. The pain slowed his progress over fallen limbs and brush, and he was careful each time he made a step. When he pivoted over a fallen tree, he landed in a hole in the sand and rolled his ankle. He came up limping and slowed his pace. At a narrow hunting trail, he emerged from the forest and made his way to his destination, two hundred yards east and then south, across the trail, fifty feet into the forest. It was a large old pine, twice as thick as a telephone pole, and 100 feet high. He looked up to check the platform; it was still intact and worth the climb. With two fistfuls of sand, he filled his front pockets and then reached for the first limb. Hand over hand, he moved up the tree to the platform. Halfway up, he stopped and listened. In the distance, Joseph was lost in the forest. He circled closer to the hunting trail and shouted in exhausted tones.

Ben started climbing again and moved up rapidly, sixty feet above the ground, to an old shooting platform made of two-by-fours and wooden planks, mostly rotten, and secured to the tree with sagging screws. It hadn't been used in years and barely had room for one hunter. Far above the terrain, a hunter would wait for deer, bobcat, and turkey to wander out from their thickets into shooting range. Quietly, Ben would wait until Joseph lost his way and gave up.

Ben climbed higher through the branches until he reached the platform. Diagonal braces held it aloft, but they were loose and old; the screws that held them to the tree were crumbling with rust. With one hand around a limb, Ben held onto a diagonal brace and shimmied upward to the hole in the platform's floor. The brace pulled away from the tree as a rusted screw broke under Ben's weight. He swung out into the air, attached to the tree only by his hand that held the limb. He grabbed another limb with his free hand and brought himself back to the tree. He hugged the trunk and then continued upward by the limbs alone until his head poked through the access hole in the platform. He pulled himself onto the planks, grabbed a limb, and held himself against the tree. The wood groaned underneath.

Below, Joseph walked out of the forest and onto the path. From his perch, Ben could see him through the canopy. Joseph stopped, waited, and listened for Ben. He looked in both directions and walked east, past the big pine. For one hundred yards in each direction, he examined the sand for footprints and broken limbs, disappeared down the path, returned, and peered into the forest. On either side, a tangle of vines and trees blocked his way and forced him back to the path. He turned his head from side to side, looking at the sand. He stopped, sank to his knees, and ran his fingers along blades of grass and pine straw. The blood was wet and bright red in the green shade. He followed the drops to the edge of the forest and picked up the trail. Fifty feet to the south, to the large pine, he moved in a zig-zag until he touched the trunk. The blood was smeared along the bark and then, when he touched it, onto his fingers. Joseph raised his head to the square platform, a black silhouette against the sky, where Ben was out of view and peered through a gap in the boards.

The man began to climb, his face turned upward. Halfway up, he pulled the stiletto from the scabbard strapped to his ankle, opened it, and locked the blade in place. As he moved through the limbs, he stabbed the knife into the trunk above him, removed it, and jammed it again, just above, so it was ready when he arrived.

Ben pulled at a rotten board on the left side of the platform and broke it free from rusted nails. He threw the board through the access hole, but it bounced off a limb and fell to the ground. Joseph stopped, watched the board fly by, and ascended quickly through the limbs. Ben pulled at more boards and freed them from the platform. He slid one over the access hole and sat on it. The others he lined up next to the left side of the platform, which had become a frame of two-by-fours, open and ready for Ben to hurl more lumber. He looked through the frame and threw another plank. It smacked a tree limb, ricocheted toward Joseph, and nearly knocked the stiletto out of the tree. Joseph pulled at the knife, wedged the blade into his belt, and continued upward.

When Joseph was within ten feet of the platform, Ben reached into a pocket, pulled out a fist of sand, and opened the access hole. He waited until Joseph looked up and then threw the sand into his face. It hit him on the bridge of his nose and sprayed into his eyes. Joseph spit and muttered in Spanish. He hugged the tree and rubbed his eyes. Ben stood on the remaining boards of the platform, just over the open access hole. Vertically, he thrust a board downward as hard as he could at Joseph's head and shoulders. It missed the head, but hit with a crack on the left shoulder. Joseph screamed in pain and held onto the tree.

Ben covered the access hole with one of the two remaining boards he had removed. With two hands, he held the other board, his last weapon, and leaned against the tree.

Joseph arrived below the platform and saw Ben through gaps in the boards. The open side of the platform, where Ben had removed the planks, was to Joseph's right, a space of open air with an uninterrupted path for the knife. A diagonal brace from the tree to the platform's outer edge was old but held the right side of the structure in place. Joseph could grab the brace, swing to the open side, and step with his right leg onto a limb on the far side of the tree. As he moved, he would have a clear path to the boy's chest, eight feet away, and nothing to obstruct a perfect throw and follow through. He had put the knife into men's bodies and heads at much greater distances. The stiletto, perfectly balanced, flew blade first in the air without rotation. If Joseph hit him in the neck, he'd pin the boy to the tree.

Joseph balanced on the limbs, removed the knife from his belt, and held the handle in his right hand. The closeness of the target meant the throw had to be in one quick motion. He would swing under the brace and use his momentum to add thrust to the knife. Joseph shifted his left foot to the limb in the center of the tree, bent his knees, and gripped the diagonal brace with his left hand. He held the handle of the knife in his right, cocked his arm, and swung out. His weight moved him like a pendulum under the brace to the open part of the platform. He saw the boy leaning forward in a crouch with a board in his hand, closer than expected, ready to attack. When his right foot landed on the far branch, Joseph threw the knife and extended his arm in a direct line to the target. The knife sliced across the side of Ben's face and ripped through his ear as the boy sent the full force of the board onto the brace. The old wood splintered around the screws that held it to the platform, and the brace broke away. Joseph's weight had pulled him in a smooth arc to the other branch, but now he moved backward into open air, the brace in his left hand and his right extended in a follow through to Ben's head. He looked at Ben, who clung to the remnants of the platform, barely attached to the tree. Joseph fell. He dropped the brace and twisted, moving his arms and legs as if to grab a limb and stop the descent sixty feet to the ground below. He landed on sand, pine straw, and dead leaves, which shot out on impact. On his back, Joseph was still, his eyes open and his arms and legs spread apart. For a moment, he could see the tree, platform, and sky.

Without the diagonal brace, the right side of the platform collapsed. Ben slid over the side, dropped the board, and held onto a horizontal two-by-four that provided the main support for the platform. He climbed back to the platform's left side, put his back against the tree, and held onto a limb. Lodged in the tree, the knife was next to his head. Ben removed it, closed the blade into the handle, and put it in his pocket. Through the access hole, he saw Joseph, who lay on his back in silence. Ben waited to see if the man moved. When he didn't, the boy descended halfway down the pine to get a closer look. He watched Joseph breathe slightly and then stop, his eyes open, as if he were looking at Ben and waiting. The man would soon be dead of internal injuries and a broken back. When Joseph hadn't moved for thirty minutes, Ben climbed through the limbs to the sand below.

XLVI
Manhattan

On the forty-fourth floor, Peyton and Ted carried three boxes into her office and found nowhere to sit. Mort Shaw leaned back in Peyton's desk chair. Dennis Upton sat across from Mort. Two members of the executive committee were on the couch. The chair of the executive committee, Ralph Draper, paced. Draper stopped when Peyton and Ted entered the office.

"Where have you been?" Draper asked, as if to a child, and caught himself but without an apology. "We need to speak about tomorrow, Peyton. Today. Now."

Peyton walked to her desk and dropped one box on the corner. Mort didn't stand. Ted put the other boxes next to the desk, and Peyton politely asked him to leave, to wait in a conference room along the hallway until she came for him. When Ted closed the door, Mort spoke.

"What's in the boxes?"

"Arthur Konigsberg's files on Iberia—some of them," she said. "There are twenty more; a courier's picking them up. These three"—she tapped a box—"were locked in a safe. According to Arthur's widow, it's the first time anyone has seen these since he died. There are things in there that could sink Maynard." She looked at each man in the room. "They could sink us." She turned to Mort. "I assume no one in this room knew about Iberia before I did, unless you tell me otherwise."

Mort glanced at Dennis, swallowed, and spoke. "I'm not sure what anyone knows. Maynard has nothing of substance on Iberia. They destroyed the files last year based on a seven-year document-destruction policy. We did too. We had virtually nothing; now we have these. That's God-damned disappointing. We were hoping to bury this."

"It's not so easy," she said. "Julian Smythe has been in Arthur's basement. He didn't get this, but he got something. That is certain. Ted knows it; I know it."

Jonah Parks, a former justice department lawyer, responded from the couch. His voice dripped with derision. "Just how bad is it? Will you tell us, or do we have to read all that crap ourselves?"

Peyton's expression never changed. "There is enough in these boxes for a federal investigation into every aspect of Iberia's operations and what Arthur Konigsberg did to help that company. Iberia worked with an organization in Ecuador. It owned land that was supposed to be for coffee but grew coca, on hundreds of thousands of acres. Iberia was the paper owner, and coca revenues were about one billion a year. If Boyle can prove that, life as we know it is over. George orchestrated Maynard's participation. Arthur was in it from the beginning. And from these files, there's a reasonable inference that Arthur's death was not a suicide."

Everyone in the room looked at her. No one spoke, until Parks, unimpressed, shot back. "Three boxes tell you that? Beyond a reasonable doubt? I don't think so. Not unless you have signed confessions in there. Did Heilman cook that up for you? Stick to civil cases, Peyton."

"The civil liability for aiding and abetting a South America drug cartel would damage this firm beyond repair. Win or lose, we'd have no future. A public investigation would destroy our client base." Peyton pulled off the top of one box, dug into a file, and removed the passport. She flung it like a Frisbee to Parks. "Read it," she said. "It's a false passport with an alias. The picture is George Harwood eight years ago. George used a fictitious person to orchestrate a transaction to separate Maynard from the cartel in 2002. It's just part of it. For twenty-five years they worked together. Ted thinks Maynard laundered money for decades."

Parks caught the passport and opened it up. He took his time, read every page, and flipped back and forth to the picture of McPhee. Parks' face was placid. He handed it to the other man on the couch, Fred Mannesmann, who smoked a pipe that floated the smell of tobacco around the room. Mannesmann looked at the passport and handed it to Draper, who leaned against the wall. The document circulated through the room until it landed in front of Mort, who was reading it when Parks spoke again.

"Why don't you tell us how you're going to handle this tomorrow? In advance, my opinion is that there is no way you can get a grip on what you've found. You're too close to it. You're too close to George. Unless there is a smoking gun—and for now, I choose to view that passport as falling short of a smoking gun—what you've told us is a theory, a hypothesis, and probably not provable fact. So with that in mind, how are you going to get that directed verdict and keep this stuff out of Stapleton's courtroom? That's your job, Peyton. It's why you get paid more damn money than most of the people in this room."

Peyton hadn't thought it through and wasn't used to re-porting to anyone but herself about courtroom strategy. "Right now, I'm not sure."

Parks stood and pointed at her. "You better be sure. If your hypothesis is even half-right, you need to control the damage and keep it out of the courtroom. Your survival—the firm's survival—depends on it."

Mort raised his hand for silence, but Peyton wouldn't be restrained. "I will not lose my license, Jonah. I will not mislead Stapleton about this stuff. There's not much of a line between arguing that Iberia is irrelevant and lying to the court." She yanked a book off the shelf. "Do we need to read the ethical rules? Iberia is not 'nothing.' It's not meaningless, and if we so much as hint that it is, we've lied—I've lied—to Stapleton. That's suspension, probably disbarment."

Parks scoffed. "Get the job done."

Mort tried to intervene, but Parks had challenged her.

"You're out of the loop, Jonah," she said. "Boyle set this up. He doesn't know as much as we do, but he's close. Regardless of what I say tomorrow, post-verdict, he'll dump as much infor-mation on Stapleton's desk as he can and argue that we lied about Iberia. That's perjury, and our motive is transparent: money and saving our skins."

Parks nearly screamed at her. "Your duty of loyalty is to Maynard and this firm. What are you going to do, jeopardize this corner office? Your astronomical percentage in this place? Your kids' future? Have you lost your mind?" Parks looked at Draper. "Take her off the case. You're litigation chair. Maynard's the firm's client too. Take her off. Step in. I'll step in. If she's in front of Stapleton tomorrow and plays a Girl Scout game, she'll hang us all. Then we're fielding subpoenas from the US attorney's office and wondering who among us will take the Fifth. There's too much at play here to let her handle it."

Peyton turned to Draper and shook her head. "You know the federal rules, Ralph. Boyle has one year from the verdict to make a claim that opposing counsel engaged in litigation abuse. Julian Smythe was in Arthur's basement." She scanned the other four faces and stopped at Fred Mannesman, who removed the pipe from his mouth. "Boxes went missing, Fred. That's why Boyle knows about Iberia. There could be just enough in what they have to hang Maynard and Arthur, which means us. And I guarantee you, all of you, that Boyle will try to hang me. He's obsessed. The truth is my only option—that's the only option I've ever had."

"How do you know about Smythe?" Mannesman was calm.

"Arthur's widow, Helen. She told me. She described Smythe and remembered his name. He had come with Helen's trust and estate lawyer, who was there to retrieve files from the basement. My guess is Boyle paid off the trust and estate lawyer to get Smythe in there. Helen questioned her lawyer but never got a straight answer."

Parks raised his voice again. "How the hell did this get so far out of control?"

"That's enough," said Mannesmann as he lit a match. Parks closed his mouth and returned to the couch. Everyone looked at the firm's internal counsel, who sat, one leg over the other, with a legal pad on his lap. He had written two pages of notes in characteristic and perfectly legible block letters. Mannesmann put the match to the pipe and puffed. As counsel to the firm, he was their lawyer, and his presence cloaked everything they said—insults, sarcasm, threats, and four-letter words—with the attorney-client privilege. He was there to render legal advice, help them decide what would happen Monday morning, and keep the entire meeting protected from discovery in any prosecution that might happen in the future.

"First," Fred said, "no one in this room has done anything wrong. Arthur went off the rails, but that was long ago." He looked at Peyton over the end of the pipe. "Mort gave you the information the firm had. Not every document, but everything he thought was relevant at the time. He could have done it differently, but on Thursday Mort knew marginally more than you did. He didn't withhold anything material, because the firm doesn't have anything material. That dissolution record was the most significant piece of information we had."

"Nothing else?" Peyton asked.

Mort answered her. "We have the underlying corporate documents from 1976, and they have Arthur's name on them. We didn't want that information going to Boyle, so we gave up the formation and dissolution records that George signed. Evidently, there's more to this than anyone suspected."

Mannesman continued. "But you did what you're good at. You went digging and found things none of us predicted. And you've kept a cool head so far. The good news is, we have most of Arthur's documents, Boyle doesn't, and they're not subject to discovery. Not yet. So it seems to me that the only course you have is the one you had Friday. That is, you're studying the situation and have concluded that Iberia is unconnected to the claims made by the Pension Fund. Iberia is not relevant to CIT four or five years after Iberia was dissolved. Discovery is closed." Mannesman waited to let the speech sink in. Peyton stood at the edge of her desk, surrounded by the men. "Tell me if you disagree."

Peyton opened the *Code of Professional Ethics*. It was dog eared with a broken spine, and colorful red, blue, and yellow stickers marked multiple pages. She flipped through the book, came to rule 3.3, and read it to herself:

(a) A lawyer shall not knowingly:
  (1) make a false statement of material fact or law to a tribunal;
  (2) fail to disclose to the tribunal legal authority in the controlling jurisdiction known to the lawyer to be directly adverse to the position of the client and not disclosed by opposing counsel; or
  (3) offer evidence that the lawyer knows to be false. If a lawyer has offered material evidence and comes to know of its falsity, the lawyer shall take reasonable remedial measures.
(b) The duties stated in paragraph (a) continue to the conclusion of the proceeding, and apply even if compliance requires disclosure of information otherwise protected by Rule 1.6 (the attorney client privilege).
(c) A lawyer may refuse to offer evidence that the lawyer reasonably believes is false.

She handed the book to Mannesman. "I'm worried about everything other than (a)(2)."

Mannesman didn't need to read the rule. "You've thought about this?"

"Since Thursday."

Fred closed the book and handed it back.

Jonah Parks looked to Mannesman along the couch and then to Mort behind the desk. "Who's doing this tomorrow?"

he asked. "With all respect, I don't see Peyton in court anymore. She's too close to George and has already equivocated. If this goes south"—he looked directly at Peyton—"your law license will be the least of your concerns. This office, this building, the entire business will be in the toilet."

Mannesman interrupted and looked at Mort. "You said Stapleton hangs on every word she says; is that still true?"

Mort nodded. "He relies on her. If the hearing tomorrow is all about Boyle accusing Maynard of operating some shadowy offshore criminal corporation, Stapleton will want to hear from her, not one of us. If she's not there, he'll know Maynard pulled her off the case. He has wide latitude. He could open up discovery and allow Boyle to amend the Complaint. If that happens, life gets much more difficult."

Parks seethed. "That's a mistake, Mort."

Mannesman replied, "There's no choice here, Jonah. We'd be foolish to change now." Mannesman looked at Peyton. "But you have your marching orders. Stay with what you've been saying. If you need to put one of your partners on the stand to explain that we know nothing, I suppose you'll have to. But stick to the script. Tell me you understand what I'm saying."

"I understand."

"Let me know if you need to talk as the evening moves on. And I'll want an expedited transcript of tomorrow's events."

Mannesman stood up and looked at the other lawyers. "Get back to work." He left Peyton's office, passed Ted, who leaned against the wall, and walked to the end of the hallway.

XLVII

Winnabow Plantation

Ben walked up a rise in the road. He saw the hurricane house, and his legs gave out. The distance from the hunting lands to the northern border of Winnabow was several miles. Through the trails and on the road, his feet had bled and swelled. He had taken off his shirt and sliced it into strips with the knife. Most were around his feet, like bandages, and one strip held the sliced ear to his head. Sitting on the ground, he tended the cuts. The strips of cloths were red and thick with clotted blood. There were puncture wounds, now black and filled with sand, on the bottoms of both feet where limbs and sticks in the forest floor had cut his skin. Deep slices were in both heels. His left foot—the one he had rolled—was swollen around the ankle and bruised yellow and violet. With less than a mile to walk, he rewrapped the cloths, tied them in place, and stood up.

It took him twenty minutes to reach the porch, where he lay in the shade and gathered energy to make his way inside to find the telephone and call his grandfather. The door was unlocked. When he opened it, he stopped, leaned against the doorframe, and slid to the floor. At the far end of the table, where his grandfather had sat the morning before, Leandro sat in a chair, bathed by the western sun. He cleaned the Herstal with a cloth and a small tool. The six-inch suppressor lay next to an open briefcase on the table. Leandro had placed Ben's map on the table in front of a chair, ready for discussion. The man never looked up. He finished cleaning the gun, picked up the suppressor, and repeated the cleaning. When he'd removed every grain of sand from both, he pushed a fifteen-bullet magazine into the handle and closed it with a snap.

Without a word, Leandro walked to Ben and stood over him. He crouched down, cradled the boy in his arms, and picked him up. Ben shuddered at how easily the man lifted him. Leandro walked across the main room and laid him on the kitchen counter, a long, wide strip of Formica that extended the length of the eastern wall. Leandro positioned the boy's lower legs and feet in a stainless steel sink, put a stopper in the drain, and turned on the spigot.

"Where is the knife?" he asked, as warm water cascaded into the sink. The voice was easy, as if he sought a missing utensil from a kitchen drawer, but his eyes were hard and efficient.

Ben felt the water surround his feet. He thought about the stiletto in his pocket and momentarily imagined his own death on the Formica. Tears came, but he pushed the thought away. It wouldn't happen here, not with the stiletto. The man had a purpose, knew he had the knife, and he could have killed him as he limped along the main road or stood in the doorway. They would go together into the forest and the black ponds, and it wouldn't be like the slave house. He wasn't like the others. There was no doubt, sentiment, or conversation. No temper. There would be no lying to "Nicolas Jackson," no deception or physical challenge. Ben could feel it when he had lifted him off the floor, the large hands around his lower legs, and the density in the man's body. He wondered whether he should have reached for the knife when the man had picked him up like laundry and arranged him on the countertop. He couldn't have done it, not against this one. The man would have acted quickly, turned the knife around, instantly calculated what he wanted, and rammed it into Ben's neck or chest.

Leandro waited for an answer. Ben leaned to one side and reached into his back pocket, pulled out the stiletto, and put it on the countertop. Leandro rolled up his sleeves to his biceps and opened the blade. He cleaned it under the spigot and set it on a dish towel at the far end of the Formica, away from the boy.

As the water rose in the sink, it surrounded Ben's feet and turned pink with blood. When the sink was full, Leandro peeled back the cloths and threw them away. He squirted dish-washing liquid into the warm water, moved his hand around in the sink, formed soap bubbles, and let the boy's feet soak. They didn't speak. Leandro washed Ben's feet with his hands. He used the stiletto to remove a shard of wood that had entered and stuck deeply just below the toes of the right foot. Ben looked at the ceiling, clenched his teeth, and let the man do his work. With gauze he'd found in a bathroom, Leandro cleaned out the puncture wounds.

With his sleeves rolled up, Ben could see Leandro's tattoo. It was on the inside of his right bicep. The characters were clear blue: the number 1 and then the letters RL, followed by another letter or number, part of which was under the sleeve. Ben stared at the tattoo as the man extended his arm into the water and opened the drain.

When the sink was empty, the feet were clean. The wounds, once black, were pink, and the water had washed the sand out of the deep cuts. Leandro dried the feet with a dishtowel, applied a topical anesthetic from the judge's medicine chest, and dressed the feet in rolls of gauze. As Ben examined his neatly wrapped feet, Leandro reached across the table to one of the chairs and pulled up a pair of boots.

"Put them on," he said. "I need you to walk." He held out the boots to Ben.

They were dark-brown leather, worn but expensive lace-ups, and neatly polished. Ben turned them over and recognized the soles, black rubber with a good tread for hiking. They had appeared in front of him, right before his eyes, and were the last things he had seen when he had screamed in terror and watched Sean careen backward in the chair. Ben had heard the man's head bounce, like two drumbeats. He had seen the soles of the shoes moving up to the ceiling and then down after the hard double thump. They had stared back at him like two black cartoon eyes rising up and then disappearing onto the floor. After that, he had been in the open, running south, Joseph behind him, fast, bearing down.

The gauze surrounded Ben's feet like white socks. He slid his feet into the boots. They fit large, so he pulled the laces tight. He walked a few steps with minor discomfort—no pain—took some strides around the kitchen, and returned to the sink. Leandro stood over him and removed the stained cloth on the side of Ben's head. The stiletto had put a small gash on Ben's face and cut the ear nearly in half. It had penetrated two inches above the lobe and made a clean slice through the cartilage, like a straight-edge razor. Blood had flowed down his neck and clotted in streaks along his shoulder and the front of his shirt. Ben stood placidly as Leandro cleaned the ear with soap and water and applied the topical anesthetic. The man's hands were almost too large for his body, but he nimbly used his fingers in the delicate task of cleaning and bandaging the ear. He wore a brown leather shoulder holster, in which he had secured the Herstal with a strap over the grip snapped at the side. Ben raised his chin cooperatively; Leandro wrapped his head in gauze to cover the wound and tightly pressed the ear against the scalp.

With his head wrapped in white, the boy looked like a patient in a battlefield hospital, wounded but ambulatory.

"You want me to find the cocaine for you, don't you?" Ben looked up, met his eyes, and then looked down to the boots. "That's why you cleaned me up. You want me to take you into the forest and find it. It belongs to you, doesn't it?"

Leandro put his finger under the boy's chin, raised the young face to his, and told him to listen. He explained who Martel was, a thief from a thousand miles away, who had been on the property earlier in the day but was no longer available, not in a position to provide any information. Gone. Done. Leandro shook his head. No more thief; no more information. Yes, it was probably a mistake, hasty, but there it was. He had killed a thief and murderer, something police officers do every day. He had to adjust. The only reason Martel was on the plantation was to find the missing cargo, the things he had stolen—the same thing Leandro was looking for. Someone had removed the cargo from the containers in the rice fields. There were three suspects: Martel; another man, also gone; and Ben. Now, he said, was when Ben stepped in, saddled up, found where Martel had hidden the product, and ended this mess. Ended it quickly. Something emphatic had crept into the man's voice.

Ben asserted his innocence, and his voice cracked. "Then you know I didn't take it. Someone else did. It's not me."

Leandro nodded. "I know. If you had something to hide, you would never have agreed to help. But here we are. Let's put an end to this, and I'll go home."

"You're not a police officer."

Leandro was calm. "I am, but not the kind you're used to."

"Then you'll let me go?" It was a meek demand.

"After we find what I'm here for. How's that?" A proposed exchange: help me, and I'll help you. Leandro's voice was practical, calculated to give the boy hope, not courage.

"I can identify you," Ben said, and his body shook in a spasm. "You'll never let me go, will you? Not if I can identify you." Ben looked to the floor, rocked with his back against the countertop, and felt the organs in his belly weaken. He kept back the tears and swallowed carefully so he didn't throw up.

Leandro was reassuring. "You'll never see me again." He pulled the boy away from the sink, turned him toward the door, and guided him into the sun.

XLVIII

US District Court, Wilmington, North Carolina

Even before he had died, Hermann Locke looked like a corpse. The emergency room photos, in color, spread his face and body across Edmund Sorel's desk and gave him the pallor of one whose blood had drained completely. His eyes were swollen. Dark circles underneath were like swipes of purple mascara misapplied. The judge looked at each photograph, twelve in all, through gold-rimmed reading glasses at the end of his nose. Agnes Pembroke and Robert Sandhurst sat on the other side of the desk and waited as Edmund turned to the report from the treating physician that stated what had happened to Hermann's eyes and brain.

"It's a murder investigation?"

Agnes nodded her head.

Sandhurst looked at Agnes and then to the judge. "Those photos show torture and murder in connection with the cocaine trafficking from South America, probably through Venezuela. Before he died, the man—Mr. Locke—was blinded and mentally disabled—brain damaged, lobotomized, whatever you want to call it—from a torture technique and chemicals. What we'd like to do is focus on the drug-running aspect of the crime to further..." Sandhurst stopped speaking when he felt Agnes's eyes on him, and he looked at her. "I apologize. Did I speak out of turn?"

"You're the witness," responded Edmund as he waved off Agnes. "Ms. Pembroke makes the presentation, but this is not a ceremony. I want to hear what you have to say and how there's a link between what I see in front of me and the warrant. Establish the connection; you'll have an expanded warrant."

Sandhurst handed the judge the data from the FBI tracking center and explained the results of the trap-and-trace device. A number with a Venezuelan exchange had called a cell phone issued to a Sutton Beach employee. Only three staff members had company-issued cell phones. Two were women; Hermann Locke was the third. This led Sandhurst to the home on Miller Street, where he had found Agnes and two City of Wilmington Detectives inspecting a house that had been torn to pieces. All the ductwork had been torn out, and the drywall had been removed down to the studs.

It was typical for traffickers to hide money, cocaine, and marijuana in the ductwork and behind drywall in their homes and apartments. The judge was familiar with their habits and nodded as Sandhurst explained what he had seen. According to Sandhurst, there were times when the ductwork in the homes became so full of cash and product that it collapsed, spilling cash and white powder into living rooms. Whoever had searched Hermann's one-story bungalow knew where to look. Behind a mirror, Agnes had found packages of pure cocaine disguised as sacks of flour. Sandhurst handed Edmund the sacks and test results from the FBI laboratory. The judge looked at the packages and read the results. According to Sandhurst, pure cocaine this far north was unusual. By the time it arrived in North Carolina, it usually had been "cut" at least once, possibly twice, with inexpensive fillers—sugar, procaine, or cheap methamphetamine—to increase the volume and street value. The cocaine was 100 percent pure, the highest quality produced anywhere in Latin America—that's what the lab tests showed—so it was a direct link between South America and the bungalow on Miller Street.

"In our view, Your Honor, there's probable cause to believe that the calls to Mr. Locke's cell phone from a Venezuelan satellite phone thirty-eight miles out at sea are directly related to what we found on Miller Street and what happened to Mr. Locke last night. It's an ongoing crime and supports an expanded warrant. We're looking for something very expansive."

Agnes added a legal concept. "We think of this as hot pursuit, Your Honor, but with a trap-and-trace device for phones. The more expansive the court can make the warrant, the more likely we'll be able to use the leads we have."

The judge looked over his glasses at Agnes and back to Sandhurst. A tape recorder took in everything they had said to preserve the statements as evidence. The expanded warrant was made. Edmund looked back to the photographs and examined Hermann's face. Wilmington was a small town. Hermann had always been part of an extended crowd at large parties, family weddings, and funerals. The judge couldn't remember why Hermann was ever at any event; he assumed he was a friend of a cousin or a cousin of a friend or married to someone who had some relative that made for the two degrees of separation on the east side of the Cape Fear River. He had noticed Hermann at the Mansion only because his presentable blond head stuck out above the crowd, and his stride was athletic. He worked at a local bank and, like hundreds of other young men, had a nice enough golf swing to teach part time at a gated community. He was recognizable, but anyone and no one, no one the judge had ever thought about until now.

"I'll grant the expanded warrant, but tell me, how far do you want to go with this?" He held up a photo. "You have your main suspect."

It was a prompt for Agnes to step in and explain the legal concept of "hot pursuit" for the tape-recorded record. Before she could speak, Sandhurst interrupted.

"They have his phone, Your Honor, and we can track it." Sandhurst blurted it out. Agnes looked at him. She wanted to reach for his arm but couldn't stop him. "Whoever tore apart Miller Street also killed Hermann Locke. Early this morning, Hermann's number lit up at the Seapath Marina in Wrightsville, but Hermann was in an emergency room in South Carolina. Someone else turned it on."

Edmund narrowed his eyes as Sandhurst explained that Hermann had been found on the South Carolina border with nothing on him but a shirt, pants, and a blue blazer—no identification, money, wallet, or a phone. Early in the morning someone at the Seapath had the phone. The FBI had located and tracked it but lost the signal when the phone went off. Sandhurst exhaled and asked for an expanded warrant that traced the location of Hermann's phone and monitored all real-time transmissions. With confidence, he politely requested the more expansive warrant for every phone with which Hermann had contact in the recent past and near future—it was something they could obtain from the service provider.

"This is a rare circumstance, sir, an opportunity not to be missed," said Sandhurst. "At any moment, the traffickers could discard that phone, throw it in the sea, and disappear. We really need this."

Edmund took off his glasses and pressed the STOP button on the tape recorder. He looked at Agnes, who straightened her back, poised for a lecture.

"Did you know about this, Ms. Pembroke?"

"Only after the fact, Your Honor. I learned that the FBI had tracked that phone earlier today when I met with Mr. Sandhurst at the Miller Street address."

Edmund turned to Sandhurst. "Your enthusiasm is admirable, but your judgment..." He didn't finish the sentence. "This court does not condone a search method that takes what law enforcement wants, violates Constitutional rights, and then asks for forgiveness. There is a reason you need a warrant to trap and trace a private citizen's phone, and you know what it is: the Fourth Amendment. You can't search and seize anything from a private citizen in this country without probable cause. You can't listen to his phone calls. You can't follow the phone. You can't read his text message and e-mails. Not without probable cause. Getting a warrant later doesn't help. The whole thing can be challenged." He looked at Agnes. "Ms. Pembroke could lose her case if the evidence becomes inadmissible."

Sandhurst hated the tired formulations. Agnes put her hand on his arm.

"Your Honor," said Agnes, "the court might want to look at it this way: this is a classic case of 'hot pursuit' but in an electronic format. I can't give you a case, not right now, but logic tells me that what the FBI did here was an electronic car chase. I understand the limits of the original warrant, but this is really no different from a car speeding away from a pursuing police officer. The police officer doesn't need a warrant to chase or search the car. Probable cause is established, and a warrantless search is justified for the trunk, for the inside of the car, and for the person." The analogy came out of her mouth spontaneously, and it sounded good. "Mr. Locke's phone is the car. The FBI had probable cause to believe that it's involved in an ongoing crime and contains substantial evidence against Mr. Locke and others. Clearly, the deceased did not do this alone."

The judge looked at Sandhurst. "You believe all that?"

"Every word."

Edmund's mobile phone rang, and he pulled it from his pocket. It was Linus, and he didn't like to wait. The judge asked Agnes and Sandhurst to be patient, stood up, walked to the other end of the chambers, and answered. Linus eased into the questions. He told the judge that Frank had called him looking for Ben. The boy wasn't at home and hadn't left a note. The tone was curious, not alarmed. Linus stood with Frank on the beach, the yacht club at their backs, and watched the surfers. A light wind from the land picked up the waves, which broke in a procession. The surfers rose up, moved rapidly north like pelicans, suspended for a moment above the water, and then disappeared.

No, Linus said, Ben hadn't taken his cell phone—it was in his bedroom—and a bicycle was missing from under the house. They'd found it leaning on a fence at the yacht club. No one had seen him; all the people doing repairs were gone for the day. He listed the names of Ben's friends and places he might be. Fifteen-year-old boys could go anywhere in Wrightsville. He could be on a sailboat, at a nearby home, or with a friend on the beach. There was no need to worry, not until the night came.

Edmund told Linus he'd call him back and returned to the desk. He looked down at the photographs. The face he'd seen the night before was barely recognizable. It must have happened suddenly, after Hermann had left the Mansion, in the hours of the night or early morning. The judge looked up at Agnes and asked her where Hermann had been found— where on the border, east or west, on the coast or inland—and who had found him. She was startled by the question but answered quickly: deep in the inland Swamps near Mannion. But they made a mistake. Whoever left him for dead failed to kill him. Hunters found him at the edge of a pond and dragged him back. She began to describe what the hunters had told the emergency room intake nurse about Hermann's behavior, but Edmund stopped her. She had given him all he needed. It was a long way to go, a methodical disposal of a body by someone who knew where to put a carcass. It was professional, smart, and creative but local, committed by someone who knew the area.

Edmund held out his hand to Agnes. "Did you write up an order?" His eyes demanded one. Agnes pulled a two-page order from her briefcase and handed it across the desk. The judge read the document and edited it with the words "hot pursuit" in a one-paragraph addition. He expanded the time period for the warrant to six full days and backdated the order to two days earlier. He signed it in a large scrawl and handed it back to Agnes. He asked her to make copies and looked at Sandhurst. "Call your people in Raleigh," Edmund said. "Find that phone and the people who did this. Contact me any time if you need to expand it." He gave Sandhurst his cell phone number and told him to use it—for this case only. Sandhurst sat erect and thanked the judge for the hearing and warrant.

He stood up as Agnes returned with the original document and laid it on the desk. Edmund scrolled through his mobile phone, distracted. He nodded to Agnes and thanked her for the presentation. "Call Raleigh now, Mr. Sandhurst." Edmund said it without looking up. "Do it now. You will please excuse me. I have to make a call."

XLIX
Manhattan

On the forty-fourth floor, Peyton paged through the daily trial transcripts and handed pages across the desk to Rachael. They engaged in banter about the evidence Joe Boyle would present, the arguments he would make about Iberia, and how she would respond. They took every fact through a standard procedure, held it up to the light, moved it through every angle, and presented various hypothetical arguments about what the fact meant to Boyle or Peyton at various points in the trial. Cases, transcripts, and trial exhibits covered the desk, sofa, and floor in what passed for a thoughtful arrangement of exhibits only Peyton and Rachael understood. The arguments flew across the desk like pellets, some hitting Peyton, others falling harmlessly to the floor. Role-playing was the rule, and Rachael played an excellent Boyle but with a beautiful shape and hair to her shoulders. When she accused Maynard of committing an ongoing crime, Rachael stepped out of character.

"The answer's yes. That's what it was. How can we say it wasn't? Boyle doesn't have the evidence to prove it, but we do."

Peyton's mobile phone vibrated. She raised an index finger and rocked back in her chair. The phone to her ear, she asked the judge how things were, and then her face changed. Rachael stopped work. Edmund explained that no one had seen Ben for three hours and that he had left his phone in his room. They had found the red bike at the yacht club, but Ben wasn't there. It was dinnertime in early August. The light would fade in an hour. Peyton thought of the water and waves and the rip currents that pulled swimmers away from the beach. She straightened the chair and leaned forward, her elbows on the desk. Edmund sensed the silence and lowered his tone, as if it would make him seem calmer. He asked questions—he was calling for advice, not to sound an alarm—where might he look, and whom should he call? Were there friends Ben knew near the yacht club, a girl he had met, phone numbers Peyton could give him?

It was the voice Edmund affected to keep people calm, a talent that qualified him for the bench. He kept it together, never seemed to crack, and acted like everything would work out. He used it more often in recent years and hid behind the judicial temperament that had won him the job. It was the same voice he had used when Paul had died. Edmund had come to the Seventy-Seventh Street apartment to comfort her and the boys with the same soothing tone, sprinkled with logic and faith, as if he were bringing wounded parties together to resolve a dispute that had ruined lives. He had been so calm that he had convinced her for a moment that they would be well, would recover, and life would be good again. Two hours later, she found him in the kitchen weeping over photographs of the family, her wedding, her mother who had died years before, and a stack of images of her with Paul on the Masonboro beach. His whole body shook. He had told her that another death in the family other than his own would be too much to bear.

Peyton listened through the phone. There was no crack in his voice; it was confident, firm, and practiced. Edmund was good. He had mediated countless cases from the bench, thrown all his credibility and intelligence into a room of enmity and hate, and walked out with a compromise. The voice was seamless; no one but his daughter could hear beneath it. She could read him on a mobile phone eight hundred miles away.

"There's something else, Dad. Something else is bothering you. That's why you called."

Edmund was seated, exactly where Agnes and Sandhurst had left him, hunched over in his desk chair, his elbows on his knees, looking down at the dark-red carpet and rubbing his forehead. He hesitated, and Peyton responded to the silence.

"Dad, tell me everything."

"I just signed a warrant to trace a phone."

Peyton raised her head. "What's it about?"

"Narcotics trafficking."

Peyton rose from the chair and stared past Rachael, who stood up with her. "In Wilmington?"

"Yes."

"Are young people involved?"

"I can't tell you, but the face and the name—you'd recognize him. He grew up here."

"Would Ben know him?"

"No. But I see this stuff, Peyton. Ben's not home. He's supposed to be home."

"Where are you, Dad?"

"Chambers."

She could hear him breathe through the receiver. "Please find Frank," she said. "Call me when you get home. I'll text you a list of places and phone numbers. Call them, and call me back. I'll make calls too. Have Frank scroll through Ben's cell phone and find the last calls he dialed and received. That might help."

Edmund agreed. He'd go back to Frank and make calls about Ben. He confessed that he had chest pains, had just taken a nitroglycerin tablet, and would lie down for ten minutes before he left for the beach. She thanked him for the call.

Rachael stood in front of Peyton's desk. "Tell me this is not about one of the boys, please."

Peyton was in the same blue work shirt she wore on the plane that morning, pressed pants, and sandals. Rachael remained silent and watched her walk out of the office and pace the hallway. She turned back, hesitated, paced again, and returned. Peyton told her to keep going through the trial transcript, pull the pages Peyton had designated, and prepare the arguments. Each set of pages should have its own folder, and she should type the argument for each section of transcript as they always did it: 18-point font, all caps, double spaced, and inserted into precisely the same folder as the part of the trial transcript the argument addressed. She needed to think, she said, and held up her phone. "I'll be on Park Avenue."

"Peyton?"

Peyton shook her head. "Just keep going. We'll finish it up when I get back. I need to be outside for a while."

The elevator doors closed, and the shiny box descended to the ground floor. On Park Avenue, the city was alive. Peyton walked north through pockets of people and noise. She wound her way through the sidewalks, moved around large groups, and rushed through pedestrian crosswalks, holding her phone. At Sixty-Fifth Street, she stopped. Two cabs had collided on the opposite side of Park Avenue; one was on fire. The engine had exploded and thrown the hood onto the median. Smoke and flames rose out of the front of the car. Police had circled the scene and waved people away. Southbound traffic had stopped. Peyton checked in her pockets and pulled out seven twenty-dollars bills, her driver's license, and a credit card. The cab exploded again and jolted Peyton back. She retreated and pressed her back against a building. Parts of the cab flew into the air and hit windows on the third floor of an office building. People screamed and ran. The police dove behind cars. Peyton turned north, took off her sandals, and ran. She raced along the avenue and weaved through the people. At Sixty-Seventh Street, she looked back at the burning cab, expecting the second taxi to explode. She put on her sandals and dialed Rachael, who answered without a ring. Peyton walked to Sixty-Eighth Street.

"I want a continuance," she said. "Write it up. Call Boyle." She gave Rachael Boyle's cell phone number. "You can do that, can't you?" Peyton raised her hand and walked off of the corner of Sixty-Eight Street into Park Avenue.

Rachael sat in Peyton's desk chair. "You're not serious," she said and heard Peyton call for a taxi.

"I'm on my way to the airport, Rachael. Put me on the next plane to Raleigh. If there's nothing to Raleigh, get me to Charlotte. Any airline will do. Just make sure I'm on the next one out. I'll rent a car."

"Peyton, what's happening?" asked Rachael. "How do I get a continuance for tomorrow morning? It's Sunday night. What if I don't get it? Who does the argument? You know the politics around here. People are scared. Maynard's not in a forgiving mood."

"Neither am I. And don't tell Jonah Parks or Mort. Do it yourself. Put me on a call with Judge Stapleton Monday morning."

Rachael had no retort. She wasn't prepared to walk into the courtroom Monday and tell everyone that Peyton had flown south to see her family and needed a continuance. She heard Peyton direct a taxi driver to LaGuardia Airport. She imagined Stapleton's face in a permanent scowl and Boyle's theatrical shrug, as if to say that his opponent had fled to another state and given up.

"You've lost me, Peyton. Please, give me something. What's happened? If you are not here tomorrow, it's the whole case."

"Ben's missing." The cab driver accelerated across First Avenue and up the ramp onto FDR Drive. Peyton liked the maneuver. "He's not home. If he turns up before the plane pulls away from the gate, I'll come right back. If he doesn't, I'm on that plane. Link me up to the courtroom at nine thirty. I'll explain everything myself."

Rachael looked at the transcripts and mountains of paper strewn around the office. The job was impossibly large without Peyton, who raised her voice one octave.

"Get me a seat on the plane, Rachael. If Ben turns up, I won't need it, but do it now."

L

North Carolina

Rachael had booked Peyton on the 8:45 p.m. flight to Charlotte, North Carolina, which landed one hour late at 11:30 p.m. Peyton called Edmund when the wheels hit the ground, but there was nothing to report—no news, no call—just a police car outside the beach house and two patrolmen and an FBI agent inside interviewing the judge and Linus. Frank lay asleep in his bed on the second floor. When the phone rang with Peyton on the line, Edmund sat on the orange couch in the living room and spoke to the patrolmen, who wrote facts on pre-printed forms and told Edmund missing teenage girls worried them, not boys. The boys usually showed up in the early morning, bruised and hungover, with a dented car. Edmund politely nodded and turned to Linus, who handed him the phone. He kept his voice steady as he said hello and told Peyton there was nothing to report. In his hand, he held Ben's cell phone, turned it over and around in his palm, scrolled through the sent and received calls for the thirtieth time that evening, and told her that no one had made contact with Ben in the hours before or after he had returned from retrieving the crab pots.

"There's nothing here," he said. "No lead. His bike was at the yacht club, but we can't find anyone who saw him. He didn't visit anyone we've called. So far, no one we've spoken to saw him in the water."

Peyton told him she was in Charlotte and would rent a car. The drive was long but under a full moon. No one would be on the road. She'd have some coffee and be in Wrightsville around 4:00 a.m. Edmund told her he'd call her every so often, that she should call him whenever a thought struck her. He'd have the phone next to the bed. Edmund thanked the officers, who waited by the front door and assured him that a patrol car would be out front all night. He handed the phone to Bob Sandhurst, the FBI representative, who stood up, cleared his throat, and introduced himself to Peyton. It was standard procedure, Sandhurst explained. The FBI investigated any threat against a federal judge. A missing family member, even a teen-age grandson who hadn't returned home on time, was something they investigated. He gave Peyton his phone number and told her to call him any time with her thoughts on where the boy might be and, if she thought it possible, who might be motivated to take him. Sandhurst looked at Edmund when he said it, and the judge looked back. The statement chilled Peyton, who thanked him, typed his number into her phone, and left the plane.

L I

Wilmington

Route I-40 was the longer drive from Charlotte by miles but shorter by time. It traversed the North Carolina piedmont through Greensboro and Durham before turning south in a straight line to Wilmington. In the early morning, the silver Chevy Impala sped at eighty miles per hour on the empty highway without provoking the traffic police who manned the road. On a Sunday night, almost all traffic had traveled north and west away from the beaches to Raleigh, Greensboro, and Charlotte. Peyton was alone, moving along the center white lines, whose reflectors clicked off the miles a tenth at a time. The summer heat had returned to the region. Hot wind blew in the open windows, whipped her hair into a tangled stream, and kept her awake.

The Chevy approached Wilmington from the north. At College Road, it glided to a stop before a blinking yellow traffic light suspended over the intersection with Market Street. On the side of the road, Peyton parked and dialed Edmund. As the phone rang, the yellow light illuminated the sign over Market, a large, green steel plate with white lettering legible for two hundred yards. On the right, an arrow pointed to

Wilmington; on the left, to Eastwood Road and Wrightsville Beach. Edmund didn't answer. She had to dial twice to wake him up. When he heard the phone, he roared up with coughs and grunts, gathered himself, and whispered the word "hello" in the dark. Seated on the bed, Edmund held the cell phone to his ear.

"It's me, Dad. I'm on College Road. I need to talk to you."

"Yes," Edmund said, partly asleep, "sure." He was there, almost, and Peyton heard groans and ruffles, the sounds of movement as Edmund adjusted his body on the bed and moved the phone in his hand. She looked across Market Street at an empty August morning. The yellow light was the only il-lumination; streetlights were off, timed to dim at two o'clock in the morning and to dim again one hour later, which left the one-story malls and parking lots in darkness.

Edmund re-positioned the phone; his voice was clear and urgent. "What is it? You have something?"

"Ben's not home, is he?"

"No."

Peyton felt it in her chest. "Dad, tell me. Who was the war-rant about?"

Edmund rubbed his eyes and took large breaths in and out to relax. He asked her why she wanted to know and what differ-ence it would make. "The warrant is sealed. I can't—"

She interrupted, and her voice rose. "Dad, don't tell me I can't know things. I'm grasping for anything. I have to find him." Tears pooled in her eyes and rolled over the lids. Her voice was near collapse through the phone. "Please tell me who was involved." She was shaking. "Anything. Please."

"Hermann Locke," he said, and Peyton's mind went blank: no face, no image. She didn't even recognize the name. "Tall blond man, appears now and then at parties, works in a bank, part-time golf instructor at Sutton Beach. That's all I know about him. He was at the Mansion Saturday night. I saw him. It was upsetting to see what happened to him. That's why I called you."

Peyton flipped through her memory of the wedding reception. George had been the central event. Every movement and image seemed to slip back to George at the table, on the porch, down the steps, and to the curb, when he grabbed her arm and warned her to drown Iberia like an unwanted cat, burn it like hospital waste, but whatever you do, get rid of it.

"What happened to Hermann Locke?" she asked. "What did you see?"

"Photographs. The FBI had photographs of Hermann taken at the hospital. He had been tortured, left for dead in the Swamps near South Carolina. You know the place. It's all bayou, no buildings for miles. Mosquitoes, alligators—local hunters use it."

"Last night? He was tortured last night?"

"After he left the Mansion. That's what upset me. I saw him. He must have left the Mansion near the end of the reception, and sometime later someone took him. The FBI found bags of cocaine hidden in his home. He lives on Miller Street near the cemetery. The house was torn up; all the drywall and ductwork had been pulled out, furniture and mattresses ripped open. And he was blind, Peyton. They had cut his eyes. He couldn't see. He died soon after they found him. Agnes Pembroke. You know Agnes, right?"

"Yes."

"She applied for the warrant. She told me he had brain damage because of chemicals injected into his system. That's what killed him."

Peyton put the Chevy in park and leaned back in the front seat. She pictured the crowd in the Mansion and retraced her steps through the great hallway and parlors. She tried to locate her movements at the bar, back to the table where she spoke with George, and then to the porches around the house. Pictures flashed in her mind as she reconstructed images of two hundred well-dressed people, many of whom she knew or recognized, in small groups and lines, seated at tables, and sipping champagne. She flipped through the images of when she had arrived. Aunt Ellen had hugged and kissed her at the front door. When she held Peyton's face in her hands, someone had passed by on the other side, a man and woman, whose face she had seen before at extended family events, where distant cousins and high school friends gathered to celebrate a birth, a wedding, a new home, or something as simple as good weather. She had black curly hair. As they passed, the man turned his head. He had thin blond hair, high cheekbones, and square shoulders.

"Was he with someone, Dad? Was Hermann with a woman with black hair, curly black hair?"

"Darla Knowles. Yes. Everyone knows Darla. She was with Hermann, but she wasn't mentioned in the warrant."

Peyton pictured him, a long image in a blue blazer that floated through the reception with Darla, attached to him like a marker buoy in a bright summer dress. Peyton followed Darla in her memory. The dress and black hair had been in front of her when she had lined up at the bar to get a drink. Darla and Hermann had spoken in low voices, clinked their glasses together, and walked off. She tried to imagine them seated at a table or talking with someone she knew but found them on a porch, Hermann on a phone, Darla wandering, spinning her hips and skirt, looking out at the lawn and torches. An image of the dance floor rose in front of her. Perhaps they'd been there, but she couldn't find them. She remembered standing alone in the central hallway and seeing Hermann and Darla in the distance but couldn't place where and why she saw them. The dance floor, long staircase, and ornate fireplace were lined with a faceless crowd. The picture focused, and they walked out. On the porch, down the path to the main gate and street, Peyton saw the print dress and Hermann's confident stride. They were in her peripheral vision as she danced with the visitor; they were leaving.

Peyton looked up at the windshield and the yellow traffic light. Steam rose off the roadway and mall parking lots. She saw the visitor in front of her and felt his lips across hers. He was bold and elegant. When he tucked the business card into her hand, she looked at it and read his name: Robert Erwin, Houston, Texas. He had to make a call and turned away. She watched as he walked to the porch, reached into a pocket, and pulled out the phone. When he made the call, Hermann and Darla were at the gate. They were in his line of sight, and he never turned back, never said good-bye. He had lightly kissed her but never said good-bye. He left the reception after Herman. He had been there for Hermann.

"Dad, did you check the house phone? Did you check the received calls on the house phone?"

"The FBI did. But there were just some numbers and no names. They wrote down the numbers. They're working on connecting them with people and addresses."

"Dad, pick up the phone next to your bed."

Edmund did as she asked. She instructed him to press a button on the lower right, which he did, and the received calls appeared on the screen. The top four were from the Wilmington Police and the FBI. The next was from 4:45 p.m. from a mobile unit identified by the number. He read her the number.

Peyton flipped the car into drive, pulled out from the shoulder, and turned right onto Market Street. She pressed the accelerator.

"That's George's cell phone, Dad. George called the house. Ben went to see George." She raised her voice and blurted it out. George had lied about Maynard and the man he had brought to the reception. George knew the visitor who had danced with her. There was a connection with Hermann. He was following Hermann. George knew something no else did. "Get the police to Highland House." She yelled it into the phone, screamed words and phrases Edmund barely understood. He could hear her breathing and the sounds of the car moving as the phone signal faded in and out.

Peyton abruptly ended the call and dialed Sandhurst's number. The call bounced into voice mail, and she cursed the air, slammed her hand against the steering wheel, weaved, and sped through a blinking traffic light. On the second attempt, she left a message: Highland House was where she was headed, and bring the police. Now.

LII

Highland House

At 4:00 a.m., Highland House was a dark silhouette against the moon. At the main entrance, Peyton brushed her finger against the doorbell but didn't press. She looked through the widows and lace curtains. The central hall was as cavernous as she had remembered, filled with a grand piano and dark portraits. Moonlight lit the elevator column and the wine-red carpet on the stairs. Peyton pulled her finger away and left the entrance portico. She walked to a side lawn and then to the rear of the house, where terraces descended to the river in steps like the gardens of a small palace. There were acres of manicured lawns under willows and oaks.

The main terrace was as long as the house. A stage paved with terra cotta tile, it rose above the lawns. Two iron tables with immense folded umbrellas were at either end. An ornate fence of molded concrete columns ran along the terrace and down the steps. Peyton looked into the windows of the first floor. The only sound was the soft pad of her sandals against the tiles. She turned the door handles and pressed up on the windows; there was no movement. She pulled her phone from a back pocket and dialed George's cell phone. It was off but still charged; without a ring, the voice mail kicked in and asked her to leave a message.

A large stone was what she needed, and in the gardens below, Peyton found one: twenty pounds, smooth, and dense. She took off the blue work shirt and wrapped it tightly around the stone. Two sharp strokes against a windowpane broke the glass, which fell to the terrace with a sound that seemed loud enough to stop her heart and wake everyone for miles. She unlocked the window and pushed the sash upward.

The library was paneled in stained oak and filled with Victorian furniture, carpets, and memorabilia. Peyton put on her shirt and fastened the buttons. When she looked up, there was an antique globe of the world next to the same carved mahogany desk over which she once had run her fingers just to touch it. Framed nineteenth-century maps of Africa and North America hung on the walls and showed vast unmarked territories. Above the maps, glass-eyed hunting trophies peered into the darkness. A taxidermist had contorted the faces of a lion, an elephant, and a brown bear in predatory snarls as if at the instant of attack they'd been beheaded and petrified.

They were remnants of staged adventures. She'd always known it. The trophies were props for stories, none of which were completely true. George had dined out on them all his life: lions in Kenya, caimans in the Amazon, and bears on Kodiak Island. They were long-winded tales of bravery, peppered with humor and an occasional toast to the safari guide. But he wasn't a real hunter. He was a wealthy tourist who paid people to take him into game parks, protect him, and make sure he bagged a trophy to show friends and lackeys. In the past, the stories were amusing, filled with embellishments, sometimes annoying in their length, but always entertaining tales of risk almost gone wrong. Now they were lies. As she moved around the room, she imagined George at the long main table at Highland House telling tales to fawning executives and cronies. The amazement and laughter rose on cue, as if George had ordered a delicious response from the menu and served it to each guest, who dutifully ate a piece to oblige the host.

He had fooled her, the firm, and the idiots who had sat before him like dogs waiting for a reward. Amiably, she had listened and nodded, patient then but cringing now—and angry, as if she had been a servant who scurried to answer "yes" whenever the client called. She had enabled him. Her perfect presentations in court and to Maynard executives were for him. They had always been for him. He had chosen her, promoted her, orchestrated who she was and where she was, as if she was his own brilliant and devoted daughter. Her credibility in the courtroom was close to perfect. If Peyton said it, Judge Stapleton adopted it. It was why they paid her so much; they'd have paid far more. It was why Jonah Parks couldn't replace her. And it was all for George. She made him look good and righteous. When she spoke, George spoke. He had designed it that way from the beginning and created for himself the veneer of a beautiful and brilliant forty-year-old woman to speak for him.

She felt the arteries in her neck pound blood into her head. When she found him, she would want to kill him. She would bring him so close to the end that his heart would give out by itself.

Peyton took off her sandals and left the library. She entered the main hallway, where the elevator column reached up to the fourth floor. She left the sandals at the base of the stairs, which she mounted slowly, one at a time, her bare feet soundlessly pressing down on the thick red carpet. On the second floor, she looked both ways and whispered George's name. The word disappeared into darkness like she'd thrown it over a ledge. She walked to the right, to the open door of his bedroom that faced the street, away from the cascading moonlight in the hallway. At the doorway, she looked at the outline of the canopy bed and said his name in an audible voice. There was no response.

Across the room, George sat in a large wing chair with his feet square on the floor, his head back and tilted to the side. In the dim light, Peyton saw him. She stepped into the room and walked to the chair. She crouched to see his face. His eyes were partly closed, as if sleep had overcome him, but stopped, the eyes half-closed and half-opened, unable to move in either direction. She dropped to her knees and touched the top of his hands, then his palms and fingers, which rested on the arms of the chair. They were cold and rigid. His muscles had contracted and stiffened permanently in a solid state from which they would never move again. She pressed up on the fingers of his right hand, which felt like plaster, without flexion, blood, or life. Perhaps there would be dust, she thought, like chalk, had she pressed too hard, pushed them back, and cracked them in pieces.

Peyton's eyes adjusted to the darkness. On her knees, she looked at George in moonlight that slipped in from the bathroom. He wore a pressed white shirt, dark pants, one leather shoe with laces, and a gold watch. The brace still wrapped the left leg. In his right arm, a needle was embedded in the vein with a syringe attached. It had been pushed all the way in, like a knife to its hilt. The syringe lay on George's arm, stationery, as if the chemistry had worked so fast that he hadn't time to remove it. Sweat beaded up on the nape of her neck and rolled over her chest. She looked back to the door and around the room in the darkness. Her scalp went numb. It was nearly perfect: an overdose of something, perhaps the same potassium ferro-cyanide that had ended Arthur Konigsberg's life and led the Upper Saddle River Police to close the case and mark it self-inflicted.

Peyton withdrew her hand as the scent of decay filled her nose. She turned away, pulled in a breath of air, and then looked behind her to what she thought was a noise. She scanned the room for movement along the curtains, an outline against the wall, or a darkness that was deeper than the room. In the corner, the closet door was open. She watched it, rose, and then moved out of the room and into the hallway. She tried to speak in the hall, and Ben's name stuck in her mouth. She cleared her throat and spoke his name, looked back into the dark bedroom, and moved away, her hand on the banister.

She heard the noise again on the floor above, loud in the quiet house, a sudden movement of furniture across the floor. "Ben." She called to him in a whisper and moved quickly up the staircase. On the landing, she stopped and listened. The hallway was flooded in moonlight. From one floor to the next, the walls had changed from red silk to lemon plaster, but the sconces were the same: ornate brass lamps with crystal hanging above unlit bulbs. The crystal shook when she heard the noise again. It came from a storage closet in the hall. From the stairs, Peyton watched the knob turn and the door open. It stopped. She stood on the stairs and called Ben's name again. Then the cries started. They came from within the closet, a whimper and groans, mixed with the movement of furniture. Peyton leapt up the stairs, opened the door, and pressed it flush against the wall. Deep and low within the closet, she saw an arm and shoulder, wedged between furniture piled up, then a head of hair and a face. It was Luisa, covered in antique embroidered linens, once piled on unused furniture, now fallen upon her in heaps. She had reached out from the furniture to push the door open, but that was as far as she could move underneath the pile of chairs and tables.

Peyton flipped on the closet light, pulled from the pile an old Victorian chair, and hurled it into the hallway. When she returned, Luisa struggled into the light. Tears streaked her face. She shook as she spoke, half English and half Portuguese. She burbled up a stream of hysterical cries, as Peyton knocked furniture and linens out of her way. Luisa cried George's name and pleaded for help, said she was hiding from the man, and then raised her hands in grief-filled sobs. "Assassinado," she said.

Peyton grabbed her arm, pulled her out of the closet, and sat her on the chair. She crouched so their eyes were on the same level and asked the woman to stay calm. Luisa breathed in and burst into tears again. A waterfall of Portuguese poured out of her mouth. Again and again, she said only one word Peyton could understand—Winnabow—and Peyton stared at her, confused, as her language morphed in and out of English and Portuguese. She described washing dishes, seeing the boy in the car, and hearing a heated conversation between George and Leandro as she hid deep in the closet on the third floor. Later, the furniture had fallen, and she thought that was the end. She couldn't move, didn't want to move, never wanted to move again. Peyton listened to the incomprehensible stream of words and felt time slip forward as if the floor were sliding away, leaving nothing. She held up her hand and asked Luisa to stop. Calmly, she asked, was there a boy, did she see a boy? Luisa stopped crying. She stiffened her back and spoke in English.

"Your boy." She pointed a finger at Peyton. "The man tell Mr. George to Winnabow. He take your boy to Winnabow."

Peyton pulled her off the chair and stood her up. Luisa stopped speaking, her mouth open. "Show me the hunting rifles, Luisa. I want Mr. George's rifles."

She grabbed Luisa by the arm and descended the stairs in seconds. The older woman nearly fell as they leapt down the last set of stairs to the first floor, where Luisa fumbled with a ring of keys she kept attached to her apron. She led Peyton to a closet in the corner of the library and, inside, a cabinet sealed with a steel bar and padlock. Luisa opened the lock, pulled the door, and revealed one rifle with a polished wooden stock that stood upright in a case lined with black velvet. It was a single-shot bolt-action Italian carbine, shorter than a standard hunting rifle, less accurate at longer distances, and made in Italy during World War II. The word "Terni" was etched into the steel plate underneath the breech loading bolt.

Peyton looked at Luisa. "Is that it? That's all he has?"

"Alligators," Luisa said. "For them. In the garden. Mr. George no hunt anymore." She pointed to one of her legs. "His leg."

Peyton ignored her and pulled the carbine out of the case, opened the bolt, and looked down the barrel. There was a shine, no dust. It had been brushed and scrubbed. She put the bolt in place, cocked it, and lined up the sights, drawing a bead on a convex mirror that hung over the fireplace. She pulled the trigger. The bolt snapped forward in a millisecond with a quick metal slap—no delay on the firing mechanism. She pulled open a drawer at the base of the cabinet and found four boxes of cartridges wrapped in cellophane. She opened a box, took out a cartridge, and loaded it into the breech. It slid smoothly into the barrel until it stopped in place. She closed the bolt and turned to Luisa.

"I called the FBI. They will be here. Tell them Mr. George is dead." The older woman held her hands over her mouth to keep in a scream and stepped back against the wall. Peyton put bullets in her front pockets and gathered up the unopened boxes. "The man, the visitor, he killed George. Tell them the visitor killed George. Ben—my son, Ben—is at Winnabow. Tell them, Luisa. I'm going to Winnabow."

LIII

Winnabow Plantation

The Chevy sped across the Memorial Bridge and went over a rise on the other side of the river. Peyton lost control in a skid, moved off the road along an embankment at the base of the bridge, and brought the car back up onto the highway. She turned south for Route 133 and left black rubber marks on the macadam as the car accelerated to one hundred miles per hour. The carbine rested against the front passenger seat, the barrel pointed to the floor. She wondered whether the weapon would discharge through the base of the car and what it would hit if it did. When she reached the straightaway to Leyland, she lost her thoughts in the speed of the car and the feeling of her foot against the accelerator, pressed to the floor, bent under the weight of her leg. She dialed Sandhurst and put the phone to her ear. He answered. An explanation rolled out of her mouth in a steady stream, propelled by adrenalin. She needed the police right away. "Bring as many as you can," she said, and George Harwood was not a suicide. It was murder.

Sandhurst tried to interview her, but she'd have nothing of it; she interrupted every question and told him to come to Winnabow. Ben was at Winnabow. The man who killed

George had Ben at Winnabow on Route 133 South. The judge would tell him how to find it. Then she ended the call and dropped the phone on the passenger seat. She held the steering wheel and looked at the speedometer hover above 105.

Sandhurst stood in George Harwood's bedroom with the police and looked at the screen of his phone. Edmund sat in a chair opposite George and leaned forward. The dead body was the first he'd seen since Peyton's mother had died ten years before. He hadn't smelled death since then. Silently, he rubbed his hands together, one over the other, around and through the fingers, as if to remove a film. George's head was pushed and tilted to the side, white and cold. His eyes were open and cast down with his head turned away from the needle. His other arm was wedged back into the fold of the chair, almost under his leg. The muscles in his face and neck had flexed and stayed stiff, frozen in place by the poison. His lips were blue. A quick death; he must have felt it enter his veins, shut down the cells upon contact, and stop his heart in the middle of a beat.

Sandhurst confirmed for Edmund that it wasn't a suicide. "That was your daughter," he said and held up the phone. "Tell me, Your Honor, where's Winnabow—because that's where she's headed."

Peyton turned south at Leyland. Half a mile later, Route 133 straightened out and ran parallel to the river. The car's speed reached 100 again through the pine forests that rose up on either side of the road. Black creeks flowed under short wooden bridges and merged with the river. Twelve miles later, the Chevy skidded onto the stones at Winnabow's main gate, and Peyton reached out for the keypad. She found nothing but air, waved her hand out of the window in the darkness, and searched for the black box to punch in the numbers and open the gate. She left the car, walked along the entry road, and looked for the device in her headlights. It was gone. The entire metal stanchion, keypad, and telephone had been removed. In the beams that lit the grass in front of the car, she found it, smashed and ripped apart. A jumble of wires stuck out of the stanchion where it had been pushed over, cut off, and removed. Peyton ran to the gate, grabbed the bars, and pushed. They were locked with a chain. On the other side, close enough that she could reach out and touch it, was the white sedan positioned sideways across the road, its tires flat. Leandro had parked it against the gates as a barrier to anyone who would try to cut the chain and break through.

Back in the car, Peyton spun the wheels in reverse onto Route 133. She drove for three miles north to the alternate entrance of the plantation, a double-track road filled with weeds and small bushes that had grown up from lack of use. The car rolled through the forest and ripped up the new foliage. As she pressed the accelerator, she prayed and shouted that the hurricane hadn't thrown a tree across the road or liquefied the tracks into holes of quicksand so deep they would swallow the tires, fenders, and engine. Two hundred yards in, she arrived at the chain, which was wrapped around two trees, stretched across the road, and fastened in the middle with a combination lock. She left the car, picked up the chain, and maneuvered seven lettered disks on the lock until they spelled "Lillian," her mother's name. She opened the lock, closed it around a single link, and dropped the chain.

Two miles of narrow tracks took the Chevy through the forest, where it scraped against the trunks of trees that tore off the side mirrors. Peyton weaved around holes and aimed for a space of light at the end of the road that would bring her into the pastures. The car flew across the fields, its headlights bouncing through ruts and past horses that suddenly woke and fled. Peyton accelerated the car when a fence appeared, broke through it, and sent boards into the air in chunks and splinters.

At the barn, she turned east to the river and hurricane house, where she brought the car to an abrupt stop in front of the wide white porch. The house was dark. She turned off the headlights and pulled the carbine from the passenger seat. She felt the bullets in her pants pocket, pulled another cartridge from the box on the passenger seat, and slipped it into the breast pocket of her shirt.

She raised the barrel, pointed it at the door, and pressed the stock against her right shoulder. The carbine was heavier than she expected. She lowered her head, adjusted the weapon, and held it tightly, ready to squeeze the trigger. She walked up the steps, stayed to the porch, and circumnavigated the house with her back along the railing. She pointed the carbine at each window, her right eye aligned with the sights, focused on whatever appeared at the end of the barrel. The screen door at the back of the porch was ajar; she slipped in, no movement of the door, and looked across the large central room to the long table where Linus had served breakfast. The sun began to rise in a line at the horizon and lit the room. The table was clear and steel sink empty; a dry dishtowel spread across the countertop.

Peyton walked to the front door and opened it to the light; hot wind blew from the impoundments. At the door, near her feet, a dark stain spread across the floor. In the small light, it could have been anything—dirt, pine tar, or traces of silt from the ponds tracked in on soles. When she turned on the overhead lights and lit the room, the stains were unmistakable: thin dry streaks of deep red. On her knees, Peyton let air out of her lungs and couldn't pull it back in. She put the carbine on the floor and pressed her hands on the stains. She hoped the substance would stick to her fingers and come up from the floor as something different: spilled food, vinegar, or mud, anything but what it was. She pressed a caked part of the stain, and it broke free. Deep and wet, glowing red, blood spotted her fingers.

She breathed in with a cough and grabbed the carbine. Room by room, Peyton walked through the house and turned on lights, the barrel of the weapon pointed out front. One shot, no chance for a second, so it had to be at close range, spot on, and perfect, no misses, no accidents. Her finger lay against the trigger, just enough to feel the metal but not enough to squeeze it, not yet, not until the target was at the end of the sights. She opened the closets and looked behind doors, breathing heavily, hoping there would be no crumpled body, no head of hair or pools of blood. She had removed her sandals. The only sounds were her breaths and the movement of the carbine, which she readjusted to the proper height against her shoulder as she moved through the house. The beds were made, just as she had left them, and the rooms were empty.

Peyton ran to the car and dialed Sandhurst. She turned south to the main road that bordered the impoundments and led to the storage sheds and dock. The yellow house was flattened. Linus had pulled the oak back across the road and collapsed the walls so they wouldn't fall by themselves on a horse or a dog. As she passed the wreckage, Sandhurst answered. He told her that he was over the bridge and almost to Leyland. He begged her to stop and wait but received an abrupt command. Come in the northern entrance, she said—her father would show him where to turn—head straight across the pastures and south along the main road next to the rice fields. No one was in the hurricane house—don't stop. He urged her to wait, but she refused, and he could hear her sob as she pressed the accelerator, yelled into the phone, and said that she was heading to the storage sheds.

One mile south, the road dipped into the trough, lower than the grade of the land, and turned east to the river along the impoundments. The Chevy disappeared into the trough and ran through pools of rainwater. Peyton followed the road along the impoundments and sped up over a rise onto the long straight stretch south to the dock.

When the car flew over the rise, the high beams caught them, like deer walking south in the dark. They pushed loaded wheelbarrows piled with White Knight Flour. Leandro walked on the right side of the road next to the forest. Ben, his ankles tied together with a length of rope and his feet bleeding into the boots, limped along the opposite side of the road, twenty feet behind Leandro.

When the headlights hit them, Leandro stopped and turned. He pulled the Herstal from the holster and aimed it just above Ben's head. He fired a single bullet, which barely made a sound through the suppressor. It passed two feet over Ben and ripped a trunk. Leandro told him to lie on the ground. Ben fell flat at the edge of the road. Leandro backed up, spread his legs, and bent his knees. He held the Herstal with two hands and lined up the sights along the barrel. He fired a single shot at the windshield to find a reference point for the second shot at a moving target. The bullet produced a perfect hole through the center of the glass. On the inside of the car, Peyton heard a small sound when the bullet entered the windshield and then a blast as it obliterated the glass behind the backseat. In a crouch, balanced forward on the balls of his feet, Leandro adjusted his aim by a fraction to the right, to the driver's side, so the bullet would hit just above the steering column.

Peyton aimed the car at Leandro. She pressed the accelerator to the floor, kept her left hand on the lower right side of the steering wheel, and leaned across the front seat, her eyes barely above the dashboard. Leandro fired as she went down. The bullet went through the windshield and into the driver's headrest, which exploded in padding. He fired again, put a third hole in the glass, and moved to the left side of the road, away from the path of the car. Peyton kept her head down and hit the wheelbarrow at ninety miles per hour. Sacks flew apart against the front of the car, smacked the windshield, and exploded. They filled the rising light with dust that surrounded the road in a white cloud. The wheelbarrow flew out at an angle like a bowling pin and hit Leandro in the chest. It cracked his sternum and dropped him against the sand, where he lay flat, unable to breathe, still gripping the Herstal, which he discharged toward the impoundments when the wheelbarrow had hit him. He blinked, covered in white dust, and exhaled in pain. Open sacks of powder lay across the road.

The Chevy veered to the right and became airborne. It flew into the trees and penetrated forty feet into the forest. It bounced over a rise, cut through limbs and saplings, caromed off a large pine, and landed with a loud pop. Every air bag released, the windshield caved in, and the steering column collapsed into the driver's side of the car. Turned on its side, the car was suspended four feet off the ground on trees that had fallen across the forest floor. One unbroken headlight illuminated the wreckage.

Leandro sat up and spat blood from his mouth. He pointed the Herstal at Ben and gestured for him to stand. Ben stood and brought the undamaged wheelbarrow to Leandro, who coughed and brushed dust from his pants and shirt. He forced the boy to his knees and pressed his face onto the sacks stacked in the wheelbarrow. He holstered the weapon, untied the boy's ankles, and tied the boy's hands to the handles of the wheelbarrow, wrapping them in coils and knots so tight that Ben gasped in pain with the last pull. Without speaking, Leandro took a flashlight from his back pocket, left Ben, and entered the forest. Every so often, he pointed the beam of light back to the boy on the road.

The car listed at a forty-five-degree angle, propped up by trees, some fallen, some still standing. Several young pines were spread across the hood. A limb had shattered the windshield, flown through the front seat, and penetrated the backseat like a spear, large enough to have cut the driver in half. Leandro climbed up on the fallen trees and looked into the open driver's side window. He expected carnage. Broken glass littered deflated airbags that covered the dashboard and seats. With his elbows on the door and the Herstal in his right hand, he scanned the empty cab. The driver had fled. He looked for traces of blood and found nothing. The carbine lay against the passenger door, covered by airbags and out of Leandro's view.

He climbed down from the trees and walked to the other side of the car. The windows had shattered and left short shards of glass that stuck up from the front passenger door, now crumpled, broken, and barely attached to the vehicle. In the beam from the flashlight, he saw the blood. The driver had moved through the window and over pieces of glass. He ran his fingers along the shards, rubbed the blood between his forefinger and thumb, and stopped breathing. He listened for sounds behind him. He turned and focused the flashlight beam along the forest floor. There were spots and smears on the pine straw and fallen leaves. A trail of blood over the ground led into the brush. He looked back at the car. The whole thing was an irrational act, not something a law enforcement officer would do, to use the vehicle as a weapon, drive it into trees, and risk near-certain death. The police didn't do that. They were predictable and careful: hostage negotiators, SWAT teams, and sharpshooters. They weren't filled with rage. This person was.

He shined the light onto the trees and moved it low around the trunks where the driver might have crawled and hidden. The flashlight shone on broken limbs, bushes, and all manner of car parts that had flown out from the crash. The trail showed that the driver hadn't crawled. He had stood up and run, somewhere in the brush, perhaps at a short distance. Leandro took a step forward and stopped. Every breath brought pain to his chest. He thought about the boy, alone on the road, and the next car to come. There had to be another one, someone to follow the driver, who wouldn't have come alone. The light was rising. He kept the beam on the forest, scanned for movement, and backed away from the wreckage, out of the clearing to the road.

Ben gripped the handles of the wheelbarrow tightly to ease the pain of the ropes, which cut off circulation and turned the color of his hands and fingers to dark purple. Leandro told him to stand up and move, to push the load forward at a run. Ben begged him to loosen the ropes or take them off. He felt nothing in his hands but pain. His feet were bleeding, and he couldn't run. Leandro pushed the barrel of the suppressor onto Ben's forehead. He pulled the boy up and pushed him forward in a slow trot. Leandro turned his head back to the crash site, which was quiet, lit only by the lone headlight that flickered in the trees. He peered north for a car in the distance, the sound of an engine, a distant light along the road. There was nothing. He turned and followed Ben.

In the water at the end of the dock, an airplane floated on its fuselage. It was shaped like the hull of a boat, a modern version of a G21 Grumman Goose. Painted sky blue, it was a sleek, floating twin turboprop with a five-thousand-pound cargo capacity and no identification numbers. It rocked lightly on the river. The wings spread out parallel to the dock and rested on retractable floats that descended to the water and bobbed up and down. The doors along the fuselage were open. Stacks of White Knight Flour lined the dock. The pilot, his hair tied tightly behind his head in a ponytail, threw the sacks, two at a time, into the plane and looked back when he heard the sounds of the rolling wheelbarrow and footfalls across the wooden planks. Ben moved slowly. Leandro followed and pushed him forward.

When they arrived at the plane, Leandro guided Ben to the open cargo hold and told the pilot to start the engines. He took up the task of loading the piles of White Knight Flour into the plane, the last load of two hundred pounds. Every so often, Leandro turned and looked back across the impoundments for movement along the road. The morning light had broadened and lit the dock and rice fields, but the forest was still dark. He could see the lone headlight of the destroyed car, a dim glow in the pines.

In a burst, the propellers began their rotation, one at a time, first the left, then the right, and filled the dock with noise. The force of the wind pushed against Ben and Leandro, strained the single line that held the plane to the dock, and pulled the Goose forward, southeast to the sea. It blew back Leandro's hair and pressed his shirt and pants flat against his frame. He heaved the sacks through the cargo door. When he turned his back to the wind and faced north, he stopped loading. In the distance where the impoundments met the hurricane house, lights of cars blinked among the trees. Out in front, Sandhurst drove his standard-issue FBI vehicle, and the police followed in cruisers with roof lights flashing. They turned at the hurricane house and sped along the main road, bouncing on the ruts, two miles away, minutes from the plane and the end of the dock.

Leandro pulled the wheelbarrow up to the cargo hold, took the stiletto from his pocket, and cut the ropes that surrounded Ben's left hand. He yelled into the boy's ear to use his free hand to throw the remaining sacks into the cargo bay. On his knees, Ben complied and threw the sacks one at a time into the compartment.

The pain along the front of Leandro's chest rose and subsided as he breathed. He spit blood into the water and looked back to the line of cars. The police lights made progress and then disappeared, one by one, into the trough along the main road.

He estimated ninety seconds for the lead car to roll to a stop at the end of the dock. As he watched the flashing lights rise up in a procession out of the trough, he felt the first bullet pass by the front of his neck. It was a millimeter away from finding its mark. Even the wind and noise from the propellers couldn't mask it: an unmistakable tiny column of lead moving at lethal speed. Leandro had felt it before; it was a memory embedded in his brain from a different time and place when he had expected to be a target from a distance. By instinct, he brought his hand up to his neck as if to protect himself, belatedly, from a lead projectile that, had it hit him, would have removed his entire throat. He looked back at the fuselage, where a perfect six-millimeter circle had formed in the aluminum skin.

At the other end of the dock, Peyton stood in the early light. She was barefoot, with blood on her shirt and pants from the shards of glass that had cut her when she crawled through the passenger side window. Her face bore cuts, streaks of sweat, and dirt. She watched Ben on his knees throw sacks into the plane and Leandro quickly turn to the fuselage and the bullet hole. She pulled back the breech, ejected the spent shell, and loaded a new cartridge. In the time it took her to adjust the carbine on her shoulder and realign the main site with the bead at the end of the barrel, Leandro turned to her, pulled the Herstal from the holster, pointed, and squeezed the trigger. He was far away and moved quickly. To hit a small target on the first shot in minimal light was nearly impossible. He aimed for her chest and missed her neck by one inch. Peyton squeezed the trigger. The second shot ripped past the Herstal and into the top of Leandro's right shoulder. A few inches to the right, and it would have hit him in the nape of his neck. His arm dropped, and he stepped back against the plane.

Ben saw the man stagger and stopped throwing sacks. He looked up at Leandro, who was suddenly off balance, leaning back against the Goose and looking at his shoulder covered in blood. Leandro dropped the Herstal—he couldn't feel his hand—which caromed off the dock and into twenty feet of water. Peyton's bullet had split the joint, shattered the shoulder blade, and exited through Leandro's back. It formed a second hole in the skin of the plane. The man dropped to his knees and tensed his muscles, prepared to use all of his strength.

Peyton walked forward and opened the breech. She ejected the spent shell, loaded another cartridge, raised the carbine to shoot again, and set her left foot forward of the right. She wanted him before he could touch the boy. Her right eye followed Leandro as he went down on the dock and held on to the front of the wheelbarrow. Leandro raised his eyes to Ben as Peyton lined up the bead at the side of his head.

She squeezed the trigger, but Leandro moved just before the hammer came forward. He was faster than she expected for a wounded man. The bullet went above him, through the open cargo doorway, and shattered a window on the other side of the fuselage. Leandro twisted the wheelbarrow and flipped it sideways. Filled with cargo, it slid over the side into the water.

Peyton kept her eyes on her target, opened the breech, and loaded another cartridge. As she gripped the carbine, Ben followed the wheelbarrow and disappeared over the edge of the dock. The boy grabbed a plank but lost his grip as forty pounds of cast iron loaded with one hundred pounds of cargo pulled him into the water. Peyton ran down the dock in a sprint.

Leandro fell back and watched her. She wasn't as he remembered, without the colorful dress, the white leather shoes, and her hair pulled back in a braid. She ran along the dock to kill him. Her hair was loose, and blood covered her shirt and pants. With his left hand, he grabbed the line that held the plane to the dock and pulled. The cargo bay floated closer. When it touched the dock, Leandro rolled into the plane; he pulled the stiletto from his pants pocket and cut the line. The pilot watched him and pushed the propellers into a new gear. The Goose plowed across the water like a speedboat to the center of the river. In seconds, it rose into the air and pointed east to the sun.

Leandro reclined and bled among the packages. He watched Peyton through the open cargo door. She dropped the carbine, leaped forward, flat against the planks, and then went over the edge into the water. With one free hand, Ben had held a joist under the dock but had lost his grip and descended with the wheelbarrow twenty feet down. When he landed on the silt, he was surrounded by White Knight Flour. Peyton swam to the bottom and found him pulling at the line that wound around his left hand and attached him to the wheelbarrow.

The cars rumbled over the dock, lights flashing. Sandhurst jumped from the car and ran to the end. He lay on the boards, his head over the edge. He saw nothing, went into the water, and swam down into a dark green haze.

Twenty feet below, Peyton pulled the knot free and uncoiled the rope from Ben's hand. They rose off the bottom. In their ascent, Peyton pushed the boy upward ahead of her, past Sandhurst, who stopped and turned back to the surface. Ben burst out the water and breathed. He was under the dock and reached for the joist he had held moments earlier. Forty pounds lighter, he gripped the wood with both hands and coughed. Peyton and Sandhurst came up next to him. She grabbed the joist and put one arm around Ben. Rapidly, she breathed in and out and told him she loved him. She kissed him on the side of his head. The words came out in a stream, choked up through her throat in a broken rhythm that shook her torso. "Nothing will ever happen to you." She said it twice. Her face was clean and wet. The blood on her forehead and cheekbones had washed away. Ben hugged her with one arm. Sandhurst hung onto a joist and watched.

"You hit him." Ben whispered the words in her ear. "You hit him."

She threw her head back, adjusted her grip on the joist, and pulled in a long, slow breath of air. The morning light slipped in through gaps between the boards and lit the three figures, just above the water. Peyton exhaled in a long, loud gasp that turned into a laugh that reverberated off the boards. Ben held onto her and closed his eyes.

Part 5

August 12, 2010

LIV

US District Court, Foley Square

Three days later, Peyton walked out of the elevator onto the sixth floor of the US courthouse on Foley Square in downtown Manhattan. Her heels clipped along the marble floor as she walked past groups of pinstriped suits in separate huddles. Whispering, they looked up, then away, and whispered again to each other. Joe Boyle left the hallway and entered a witness room, followed by a young woman with a stack of documents and a briefcase. Julian Smythe turned to Peyton with a smile and perfect teeth. He made the skin on the back of her neck tighten. He nodded and tracked her with his eyes as she walked to the courtroom door. She moved past him and nodded a perfunctory good morning.

She entered the courtroom, where Rachael stood at the defense table. In a brown jacket and black pants, Ted sat on the first bench. He rose when he saw her. Peyton carried a soft leather briefcase with five folders. Within were copies of the dissolution record for Iberia, the documents Ted had found in Bermuda, and typewritten notes of precisely what Peyton intended to say to Judge Stapleton about each document and every remaining issue. The notes contained citations to cases, direct quotations, and argument. Rachael stood and slid two folders in front of Peyton as she arrived at the table. One contained the motion for a directed verdict, written the week before, and a copy of Boyle's memorandum opposing the motion, which Rachael had picked apart on three sheets of typewritten notes. The second had the letters "HK" in black marker written on the front.

"It's all there," Rachael said, touching the folder. "Just like you wanted it." Peyton nodded.

At the back of the courtroom, Eric sat on a bench. Peyton raised her hand to say hello and motioned for him to approach the defense table. He stood and walked to her. He spoke first, told her how sorry he was, and asked about Ben, Frank, and her father. She thanked him, patted him on the lapel, and asked him if he was ready. He pulled out his cell phone from the inside pocket of his jacket, showed it to her, and then slid it back in. She nodded and thanked him.

On Boyle's side of the courtroom, technicians set up a projector and screen operated by a laptop. On the screen, the projector displayed the schematic triangle of George's transaction to dissolve Iberia. She watched the technician center the image on the screen as Smythe passed behind her. "Beautiful," he said over her shoulder, "isn't it?"

Peyton ignored him and arranged her folders in the order she would use them. She opened the last folder labeled HK, reviewed a list of questions, and positioned it on the bottom of the stack.

The court clerk announced the arrival of Judge Stapleton, and the lawyers put down their papers. Everyone stood at attention. The technicians shut down the projector and headed to the first row of benches.

"Welcome," Judge Stapleton said from the bench. "Please sit down." The lawyers and parties sat. Stapleton waited for a nod from the stenographer and court clerk and then began the proceedings. He addressed Peyton. "From the reports I've received, much has happened since Friday, Ms. Sorel."

"Yes, Your Honor."

"In light of that, do you still wish to proceed this week?"

"We do."

"You know you don't have to. I'll give you more time if you'd like."

"Thank you. We're ready to go."

"Very good. Mr. Boyle and all counsel and parties present, this is a hearing on multiple issues. Before the court is a motion from the plaintiffs to reopen fact discovery based on recently acquired information and a competing motion for a directed verdict from the defendant. The court asked counsel for the defendants to be prepared to discuss the issue of Iberia Corporation so the court can determine whether the facts and circumstances of that company could be related to the claims and defenses in this case. Is everyone prepared?"

The lawyers said yes in unison.

"Ms. Sorel, what do you have for us?"

Peyton rose and walked to the lectern. She wore a small Band-Aid on the largest cut on her forehead. A bruise on her right cheekbone and jaw had yellowed. Otherwise, she was the same, in a dark-blue suit and off-white blouse with no collar. Judge Stapleton looked up as Peyton raised her head from the papers.

"It's good to have you back. Are you ready?"

"I am."

"The time is yours."

"Thank you, Your Honor. First, I'd like to address the question you raised last Friday." She turned to Eric Olsen, who sat on the first bench. "The defendant calls Eric Olsen."

Eric rose and walked to the witness stand. Peyton watched him adjust the microphone and place his hands in front of him.

The direct examination was simple. "Mr. Olsen, could you explain for the court your responsibilities and the date those began."

Eric explained that he had come to Maynard as chief financial officer and treasurer in 2002 and supervised all financial affairs worldwide since November of that year. He explained how he directed a team of accountants to prepare annual and quarterly budgets, enforce regulatory compliance within the company, and prepare financial forecasts and statements that addressed rent, equity, and pricing calculations for all assets.

"In all the time you've worked at Maynard," said Peyton, "have you ever heard the word 'Iberia'?"

"Not until last week."

"Why is that?"

Eric turned and looked directly at Judge Stapleton. "It was dissolved before I arrived."

"May I approach, Your Honor?"

Judge Stapleton nodded, and Peyton handed Eric and Judge Stapleton copies of George Harwood's cover letter and Iberia's certificate of dissolution dated August 2, 2002.

"Please identify those for the court, Mr. Olsen."

Eric complied and explained what they meant.

"Did you find those documents?"

"No. Counsel found them."

"In counsel's files?"

"Yes."

"Does Maynard have any files related to Iberia?"

"No."

"Why not?"

"They were destroyed as a routine matter approximately one year ago."

"Please explain for the court why that happened."

Eric cleared his throat. "We have a standard seven-year document-destruction policy, the same as almost every sizable company. Although we are supposed to preserve all documents associated with the claims in this litigation, we understood that documents completely unconnected with the claims in this case could be subject to the destruction policy. Since Iberia was dissolved three years before Maynard ever made the loan to CIT and five years before any of the events related to this case, no one in our company ever thought that the Iberia files would be subject to this litigation. I can't see how they could be."

"That's for me to decide."

"Yes, Your Honor."

Peyton handed up the internal Maynard document prepared by Dennis Upton that showed authorization and destruction of all Iberia files. Eric identified the document and explained the procedure. She showed him the written policy for document destruction, and he explained it.

Rachael picked up three boxes, arranged them on the table, and stood over them.

"Mr. Olsen," Peyton said, "did counsel for Maynard investigate Iberia since last Friday?"

"Yes, you did."

"Did you personally review those files?"

"Yes, with you."

"What are they?"

"Miscellaneous documents for the sale of land in Ecuador in 2002."

"How much land?"

"Three hundred and forty thousand acres of agricultural land."

Judge Stapleton visibly stiffened.

"Had you ever seen those documents before I showed them to you?"

"No."

"Had you ever heard of the transaction before I identified it for you?"

"No."

"Do the documents you reviewed appear to be complete?"

"No."

"Do the documents tell you the total sales price of the land?"

"Yes. Two hundred and fifty million dollars."

"Your Honor, I have no other questions at this time."

Stapleton looked at Boyle. "Would you like to cross-examine?"

Joe Boyle stood up. "No, Your Honor. We have nothing for this witness. We will proffer an analyst who will explain the documents and tie them to ongoing activities of Maynard. It's why we set up the screen. We'll show the court all the documents. We'll explain each one."

Stapleton told Eric he was excused, and Eric stepped down. "Ms. Sorel, anything further?"

"Yes, the defendant calls Julian Smythe."

A murmur rose in the courtroom, and the word "what" silently formed on Smythe's mouth. Boyle stood up. On the last row of benches, Jonah Parks wrote a note on a legal pad and handed it to Fred Mannesman, who was seated next to him. "She tell you about this?"

Mannesman wrote back. "No."

"Your Honor," said Boyle, "Ms. Sorel is playing a game. I respectfully request that the court make her stop. My colleague is not a witness to anything. He's the Fund's lawyer. He has no direct knowledge of any fact, and he has no qualifications as a financial expert." He addressed Peyton. "Stop the tricks; make a proffer. What could Julian possibly say on the stand that's relevant to why we're here today?"

Stapleton took off his reading glasses and spoke. "Ms. Sorel, I assume you have a proffer."

"I do. Mr. Smythe independently obtained the Iberia documents outside of the discovery process. We did not furnish them, because we had virtually nothing, and there was no reason to think they are relevant. Mr. Olsen just testified to that. Neither Maynard nor its lawyers knew anything about Iberia until last Thursday. How Mr. Smythe obtained the documents should be a matter of record. If he acted properly in obtaining them, he should have no problem taking the stand and explaining it to the court."

Stapleton nodded. "Mr. Boyle?"

Boyle asked the judge for a moment and spoke with Smythe, who whispered to Boyle, nodded, and buttoned his jacket. He was dressed in a khaki suit lighter than his tanned face.

Smythe walked to the witness stand, raised his right hand, and swore to tell the truth. He sat down and unbuttoned his jacket.

Peyton started with easy questions and called Julian by his first name. "Where do you work?"

"Boyle and Price."

"Are you a partner?"

"Yes."

"Does all of your compensation as a lawyer come through that firm?"

Boyle sat up.

"Yes."

"So you don't receive any salary or bonus from any other firm, do you?"

Smythe leaned toward the microphone. "No."

"Are you associated with or do you hold a position with any other firm?"

Smythe hesitated, looked at Boyle, and answered truthfully. "No."

With the next question, she allowed him to say anything he wanted. "Julian, please tell the court where you obtained the box of documents you showed the court and jury last Thursday."

"A confidential source." He had not formulated an answer and instinctively resisted.

"Who?"

"A whistleblower." Smythe could think of nothing else.

"Please name the whistleblower."

Boyle spontaneously played his part and objected. "Your Honor, evidently the identity of the person is confidential. Ms. Sorel shouldn't even ask the question."

She pushed harder. "We can clear the courtroom, Your Honor. The court should hear what Mr. Smythe knows."

Boyle objected.

Smythe looked at the judge and answered. "From a whistle-blower, sir."

Peyton followed. "Did you obtain them from a private home in Upper Saddle River, New Jersey?"

Smythe looked at Peyton.

"You can answer that, Julian, can't you?"

Stapleton interjected. "You don't have to reveal the source's identity."

"I cannot answer, Your Honor. It could reveal the source's identity."

"You found them in the basement of the home?"

Smythe had no choice. "I cannot answer that."

Mannesman and Parks sat up straight on the back bench; Parks wrote, "Why is she doing this?" on the legal pad and passed it to Mannesman, who shook his head.

"Is it fair to say," asked Peyton, "that the source authorized you to take the documents?" There was only one answer.

"Yes."

"You're certain."

He had to say it. "I am."

"Julian?" Peyton asked.

"The source is confidential."

It was all she needed. "No further questions."

Parks sat back on the bench. He wrote on the pad "WTF?" and underlined the letters and question mark twice. Mannesman shook his head.

Boyle stood up. "No questions, Your Honor."

Smythe stepped from the witness stand, returned to the plaintiffs' table, and sat down.

Stapleton wiped his reading glasses on a cloth. "Ms. Sorel, anything further?"

"Yes, Your Honor." She nodded to Rachael, who left the courtroom.

Moments later, Rachael held the courtroom door as Helen Konigsberg walked in on aluminum crutches. One step at a time, she proceeded to Peyton, who stood at the lectern in the center of the courtroom. Maddie walked next to her and carried a portable oxygen tank and mask. Except for the light metallic click of the crutches, the courtroom was silent. She wore a cobalt-blue summer suit, a strand of white pearls around her neck, and long white gloves. Her hair was done in silver waves. Her eyes and cheekbones were painted in mild makeup that gave color to her face. The gait was labored and frail but elegant as she maneuvered to the center of the courtroom. She stopped before Peyton and nodded.

"The defendant calls Helen Konigsberg." Peyton stood aside as Helen made her way to the witness stand. Rachael and Maddie helped her up the two steps and leaned the crutches against the back wall. They arranged the oxygen tank next to Helen on the chair and handed her the mask. Helen offered her hand to the judge, and he waved back.

Boyle stood. "We object. She's not on any witness list."

"This is impeachment," Peyton said from the lectern. She laid the folder marked "HK" on the lectern.

"Overruled. Swear in the witness," said Stapleton.

Helen swore to tell the truth, and the judge asked Peyton to proceed.

Sitting at the plaintiffs' table, Smythe stared straight ahead at Helen. Boyle whispered to him. Smythe didn't react.

Peyton began. "Mrs. Konigsberg, would you please introduce yourself to Judge Stapleton."

Helen took a breath of oxygen and spoke. She gave her name and address.

Peyton asked her about Arthur, his professional interests, how long they were married, and the home they shared in Upper Saddle River.

"When did he die?"

"In 2002."

"In 2002, did your husband have any files he had brought home from his office?"

"Many."

"Where did he keep them?"

"In his home office and the basement." Helen took some more oxygen.

"How many files did he have in the basement?"

"Thirty boxes."

"Exactly thirty?"

"Yes, they were numbered on the lower-right corner of the front of each box. He was obsessive about order." Boyle looked at Smythe.

"Did your husband keep a list of those boxes?"

"He did."

"Do you have a copy?"

Helen reached into the pocket of her suit and pulled out a folded, double-sided typed sheet of paper with thirty numbered entries.

"Is that it?

"Yes." Helen took another breath of oxygen.

"Please give it to Judge Stapleton." Helen handed it to the judge, who reviewed both sides.

"Have you ever met a lawyer named Julian Smythe?"

"Yes."

"Can you identify him?"

Helen leaned forward to the microphone and pointed. "The blond man in the khaki suit."

"How did you meet him?"

"He came to my house with my estate lawyer, Christopher Holland."

"Had you invited him?"

"No, not him. I'd asked Mr. Holland to retrieve some trust and estate files in my basement. I'd recently changed lawyers."

"Had Mr. Holland ever been in your house before?"

"Yes."

"Had he ever been in your basement before?"

"Yes."

"Why?"

"To identify and inventory the estate files. He came back to collect them."

"Did Mr. Holland explain why Mr. Smythe was there?"

"Yes, to help remove the files."

Peyton turned a page within the last folder to a new set of questions. "Did he tell you that Mr. Smythe worked with him?"

"Yes, they both did."

"What did they say?"

Helen looked at Smythe. "Mr. Smythe said he worked with Mr. Holland."

"Did they take the estate files?"

"Yes."

"How many boxes?"

"Five."

"How do you know?"

Helen pointed to the list in Stapleton's hand. "The first five boxes on the list; I gave a copy of the list to Mr. Holland the first time he came to the house. I told him to take the first five boxes. They all had numbers."

"Did he take only five boxes?"

"No. He took boxes twenty-six and twenty-seven and part of box twenty-eight." She pointed to the list.

"What does the list say about boxes twenty-six through twenty-eight?"

The judge handed her the list, and she took another breath of oxygen. "All three are designated 'Bermuda Company.'"

"Do you know what 'Bermuda Company' means?"

"No."

"Was it connected to your estate plan?"

"No. Those were Arthur's files from work."

"Did Mr. Holland acknowledge to you that he had taken the wrong files?"

"No. He denied it. He said he'd only taken the estate files. But miraculously, they reappeared once he returned the first five boxes. They're in the basement now."

"Have you terminated Mr. Holland as your estate lawyer?"

"Yes."

Peyton turned the page to new questions.

"Do you know Mr. Boyle?"

"We're acquainted. He and I belong to the Polo Club. It's near my home. I know his reputation."

Peyton addressed Judge Stapleton. "I'll turn this witness over to Mr. Boyle now."

Joe Boyle couldn't resist, and Peyton knew it. He'd sliced up so many elderly witnesses he couldn't keep track of the number. Weak memories, confusion, medication, and bereavement—they added up to a line of cross-examination Boyle had practiced for thirty years. He could do it standing on his head. Peyton rocked back in her chair and let him go.

Jonah Parks wrote a note and handed it to Mannesman: "This could be ugly." Mannesman put a large X through the note and handed it back.

Boyle was delicate. "How do you do, Mrs. Konigsberg," he asked, and she responded that she was feeling as well as could be expected. She took a breath of oxygen.

"You suffer from emphysema?" He knew the answer.

"Yes."

"Are you on medication?"

"I am."

"Please tell the court the medicines your take."

Helen responded. The list was long.

"Are there any side effects?"

"Yes."

"You sleep a lot?"

"Yes."

"You're disoriented?"

"Sometimes."

"And you have balance problems?"

"Yes."

"Ever fallen?" He knew that answer too.

"Yes."

"Have you hit your head?"

"Once."

"Were you hospitalized?"

"Yes."

"You saw a neurologist?"

"Yes."

"That was four months ago?" He knew it all.

"Yes."

"Helen, how old are you?"

She glared at him. "Seventy-nine."

"Do you spend any time with people your own age?"

"Now and then."

Peyton sat back in her chair and watched. Jonah Parks leaned forward on the back bench.

"Do they have any memory problems?"

Helen took a breath of oxygen. "They do."

"What do they forget?"

"Appointments, the time, sometimes the names of friends and family. They lose things now and then."

"Like what?"

"Wallets. Handbags."

"How about you? Do you have any memory problems?"

"Somewhat."

"How long ago did Christopher Holland and Julian Smythe come to your house?"

"Approximately two weeks ago, perhaps. I'm not sure. It's on my calendar."

"Have you ever failed to remember clearly anything recent that had happened two weeks in the past?"

Helen stared at him and hesitated.

"You are under oath, Mrs. Konigsberg."

Helen was honest. "Yes."

"You didn't actually go down in the basement and check the boxes that you claim were missing, correct?"

"No, I did not."

"You sent your servant?"

"Yes."

"Her name is?"

"Maddie."

"You're relying on Maddie to tell you that the files were missing, correct?"

"Yes."

"Maddie's not a lawyer, is she?"

"Of course not."

"She's not a paralegal."

"No."

"Did Maddie ever graduate from high school?"

Helen was silent. Peyton looked straight at Helen. Jonah Parks had his hands over his mouth.

"Forgive me; I'll rephrase it. Do you know one way or the other whether Maddie ever graduated from high school?"

"I do not."

"And the files you claim were missing are now on the shelves, correct?"

"Yes."

Boyle looked at Judge Stapleton. "That's all I have." He turned back to the plaintiffs' table and Smythe.

Parks and Mannesman leaned against the bench. Parks exhaled and looked at the line of suits along the back wall and saw Mort Shaw, who wrote on a pad.

Peyton rose. "Redirect, Your Honor?"

"She's your witness, Ms. Sorel."

"Mrs. Konigsberg, do you regularly allow people to examine files in your house?"

"No."

"Why not?"

"Many reasons. I'm a very private person, and I have many valuable objects, paintings, and sculpture I've collected over time. I don't want things to go missing."

"How about lawyers—do you ever let them in your house?"

"Only if I have to."

"When have you had to do that?"

"Recently, for estate reasons, appraisals, that sort of thing."

"Do you require that they identify themselves first, before they come to your home?"

"Yes."

"Why?"

"I want to know who I'm hiring."

"Did you require that Mr. Smythe identify himself?"

"Yes."

"Had you known Mr. Smythe worked with Mr. Boyle, and not Mr. Holland, would you have allowed him to review private files in your home?"

"No."

"Had you known that Mr. Smythe was trying a case against your husband's former client, would you have allowed him to review private files in your home?"

"No."

"Did you require lawyers who entered your home to present a business card?"

"Yes."

"Did Mr. Holland know that in advance?"

"Yes."

"How did he know that?"

"I told him."

"Did Mr. Smythe give you a business card?"

"Yes."

"Do you have it?"

"Yes."

"Please show it to Judge Stapleton."

Helen reached into the pocket of her jacket and pulled out a white card. She handed it to the judge. Boyle turned to Smythe, who looked straight ahead.

"Is that the card he gave you?"

"Yes."

Stapleton read the card, and Peyton continued. "What does it say?"

"It says Mr. Smythe works at Holland and Wright."

"Is he a partner or an associate?"

Stapleton answered for her. "Partner."

"Does Mr. Smythe have an office at Holland and Wright?"

"No."

"How do you know that?"

"When I learned from Maddie that the boxes were missing, I called. Mr. Holland claimed nothing was missing. Later, I called for Mr. Smythe. They said no one by that name worked there."

Judge Stapleton pointed the card at Smythe. "Stand up and approach the bench." He looked at the name. "What's your middle initial?"

Smythe stood and approached, but said nothing.

"Mr. Boyle," said Stapleton.

"Yes, Your Honor." Boyle stood and walked to the bench.

"Did you or Mr. Smythe have this card printed?"

Boyle put his hand on Smythe's elbow, and Stapleton glared at Boyle. Boyle took the card, examined it, and gave it back.

"Answer me," said Stapleton.

Smythe and Boyle were silent.

"By your silence, Mr. Smythe, I infer that you are invoking the Fifth Amendment protection against self-incrimination. Is that true?"

Smythe remained silent.

"Mr. Boyle, to your knowledge, has Mr. Smythe ever been associated with Holland and Wright or been a partner at Holland and Wright?"

Boyle looked at Smythe and back to Stapleton. He remained silent.

"I see," said Stapleton. "You'll both need lawyers. So will Mr. Holland." The judge looked to Peyton, who stood at the lectern. "What's the next item on the agenda?"

"Our motion for a directed verdict."

"Indeed. I've reviewed the papers. The motion is granted. A written opinion will follow." He spoke to the bailiff. "Court is adjourned. Dismiss the jury, and thank them." Stapleton slammed the gavel, stood up, and pointed to Boyle and Smythe, the card still between two fingers. "We will see each other again." He disappeared to his chambers behind blue curtains and the back wall of the courtroom.

LV

Foley Square

When the judge departed, the courtroom cleared. Smythe left without speaking; Boyle sat at the plaintiffs' table alone with his palms on his bald head. He stared straight ahead at the court clerks, who cleaned their desks and shut down their computer terminals for the day.

Rachael escorted Helen Konigsberg to the hallway, where Maddie was waiting with a wheelchair. They entered the elevator, descended to the ground level, and rolled out to a waiting car. Rachael returned to place papers in briefcases and boxes. She directed two men in suits to pack up exhibits and make sure they safely arrived at the Park Avenue offices. Every box was to go into Peyton's office. She held a key in her hand. "Lock the office," Rachael said to the men, "and return the key to no one but me."

Fred Mannesman approached the defense table. He shook Peyton's hand—for Fred, the gesture was as warm as he ever could be—and asked her to come to the windowless conference room outside in the hallway to speak. "Short debriefing," he said. "That was masterful."

She smiled and thanked him. She had anticipated the request and put the HK folder and Iberia documents in her briefcase. Mannesman walked to the doors of the courtroom and looked back. Five other suits from Stewart & Stevens filed out with him, Mort Shaw and Ralph Draper among them. Mannesman called to her from the door. She looked up and said yes.

"Do you want me in there with you?" asked Rachael.

"No, you're safer outside."

"You need a witness?"

"I'll be fine." She handed Rachael the briefcase.

Eric stood in the back of the courtroom and watched Peyton. He walked to her and held out his hand. She shook it. He congratulated her, thanked her, and offered pleasantries, which she accepted graciously with a nod and smile. He pulled out his phone and turned it on. She watched him type an e-mail to Maynard's representative in a Manhattan bank. The e-mail authorized the transfer of funds from Maynard's account to Peyton's in the same bank: $10 million in cash, a journal entry from one account to another—it would be completed in minutes. He copied Peyton on the e-mail. She turned on her phone and waited for the authorization. It appeared and contained a request for confirmation directly to her when the transfer was complete.

"Were they waiting for this?"

"Yes," Eric said. "I told them to expect it. Actually, I told them it was likely."

"When does the confirmation come in?"

"A few minutes. It's fast."

Peyton thanked him.

Mannesman opened the courtroom door. He asked her to enter the counsel room in the hallway. She nodded to Fred and left the courtroom.

Body heat had already warmed the room. A rectangular table with steel chairs was in the center. Piles of exhibits were on the table, and stacks of white boxes lined the back wall, stuff Peyton would have used had the case gone forward. She was looking at six men in $4,000 suits. Some leaned against the walls; others sat on chairs. Each one had a perfect haircut. Mannesman sat at the table and lit his pipe. She closed the door, leaned back, and gripped the door handle. In her other hand, she held her phone.

A stream of smoke from Mannesman's mouth formed a cloud. "First, let me say that what we saw was textbook perfect. I've seen some great moments in a courtroom, but none better. And you did it against the best. Joe's probably ruined for years, possibly forever. Smythe?" Mannesman shook his head. "He may never practice again."

The other five agreed and congratulated her. She thanked them and kept her back against the door. She watched Mannesman's cloud of smoke hit the ceiling and spread apart. She felt hot and thought of the last moment in moonlight when Leandro must have stood over George in the bedroom at Highland House, pulled cyanide into the syringe, and felt for the vein. According to the coroner, it had taken him instantly. She had arrived nine hours later and kneeled in front of him in the dark. In her memory, she could still smell the first foul odor of decay.

Mort Shaw sat at the far end of the table. "We need a plan," he said. "How do you think we deal with this?"

"Just a preliminary discussion," Mannesman said.

Standard strategy, she thought, an invitation for a constructive proposal, to be part of an agreement to protect everyone, bury the inconvenience, and move on. The alternative was unspoken. She either agreed or risked being the first under a wheel, before she knew or could stop it.

"What are you thinking about?" Peyton asked.

"I'm thinking about getting our arms around this and moving forward," Mort said. He had perfected the equivocal euphemism. It was code; they all knew it. Just as well, they knew how to deny it.

Jonah Parks leaned against a wall. "I'm thinking about how not one of us ever has to lawyer up and take the Fifth." He laughed when he said it.

Mannesman raised his head to Parks and took the pipe out of his mouth.

Parks feigned surprise. "We're making it plain here, aren't we?"

Peyton wished for a recorder.

Mort looked up at the ceiling and thought out loud. "All but a few documents are gone, and Arthur and George are dead." His eyes fell on Peyton. "What does that tell us?"

"It's a tough case for a prosecutor," Peyton said. "Without more, it probably goes away."

"Then why," asked Mannesman, "would we give them anything more?" Mannesman held the pipe in his mouth and puffed smoke from the side.

"I'm a material witness to murder."

"Suicide," Mort said.

"Two murders, eight years apart."

"Not provable," said Mannesman.

Peyton shook her head. "Money laundering on an unimaginable scale. Law enforcement will want to know about that, even if everyone is dead, every document is shredded, and there's no one to prosecute."

Mannesman responded. "I agree that Ted is very good. He's brilliant. But I doubt anyone can prove what he's told you. It's a theory without evidence." Mannesman put a match to the pipe again.

"If that's what you want," Mort said, "let's do it together and not rush into it. You don't have to be on your own. We'll insulate and protect you. Take eight weeks. Fred will prepare an internal report. It will be attorney-client privileged. We can discuss it when you return. We'll be up front with Maynard and give them the full truth. They deserve to know how exposed they've become. And Jonah's already volunteered to draft an ethics complaint against Boyle and Smythe. Knowing Stapleton, he'll probably have their licenses suspended. This case won't come back."

"Protect me from what?"

"I don't know," offered Mort. His role playing was impeccable; he was an actor without face paint. "Once these things start, it's impossible to predict where they'll go. You've been Maynard's exclusive trial counsel for more than a decade. George made your practice. He was your book, millions every year. You have a family relationship. What will the authorities do with that? They'll want to know what you knew. You sure don't want that—the authorities parsing through every verdict you won, every piece of information you knew or didn't know, all your e-mails and phone calls with George. I don't want that. I don't think you want that. Getting things organized now may be your best opportunity."

The threat was unmistakable, like sudden, oncoming traffic, about to hit her on Park Avenue. They kept talking, but she didn't hear them. She was back on Forty-Eighth Street, Sunday night, at the crosswalk. The two cabs were on fire, and this time she walked to the median for a closer look. Columns of accelerating cars appeared on the street. They raced forward. She ran to the median and felt the heat of the burning cars. Then she was heading for the plane and sitting in the rental car at the corner of Market Street and College Road in Wilmington. The blinking yellow light pulsed in the darkness over the intersection. She left the median on Park Avenue and faced south. Chrome grills and headlights flew forward. They almost hit her, passed by, and she turned and watched the red taillights head north to Harlem. One of the cars exploded. Like the taxi, its hood shot into the air, then the windshield and trunk lid. One at a time, the cars exploded without a sound, red and yellow, in rolling flames that billowed up into black. Their hoods and doors flew onto the sidewalks and into the glass of office buildings. Spinning wheels hit windows and took down awnings. The explosions split the cars in half and lit them on fire. They blew skyward and took down stoplights. Again and again, flames and burning pieces of cars lit the darkness.

She put her hand on the left side of her chest and felt for the six-millimeter bullet in the pocket of her blue work shirt. It wasn't there; she was dressed for court. She'd put it in the breech and fired it as the second shot on the dock, the one that had hit Robert Erwin. Sandhurst had taken the rest with the carbine she'd dropped on the dock. They'd walked into the trees and collected the box of bullets from the car, still suspended on trunks and broken limbs. Everything was in an FBI evidence locker, even the discharged shell casings. She'd returned to Highland House with Sandhurst and met with Agnes. They'd watched the coroner collect George's decomposing body. By the time she'd arrived, he was on a rolling stretcher, covered by a sheet. She had told Sandhurst and Agnes that it wasn't a suicide and recounted Arthur's death and the documents found in Helen's basement. The coroner in the bedroom had confirmed a suspicion of homicide. He had found constriction of George's throat but no hand marks, more likely a wet towel from the bathroom used as a tourniquet around the neck to pinch the carotid artery. George was partially conscious when Leandro had administered the cyanide. Sandhurst and Agnes listened; another agent took notes. It had lasted hours and filled three notepads. Ben was in the dining room with medical technicians, who tended to his feet and ear. The FBI had interviewed him later in the morning. She'd been there with him and heard the story of George and Leandro, Sean and Joseph.

"I don't need protecting," Peyton said. Her phone vibrated. An e-mail from the bank confirmed the transfer of $10 million. She glanced at the message; the money was in her account.

Mannesman puffed out a thin line of blue smoke. "Then you'll be fine. There's no need to take this outside the firm."

"I'm a material witness to murder and money laundering. I'm not here to protect criminals or destroy evidence for clients. I can't. All of you know I can't. How do I do that? How do I go back to my office, throw it all in a vault, and lock it down? When you have an answer, let me know."

Parks couldn't help himself. "You're willing to give up your corner office?"

Mannesman pulled the pipe out of his mouth. "Would you shut up?"

"How about that ten-million-dollar success fee? You giving that up too?"

Mannesman stood up, and Parks stopped.

"Sleep on it, Peyton," said Mort. "Take eight weeks. We'll work with Rachael while you're away."

Rachael was coming with her. "I'm not an accomplice," she said. "I wasn't then, and I'm not now."

Mannesman began to speak, but Peyton ignored him. She pushed down on the door handle and leaned back. Halfway down the hallway, she heard the door close.

Rachael stood outside the courthouse at the top of the steps. Light rain fell on Foley Square. Peyton walked out the front door and waved; in a few strides, she was at the top of the steps. Rachael moved into the rain in front of her, one step ahead. Peyton opened her palms, gathered some water, and ran her hands through her hair. The steps were crowded with lawyers and court employees. Some were descending next to Peyton; others walked up the steps. The tops of black umbrellas popped open in the rain.

When they reached the sidewalk, Peyton's phone vibrated in her suit pocket. She and Rachael kept walking and weaved in and out of the black umbrellas. They headed to the car at the front of the line, a Lincoln Town Car with no medallion. Peyton felt the vibration and pulled the phone out to look at the screen. The rain had grown heavier. It soaked her shoulders and covered the screen with drops. Peyton told Rachael to stop. She didn't move as water rolled down her forehead and over her nose. The face on the phone was George, age sixty and smiling, the same black-and-white public relations photo he'd used for years. She'd seen it with his number and name when she called him Thursday night. His cell phone was calling her, the one he said he had lost but used to dial Edmund's house on the beach and contact Ben. She answered the call on the third ring and said nothing. On the other end, there was silence, not even breathing, as if George's phone was on mute. Rachael stood in front of Peyton, her back to the square. A crowd of men passed by and raised their umbrellas above the women's heads. Other black Town Cars had pulled up alongside the yellow taxis; they doubled parked and discharged passengers. The crowd had doubled in size.

Peyton grabbed Rachael's jacket and pulled her away from the curb. She scanned the windows of the cars to see if any drivers were missing and raised her head to the windows in the buildings across the square. She moved quickly with Rachael into a crowd of umbrellas, everyone walking north away from the steps of the courthouse. They stayed within the crowd. Peyton held the phone to her ear.

Leandro sat in a booth at a coffee shop. It was noon. Two phones were on the table in front of him. With his left hand, he turned off George's phone, broke it in half on the corner of the table, and put it into the side pocket of a blue windbreaker he had worn for the weather. His right arm and shoulder were wrapped in gauze and medical tape. Underneath the windbreaker and tight to his body, his right arm had grown numb. He turned off his satellite phone, put it into a back pocket of his pants, and stood up.

At Lafayette and Worth Streets, on the northwest corner of Foley Square, Leandro walked out into the rain. He pulled a blue baseball cap down over his forehead, dug into the pocket of the windbreaker, and pitched George's broken phone into the back of a trash truck. He raised his left arm for a cab.

Across the square, Peyton and Rachael stayed within the crowd. In between the people and umbrellas, Peyton scanned the rooftops and then the sidewalks, which were filled with pedestrians and open umbrellas. At the northwest corner, she saw the man in a blue pullover and baseball cap walk along the pavement and enter a taxicab. She tracked the vehicle with her eyes. It drove south along the other side of the square, down Lafayette to the Brooklyn Bridge, where it merged with traffic heading to the Brooklyn Queens Expressway. Peyton wiped water off the screen of her phone and called home.

45088988R00316

Made in the USA
Middletown, DE
13 May 2019